T0191445

By ELLE E. IRE

Reel to Real Love
Vicious Circle

NEARLY DEPARTED
Dead Woman's Pond

STORM FRONTS
Threadbare
Patchwork
Woven

Published by DSP PUBLICATIONS
www.dspublications.com

REEL TO REAL LOVE

ELLE E. IRE

DSP PUBLICATIONS

Published by
DSP Publications

5032 Capital Circle SW, Suite 2, PMB# 279,
Tallahassee, FL 32305-7886 USA
www.dsppublications.com

This is a work of fiction. Names, characters, places, and incidents either
are the product of author imagination or are used fictitiously, and any
resemblance to actual persons, living or dead, business establishments,
events, or locales is entirely coincidental.

Reel to Real Love
© 2021 Elle E. Ire

Cover Art
© 2021 Cover Art by Tiferet Design
http://www.tiferetdesign.com
Cover content is for illustrative purposes only and any person depicted
on the cover is a model.

Mass Market Paperback ISBN: 978-1-64108-260-0
Trade Paperback ISBN: 978-1-64405-979-1
Digital ISBN: 978-1-64405-978-4
Mass Market Paperback published July 2022
First Edition
v. 1.0

Printed in the United States of America
∞
This paper meets the requirements of
ANSI/NISO Z39.48-1992 (Permanence of Paper).

To the one person who can read my first draft, tell me what's wrong with it, suggest how to fix it, and not make me angry—my amazing spouse. I love you so very much.

ACKNOWLEDGMENTS

FIRST THANKS go to my former writing group: Ann, Evergreen, Amy, Mark, Joe, Jan, and Jennye. This book wouldn't have an ending if not for all of you. Thank you for helping me brainstorm who dunnit. There's nothing quite like writing your first murder mystery and not having chosen the murderer in advance.

Thank you to my intrepid agent, Naomi Davis, for your negotiating skills and limitless optimism. You are awesome as always.

Thank you to everyone at DSP Publications. First, my editing team: Gus, Yv, and Brian. Any remaining errors are entirely my own. Thanks to my promotions guru, Naomi, my blurb and back cover copy wizard Ginnifer, and my unbelievably talented cover artist, Anna Sikorska. And thank you to DSP in general for giving my work a home.

Finally, thank you to my readers for your enthusiasm and encouragement. Stephanie, thank you for entering my contest. I hope you enjoy the character I named after you.

CHAPTER 1
DEATH BECOMES HER

"CANCER RESEARCH, canine abuse prevention, cloning advancements." Harriet (Harry) Kane stabbed at her desk touchscreen with one manicured forefinger, then reached up and unclipped her personal transmitter from her ear, effectively cutting herself off from the Leviathan corporation to deal with her wife, Elaine. "Cute," she growled, laying emphasis on the *c*. "Think you could pick a charity beginning with a different letter of the alphabet? *Y* maybe? How about *x*? I hear *x* charities are woefully overlooked." She waved her right hand over the glowing blue sanitizing unit beside her, erasing any trace of stray rads her equipment might have gotten on her skin.

Better tech meant greater exposure to the recently discovered particles and bigger risks of sterilization. Birth rates had steadily declined until the invention of the decontaminators—a Leviathan product. But everyone dealt with it. At least it wasn't all tech, just the best and fastest processors, the high-speed communication devices. Humanity had three choices: use the decontaminators, wipe out the human race, or go back to the Stone Age. And only a few fanatics had taken such drastic measures.

Elaine stood, her arms folded over her chest, and faced Harry across the desk. "It's a gimmick, honey. A promotional quirk. Last year we gave to Boys Town, the Beirut Meltdown Survivors, and research to prevent some of the more stubborn forms of blindness."

"Clever, Lanie, clever." Sarcasm dripped from every *c*.

"I hate it when you call me that."

Harry continued as if Elaine hadn't spoken. "Doesn't matter what you've got on the donations list. We're not giving anything this year. Profits are down."

Elaine met her spouse's glare head-on. "That's not what you sent out in the stockholder newsletter."

"Good spin can make loss look like profit." Harry leaned back in her black leather swivel chair, a slap in the face to Elaine's charity drives to prevent the slaughter of animals for the making of furniture and clothing. Seven species gone extinct in the past five years, and Harry was buying leather chairs.

Harry kept talking, oblivious as always. "I hire the best writers for our company literature. And by the time the lawyers work out a translation, we'll have regained what we've lost."

"That's all a load of crap. This company makes millions."

"Oooh, crap. Good *c* word."

Elaine clamped her mouth shut on another retort. No use arguing when Harry had made up her mind. Elaine might hold controlling interest in Leviathan Industries, but her spouse would make living with her a total hell if Elaine clung to her charitable "whims." Honestly, there were times when Elaine wished Harriet would just—

The bullet wrought destruction upon windowpane, human skull, and brain matter. The glass popped at the point of impact, its surface crackling outward in a snowflake pattern of fractures. The dull thud as the hollow point pierced the soft area at the back of Harriet's head echoed through her office like a distant thunderclap. Blood splattered across her desk, her body falling forward into the gruesome mess. Elaine's scream reverberated off the office walls and caused already loosened shards to drop from the window to the tiled floor.

The bullet embedded itself in the *real* wood paneling of the wall closest to the entry (another indulgence of Harriet's, while the cities encroached farther upon the few remaining forests every year). It lodged a mere hairsbreadth from where Elaine stood. She stopped thinking about the forests and realized she'd been in shock to have focused on trees of all things.

So close.

Too close.

The viscous fluid flowed across the surface of the onyx desk, disturbed by the occasional bit of gore and forming a ripple around each one like a stream over stones. It seeped into the Leviathan logo, a tentacled sea creature etched into the desk's surface, filling the grooves.

Oh God.

Elaine dropped flat, bruising elbows and knees on the tile as another projectile whined overhead, passing right through the space where her face had been. Her breath came in rapid gasps. Her pulse thrummed like a hovercar engine. Security pounded on the thick metal door, making her jerk and yelp for the second time in the span of a minute.

"Ms. Kane! Ms. Kane, are you all right?" A pause. "Ms. Kane?" Shuffling and scraping outside the door.

Elaine made no move to respond. She raised her head, the desk acting as a protective barrier between herself and the broken window. Her gaze fixated on a thin stream of blood running from the corner of the polished onyx to hit the floor and stain the grout.

Was this what shock felt like—this detached one-way trip down a tunnel of blocked emotions and too-focused vision?

Elaine forced herself to place one knee in front of the other, crawling the distance to her spouse's body in three strides and making certain she kept her head beneath the edge of the windowsill. Now she understood the actions of all those airheaded heroines in every murder-mystery vid she'd ever seen. Cliches didn't create themselves.

At Harriet's side, she hesitated, not out of squeamishness, though there was that too, but fear of rad transference. Some scientists suggested bodily fluids could transmit rads from one person to another, and Harriet loved her tech.

Elaine shook it off, furious with her irrational fear at a time like this. She reached up to press her fingertips against Harriet's carotid artery, red blood flowing over red fingernails. Warm stickiness.

Elaine gagged, then vomited, adding her mess to Harry's and further contaminating the room, if the scientists were to be believed. The robocleaners and sanbots would have an electronic fit cleaning this up.

And what a world she lived in where such concerns warred with the sudden murder of her spouse.

Falling back, she clamped her palm over her mouth. Hot tears streamed across the back of her hand. This wasn't what she'd wanted. Not this. Nothing like this. The trembling in her limbs increased from minor vibration to earthquake. Her spouse was very, very dead, but she'd needed the confirmation. Now she paid the physical price for her stupidity.

She stared around the normally pristine, professional space, trying to make sense of something, anything in the crazy scene. The shattered window drew her gaze, though from her vantage point on the floor, all she could see was empty, peaceful sky, clouds slightly distorted into blurs by the protective climate-controlled dome that shielded the city from the rest of the world's pollution. The pounding in her chest skipped a beat in its staccato.

Was the killer still out there, waiting, watching for her?

Nothing but New York City rooftops for miles, she knew. Nice flat surfaces for balancing a rifle.

She heard the override on the office door's lock buzzing a second before Daniel and Stephen, her spouse's most trusted and dependable bodyguards, burst into the room. The decontaminator built into the doorway buzzed, casting their already bleak expressions in the gray-blue of its beam. In the hallway beyond, a crowd gathered. She registered Stephanie—Harriet's personal assistant and Elaine's own best friend. The rest were blurs wearing corporate blues and grays. Elaine shifted her hand from her mouth to brush the tears from her vision, swiping a smear of stickiness across her face. A wave of cold flowed from her chest outward to her extremities, and she slid sideways. The tile rushed up at her in a haze of even squares.

Strong hands caught her shoulders. She saw Stephen gazing down at her, forehead creased with concern. A number of other figures rushed past him, brushing her, bumping her, almost stumbling over her in their hurry to examine the body and secure the room. Then everything faded.

ELAINE RUBBED the fingers of her right hand together, then brought them to her face and inhaled. Moist towelettes from some helpful assistant's purse, or maybe her own. No, not her own. This one carried the scent of Tepsin, a product some drug company claimed could reduce rads on skin and which had been proven to be a total hoax. Didn't stop it from selling.

Well, at least someone had cleaned her up. She brushed her palm across the damp hair on her cheek. That blood smear was gone too.

The creaky leather couch, probably the one in Harriet's outer office, clung to the skin of her back where her shirt had ridden up. But that was from her sweat, nothing more. Her clothing would absorb it, or the sanbots would scrub it clean later.

Elaine opened her eyes, swung her feet to the floor, and sat up. Her head turned robotically toward the inner office door, but a gaggle of uniformed officers and company staff blocked her view. Thank God.

The trembling returned to her limbs, and she heard herself babbling, though she couldn't do a damn thing to stop it. "I don't... I can't...." Words tumbled from her lips in incoherent spurts. "The window... didn't see... so fast...." When a couple of cops turned to frown at her, she lapsed into stupefied silence. Her body wanted to rock, but she willed herself to stillness. Someone had removed her shoes. She dug into the thick synthetic carpet of the outer office with her stocking-covered toes, trying to get a grip, to make sense. A million things to be done. Arrangements to be made.

"Out of the way," came a sharp voice from the outer hall. "You people have no compassion. Standing around gawking at the dead while the living suffer. She needs a sedative and a friendly face, and you all sure aren't going to give them to her. Can't you see she's in shock? Good Lord!" Stephanie pushed her way through the other crowd at the office suite's entrance and crossed the room to plunk herself down beside Elaine. Next to the rock that was Stephanie, Elaine found strength.

Elaine knew the police would be within their rights to arrest Stephanie for her interference, but they wouldn't. Leviathan employed a number of off-duty officers as their night security and handled a lot of police and other government contracts. When Stephanie got pissed off, things that needed doing didn't get done. Always better to work with her than against her.

"Water. Absorbers," Stephanie snapped, and one of the office assistants in the doorway went running, nearly knocking over two secretaries in his haste.

Absorbers? Was she crying again?

Elaine touched her cheek, the wetness surprising her. "How do you do that?" she muttered, seizing upon the distraction and waving a vague hand toward the door.

Her friend smiled a barracuda smile. "Everyone knows the boss's personal assistant runs the company." Stephanie tossed thick curls of blond hair over one shoulder. The college student intern reappeared and set down a box of Kleenex-brand absorbers, guaranteed to reduce rad transference through tears, and placed a paper cup on the table beside them, then fled. "Smart young man," Stephanie murmured. She drew a deep breath. "Everybody else, out!"

The remaining officers and personnel scrambled, some stepping inside Harriet's inner office with the body, others retreating to the hallway. None of them looked back.

Only Stephanie Spier could clear a room of crime investigators and not get herself handcuffed for it.

Stephanie took both Elaine's shoulders in her hands and turned her so she faced her friend. She waited until Elaine had dried her face and could look her in the eye before speaking.

"I know that every piece of you wants to come apart right now, and you can't do it. Not here. Not in front of these people."

Elaine shook her head. "Doesn't any of this bother you? You knew Harriet, worked for her…."

Stephanie jumped on her words. "Yes, worked. She was my employer, not my friend. *You* are my friend." Her tone softened. "And now you need to listen to this friendly advice."

To hell with the absorbers. Elaine had passed through the doorway decontaminator when she came in, and she hadn't used Harriet's computer. She tossed the used Kleenex into the disposal unit under the table and wiped tears on the back of her sleeve. To her satisfaction, Stephanie didn't flinch away.

Elaine had left a wet stain across the blue-and-silver fabric. The blouse had been expensive, a gift from Harriet. Elaine had worn it for her because Harry asked her to. Lunch today was with several other executives and their wives. Harriet expected her to look presentable. The tears welled up anew.

"No, not now," Stephanie commanded, the sharpness returning.

Elaine felt compelled to obey that command, but she shot her friend a look of confusion. What difference did it make, now or later? Here or at home? These people all knew her, had known her for years. She couldn't remember ever crying in front of them. She'd never had a reason to. But what did that matter?

Harriet was dead. People cried when they lost their spouses.

Stephanie allowed a touch of pity to enter her expression. "Ah, honey, you really haven't realized it yet, have you? Leviathan's yours, sweetheart. Every desk, chair, and plastic fern. Every employee, deal, and dollar. I notarized the will, sweetie. From this moment on, every action you take, every word that comes out of your mouth, is a public statement. You are the new face of this company. And that means displays of weakness happen in private. Stocks have been known to plummet for less."

Elaine swallowed as more reality hit. Half the corporation had always been hers. Her late father had owned controlling stock in a number of Leviathan's partners. Shortly after she'd married Harriet, the

companies had merged, giving Elaine half control over
Leviathan itself. Of course she let Harriet handle the
business dealings. Elaine never had an interest in mergers and takeovers. It bothered her to seize a business
that had been in someone's family for generations, and
she'd quarreled with Harriet about it often, but Harry
was the businesswoman. Now, however....

As if on cue, a team of news vid reporters appeared
in the hallway, lights glaring and cameras recording everything they could scan. The police halted them before
they could enter, and Stephanie kept much of their view
of Elaine blocked, preventing her disheveled appearance from ever making it on the evening broadcast or
worse, directly transferring to the 24-hour newsnet. In
that moment, she gained an even greater appreciation
for Harriet's secretary.

"Time to get you out of here." She hauled Elaine
up, pausing only long enough for her to locate and retrieve her missing shoes. Then the two women returned
to Harriet's inner office, Stephanie standing between
Elaine and the body.

A detective followed, shouting down the press outside the doors and blocking their access. He sealed the
door. "Our questions will wait. I'll contact you at your
home, Ms. Kane."

He escorted both women to Harriet's private anti-grav lift, accessed via a sliding panel in the far corner of the office. Stephanie produced a code key from
her skirt pocket and slipped it into the appropriate slot,
activating the elevator's controls. She hit the button
for the garage, and they plummeted the 105 floors to
the primary parking area of the Leviathan Industries
headquarters.

Elaine counted the number of police hovervehicles patrolling the parking garage. They skimmed above the concrete surface on cushions of air, dozens of them circling like sharks now that blood had hit the water.

She only hoped she wasn't the next source of chum.

"RICHELLE" WATCHED as "her" guest paused in the *Nebula*'s corridor and turned to peer at the closest emitter camera. Hope surged, blending with the electrical vibrations of the starliner's constant humming. Did she realize then, finally? Too late, but encouraging nonetheless. But no. The guest laughed at herself, passed under the blue decontaminator lights, and moved on to disembark. Constructs like Richelle didn't merit acknowledgment, no matter how much fun she'd provided the guest. Designer-label travel pack over one shoulder, the passenger slipped through the airlock hatch and with a whoosh, disappeared behind the sealing metal.

Depression and loneliness crashed in, as they always did at the end of a voyage. Oh, Richelle had tried to drop subtle hints, bits of insight, creativity, emotion, to indicate something more lay behind her protective veneer, all in vain. And "the rules" prevented her from anything further.

Too many rules. Too many restrictions. Damn them all.

No matter how frequently she got to play in their world, without companionship, she was still half a being, half-alive. Bonding meant growth and enlightenment, experience and enhanced existence. It *was* life.

"Dangerous thoughts, my friend. Some might even say treasonous. And bonding? Really? With *that* woman? That one wouldn't have had you even if you were flesh and blood."

The disembodied voice carried across the ether, not sounds but pulses, sinking into Richelle's existence like boots in mud. If she had boots. If fancy starship passenger liners had mud. They trod a dirty path through her thoughts, leaving smudges wherever they passed.

"I've done nothing," Richelle answered the voice, feminine in feel and quality. "You know that. You watched, like you always do." Since she couldn't glare in this form, Richelle layered her words with sarcasm.

"You mean you weren't successful. It wasn't for lack of trying. You dropped enough hints to fill a hypothetical bucket. And yes, I popped in from time to time. Have to keep an eye on everyone, you know."

"It's rude."

"It's my purpose."

They could both have better purposes if they allowed themselves to bond once more, to interact fully with those outside themselves. To have permanent access to sensations like taste and smell. If Richelle could convince the council....

It would have to wait. Even now, the generator at the core of the ship drew on her, calling her to the source, shutting down to conserve power between flights, forcing her to compact herself and hide within other systems, in order to avoid full dispersal.

Maybe, Richelle thought, as her consciousness turned to concealment, maybe on the next trip out....

CHAPTER 2
SIX DAY
SEVEN NIGHT ESCAPE

ELEVEN MONTHS had passed since Harriet Kane's murder. Eleven months Elaine had spent cooped up in her mansion, relying on robotic servants and occasional visits from Stephanie and her personal psychiatrist to break up the monotony.

Now she sat, muscles tensed almost to the point of trembling, staring out the bulletproof windows of the hoverlimo on the two-hour drive into New Jersey. The turbulence compensators kept the ride smooth as imitation silk. Elaine almost wished the vehicle would jounce a little. It would have better suited her mood.

Damn Stephanie for insisting on this, for dragging her out here when she could be safe at home. Elaine glared at the vacant seats of the otherwise empty limo, wishing her friend were present to feel her wrath, but they'd agreed to meet at the port.

They pulled up at the departure terminal. Hundreds of acres of corn, tomato, and strawberry crops had been replaced by individual concrete landing disks for each of the fleet of small shuttlecraft. Elaine missed the "pick your own" strawberry fields she had frequented as a child. Now one could hardly call it the "Garden State." And even if there were still berry fields, there wouldn't be many children.

No matter how the government tried to claim they'd solved the rad problem, they couldn't hide the declining birth rate.

Elaine drew a breath of unfiltered air, detecting hints of oil, shuttle fuel, and her own nervous sweat. No protective domes out here. You breathed what you got and took chances with that as well.

She glanced down at her blouse. The sweat-retardant fabric didn't show perspiration stains, but it couldn't entirely hide the odor. With the exception of the rads, she preferred the offerings of the dome-covered city—dome courtesy of Leviathan Industries—with her mansion on its outskirts but still tucked safely and sanitarily inside.

A few extremist groups had established colonies without heavy tech in obscure locales like the Arctic, a few isolated islands, and the remnants of the rain forests. Hard to reach, out of contact, and primitive. And there were some off-world colonies with advanced technology on planets whose environments naturally dispersed rads to humanly tolerable levels.

Elaine stepped through the entrance to the shuttle terminal, the blue decon light humming overhead, and sighed. Stephanie had fought to get her to take this vacation off-world, and she'd agreed, but no matter how bad things got, Earth would always be home.

Porters vied for her attention, stumbling over one another in their haste to whisk her luggage away for storage and loading. She tipped generously. Cheap travelers might find themselves in the elegant dining hall that evening wearing the same shorts and sport shirts in which they'd boarded when their luggage didn't arrive at their cabins early enough for them to change.

Elaine tried to avoid the press of the bustling crowd and wondered where to find Stephanie. Stephanie, who'd talked her into this nightmare. She clutched her universal identification in one hand, hating the necessity for the losable item, but like the previous generations' passports, it was required. Not all worlds had the same level of technology as Earth, and a physical identifier was often necessary to prove people were who they said they were. Elaine scanned the hundreds, if not thousands, of other travelers for her friend. With her impressive height and striking good looks, Stephanie tended to stand out in large groups, but Elaine doubted she could have spotted her own mother in all this movement and noise. That thought sparked another fond childhood memory, and she felt a smile drift across her face.

She was a grown woman. She needed to pull on her big-girl panties and get moving.

"Okay, Mom," Elaine whispered. No one would hear her in this overwhelming shoutfest. No one living, anyway.

A momentary terror surged through her veins, and Elaine froze in place. Tourists cursed under their breaths as they swerved to avoid crashing into her. Her gaze darted from face to face, analyzing potential threats. What if another assassin had been waiting all this time for an opportunity? They'd caught the murderer who'd shot Harriet, but not whoever hired him. Detective Niles thought Elaine might be a secondary target.

Any number of people had any number of reasons for wanting Harriet dead. She ran Leviathan. Leviathan ran practically everything else, often with an iron fist. Even their marriage had been a carefully planned business maneuver. It had taken years for Elaine to see beyond the suave words and good looks, but Harriet had wedded her for the stocks Elaine got when her parents died. For the companies Harriet could take over, through Elaine.

Elaine hadn't been entirely fooled by Harriet's charms. Elaine kept those stocks in her name. Harriet ran it all, but Elaine owned half of Leviathan and could have fought Harriet on numerous dealings, had she been so inclined.

She didn't have those inclinations.

After Harriet's death, Elaine hadn't wanted to know the details of Harriet's dark dealings, never had any interest in becoming a business mogul. But even though she'd turned the decision-making over to the board of directors a week after the shooting, Elaine now owned all of Leviathan.

And someone didn't like Leviathan very much.

Her psychiatrist would have a field day with this reaction. "Get out of the damn house," he'd told her during his last house call. "I'm not coming back here.

You'll have to come to me if you want further treatment." Then Dr. Greenburg winked, and his expression softened. "I don't care how much you offer to pay me. You need to get out, for your own good. This continued fear is irrational."

She'd promised to make an office appointment... three weeks ago.

As a personal compromise, she'd agreed to this singles' starship cruise. Big mistake.

Elaine squeezed her eyes shut, drawing in rapid breaths as her knees threatened to buckle beneath her, right there in the middle of the terminal. Goose bumps rose on her arms and legs, responding to the ice in her bloodstream. *I'm standing in a crowd*, she told herself. Picking her out as a target would be very difficult.

But Harriet's killer had hit her square in the head from an office building across the street. Across the fucking street. Dear God.

Elaine lost her battle to remain upright and would have hit the floor in a heap if a strong hand with sharp, manicured fingernails hadn't gripped her upper arm. She shrieked at the sudden physical contact and tried to twist away.

"El?"

Elaine's eyes flew wide. She looked into Stephanie's concerned expression, then felt the heat flood her face when she saw all the passersby staring at her.

Stephanie followed her gaze and frowned, red lips pouting. "She's just a little flightaphobic," her friend improvised. "Go on! You'll miss the free drinks on deck two. Martian Mamas today!" Stephanie clutched a glossy schedule of events in her free hand.

When the crowd refused to disperse, she released Elaine's arm to flick her fingers at them in a dismissive gesture. "Shoo! Shoo! She's not a tourist attraction!" Stephanie turned her back on their audience, giving all her attention to Elaine. "You okay, hon? Sorry I didn't meet you at the entrance. Had to take care of some last-minute details at work. Secretaries run the world, remember?"

Stephanie pulled Elaine toward the check-in desk and a poster-worthy young man in a Transgalactic Star-lines uniform. His perfect white teeth gleamed in the overhead lighting as he beckoned to both women.

"IDs?" he asked. His accent placed his origins somewhere in Europe.

Stephanie passed hers over, but Elaine held up her empty hand and stiffened, then turned to where she'd had her panic attack. Dozens of people tromped over the spot of polished tile, their feet making a proper search impossible. Among them, she spotted a cleaning bot and her heart sank. By now, the device would have picked up and disintegrated anything she'd dropped.

"Excuse me, ladies?"

Elaine yelped again and mentally kicked herself for the reaction. A dark-haired gentleman in his early thirties stood just behind Stephanie's right shoulder. He reached a hand into the pocket of his shorts and with-drew Elaine's ID. Deep brown eyes focused all their attention on Stephanie.

Figured. No one noticed Elaine when the buxom blond Stephanie was around.

"Did one of you drop this?"

"I wish I had." Stephanie took the card from the man's fingers, allowing her own to linger a moment be-fore passing the ID over to Elaine.

Elaine couldn't resist a snicker. Every ID had the owner's photo emblazoned on its surface. This handsome stranger knew exactly to whom the card belonged. It was a clever way to make Stephanie's acquaintance, but not *that* clever.

"I'm Jay Grego."

"Stephanie Spier."

"Elaine Kane." Ugh. She hated the sound of her full name spoken aloud. Too rhymey and singsongy. But no point in hiding what he already knew, if he'd read the card.

His attention turned to her. "Kane?" he repeated and took the opportunity to scan her from head to foot, gaze resting a little too long on her legs and breasts for her comfort. When he refocused on her face, recognition widened his eyes. False recognition, Elaine suspected. But she'd play along like the good third wheel she was. "Of Leviathan Industries?"

Elaine suppressed a groan but nodded. The media circus had died down a few months after Harriet's death. Plenty of other corporate scandals demanded the public's attention. But not everyone forgot.

A strange progression of emotions passed over Jay's features, so fast Elaine couldn't identify them. Surprise that might or might not be real, but something less innocent as well. Jay wasn't the best actor. He recovered quickly, schooling his expression into one of sympathy. "Your spouse used to be my boss," he admitted with a halfhearted shrug of one shoulder. "Apparently I'm not cut out for mergers and acquisitions. To be honest, I'm glad she let me go soon enough for me to pursue my true calling in THI sales over at Biotech."

Elaine's newly trained corporate ears perked up a bit. Biotech. One of Leviathan's leading competitors.

"Most of the programs you'll see running on this trip were sold to Transgalactic by yours truly, and of course, all of them rad-free." He placed a palm against his chest. "Can't complain about that kind of success." Jay reached out to touch Elaine's arm. She felt the warmth of his skin through her blouse. "I'm sorry for your loss."

Did everyone have to say those same five words? And in such a smarmy tone? Jay was trying way too hard to ingratiate himself, and all the physical contact seemed inappropriate and borderline creepy. He reminded her of a male Harriet. It surprised her they hadn't worked better together. Then again, Harriet eliminated anyone who might become competition for her brand of charm-wielding.

The attendant behind the counter cleared his throat, and Elaine realized with some embarrassment that the line behind them had grown quite long.

Jay excused himself, disappearing into the crowd while Stephanie tossed him a flirty finger wave, and Elaine almost sagged with relief. Stephanie dealt with the identification procedures and collected their stateroom scan keys. She hooked her arm with Elaine's. They proceeded to VIP boarding, Stephanie chatting all the way and Elaine tuning her out.

WHEN SHE had the brilliant idea to hide in an unnoticeable data feedback loop in the *Nebula*'s intercom system, Richelle never imagined she'd be tortured with the inane interactions between guests and crew, and among the crew themselves, for the next eleven months. Time didn't pass the same for her as it did for corporeal beings, and hours shrank to minutes in her perception, but if she had to listen to passengers complaining about the runny eggs from room service or the overly loud toilets that *must* be in need of repair despite the fact that everyone's toilet sounded like that, she thought she might lose her sanity. Moving to a different system might send up red flags in the ship's maintenance sweeps. She couldn't risk that.

She could, she supposed, have switched to a different camouflage persona, taken on a new entertainment personality to use to come out of hiding and mingle once more with the guests in a capacity that went beyond their complaints and crew orders. But she'd grown fond of the Richelle program. All the entertainment programs could walk, talk, taste, feel, hear, see, smell. They could experience the senses through actual simulated sensory *organs*. But as Richelle, she could joke! She could dance!

And she wasn't too perfect like so many of the others: teeth not quite straight, hair a little mussed, not homely but not gorgeous, a little clumsy at times. She liked that. A lot.

The downside was, most guests wanted perfection. Perfect looks. Perfect personalities. No awkward moments. No mistakes.

They wanted reality, but not too real.

And that meant Richelle's program didn't get called up as often as the others.

Sometimes not for eleven months.

But something had drawn her out of her holding pattern. A signal. A command to activate. Richelle accessed her instructions. Another singles cruise. VIP accommodations. Female passenger.

She tapped into the central database along with all the other programs, calling up everything available on her upcoming guest, and a few files not so available that only she could download.

Other companion programs knew their guests well. Richelle always knew hers intimately.

ELAINE WATCHED, fascinated, as the starliner grew larger and larger outside the shuttle's viewport by her seat. A class-five LVN resembled an overweight bovine. The "head" jutted out at one end, housing the bridge. A "tail" of a massive engine extended behind. Elaine would never comprehend how it all worked to move the ship through "bent space." Harriet would have expounded at length about distance compression and time distortion, but Elaine's brain shut down during such discussions. Polite nods and smiles at calculated intervals kept her spouse satisfied and babbling tech-speak for hours. Despite Harriet's general indifference toward Elaine's feelings and interests, she would have given anything to hear that babble right now. It would have been something familiar to focus on.

"I'm hooking up with that one," Stephanie spoke up from the seat beside her.

"I'm sorry?"

"Jay Grego. The guy from check-in? Lesbian or not, surely you haven't forgotten someone so delicious."

Elaine inwardly groaned. "Steph, you'd hook up with anything male and reasonably decent to look at."

Her friend laughed. "True, hon. Very true. But really, Jay looks like a keeper."

"For one night, at least." Elaine fixed Stephanie with her best heart-to-heart stare. "Be careful with that one, Steph. He's smooth."

Stephanie wriggled suggestively in her padded chair. "Oh, I hope so."

Elaine rolled her eyes and pressed her fingers to her temple, trying to relieve a threatening headache. She felt the thrum of the shuttle's engines cycle down, and the transport hovered alongside the massive cruise vessel. A transparent pressurized docking tube extended from one to the other, and a series of mechanical clanks and whirs signified the completed connection. The shuttle crew called out row numbers, and passengers made their way to the hatch to pull themselves, one at a time, along the handrails lining the twenty-meter length of tube.

Elaine's stomach clenched. She hated this part. Zero-g nauseated her, and seeing empty space all around brought on horrific vertigo. Opaque tubing caused many passengers claustrophobia, so the starliners went with this supposedly lesser of two evils. The steward called her row twice, and Stephanie had to take her arm before she responded.

"I'll go first. It'll be fine." Stephanie knew all about Elaine's fears. They'd traveled to the Mars orbital station on a college field trip, and Elaine had vomited for an hour after arrival. She'd enjoyed the rest of the visit, but getting there.... She mentally kicked herself. In all the rush and nervous tension built up for this trip, Elaine had forgotten to take her antinausea meds.

Elaine nodded and waited while Stephanie stepped through the hatch. Her friend pressed the touchplate to cycle it closed behind her and stood a moment in the airlock, then opened the second door to the tube. Elaine watched her progress through a small window in the portal. Athletic and graceful as always, Stephanie pulled herself, hand over hand, until she reached the opposite access. It opened and Stephanie passed into the starliner's lock, where Elaine spotted the glow of the decontaminator beam. Her friend disappeared behind the closed hatch. Elaine breathed a sigh of temporary relief.

If she really freaked out, she could use the "alternative connection module" provided by all starliners and built, of course, by Leviathan. Every shuttle had one of the modules attached to the top of its hull for use by physically challenged passengers, or those so overcome by the terror of the crossing that they couldn't manage it. Use of the module meant riding a tiny elevator into it from the seating area, along with one of the stewards, who would pilot the small self-propelled egg-shaped transport to a special airlock on the *Nebula* it could connect to directly. The shuttle was too big to manage such a connection. Doing so would be too risky. But the modules would do little or no damage if they collided with the starliner's hull. It would take a lot of time, probably affect the shuttle's schedule, and be very, very humiliating, at least in Elaine's head.

The steward opened the access on Elaine's end, then paused to examine her face. "Here," the young man said, taking her icy cold hand between his warm ones. He walked her into the shuttle's airlock. "The bars are evenly spaced about forty centimeters apart. Close your eyes if you need to. You can feel for them. Departure isn't for hours yet. We're not in any particular rush." He turned back to the twenty or so passengers waiting behind Elaine. "Right, folks?"

The other tourists mumbled their grudging assent.

"There, you see?" The steward smiled and lowered his voice. "Don't worry about them. I'll hand out some free drink chits while you're crossing. They'll thank you later." He released Elaine's hands and patted her shoulder. "If you panic halfway, I can come after you, but the tube isn't designed to support two, so it will get stuffy pretty fast. You sure you don't want the module?" His tone spoke volumes about how little he wanted to deal with the hassle of using the smaller transport vehicle, and Elaine shook her head. "Well, off you go, then." He stepped back into the shuttle, closing the hatch afterward. Elaine drew a breath and opened the access to the tube. She gripped the first rung, felt her shoes leave the deck plates, and before she could change her mind, she slapped the sealing panel, closing the hatch behind her.

At first she tried to focus on the metal hulk of the starliner. It was so close, yet it seemed kilometers away. The stars whirled around her, and the emptiness above and below threatened to swallow her whole. She squeezed her eyes shut and reached blindly for the next bar. Elaine counted them one by one, anything to distract her. She wished she'd paid more attention as Stephanie crossed. She had no idea how many there were. "Twenty, twenty-one, twenty-two...."

How far had she gone?

"Fifty-four, fifty-five, fifty-six...."

The tube jolted.

Her imagination had to be playing tricks on her. She pulled herself faster.

An alarm sounded. The wailing siren seized her heart and wrenched it. Elaine opened her eyes. The opposite hatch stood closer than she'd expected, closer than turning around. She could see Stephanie and a strange man, probably ship's crew, staring at her through the window in the door. Red lights flashed above the portal. An onyx disk of a camera lens was embedded between the dual beacons. Over the sound of the alarm, she made out the high-pitched hiss of escaping air.

Oh God.

Why hadn't anyone come in to assist? Did they want to avoid losing a second person? She risked a glance backward and saw the steward who'd sent her off, his face pressed against the window in the hatch at his end. Pounding echoed, barely audible, and Elaine had the impression that entry had jammed.

Arm muscles tensing, she hauled herself forward. Stephanie vanished from the window, but the crewman on the starliner waved at Elaine, beckoning her onward with frantic gestures. The hissing rose in volume. She couldn't tell where it originated from, but her ears rang, and the dizziness increased. Panic? Lack of oxygen? Impossible to tell. The clanging of metal on metal reverberated through the tube. She thought it came from within the starliner's airlock. Had both hatches become locked somehow? Some kind of emergency shutdown to prevent further damage? What about her?

When Elaine felt certain she couldn't reach for one more rung, the red lights flashed to green, and the hatch on the *Nebula*'s airlock opened. The muscular crewman grabbed her by the waist, hauling her into the lock seconds before a howling shriek came from the tube. An overpowering sucking sensation yanked Elaine backward, but the man had a firm hold with one leg wrapped around a protruding bar, one arm around her midsection and the other elbowing the pressure panel to seal the door. His positioning was statuesque, like a dancer's, but when seal integrity cycled to 100 percent, the pair fell into a heap of twisted limbs, Elaine's hair covering her face and eyes.

Her rescuer released her, and she parted her long brown strands with trembling fingers to meet his relieved and worried gaze. At that moment, the blue light of the decontaminator was the most beautiful thing in the universe.

"Are you all right?" His green eyes scanned her, searching for injury.

"Yes, thank you," Elaine panted, her heart still racing. Now that she could get a better look, his age surprised her. The crewman couldn't have been more than twenty-one or twenty-two, a very junior employee of Nebula Starlines. He seemed as flustered as she was, uniform disheveled, hair mussed. "I owe you my life…."

"Lansington, ma'am. Arnold Lansington." He managed a sheepish smile. "Wasn't all me, though. I cleared the lock, but the tube hatch on this end was stuck tight. I tried everything in the manual to override it. Nothing worked. Guess they got the thing open from the bridge. Then I grabbed you." He heaved a shuddering breath, and Elaine realized his fear had equaled hers. "They make everyone study the airlock manuals, from cabin boy to captain. Never thought I'd need it, though."

"And which one are you, cabin boy or captain?" Her attempt to regain normalcy failed when her pitch wavered, and she fought to still her shaking hands. She got to her feet, testing her arms and legs for damage. Other than a tear in her navy skort (one didn't wear skirts in zero-g) and a bruise on her forearm, she thought she was, if not fine, then at least otherwise unharmed.

Lansington's smile grew wider. "I'm a waiter, ma'am. I serve drinks to the boarding passengers.

Sometimes I tend bar. I just happened to be the closest crewman to the lock."

The inner hatch opened, catching her by surprise. She'd forgotten they were still only in the airlock. Elaine spotted those drinks, the glassware, tray, and liquids scattered over a red carpet where Lansington must have dropped them at the sound of the alarm. Emergency personnel swarmed the small space, but Stephanie shoved her way through to envelop Elaine in a bear hug. She would have thanked Arnold Lansington further, but higher-ranking officials drew him aside to get his accounting of the events. One thumped him on the back good-naturedly. She heard another suggest he would receive a promotion.

The next twenty minutes filled quickly with apologies and promises of complimentary service, including an invitation to dine at the captain's table presented by the captain himself. Elaine tried to focus on the portly white-haired gentleman with all the stars and stripes on his uniform, but the scene reminded her too much of Harriet's death, and exhaustion threatened to overwhelm her. When her identity as Leviathan's primary shareholder came to light, she had to ask him to leave to avoid further obsequiousness. She sagged against the corridor bulkhead when he retreated.

Stephanie explained how the shuttle would return the remaining passengers out of orbit and down to Earth, where they would transfer to a different vehicle with a working connection tube. Elaine cut her off midsentence.

"Steph, what's a Martian Mama?"

Stephanie examined her friend's face. "Something I think you could use right about now." She scanned the rows of uniformed crewmen. "Where's a bartender when you need one?"

Elaine just smiled.

SHIT, WHAT had gone wrong?

Richelle couldn't curse in front of the guests, but here, in her own consciousness, she could think whatever the hell she wanted. And this moment warranted profanity.

She materialized in her guest's as of yet unoccupied quarters, then crumpled against the king-size bed, parts of her humanoid form passing through it to dump her on the floor at its base.

She focused, hurrying to solidify the transparent bits before she sank beneath the deck itself and had to start over. Even once capable of clutching the trailing ends of the deep blue bedspread, her fingertips and the toes of her loafers shimmered at the edges.

Really, she shouldn't have taken on this form at all, not until she recovered. She'd fought against waves of conflicting data, expending energy and stripping away strings of code to get to the original pattern and open the damn airlock door before that guest, *her* guest, died a horrible, corporeal death in the vacuum of space.

Biological life-forms possessed such tremendous beauty and such delicate frailty.

Elaine Kane had been so frightened, an emotion familiar to Richelle, though its physical manifestations were not, despite multiple incarnations of the Richelle persona. Pounding heart, rapid breathing, sweating palms. The absolute invigoration of it all. The overwhelming relief to discover you'd survived! Richelle never experienced any of that. Was it possible to pity and envy someone at the same time?

She laughed at herself, and the tremulous quality of her own voice surprised her. No, she should have waited and drawn more energy from the generator, but she had no idea when Ms. Kane would arrive in these quarters, and Richelle wanted to be ready.

Richelle couldn't wait to meet her, this woman who had fought for survival, who hadn't given up in the access tube but instead had dragged herself hand over hand, away from certain death.

ONCE THE anxious medical team from the ship's infirmary released them, the two women finally took the twenty steps down the short corridor into the starliner's receiving area. A server appeared at Elaine's elbow and pressed a crystal glass of red liquid into her hand. "If you would like another, wave at any of the camera disks." The waitress gestured toward the onyx circles embedded at intervals along the walls, like the one Elaine had seen in the airlock. "I'll be watching for you." The young woman bobbed a graceful curtsy in her flouncy black-and-white skirt, amazing Elaine with her ability to keep her tray of glassware balanced through the maneuver.

Elaine took a tentative sip, then a heartier second as the fruity alcoholic mixture revitalized her. No watering down of the drinks here. The sweetness tingled on its way down, easing, then stilling the lingering butterflies in her stomach. She'd need to watch herself or the self-control she'd regained after her harrowing experience would get shot all to hell.

The entry alcove led to a short hall that ended in an enormous atrium. Elaine swallowed fast to keep from sputtering. They stood in the heart of the vessel, about midway down in its "body." She looked up, up, and up. Level upon level of balconies and glassed walkways lined and crossed the atrium on each upper deck. She could make out small groups of people strolling back and forth, some pausing to look down at the new arrivals. They seemed oblivious to the ordeal she'd endured. The crew must have scrambled to put a lid on the accident.

Ornate gold and silver metalwork swirled to entwine every railing. Holos of constellations and planets floated in the empty space, so real Elaine found herself straining her eyes for signs of life on them. She recognized recreations of the celestial bodies in Earth's solar system. Another planet, farther up, glowed in brilliant lavender. That would be their main stop on this cruise—Gratitude. She couldn't identify other worlds beyond, swirling like the colored shapes in a kaleidoscope, but the effect impressed her.

The peak of the atrium made Elaine forget to breathe. Instead of a metal bulkhead or even a viewport to space, the highest point of this central core of the ship hid itself behind a virtual starfield, each pinpoint of light glowing in luminescent splendor. Passengers on that level walked among the heavens.

Stephanie tugged on her arm, drawing Elaine out of the universe and into reality. More personnel in sharp, pressed black-and-white uniforms unmarred by a brush with death beckoned the travelers to break into small groups, about ten tourists per crew member. They gathered in front of a central bar where the wandering waiters filled their drink trays. "A tour?" Elaine guessed.

"Can't we skip it and go to our rooms... I mean cabins?" Her voice sounded weary even to herself.

"'Fraid not, hon." Stephanie reached out to smooth some of Elaine's long brown hair into place. Her sympathetic smile helped a little. "Starship tours are required by interstellar travel law. In case of emergency, we have to know where to go and what to do."

"I'm not sure I can handle another emergency." She shivered and wrapped her arms around her own shoulders, wishing for the sweater she'd packed in her suitcase.

"What are the odds?"

Elaine glared.

"The man I spoke to said it was the shuttle, not the starliner." When Stephanie's comment failed to get Elaine's muscles to untense, her friend smiled and leaned close to her ear. "I think they're more worried about pirate attacks."

Elaine slapped her lightly on the shoulder. "Quit it."

Hands on hips, Stephanie faced her. "I'm not kidding. You've been out of touch in your hidey hole, sweetie. There have been several raids on starliners over the past six months. I'm betting they're hiding out on Gratitude. There's even some hypotheses about them building their numbers by recruiting from the gem miners in the asteroid fields near there. Rough bunch, and angry about low wages and poor benefits."

And they were going to Gratitude. Wonderful.

Elaine didn't need the extra stress, but her friend was oblivious. To Stephanie, danger meant excitement. Oh, she'd shown genuine concern for Elaine's safety during the tube accident, but the *idea* of a thrill stimulated Stephanie more than anyone Elaine had ever met.

Stephanie and Elaine moved to stand in front of a male crew member whose dark skin set off his uniform nicely. More perfect white teeth greeted them with a smile. Dental work must have been a requirement for employment. Elaine ran her tongue over her own teeth, hoping none of her rarely applied lipstick had smeared on them. The tear in her skort bothered her. She knew it was irrational. No one would blame her. But focusing on what happened would push her into hysterics. Better to worry over the little things.

As their guide began his spiel about the atrium and how the holographs functioned, Stephanie leaned in for the last word. "If we are attacked by pirates, I hope they're as cute as the ship's crew."

THE TOUR proved more entertaining than Elaine would have imagined, and a welcome distraction from her arrival incident. *Accident*. No foul play. Accidents happened all the time, right?

The Martian Mamas (she was working on her second now) lightened her sore feet and had her giggling at the tour guide's scripted jokes. Familiarity with large public areas, especially locations such as the Milky Way Bar, the Celestial Theater, the Starlight Dining Room, and the Comet Gym and Spa would be helpful to prevent her from getting lost.

Stephanie, who had taken several of these cruises, spent the time flirting with the host. Elaine would have sworn she slipped him her cabin number halfway through the tour. Good thing she insisted on separate staterooms. Stephanie's should have a revolving door.

"Where are the THIs?" someone asked from the rear of the group.

Wait. What?

Jay Grego had mentioned something about having sold the THI programs running on the *Nebula*, but Elaine had been too distracted by her port panic attack and Stephanie's flirting to think much of his announcement.

Elaine leaned over to whisper in her friend's ear. "Steph, what have you gotten me into?"

Stephanie didn't look the least bit apologetic. "It's a themed cruise, hon. Film stars and characters from the twentieth century. THI companions for all the singles. Every girl gets her dream date. And no rad risks." She practically wriggled in anticipation.

THI—Tangible Holographic Image—technology was defined as a "found" technology, discovered in the abandoned ruins of an ancient alien civilization on…. Elaine thought back to the newsvids she'd seen years ago… yep, Gratitude. Xenoarchaeologists and scientists suspected its purpose had been for entertainment originally, and they'd adapted it for use with human-made computers, tweaking the systems and eventually reproducing them. Alien-made hardware intrigued Elaine, but the speed with which it had been introduced to the public made her a little nervous. Everyone wanted it, and fast, especially when it proved to be rad-free and rendered the systems it ran on rad-free as well.

Sadly, it only ran with the outrageously expensive entertainment systems, almost as if the THI tech had a mind of its own.

The military first sought uses for it, but it had built-in failsafes preventing aggressive applications from being developed. Every effort they made resulted in cataclysmic failure, erasing entire hard drives despite all kinds of protection. It defied explanation. Researchers reverse-engineered the technique and made their own versions, and still it failed in every military trial. Again, one more reason for Elaine to wonder if they'd analyzed it fully enough. Potential profit had an unhealthy habit of overruling common sense.

The crewman paused in his explanation of early and late dinner seatings to favor the inquisitive teenager who'd asked about the THIs with a polite smile. "The THIs are all around us." When first-timers turned in circles like they rode an invisible merry-go-round, he laughed. "You just can't see them yet." He pointed at a small black disk embedded in the wall about five centimeters from the ceiling. "Those are not only our vid cameras, but also our THI emitters. Your personal THI escorts activate when you first enter your staterooms. In addition to the questionnaires you filled out online, the system is gathering information about each of you even now, fine-tuning and tweaking the programs to your individual quirks and habits."

"What questionnaires?" she growled to Stephanie grinning beside her. This is what she got for letting someone else book the cruise and handle the details.

"Oh, don't worry," her friend whispered back. "I was completely honest about you. I'm sure they'll pair you with a very compatible, very polite, very boringly *normal* THI companion."

Elaine resisted the urge to kick her friend in the shin.

The guide continued, "The THI system also serves as internal security." He shot Elaine a quick glance before focusing on another guest. "It alerts the crew to your needs and any problems that might arise." He patted the wall fondly, as if it lived and breathed. "We're very proud of our system. It's the best of its kind. You won't be able to tell your escorts from real people."

Ancient celluloid films remastered in Tangible Holographic Imagery had been the fad on Earth for the past two years. The THITs—Tangible Holo-Imagery Theaters—capitalized on that popularity. Patrons sat or even walked through the actual settings of the films, participated in the action, interacted with the characters. Elaine had never attended one but assumed this cruise experience was designed similarly.

Like she wanted to have physical contact with images of actors who'd been dead hundreds of years.

And not knowing who was real and who wasn't—it unnerved her. Maybe with a THI partner she didn't have to worry about residual radiation, but there were other considerations, more important ones, at least to her. She raised her hand for attention.

"What if we want to know if someone is a THI? I mean, I wouldn't want to start a relationship with someone who was going to just disappear." Elaine felt the heat rush to her face as she blushed. She hadn't meant to imply she was thinking of relationships at all. And Harriet's assassination proved to her that quick disappearances via unexpected death could and did happen. It wasn't an experience she cared to repeat, in any form.

"Why the hell not?" Stephanie laughed, nudging her arm with her shoulder. "That would describe half the guys I've dated!"

The guide joined the group in a good chuckle, then raised his voice to regain their focus. "In all seriousness, you *can* tell them apart, not by appearance but by their expressive personalities. The theme is film characters and actors of the twentieth century. If someone behaves in a particularly dramatic manner or bursts into spontaneous dance or song—" He paused for more laughter. "—that would be a good indication you are dealing with a THI. But if you are particularly paranoid—" He glanced again at Elaine, but his smile gentled the rebuke. "—wait for an intimate moment and look behind your partner's right ear." He waggled his eyebrows.

"What for? Hickeys?" The teenager earned herself a laugh.

"Nope. The Biotech logo."

Elaine nodded with the others. Like the Leviathan sea-monster design, everyone knew Biotech's signature image, a single flower with a power cord for a stem and its three-pronged plug for roots.

They finished their tour on a more somber note, one of the lifepod decks. Centrally located amidships, the lifepods formed three globular rings around the starliner's exterior. Their guide paused at the access hatch to one of them and tapped a complex code into a numbered panel beside it. A high-pitched alarm sounded. The tourists covered their ears with hands and forearms, one man spilling his drink. The siren screeched for several seconds before the host turned it off. Elaine thought she might be ill. Hearing that sound again so soon set her nerves on end. She swallowed hard, took even breaths, and counted to ten.

A whirring noise made them all turn to see a robo-cleaner approach. The low-to-the-ground circular device hummed over the puddle of Martian Mama. When it left, the spill had vanished.

"Sorry about that, sir," the crewman apologized. "We'll get you another one of those at the completion of the tour, on the house of course." He turned to the group. "Now, if this had been a real emergency, that alarm would have come through every speaker on all twelve decks of the ship. Your THI escorts would lead you to your designated lifepods. If access to your pod is restricted due to the emergency, then it will take you to the nearest pod. In the event of a major power failure, back-up generators will activate, and glowing red arrows will direct you to your pods."

"And if all power fails?" Elaine asked.

The crewman opened his mouth to respond, but Stephanie cut him off.

"Then screw the closest willing partner, 'cause you ain't got a prayer."

THEIR STATEROOMS turned out to be on the Starfield level, deck one, the concierge section. She'd told Stephanie to book this trip without a thought to cost, and her friend had followed her instructions like the good personal assistant she'd trained to become.

A white-coated butler led them across the walkway that bridged the atrium, and Elaine resisted the urge to look over the railing. Height was not her friend.

"Ooooh, pretty!" Stephanie squealed, pulling at her sleeve.

Elaine's hip bumped the guardrail. "Steph, I don't think—"

"Oh, lighten up and look, sweetheart."

Elaine allowed herself a glance over the edge and caught her breath. No dizziness, no nausea. As well as being decorative, the holographic starfield served a practical purpose. The swirling nebulae and occasional vapor-trailing comets softened the immense drop, allowing her to experience the spectacle without the feeling of falling to her death.

They continued across the abyss, entering a long corridor lined with hatches numbered in gold filigree on either side. The butler halted between 134 and 135, with 134 being an exterior cabin and 135 an interior. Elaine had the outside stateroom, of course. It was her credits paying for the trip, after all. She wasn't certain she appreciated the luxury. Exterior meant view, and view meant potential vertigo.

The butler pulled a handcomp from his inside jacket pocket, consulted it, and turned to the two women. "Your luggage has already been delivered and awaits you inside. Departure is at three. Dinner this evening is at 6:00 p.m. Attire is semiformal. Complimentary beverages and hors d'oeuvres are served on the walkway at five fifteen. I hope you'll join us. If you need anything further, the call switch is located right inside the hatch." With a nod to them both, the butler strode away, stiff-backed and formal.

Stephanie yawned. "Well, honey, I'm in for a nap, a shower, and dressing for dinner. Meet you at the cocktail party?"

Elaine covered the copycat yawn behind her hand and consulted her watch. "It's one now. Sounds good."

A hatch across the hall and two rooms down cycled open, and a familiar face leaned out. Jay Grego's cheeks dimpled charmingly with his wide grin. "Isn't this lucky for me! Always nice to know your neighbors."

Too lucky. Elaine suspected a bribe might have crossed the check-in desk after they left.

"How about me coming over for a neighborly drink?" Grego's voice flowed silky smooth.

To Elaine's surprise, Stephanie hesitated, glancing between Jay Grego and Elaine, a torn expression pulling down the corners of her mouth. Her friend crossed to her, blocking Jay's view of their faces and lowering her voice so he couldn't hear her. "This might take a while. Forgive me if I'm a little late for drinks and hors d' oeuvres?"

Elaine fumbled in her skort pocket for the keycard Stephanie had given her. "Don't worry about it," she said, giving her friend a gentle nudge with her toe. "I'm fine by myself for a while." At Stephanie's look of relief, Elaine turned and inserted the keycard in its slot, urging the hatch to open faster. She'd given Stephanie the "be careful" lecture. Time to escape the awkwardness of hallway voyeurism. When the thick slab of airtight metal slid into the bulkhead, she stepped inside, passed under the decontaminator light, and let it close behind her. Its clang drowned out Stephanie's giggle and Jay's throaty laughter.

She leaned against the sealed hatch, closing her eyes with a sigh. Not that they even noticed her, but Elaine also wanted to avoid any further discussions about her late wife and Leviathan's hiring and firing policies.

Beyond all that, after the day she'd had, she needed some time alone.

She opened her eyes, taking in the large suite at a glance. She stood in a small alcove, her luggage just inside the entrance. The short hall opened into a sitting area with a viewport that showed the darkness of space and a few stars. An open door on her right revealed the sanitary facilities. An archway to the left likely led to the bedroom, but with the lights out in there, she couldn't be sure.

Elaine set her empty drink glass on a shelf beside the entry. She turned to enter the small but efficiently designed bathroom, stepping around her suitcase. Unpacking would wait until after her nap.

A tousled head of short, thick brown hair leaned around the edge of the bedroom archway. The androgynous but striking face turned in Elaine's direction, lopsided grin spreading across the handsome features. "Well, hello!" the stranger said in a low but distinctly female voice.

Elaine jumped, tumbled over her own luggage, and landed on her ass.

CHAPTER 3
WHEN RICHELLE MET ELAINE

"OH! OH, for goodness' sake!" The stranger rushed to Elaine's side, extending a hand to help her up. Elaine scrambled backward like a crab, and with no one to grab on to, the unknown woman overbalanced and fell over the suitcase herself to join her on the floor.

She shoved at the stranger's shoulder hard, forcing her to roll. "Get away from me! I've had karate training." Elaine's spine connected with the wall. She couldn't go any farther, and this woman sat between her and the door.

The woman tilted her head to one side. She paused, staring at Elaine. Soft brown eyes met Elaine's wide ones. Then the woman sat back, drawing her knees up and resting her open palms on them. "No, you haven't."

"What?" The single word came out in a screech.

"Karate. You haven't had any. I doubt you've ever even watched it done. It's not in your character."

"My—" Elaine blinked, then exhaled. Her bangs rose and fell on her forehead with the rush of air. "You're my THI." Her respiration returned to normal. "Damn Stephanie and this whole stupid idea." She stood and righted her fallen suitcase.

The tangible hologram got to its feet with more difficulty, long legs a little awkward under the lean frame. Funny for a hologram to be awkward. Elaine guessed it made for better realism. It extended its hand, this time in greeting. "I'm Richelle, ma'am. Back in the bigtime era of movie musicals, people used to shorten that to Ricky, which is what I'd prefer if you're willing."

Bullshit. THIs couldn't *prefer* anything. Elaine ignored the outstretched hand and focused on her luggage. "Go away, Richelle," she said pointedly. The floral pattern of the retro fabric suitcase had been scraped and scratched by the double falls and recent use. She fingered a small hole near the handle and wished she'd brought durahard bags instead.

Richelle moved to look over her shoulder at the damage. Elaine suppressed a shiver at the close proximity. God, she could feel its breath on her neck! Too much realism. Way too much.

"I'm sure the butler could have that fixed for you. After all, it was my fault."

Elaine turned and studied the holographic image. She didn't know how the unknown and long-gone aliens had made THI tech work. She'd read an article explaining in layman's terms that it had to do with mass particles created in a centrally located generator and then transferred via light waves, recombining in a programmed pattern to simulate anything the programmer desired. It required a tremendous amount of power to operate, and Elaine privately suspected the scientists themselves didn't fully understand how it all functioned. But they were willing to use it to make money when Biotech offered to fund their research.

"I asked you to go away." Elaine met the THI's eyes, having to look up to do so. "You can do that, can't you?" Richelle stood almost a head taller than her—at least five nine, maybe more. Toned and fit. Not much in the way of muscle, but not an ounce of flab either. Richelle's simple white button-down shirt had come untucked in the fall, and the tailored cut draped over small, firm breasts and tapered at a slightly narrower waist.

Richelle followed Elaine's gaze and shoved the shirt into the waistband of the now-rumpled gray trousers. "Yes, ma'am." The voice went soft. "I can do that."

But it didn't. The hologram continued to watch her. Elaine pushed a few strands of hair behind her ear and stepped to the entrance. "Do you use the door, or…?" She glanced toward the ceiling and spotted those same onyx disks. Her gaze traveled around the room, following the sequence of them, embedded in all four walls. Good God! Did this thing watch her in the bathroom too? She hadn't paid attention. She leaned a little, trying to get a glimpse inside the sanitary facility from her current location.

Richelle leaned with her, mimicking her actions and blocking her view. "There aren't any in there," the THI said with a grin.

Elaine jolted.

"It made some guests uncomfortable. And to answer your *spoken* question, I don't just disappear. I'm not a magician or anything."

"No, you're a THI." Elaine turned and walked into the sitting area. In the mirror over the couch, she watched Richelle place hands on narrow hips.

"And you're afraid of me. Why?"

Subtlety wasn't this thing's strong suit. "I'm not afraid of you." Okay, she had been, but a THI wasn't nearly as intimidating as a human stranger in her room. Elaine sank onto the couch. It conformed to her body, cushioning the bruised areas from both of today's falls. Its deep navy velvet complemented the sky-blue decor of the suite. She ran her hands over the material, letting its softness soothe her shattered nerves. Elaine looked out the viewport at the starfield beyond. The starliner's orbit made the pinpoints of light appear to move, making her a little nauseated. Maybe she should take a sedative. Not a bad idea, given the day she'd had.

Richelle studied her from the alcove. The scrutiny unnerved her, and she was already unnerved enough. "You fell on your, um, well—" Richelle pointed to its own backside. "—while trying to get away from me."

"I thought you were an assassin."

That comment doubled the hologram over in hearty laughter. The sound rolled through the room, carrying to every corner. Thank goodness for insulation or it would disturb neighboring guests. A full minute passed before it got hold of itself, quite literally, with both arms wrapped around its midsection in an attempt to stifle the guffaws. By the end, it could barely breathe, or, well, simulate breathing. "An assassin!" It chuckled a bit more. "You give me far too much credit, ma'am."

Elaine's stresses hit her with a force like a falling anvil from some black-and-white 2D film. How dare this thing belittle her fears! The strain of the day, the trip, all these people, the accident, this stranger in her room. Too much. Her lower lip trembled, and she bit it hard enough to taste blood, trying to stifle tears. This would never do. She didn't even see a box of absorbers in the room.

Richelle ceased its laughter and sat on the floor in front of her, folding legs beneath itself like closing an old-fashioned ironing board.

Its height intimidated her, and it seemed to know it. Normally, she preferred tall women, and Stephanie had likely said so in the survey her friend had filled out for her. Harriet had been tall. Today tall bothered her. It had seated itself to make her more comfortable. That was... well, if not "nice," at least some damn good programming.

"I'm sorry," Richelle said, voice low. "I wasn't making light of what happened to you today."

"You know?"

Richelle cocked its head toward the upper walls and the onyx disks. "I saw. You must have been very frightened." It reached out as if to take her hand.

She yanked both of them away. They clenched into fists. Her face grew hot. "Don't patronize me." She jerked to her feet. Even with it seated and her standing, its head was higher than her waist. Geez. "Do you even know what fear is? Of course you don't. You invade, you analyze, you pronounce." Elaine shoved past it and stormed to the entry hatch. She pointed at the door. "Get out. Disappear, fade away, disintegrate. I don't care. Just go!"

The THI stood and walked past her. It did not avoid her, though, and its arm brushed her shoulder. Even through clothing, the heat of its body transferred to her. It sent a warm wave from neck to hip before it faded. *Damn* good programming.

And alien technology, Elaine reminded herself, suppressing a shiver.

Richelle opened the hatch and stepped over the threshold, but paused halfway out, the blue decon light remaining on while it hesitated. THIs didn't give off rads or absorb them, but it was apparently solid enough, real enough, to trigger the decontaminator. It leaned to look at her, exactly the way she'd first caught a glimpse of it through the bedroom arch. "I'm not your enemy." It spoke with assurance. The intensity in its eyes compelled her to listen, but she fought it and turned away.

The voice grew softer. Elaine assumed it stood in the exterior corridor now. Its words wafted to her over the hallway foot traffic. "Who do you think unlocked the jammed airlock door?"

"Wait, what? How?"

But her questions went unanswered.

TOO FAST. You're moving too fast.

Back in the flow of electrons and protons, Richelle could have kicked herself, if she still had legs.

She'd reached Elaine. She'd reached her with her concern, albeit briefly, and then blown it. Organics couldn't accept emotions from Richelle, no matter how deeply she felt them.

Well, at least Elaine had spoken to her, harshly or not. Elaine Kane had not ignored her. And for all her posturing and determination to do otherwise, she had, at intervals, interacted with Richelle as if she were a person and not a thing. Not a mere servant or slave.

Baby steps.

Frustration roiled through her, particles flowing faster, swirling in circles through the emitters' conduits. One couldn't take baby steps when one had only a week.

Richelle didn't want to scare her, but dammit, she liked Elaine. And she had reached her. She'd looked at Richelle, not through her. And for the first time in a long time, Richelle felt alive.

Somehow, she'd get Elaine to make her feel that way more often.

The rescue. That surprised Elaine. If she believed Richelle. Damsel in distress, and she'd saved Elaine's life, or at least made saving her life possible.

Richelle brought up information on classic heroes—strong, masculine individuals who rode in on white horses in the nick of time to save the girl. Not many (any) female examples from her film-era origins. Her current persona didn't really measure up, but she'd do her best. Thank goodness humanity had progressed from those chauvinistic origins. Too bad Richelle's character selection didn't include enough of that progression. If she pushed it too far, she'd give herself away, and that, she could not afford.

ELAINE STOOD beside the alcove, Harriet's urn centered within it. Caretakers had polished the brass surface to such a sheen that Elaine should see her own face reflected. Only it wasn't her face she saw.

It was Harriet's.

"Where am I, Lanie?" Harry's voice demanded, the mouth of the reflection motionless, the whisper escaping from the vessel's lid. "Where am I?"

Elaine shivered, wrapping her arms around herself in the black dress she'd worn to the funeral. "I don't know," she whimpered.

And she didn't.

After Elaine and Stephanie left the murder scene, during a brief moment while the detectives were fending off the press and everyone was out of the office, the corpse had disappeared. Just vanished. Investigators suspected the private anti-grav lift, but security cameras showed no one entering or leaving, and between one frame and another, the late Harriet Kane was gone. The bloodstains and brain matter remained on the floor and desk, but the samples taken and packed into cases also vanished, and by the time the forensic scientists figured out they'd been taken, the office had been cleaned. Whoever tampered with the office recordings must have been very good. None of the police techs could find evidence of it. Someone had to be working on the inside. Someone didn't want any further investigation of the murder.

As she watched, wide-eyed, the urn rocked, back and forth, back and forth, picking up intensity until it toppled onto its side and the lid fell the three feet from the alcove to the stone floor with a resounding clang.

Elaine stared into its empty depths, fingernails digging into the fabric of her sleeves.

"Where am I, Lanie?"

SHE SAT up in bed, panting, her breath coming in a hiss too reminiscent of Harriet's whisper.

The chiming of the bed's headboard clock sounded like ship's bells on an old Earth sailing vessel. Elaine steadied herself quickly. Nothing new about the nightmares. She'd had a variety of them since the murder eleven months ago. The whispering-urn scenario was a favorite of her subconscious.

Elaine glared at the glowing red clock face numbers, an inch high, embedded in the wood behind her head. She blinked to clear her vision, then blinked again. Shit. Four thirty. She'd set it for four and slept right through it. Now she'd have to scramble to shower and change before the cocktail reception on the walkway.

Being late didn't make it easier for her to move faster. Her muscles complained when she stretched to turn off the alarm. She flopped on the mattress for a few more moments and sighed, Harriet's voice still echoing in her ears. The king-size bed had a Smart Mattress, a Leviathan innovation. Hard to detach herself from her late spouse when everything around her came from Harry's, now her, corporation.

Elaine became aware of the subtle vibration of the ship's engines traveling through the bed's frame. A quick glance out the bedroom viewport confirmed departure, but she turned away before the swirling stars could make her space-sick. The *Nebula* had top-of-the-line inertial compensators. At the faster-than-light speeds they traveled via the singularity drive, every living thing would have been paste on the bulkheads without them. But the sight of such movement played havoc with her senses. She'd always been susceptible to such things. Ground and aircar travel bumped her around enough to make her sick.

Resigned, she swung her legs over the side and stood. Her rumpled skort and blouse fell into place around her, but she cast a glance at the THI emitters anyway. How much of her skin revealed itself during sleep? She'd clearly tossed and turned, the blankets dumped on the floor and the sheets tangled at the foot of the bed. Exhaustion hadn't overcome her nightmares.

She peered through the arch into the sitting area, searching for any sign that another entity occupied the suite. She crept to her suitcase and pulled out her LBD (little black dress) but waited until she'd entered the bathroom and shut the door before removing her day clothes. Hologram or not, it wasn't watching her undress. She didn't want to see its realistic reaction to her nakedness.

How did the technology work? She guessed her arrival triggered its initial appearance. One of the crewmen, the tour guide, maybe, had said as much. What would bring it back? More importantly, what would keep it away?

Still, she couldn't help her mind cycling over and over again to its final pronouncement, that it had saved her from the airlock and a gruesome death in the cold of space. How? Could a sophisticated enough THI override some code in the airlock release? The ship guide said the programs ran everywhere, acted as backup security, gathered information on the passengers from their actions. If it could do all that, then playing her savior didn't seem so far-fetched. Clearly, Richelle was an "intelligent" program, more complex than a glitching computerized hatch lock.

Rescuer or not, she wanted it to leave her alone.

Elaine sighed. She wanted everyone to leave her alone. A wave of irritation clenched her fists at her sides. Stephanie engineered this excursion, and now she was off with her new fling, leaving Elaine at the mercy of whatever the ship's programmers decided to toss her way. Not her idea of rest and relaxation. Maybe she could lure her friend away for some spa time or dancing. Dancing would be fun.

After a hasty shower, Elaine slithered into the spaghetti-strap three-tiered knee-length dress, hearing the silky fabric rustle around her. She examined her reflection in the mirror. Harriet had liked this dress, though she'd complained it made her upper arms look too big. Elaine had worked out with weights for three months after that offhanded remark. She quirked a grin. No flabby arms now. She did hair and makeup without her usual precision, going for free-spirited rather than polished, and finished with black heels, adding an inch and a half to her height.

A quick glance told her the sitting room remained empty, and she blew out an impatient breath. This was ridiculous, having to sneak around her own stateroom like a cat burglar. She'd speak to the cruise director, ask if the THI emitters in her cabin could be disconnected. After all, they owed her, and she could still sue over her earlier frightening experience. Determined to assert her dominance, Elaine stomped about the entry alcove in her heels, letting them click loudly on the polished floor, then marched through the living space, placing each foot with such force that she left indentations in the plush carpeting. She didn't call the hologram by name, but she glared at each onyx disk, daring it to appear. When it didn't, she caught a glimpse of herself in the small mirror inside the entry and laughed almost hysterically at her fierce expression.

It was just a computer program. A very sophisticated, alien-enhanced program to be sure, but she'd told it to shut down, and it had obeyed her command.

Elaine checked her diamond-and-silver watch, another gift from Harry. Late. She'd never been late to anything while her spouse lived. Between Harriet's inner clock and a dozen aides, they'd never missed an appointment time. Since her death, Elaine hadn't attended many functions. Come to think of it, she'd been late to Harry's funeral. Even without a body to cremate, the media and Harriet's family expected the performance of all the traditional rituals, including the ceremonial, though empty, urn. Pushing the memory away, Elaine hurried to the hatch.

It cycled open, sliding into the bulkhead with a mechanical growl while the blue decon light bathed her in its glow and washed out her skin, already set off a bit pale in the black dress. Couples in an array of fabrics and fashions ranging from gorgeous to garish strolled past en route to the walkway cocktail reception. Elaine studied them as she waited for each pairing to pass.

Telling the THIs from the living, breathing human beings proved less difficult than she would have expected. On the whole, THIs had more polish, more pizzazz. They were larger than life. Modeled after movie stars and the characters they played, they possessed that "star quality" that catapulted them to fame in the twentieth century. They might have been indistinguishable from their originals, but next to average tourists, even wealthy ones, they stood out.

An impeccably dressed gentleman in a black tuxedo extended his arm for his lady companion to take. When he did so, the movement of his jacket revealed an ancient revolver tucked into the waistband of his trousers.

Elaine blinked. That couldn't be real. Bullets on a starliner were dangerous things. One misfire could pierce the ship's hull and compromise atmospheric integrity. The buxom redhead with him didn't seem to notice the weapon. She giggled and wrapped herself around the offered arm. The man winked at Elaine as they passed, and the redhead smiled, then frowned, glancing over Elaine's shoulder and raising an eyebrow. Elaine turned, expecting to find that Richelle had appeared, but saw only empty space. She shrugged at the curious woman. The couple moved on.

Next came a portly gentleman managing to look neat and distinguished in a formal suit and tie despite his bulk. Elaine credited his tailors with the accomplishment. The lines of the gray-and-black ensemble hid the worst of the bulges and flattered his better features. However, it didn't compensate enough to warrant the young, flirty platinum blond pausing to blow in his ear. She planted a peck on his cheek before they proceeded past. Nope, no fear of rad transference with THIs. Her white cocktail dress flared at the hemline and plunged at the neck, showing enough leg and breast to attract the attention of every man in the corridor. She blew kisses at them and waved.

Elaine frowned. Everyone had a partner. No one walked alone. She thought about chiming Stephanie's cabin, but if she and Jay were occupied, that might turn out embarrassing. Elaine would be horribly obvious if she went to the reception unattended, which was, she supposed, the point of this themed cruise for singles. Opening her mouth, she drew breath to call for the THI—

And felt a tap on her shoulder.

Aware of the sophisticated clientele around her, she managed to stifle her squeak of surprise, but she took an involuntary step and stumbled in the high heels (well, high for her). Steadying arms wrapped around her waist, preventing her from falling over the raised threshold. Elaine inhaled the scent of a pleasant musky cologne applied in the perfect amount to not overpower or make her sneeze.

Smells too? Well, it made sense. The molecular structure of each piece of a THI was recreated to match an original identically. The generator, wherever on the ship it was located, was told what to produce. And if its molecular structure gave off a scent, then the duplication of those same molecules in that same combination would give off the same scent.

Richelle drew her up against it, pressing Elaine back against its chest and holding her there. For a moment, just a moment, Elaine allowed herself safety and protection in those encircling arms that felt so very real.

Could she pretend? For the duration of this seven-day excursion across the stars, could she imagine herself involved in a vid-worthy romance?

Then what? One empty relationship was enough. Her marriage to Harriet had been no happily-ever-after—more of a convenient toleration. Elaine pressed harder against Richelle to gain the leverage to push away. She heard its grunt of surprise and felt it stagger a bit to maintain its own balance. Guess it didn't know everything about her, after all.

Elaine faced it. "Stop sneaking up on me." She plunged into the procession of passengers, not bothering to check if her companion trailed her or not. Heavier footfalls in dress shoes assured her it did. In fact, she bet its stomps were for emphasis, so as not to sneak up on her.

When the passage opened onto the wide catwalk over the starfield holographic display, she paused and scanned the crowd of guests for Stephanie. Dozens of couples strolled back and forth, some pausing to admire the atrium view, others rocking gently to the classical music that gave the scene an almost eerie soundtrack. Elaine couldn't spot her friend anywhere. With Stephanie's height, that meant she wasn't present.

"She's in her suite. With a Mister Jay Grego. I can fetch them, if you want."

Elaine stared at it. Was that sulkiness in the THI's voice? Seriously? Richelle's emotional algorithms needed tweaking if she could hurt its "feelings" with a shove and a simple rebuke.

"If they're still in her suite, they don't want to be disturbed."

Stephanie didn't concern herself with the risk of rad transference. Sterilization didn't worry her. She was an upwardly mobile executive assistant and had no desire to have children. And the government's pleas for caution and encouragement to women to produce multiple babies held no sway with her. She'd sleep with whomever she wanted, whenever she wanted.

"Oh? But they'll miss the—" The clouds cleared. "Oh! Of course!" A blush crept from beneath its collar. "Well, I don't mean 'of course' like that's her usual behavior or anything. What I mean is—"

"That *is* her usual behavior." Elaine laughed. The blush was a nice touch, made it more endearing. More human. She cleared her throat, then coughed to hide her reaction.

"I—I'll get you a drink." The hologram maneuvered its way into the crowd of milling guests and other THIs.

Which left Elaine alone in a crowd of strangers. Though she hated it, this was familiar territory. Harriet often escorted her to events and functions only to vanish when her comm chimed or an aide needed her or a business associate beckoned. Shy by nature and awkward throughout her teens and into young adulthood, it had taken Elaine years to develop social skills. Now the routine reminded her of a set of dance steps. Performed in the correct sequence, it charmed your audience. One misstep and you fell flat on your face.

She usually began with a drink to give her something to occupy her hands so they wouldn't hang at her sides like withering leaves. But liquids involved risk. One could spill a drink and end up with stains in odd places. More dangerous for men than women, really, but she wasn't ready to take the chance just yet. A passing server offered a tray of hors d'oeuvres, but she declined. Depending on the quality of preparation and the ingredients, she could wear a variety of flavors and smell of pungent spices for the remainder of the evening.

You're overanalyzing, Elaine.

Well, what else was she going to do, hit on someone? She flushed a little at the thought. Such an action would have been totally out of character for her. That was Stephanie's talent. Besides, Elaine already had a "date."

Elaine spotted Richelle on the far side of the walkway, waiting in line at a temporary bar set up for this occasion. The THI stood several people back in the queue. It would be a while before it got her drink. She smiled to herself, betting it even knew her preferred wines and cocktails. Harriet never got it right, always bringing her something too strong for her taste. Elaine suspected she thought it would make her more amorous in bed. More often than not, it put her to sleep.

Time for the sashay. She smiled at one guest and then another, testing each one for an amiable response. An older woman returned the smile, raising her glass of white wine in greeting, then beckoning Elaine over with a wave of a bejeweled hand. Each finger wore a ring with a different colored gemstone. Bracelets of amethysts, topaz, emeralds, and sapphires ran up her arms, almost succeeding in hiding age spots beneath their finery. Strands of multihued crystal beads diverted attention from sagging breasts and stood in stark contrast against the simple yet elegant black dress she wore. Her angle revealed more crystals woven through a long braid of salt-and-pepper hair, which followed the barely noticeable curvature of her spine. Elaine appreciated the effect. What would have been gaudy on anyone else worked for her. And even better, the woman appeared to be alone.

Just to be certain of what she was dealing with, Elaine leaned a little, trying to steal a glimpse of the bare skin behind the woman's right ear.

The older woman laughed. "Just moles and a freckle or two. Though I've got a tattoo at the nape of my neck that might be of interest."

Elaine smiled and shifted her focus to the woman's eyes. "You caught me. Sorry."

The woman extended her free hand and shook the one Elaine offered in return. "I'm Muriel Debois. No need to apologize. This your first THI cruise?"

Elaine nodded, then blinked. "Debois? The artist?"

Muriel gave a slight bow. "In the flesh."

"I have one of your sculptures in my living room. It's a dolphin, blue crystal, with white foam and—"

"*Leviathan's Prey.* I remember that piece. One of my favorites. Which means you must be Ms. Kane." She paused, placing a finger to her temple as she thought a moment. "Elaine, isn't it?" At Elaine's start, she added, "I never forget a customer. I fill the orders myself. And though I only interacted with you by email, I appreciated your sense of irony." She gave Elaine a knowing look, then extended her arm to encompass the starliner in all its glory. "I guess the prey escaped after all."

Yes, Harriet's death had freed Elaine, in a way. Muriel had cracked open a door Elaine preferred remain closed. Time to do a little sidestepping. "So, where's your…?" She let her voice trail off but stared at the empty place at Muriel's shoulder.

"Oh, Marlon? He's fetching my shawl. This atrium gets terribly drafty with all the air circulation."

Come to think of it, the walkway area *was* cold. Elaine felt goose bumps rising on her bare shoulders and forearms. A breeze carried over the balcony, and she shivered.

Something warm and heavy dropped around her. She looked down at her arms to see a tweed jacket draped over her shoulders. So THIs could separate into parts, the jacket and the rest of Richelle. Interesting. She supposed as long as the emitters surrounded her, such a thing made sense. Richelle handed her a sparkling deep blue liquid in a champagne glass. She cocked an eyebrow at it.

"Blueberry champagne," it explained. "Made not too far from our launch site, in Egg Harbor City, believe it or not. New Jersey may not be known for its wines, but they do know how to grow blueberries."

And how did a THI know that? Certainly a twentieth-century film character wouldn't. At least Elaine didn't think so.

Elaine took a tentative sip and grinned. Light, sweet, perfect. "It's wonderful," she admitted. She held the glass up to admire the beverage's shimmer in the light.

The aforementioned Marlon arrived, a large, burly man with an olive complexion and dark slicked-back hair. Muscles stretched his formal wear to its limits. Elaine smothered a laugh at the incongruity of the lacy black shawl he had draped over one arm. Marlon passed the shawl to Muriel, who took it and ignored him. Instead, all the older woman's attention focused on Richelle.

"You've never had Renault champagne before, have you?" Muriel asked. She directed her question to Elaine but continued her examination of Elaine's THI.

"No… why?" Had she committed some faux pas? Was blueberry champagne the latest "in" drink among the elite? Locked in her home for the past eleven months, Elaine had lost touch with the trends.

Muriel circled Richelle, taking in every angle. It tried to watch her out of the corner of its eye, a disconcerted frown on its face. When she pulled its right ear aside to look behind it, the THI flinched, then batted her hand away. "Excuse me, madam!"

The artist placed the swatted hand on her hip. "Well!" she exclaimed with a huff. "You got yourself a good one!"

"I'm sorry?" Elaine moved to Richelle's side and took her arm possessively. When she realized what she'd done, and that she'd thought of the program as "her" rather than "it," Elaine blushed but didn't let go. Richelle glanced down at her with a slight smile.

"Now, that's real artistry. An upgrade or something. Most of these clods can't think past their programming." Muriel jerked a thumb at Marlon, who'd watched the proceedings with complete lack of interest. "Oh, they're good at some things. They do what you tell them. They're gallant and charming." She leaned toward Elaine. "Sex ain't bad, either, believe me. I've done this trip a few times. Every time, I change some of my survey answers to get a different character. None of them fail you in bed. Even the ones that were heterosexual in real life are programmed to please both sides. And it's nice not to worry about potential rad transference." She paused and blinked up at Richelle. "I haven't had you, though. What's your specialty?"

Richelle shifted, coughed, and cleared her throat. She could turn an impressively bright shade of pink.

Elaine rushed to her rescue. "You were saying something about artistry?"

"Hmm? Oh, right. Extrapolation from accumulated data. You like champagne. I'll bet you like blueberries too."

Elaine nodded.

"I'll even wager your favorite color is a shade of blue."

Elaine held out her glass. "Yes, this shade."

Muriel nodded. "Like I said, extrapolation. It's all logical, the combination of information. But Marlon here brings me the same damn white wine over and over again. It's my favorite drink. It's on one of the checklists I filled out for one of these cruises. It's stored somewhere." She took a breath and expelled it. "It's boring!"

Well, one thing Elaine could confirm about her time with Richelle so far. She was anything but boring.

"Yep," Muriel concluded, "you've got one of the good ones."

CHAPTER 4
THE GOOD ONES,
THE BAD ONES,
AND THE BALD ONES

AS THE evening wore on, Elaine became more and more aware of what having a "good one" meant. Richelle escorted her to dinner, seated her at the captain's table, and even reminded the waiter that she didn't care for too much Worcestershire sauce in her cheese fondue appetizer.

Elaine blinked at that. The questionnaire Stephanie had filled out for her must have included food preferences and dislikes, but the THI's insight continued to amaze her. She supposed it could have extrapolated

again, from the combination of flavors checked in the
negatives column, but…. Very impressive. And a little creepy. Still, she was happy to let someone else be
picky with the waiter instead of having to annoy the
white-coated young man herself.

The other six chairs remained empty. The captain and first mate stood at the entrance to the Starlight Dining Room, greeting and schmoozing with the
guests. The line to shake their hands extended so long
Elaine doubted they'd make it to their seats before
dessert. Stephanie and her THI had yet to appear, and
Elaine had no idea who their other dining companions
would be.

Richelle engaged her in conversation. "What differences do you perceive between living within one of
the biodomes and your childhood outside one? Do you
think being enclosed all the time has an effect on a person's psychology?"

Elaine just managed to keep her mouth from dropping open. Okay, not exactly in character with the twentieth-century persona, but an intriguing topic. They discussed humanity's loss of connection with nature and
her desire to lie on a beach that hadn't been dominated
by homes and hotels. She wanted to swim in an ocean
untainted by pollution.

"So, you enjoy swimming. And dance, if I recall
correctly?" Richelle spoke like an old friend who'd
known her well once but hadn't seen her in years.

Despite seeing the wheels turning, Elaine found
herself caught up in the exchange until Richelle mentioned hobbies of her own.

"You have… hobbies?"

Richelle fumbled her fork, spattering a bit of cheddar on her white shirtsleeve. She dabbed her napkin in

her water glass to wipe it off and didn't meet Elaine's eyes when she spoke. "Yes, I have hobbies. I like to learn new things."

Elaine leaned forward, placing both elbows on the table without concern for etiquette. She took a sip from her second champagne (or was it her third?). The starliner no longer seemed so chilly. Probably the alcohol. "What kinds of things?"

Richelle gestured in an offhanded manner, nearly knocking over Elaine's long-stemmed glass. Elaine steadied it with her fingertips. "Sorry," the THI muttered. "I like to learn about people and different places."

Elaine stiffened. "You gather data, you mean. Like our conversation just now. You're learning about me so you can improve on your programming." She looked around the room at the other couples, real and fake, human and hologram. As others shared a kiss (a wild public display between casual acquaintances in this era of rad risk, but inconsequential with a THI) or swirled across the central dance floor to some twentieth-century ballad, many seemed devoted to each other. But they couldn't be. The designers engineered it all.

Richelle caught Elaine's hand in her own, drawing her attention. The gentle fingers were cold around hers. "I'm learning about you because I'm interested." Her eyes searched Elaine's face. Richelle frowned at what she saw.

"Because you're programmed to be."

"I'm more than that. And you're stubborn."

"And you eat. How does that work?" Elaine waved at her companion's half-consumed appetizer.

Richelle's frown grew deeper. "My body can do anything any human female's can do." She shifted in her chair.

"I'll just bet it can!" came Stephanie's chipper voice as she arrived with a good-looking man wearing a white tuxedo, followed by Jay Grego and a striking brunette in a silver evening gown. And how had *he* finagled a seat at the captain's table? Elaine had to think for a moment. Ah, he sold the THIs to Nebula Starlines. That would do it.

"Hello, Ricky!" Stephanie's date extended a hand.

THIs recognized one another. If a central processor produced them all, then it made sense. Elaine wondered if two THIs having a conversation resembled talking to oneself, or if they were completely separate programs running independently.

"John," Richelle acknowledged, then nodded to the brunette. "Lara."

More first names, Elaine noted. She wondered if that were a conscious choice to foster familiarity between humans and their THIs, or maybe a copyright issue with some of the film production companies?

Dinner proceeded, interspersed with peaks of tension. Jay snapped his fingers to gain the attention of the bar waiter—an annoying habit Harriet had shared, treating servers like slaves. He placed a drink order for Stephanie without asking her preference, and when it arrived, she laughed at its potency. "It's a little late to be breaking down my inhibitions through alcohol," she declared. Everyone laughed except Elaine. And Richelle.

Further irritations arose when Stephanie spent most of her time talking with Jay instead of her THI. Apparently holograms could feign jealousy. John tried to tell jokes to get Stephanie's attention, while Lara pouted. Maybe Stephanie and Jay got off on that.

"And how are you two getting along?" Stephanie asked, smiling while Jay nuzzled her ear.

Elaine glanced at her date, who raised her eyebrows in anticipation of Elaine's response. "It's been… interesting."

Richelle's face fell. Elaine's gut twisted. This patchwork of electrical impulses was manipulating her. That didn't change her irrational desire to take back her words.

"Have you tried her out in bed yet?" Stephanie waggled her eyebrows.

Even though Richelle was a computer construct, that sort of crassness bothered Elaine. It implied things about *her* as well as the hologram, and she frowned.

Stephanie studied her expression. "Sorry, honey. I didn't mean to embarrass or insult you. You know me. My mouth runs off without my brain. And the liquor is talking a bit too. But seriously, it's expected. You paid good money for this trip. It's like buying a high-priced escort without the guilt or any risk of disease. All the fun and none of the worry."

Such a statement reminded Elaine of why she and Stephanie had become friends in the first place. Back in college, she'd depended on Stephanie to draw her from the dorms, get her eyes off her computer screen and her mind away from her studies. Stephanie taught her a lot about flirting and social life in general. But Elaine had never gone in for the supposedly guilt-free fling that rads had made less and less socially acceptable over the past few years, and that guilt niggled at her now, especially when she saw Richelle's hand clench into a fist before she caught herself and released it. If the program could extrapolate from acquired data and learn new things beyond its programming, could it acquire opinions of its own?

"We're thinking of having a foursome later. Care to make it a sextet?" Stephanie laughed at her own pun.

That was crass, even for Stephanie, and the blood rushed to Elaine's cheeks as she looked for the others' reactions. John grinned wider than a hoverlimousine's front grill. Jay tilted forward in his chair, waiting for her response. Lara appeared nonplussed but didn't argue. Richelle focused all her attention on her salad, sending bits of lettuce flying onto the stark white tablecloth while she tore it apart with knife and fork. The suggestion was bad enough, but Elaine's mind wandered down the same path it'd taken earlier. If two THIs talking was like talking to oneself, were two THIs in bed a twisted form of masturbation? She turned to Grego and changed the subject.

"How are the THI sales going?"

To his credit, Jay paused only a second before picking up the new thread. "Very well, thank you." He dabbed at a bit of salad dressing on his chin, then laid the napkin across his lap. "We're making some incredible progress with the technology. All sorts of innovations."

Ah, perhaps he could clarify the suggestion that she'd gotten some sort of different model. "What kind of innovations?"

The salesman glanced dramatically over his shoulder, then leaned forward, elbows on the table. His voice dropped to a conspiratorial whisper. "Well, I'm not supposed to share company secrets, but word is, we're going portable."

Beside her, Richelle straightened in her seat, then tried to appear nonchalant, polishing a smudge off the handle of her salad fork. The other THIs seemed disinterested in the conversation as a whole.

"Portable?" Stephanie chimed in.

"I have a friend in research and development who claims they're working on miniaturizing the THI generators, making them pocket-sized, even wearable like jewelry. A phenomenal breakthrough, if it happens, though we're years from actual mass production, and the cost will be horrifically expensive for years after that."

Fascinating, but this wasn't the sort of thing Elaine most wanted to know about. A tap on her shoulder prevented her from asking further questions. She glanced up, expecting waiters with their entrees, but instead found Arnold Lansington, her bartender-turned-hero.

"With my compliments," he said, placing another glass of blueberry champagne next to her plate. "I wanted to stop by to see how you were doing."

"Better after several of these." Elaine laughed, holding the glass with one hand and flicking her fingernail against the crystal with the other. It chimed with the tone of good quality. "Really, I should be buying *you* a drink. After all, if it hadn't been for you and Richelle here—"

Ricky's hand closed over hers in what, to any outside observer, would have appeared to be an affectionate gesture. But the fingers tightened to a point of nearly causing her pain. Elaine sucked in a breath but managed to maintain her composure.

"Richelle?" Lansington asked, examining her dinner companion.

"Oh yes," Elaine stammered. She bought time with a sip of champagne. "You to rescue me and Ricky here to, uh, distract me afterwards." Smoothly done! She gave herself a mental gold star on the forehead.

The bartender raised his eyebrows and blinked while the rest of the table laughed. Elaine flushed when she realized where their collective minds had taken them, not difficult at all in light of the previous conversation. "What I meant was—"

"What you meant," Richelle interrupted, standing and drawing her from her seat by the hand she gripped, "was you would really like me to ask you to dance." She bowed from the waist, gallant and charming. "Which I am."

Elaine blew out a breath. "I accept." Taking the proffered arm, Elaine tried to ignore the way the dining room tilted as she walked. Chatter and laughter rose and fell from the surrounding tables. The twinkling of the overhead lights blurred at the edges of her vision.

"I believe that you are tipsy." Ricky twirled her onto the dance floor, sliding them in between two couples engaged in a graceful waltz. With Elaine's hand in hers and Ricky's arm at her waist, she managed to keep from losing her balance.

"The word you're looking for is 'drunk off my ass.'" Really, she'd been hanging around Stephanie too long.

"That's four words."

"My point exactly."

Richelle led her about the intricate parquet floor, her steps sure and even, her moves agile, her guidance and pressure perfect. For someone who gave the impression of clumsiness in every other situation, the woman could certainly dance. Elaine lost herself in the flow of motion, years of lessons from her younger days resurfacing. Few of the other couples seemed as well-matched. One or the other could dance (likely the THI), but not both. She and Richelle made quite the pairing, and she noticed several onlookers had turned their attention to them.

Before Elaine could become embarrassed, the music began anew. This time, sultry jazz caressed her. Ricky swept Elaine into her arms, holding her close and rocking her gently from side to side, Elaine's cheek pressed against the starched white of Ricky's shirt. She could feel Ricky's heart beating beneath the coarse fabric. It seemed faster than would have been the norm. Or was that hers?

Well, they *had* been dancing.

Isolated from the world in Ricky's arms, Elaine turned her face up to hers. Ricky gazed down at her, a fond smile turning up the corners of her lips, and leaned a little closer.

"So, you want to tell me what crushing the bones in my hand was all about?"

From her raised eyebrows, that was clearly not the question Ricky had expected Elaine to ask, if she'd expected one at all. Richelle straightened, her movements becoming stiffer, more mechanical in their precision. She didn't make eye contact when she spoke. "If you don't know who your enemy is, should you advertise your allies?"

Now Elaine was the one crushing *her* hand. "You're saying this morning really wasn't an accident." She'd suspected as much but didn't want to seem paranoid. Besides, she'd desperately wanted it to have been accidental.

Elaine watched Richelle's expression shift. Though her steps never faltered, her sight seemed to turn inward, pupils dilating in a most disconcerting fashion. Her voice sounded distant when she responded, "I'm saying the patterns don't add up. The *Nebula*'s mainframe connected with the shuttle's onboard computer. Maintenance checks on the boarding tube had been performed according to safety regulation schedules. Scans detected no technological failure, though if the scans themselves were faulty…." She trailed off as the music changed to an upbeat tune with a driving rhythm and lots of horns. "Damn."

None of her previous speech sounded like something a twentieth-century actor would say. At least Elaine didn't think so. Her knowledge of such things was admittedly limited. Elaine opened her mouth to question her further, but Ricky led her to the edge of the dance floor, leaving her standing just off the wood squares. Summoned by the music, other THIs approached from every corner of the dining room, their partners remaining in their seats or standing alone like Elaine. The holograms gathered in the center of the dance area, lining up in two rows, one of men and one of women. In all their physical attractiveness and flair, they made an impressive sight.

At first glance, Richelle paled by comparison. Her height made her stand out in the first row, as did her appearance, more masculine than the other gathered women, but otherwise, she was somewhat dapper butch-next-door ordinary. And yet that ordinariness drew Elaine's attention to her all the more. Wealthy and impressive hadn't worked out for her.

The captain strode to the center of the floor. As he passed her, Elaine spotted a microphone chip adhered to the corner of his mouth, no bigger than a tiny mole and indiscernible from a greater distance. Hidden speakers projected his voice throughout the large space, loudly enough to be heard over lingering conversation and the clatter of dishware.

"Ladies and gentlemen, it is my great pleasure to welcome you all aboard the *Nebula*. I hope you have enjoyed your evening so far. In keeping with our theme of twentieth-century film classics, I now present a medley of songs from Hollywood musicals." The captain clapped twice in quick succession, and the lights went out.

When they came up again, the THIs had switched positions, scattering themselves in pairs around the dance floor. Ricky had partnered with a dark-haired woman in a floor-length green gown that shimmered when she moved. She was gorgeous, of course. Elaine frowned, then caught herself, laughing at her moment of jealousy—jealous of a pair of THIs. Ridiculous.

Long, shapely legs made the brunette a perfect dance partner for Richelle. It made practical sense. Elaine spotted John and Lara, paired with each other. To Elaine's surprise, the somewhat goofy John turned out to be an exceptional dancer as he "boogied" (at least she thought that was the appropriate term) his way across the floor. He twirled Lara, then sent her spinning away while he finished with a struck pose, one hand on his hip, the other pointing a finger diagonally into the air. Lara held her own, but lacked a dancer's pure grace, moving more with the litheness and purpose of a martial arts master. In one of her twirls, Elaine could have sworn she spotted twin thigh pistols strapped to her long legs, revealed by the slits in the silver dress. One more testament to "movie magic" or the THI technology that the weapons didn't ruin the lines of the form-fitting gown.

The music shifted, and Elaine caught Richelle's eye. She gave Elaine an apologetic smile as a crewman tossed Ricky a polished cane. Then Ricky launched into a rousing, thigh-slapping dance number, spinning the cane, jumping over it, passing it over her back and between her legs. Even the most sophisticated guests were hooting, hollering, and clapping to the rhythm. Everyone except Elaine.

None of the performers missed a step or soured a note. Though corny, each sequence in the medley impressed as much as the last. Precision, timing, choreography, enunciation, clarity: the THIs were flawless.

As their programmers designed them to be.

This display of holographic prowess did nothing for Elaine except shatter the illusion. It heightened the artificial nature of the THIs, placing them on pedestals no average human being could ever hope to climb. They were as unobtainable as their originals. They might as well have set up a screen and showed her a 3D film. Maybe these other guests thought this was as close as they'd ever get. Maybe it was enough for them to fool themselves. But not Elaine. THIs weren't real people.

She left the dining room before the waitstaff served the main course.

RICHELLE WATCHED Elaine flee the dining room and got three paces off the dance floor before a strong grip caught her shirtsleeve. "What do you think you're doing?"

She turned to face Lara, and a tingle of energy passed between them where they touched. Not difficult to recognize the councilwoman, Fzzd, behind the Lara disguise. The rest of the THIs rejoined their human companions and refilled the dance space with more mundane steps.

"I'm seeing to my guest."

"She doesn't want to see you." Lara/Fzzd placed one hand on her silk-covered hip, her lips downturned in a frown. "And I wasn't referring to just now. You're up to your usual tricks. Don't think I can't tell. That dance floor conversation looked far too intimate for small talk."

Well, at least Fzzd hadn't listened in, like she did whenever she wasn't too distracted by her own guest duties.

"And I know you had something to do with saving Ms. Kane's ass this morning."

And a nice ass it was.

Ricky blinked to clear her surprisingly human thoughts, pleased they'd wandered in such a way. She narrowed her gaze on the woman in front of her. "You expected me to let her die?"

Fzzd glared. "I expected you to let matters run their natural course while you gathered information. That's what we're supposed to be doing."

Richelle almost suggested that morning had been anything but natural, but something stopped her. Fzzd had access to the passenger/THI roster. She had to have known Elaine was assigned to Ricky. Surely Fzzd wouldn't go to such extreme measures to prevent Ricky from interacting with another human.

Would she?

No. She would have left some trace in the data stream, something Ricky would have recognized. Still, she kept it to herself.

"We value life, Fzzd. In all its forms. It's our foundation. That hasn't changed, regardless of the council's new mandates." From the corner of her eye, Richelle spotted Jay Grego heading toward them, and even as she watched, Fzzd's expression shifted from intense to bland, a sultry smile replacing her frown. She greeted the Biotech salesman with an outstretched hand.

"Take *care*, Ricky," Fzzd warned her, slipping from her Lara guise for one last instant. Grego slid his arm around her waist and led her away.

And Elaine was long gone.

IN HER inebriated condition, Elaine had difficulty finding her way to her stateroom's level. She took three wrong turns, almost walking into the infirmary. She tripped over a robo-cleaner and caught herself on a handrail.

The onyx disks mocked her from above, and she expected security personnel to appear at any moment to guide the stupid, drunk rich girl to her suite.

They never showed up. Elaine supposed as long as she avoided restricted areas like engineering and the bridge, and didn't try to jump off any walkways, they'd let her fend for herself.

Fending for herself sucked.

At last the lift opened, and she peered out to see the holographic starfield floating below the crosswalk to the corridor of suites. She walked across, her vision clouded by the tail of a passing comet and her own tears of frustration, and collided with a couple locked in an amorous embrace outside her stateroom, blocking her entry.

"Sorry," she muttered.

The man held her at arm's length until she steadied herself. He was nearly bald, and with little hair to hide it, Elaine noted the Biotech logo behind his right ear.

She jerked from his grasp. "Don't they need you for the grand finale or something?" Her words grated from a throat tightened by disgust.

The man watched her, a bemused expression on his face. Despite the baldness, his features were striking. He carried himself with an air of authority, and his formal wear in red and black hinted at military origins. He tugged his tunic down at the waist to straighten its lines.

"Jean-Luc doesn't dance at their command. Just mine." A woman put a possessive hand on the THI's arm.

Only now did Elaine notice the hologram's human companion. Elaine recognized the woman from advertisements for her e-books. Denise Lazaro had sold her series rights to vid, and her tie-in merchandise broke sales records worldwide. Her fortune didn't come close to Elaine's, but she'd done well for herself. Elaine would have been happy to sell just one of her little hobby stories.

"I love your work." Yeah, Elaine, you and every other vapid fan back on Earth. Could she possibly sound more foolish?

The author pulled a loose strand of her unnaturally auburn hair behind her ear and smiled. "Always good to hear." She looked over her shoulder at the stateroom entry hatch. "Yours?"

Elaine nodded. The couple moved aside, then headed down the corridor.

As Elaine fumbled her keycard into the slot, she called after them, "How did you manage it?"

"Hmm?" Denise turned to face her.

"The THIs work for Nebula, right? I mean, the cruise line programs them for us, but if the captain calls, don't they have to…?"

"I bought the rights. Jean-Luc's program works for me, exclusively. He's only available when I cruise, and only to me." The author winked. "I don't like to share." They walked off arm in arm and disappeared into a suite five hatches down.

Well, if the THIs really did go portable, Elaine knew Denise would be their first customer.

CHAPTER 5
ERIS HOLIDAY

HER LUNGS burned. Her arms ached. The blaring alarm deafened her. Above the hatch, the red light blinked, teasing her with its inaccessible nearness. The hiss of escaping oxygen rose above the other clamor and the pounding of her pulse in her temples. She wasn't going to make it, wasn't going to....

"Let me in!" she screamed, pounding her fists against unyielding metal. "It's coming apart! Let me in!"

Elaine sat up, gasping. Her pulse raced. Sweat dampened the sheets, and a small part of her mind made a note to put them through the recycler later, where they could be decontaminated if she'd picked up any rads lately. She hovered in the nightmare-fog, trying to re-acclimate to the here and now.

Elaine usually slept lightly. While that trait benefited her in college and forestalled any number of dorm pranks targeting her, it made married life difficult. Harriet preferred to work late. When she'd come to bed in the wee hours of the morning, she'd wake her no matter how hard she tried for silence. After their first three months of marriage, Harriet had given up trying.

Even the absence of regular sound would stir Elaine to full wakefulness, like now.

The ship's engines altered their rumbling pitch as they shifted from propulsion to idling. A subtle bump reverberated throughout the vessel, twanging the metal like a muffled gong.

Their first port of call was Eris's orbital station. They must have been in the process of establishing the connection.

Elaine swallowed a sudden mouthful of bile, the memories of her nightmare flooding back to her. If she wanted to get off the ship, she'd have to cross another tube. More weightless vulnerability. Her head pounded; then the room spun, corners rocking at the edges of her vision. She was going to be ill.

Bolting from the bed, she raced across the suite, through the sitting area, and burst into the sanitary facility. Her shoulder slammed into the edge of the entryway, but she ignored the pain and focused on not showering the bathroom floor with her meager dinner and the large quantity of alcohol from the previous night.

Elaine vomited until nothing remained in her stomach, then continued to dry heave for several more tortuous minutes. A blue light from beneath the toilet's rim decontaminated any rads that might have been in her vomit. She hadn't even known that particular decon device was there. Not something she would have easily spotted under normal circumstances. The cruise line wasn't taking any chances.

Her tremulous hand activated the suction system, whisking away the mess and the smell in a loud roar of rushing air through the ship's plumbing network. Then she collapsed against the cool tile wall, gulping oxygen through her mouth and nose. She pressed her cheek against the smooth surface. The chill drove away some of the fuzziness in her head and cleared her vision. Now her bruised shoulder throbbed, and she rubbed it with one hand, using the other to push herself to her feet.

She'd moved three steps into the sitting area before she noticed Richelle standing at the bedroom archway, eyebrows drawn down with concern. The painkiller tablets in her extended palm called to Elaine, but she froze like cornered prey. Elaine's nightclothes, satiny blue shorts and a matching sleeveless top, revealed far more skin than she'd prefer any woman of such brief acquaintance to see. Hands fluttered to cover herself, then dropped at the pointlessness of it. She might not be well-endowed, but she couldn't hide what she had.

"I can't see through fabrics, you know." Richelle gave her a lopsided smile. She passed Elaine the pills.

The analgesics dissolved on her tongue, easing the pain within seconds.

"There's nothing to be upset about."

Elaine's head shot up. How could Richelle even know the cause of her distress? She glared at the THI. Was Richelle going to make fun of her? Elaine's mouth opened to order it from the room.

Richelle held up both palms in a defensive gesture. "I mean there's no boarding tube. I heard you shouting in your sleep and made an educated guess."

She'd shouted? She remembered her dream self shouting. Maybe she'd done so out loud as well. And Richelle had been listening? "You watch me sleep?"

"Of course not," she hastened to explain. "But if our audio receptors detect notes of distress, we check in to make sure you're not in any danger. We've prevented several heart attacks and other life-threatening situations from becoming fatal that way." The THI straightened with pride.

Elaine released some of her anger. She supposed it was an effective security system.

"As I was saying, Eris Station has a permanent walkway that connects to the *Nebula*. It's got gravity and everything." Richelle reached into a back pocket of her khaki cargo shorts and removed a long, thin box like a container for bracelets. "Besides, I'll be right there with you."

Richelle opened the black velvet box. Inside rested two white bands and a brooch. The wrist-diameter bands had onyx disks embedded along them. The pin featured one as well. If one didn't know their purpose, they might be mistaken for simple costume jewelry. "These tap into the ship's generators and will let me tour the station with you."

Elaine backed away from her. "You think I'm taking you with me?" Presumptuous, arrogant caricature. The qualities reminded her too much of Harriet, though really the two women had little else in common. Elaine tried to shake it off, but the irritation lingered. "You assume a lot."

Richelle spread her arms wide. "I assume nothing. I simply thought you might appreciate the added protection, under your particular circumstances."

She referred to the attempt on Elaine's life, or at least the supposed attempt. Which brought back the transfer tube memory in full detail. Elaine swallowed hard.

"The station's fairly safe, but there are some rougher areas, and a few wealthier visitors have had unfortunate experiences," Richelle went on, for once oblivious.

"Like what?" Elaine slipped one of the emitter bracelets over each hand, checking the fit. She kept the pin to attach to her day clothes later.

Richelle frowned as she considered it. "Muggings mostly, pickpocketing, a few more violent crimes—typical tourist town stuff—unwary visitors, savvy local criminals." She gestured to Elaine's new jewelry, smoothly shifting the topic. "I'm still tied into the ship's generator via wireless connections, so it isn't foolproof. You can't hop another ship and expect me to stick around. The range is extensive, but it has limits. You also need to keep me to either side or in front of you, within the projection radius."

And if she didn't, Richelle would vanish, at least until she could re-coalesce. Great.

"Here on the ship, the massive generator and the wealth of emitters maintain a projection 'field' carrying the alien-engineered particles over a variety of wavelengths including the full light spectrum, the subtlest of sounds, heat waves, background radiation waves, etc. It uses wave front technology to extrapolate THIs beyond the limitations of line-of-sight. Off the ship, with so few emitters, it's far more limited."

"Why not get more pins?"

Richelle's grin turned sheepish. "Each guest is entitled to two. I, um, appropriated the extra bracelet."

"Ah."

Elaine looked her up and down, raising a skeptical eyebrow. Richelle didn't have muscles per se, but she was taller and fit. *Very* fit. She shook herself to bring her thoughts back on track. The illusion of having someone else with her would deter most thieves.

Richelle frowned, guessing her thoughts. "I'm stronger than I appear."

Yeah, she probably was, assuming THIs possessed some control over their own structures.

Elaine sank down on the couch, rubbing her shoulder and wishing for coffee. "You know, it would have been good to know all this *before* the worry made me throw up." She nodded toward the bathroom.

Richelle pressed her lips together. Her eyes were sympathetic. "I would have, but...." She looked at the black emitter disks near the ceiling.

No THI emitters in the sanitary facility. Right.

"And it was in the online brochure."

So much angry heat flushed Elaine's face, she thought lasers might shoot from her eyes. "And I'm just a stupid tourist who rushes headlong into things and panics unnecessarily. Correct?"

Where was that coming from? None of this was Richelle's fault. She didn't know Elaine hadn't wanted any of this. Or maybe she did. Richelle seemed to know everything else.

The hologram threw its hands up and turned away. "Look, if that's how you're going to be, then be by yourself. If you want my company, call me when you're ready."

She expected it to dissipate or blink out or something. Instead, it went to the hatch, opened it, and stepped into the corridor beyond, shutting it behind her. Realism.

When Elaine emerged from her shower, a mug of steaming coffee waited on the sitting room table. She gave the onyx disks an apologetic smile.

PROGRESS AND opportunity. Elaine would take Richelle with her. Despite Elaine's brief bout of anger, with her eyes flashing in such beautiful, fiery fury, Richelle would accompany her to the station. She knew it. She saw it in that last smile.

Elaine had smiled at her! And in her face, Richelle had seen regret for her outburst, if she read Elaine correctly. Amazing, the powers of caffeine and compassion. But concerns threatened her enthusiasm.

Though the extended contact would give her more chances to get to know Elaine, the venue left much to be desired. Those damn wireless disks functioned so poorly, they were bound to draw more attention to her lack of substance. One misstep, one turn of Elaine's back toward her and Richelle would vanish, to reappear in an entirely new location in front of Elaine. And here Richelle had gone to such pains to avoid doing just that, to make herself more human in Elaine's eyes.

Well, Richelle would have to be especially light on her feet for the next few hours.

Elaine had accepted her as a protector. Richelle would not mess that up.

CHAPTER 6
A HOLOGRAPHIC
WEREWOLF ON ERIS

ERIS STATION bustled with vibrant activity. Many starliners en route to interstellar destinations stopped there on their way out of the solar system. Tourists, asteroid miners, explorers, scientists, even military personnel frequented the orbiting facility. It provided a final opportunity to top off fuel and supplies, to trade exotic goods, and to get a relatively stationary surface under one's feet for a little while before the next long haul. Being much larger, and lacking propulsion, the station simulated the stability of a planet-bound installation with great success.

It also advertised a wide variety of entertainment options, some of which were outlawed on Earth.

The station resembled a small city trapped in a bubble dome, with spokes extending outward for docking ships. Elaine had spotted the multicolored twinkling lights of the businesses from her stateroom window. Some of the neon glowed in letters tall enough to read even from that distance. Promises of gambling, strong drinks, lavish meals, and erotic pleasures ran in red digital letters along the walkway from the ship to the station. Pictures accompanied a few of the ads, and she studiously avoided looking at them or Richelle as they strolled along surrounded by other passengers off the *Nebula*.

Stephanie and Jay planned to spend the day shopping, then meet up with Elaine and Richelle for dinner at someplace Jay recommended called the Astrogator. They'd left their THIs behind, having each other for company. Elaine wondered how John and Lara felt about that, or at least how the programs would act upon Stephanie and Jay's return.

"So," Richelle announced once they'd cleared the walkway and a security checkpoint with a lengthy decontamination at its end, "what would you like to see? I'm an excellent tour guide."

Some of the tourists from other ships that lacked THI technology carried hand-held compumaps loaded with directions and descriptions of all of Eris Station's offerings. They bumped into displays and each other, trying to read as they walked.

Elaine had Richelle.

"I've heard the asteroid miners produce some pretty jewelry from some of the minerals. A souvenir would

be nice. Rastozite is teal blue." Elaine's favorite color.
Which Richelle already knew.

Richelle took her hand, holding up Elaine's wrist
to display the emitter bracelet. "Don't you like the jewelry you're wearing? I'm crushed." She placed her free
hand over her heart and pouted.

Elaine giggled. She couldn't remember the last
time she'd sounded so girlish. When Richelle let her
arm drop but didn't release her hand, Elaine didn't
pull away.

They made their way up one "street" and down
another. The station city towered above them—huge,
sprawling hotels and casinos built beneath the dome.
Hovercars whizzed by on their antigrav cushions.
Crowds of tourists milled about. The recyclers couldn't
quite filter all the smells wafting from dozens of restaurants. Some scents, Elaine could identify. One meaty,
spicy odor reminded her of her mother's homemade
beef stew. Others made her queasy. Overhead the transparent synthplas would have revealed the heavens in
all their glory, if light pollution weren't interfering with
the view. The station existed in a permanent "night,"
holding in a stationary orbit at all times over the side
of Eris facing away from the sun, and each establishment's lighting rivaled the blotted starfield above.

The gemstone and jewelry district sat a few streets
off the main strip. Here, the buildings rose only a story
or two above "ground" level, as opposed to the domes-
craper hotels and casinos. Richelle and Elaine browsed
through one shop and then another, avoiding overly so-
licitous sales personnel. Fierce competition drove the
market out on the edge of the system, and judging from
the shabbiness of the stores and the desperate nature of
the shopkeepers, that market had faltered.

Elaine felt for them but didn't intend to spend money on something just for the sake of spending it. If she made a purchase, it would be something she really wanted and would wear with some frequency. She'd never developed an excessive taste for accessories. Stephanie taught her a few tricks with scarves and belts that helped spruce up her wardrobe, but while Elaine always presented a neat appearance, one would never call her a fashion expert.

Her family held on to its fortune by avoiding most frivolous pleasures and didn't clutter their lives with the collection of things. Other than her wedding ring, her mother had owned few precious stones—enough to rotate through the occasional formal gathering, but no more. She, like Elaine, preferred experiences. She'd traveled the world, right up until the weeks before her death. Elaine wondered what she would have thought of off-world cruising.

"Everything all right?"

Richelle's voice brought her back to the case of bracelets she'd been scanning.

"Yes, fine. Sorry." Though she tried to mask it, her melancholy mood came through in her tone, and Richelle squeezed her hand. Elaine expected her to place an arm around her shoulders, then realized why she couldn't. That would put Richelle's arm behind her, where she wore no emitters. The limb would vanish as soon as it left the range of the three onyx disks.

A bright teal bracelet of oval stones caught her eye. She pointed at it, eager for the distraction. Richelle nodded, and before Elaine could look up, two salesmen skittered from the showroom floor like cockroaches out of wood paneling.

Richelle was a pitiful negotiator, and it wasn't Elaine's strength either. Elaine ended up paying full price, though she didn't mind. The salesmen demonstrated how the unusual precious stones changed color depending upon the source of ambient lighting. Within the shop, the gems were teal, but under a sunlamp—and one salesman nearly sprained Elaine's wrist in his urgency to demonstrate using a small solar light at the rear of the store—the different lighting turned the color a pale blue resembling an unpolluted spring sky. Money paid for something she really wanted and would actually wear was, in her opinion, money well spent.

As they left the shop, bracelet glittering above the emitter strap on her right wrist, three burly men in gray miner coveralls fell into step behind them. Elaine tried to glance over her shoulder, but Richelle clamped on to her hand like a vise, urging her down the walkway between two storehouses that would return them to the main thoroughfare. Richelle whistled off-key, for all the universe oblivious to their pursuers.

Elaine thought about ducking into another store, but the walls on either side held no entrances or exits, only flat, featureless surfaces. And the men hadn't done anything overtly threatening—

"Hey, honey, wouldn't you like a *real man* instead of particle girl?"

The second miner barked while the third hooted and made growling noises. Elaine sensed Richelle's muscles tightening, though her whistling never faltered. Elaine cast a quick look behind her.

The trio had moved closer, forming a triangle. They must have known how the emitters worked. In the disks' blind spot, they could taunt and tease without fear of physical repercussions.

Ahead, Elaine could make out the end of the alleyway and crowds of tourists passing back and forth across the opening between the two buildings. Noise increased as the sounds of aircar traffic and distant conversations drifted along the passage.

"That's a pretty sparkler you're wearing," the leader remarked. Elaine assumed he referred to her recent purchase. "You know how much we make when you buy one of those?" He didn't wait for a response. "Ten percent. Ten percent for risking our lives on floating rocks wearing worn-out spacesuits with holes patched up using duct tape."

"And if she hadn't bought it, you'd get nothing." Richelle staggered forward, yanking Elaine along with her. At first Elaine thought she'd tripped yet again. Then she realized one of the miners had shoved Richelle as the man withdrew his hand. She smelled sweat and dust and foul breath.

"I'll get a lot more if I sell it myself." Dry, callused fingers closed around Elaine's right wrist and yanked her so hard her arm nearly dislocated from its socket. She lost contact with Richelle as the miner twisted her around to face him and drew her in close. Out of the corner of her eye, she saw the THI flicker, molecules dispersing out of the emitters' lines of sight. There wasn't enough space between herself and the miner for Richelle to reappear in front of her. Elaine extended her free arm backward and turned it while she held eye contact with her assailant.

Richelle's form solidified in time for her to throw a punch at the lead miner. The THI's fist connected with the block jaw, eliciting grunts of pain from them both. The miner lost his hold on Elaine, stumbling two steps back, while Richelle shook out her bruised hand.

The twentieth-century actor clearly hadn't done action films. "Surely we can avoid further unpleasantness?" Richelle cradled her injured knuckles.

Unpleasantness? Seriously? Elaine inwardly groaned. She chose *now* to behave like a caricature?

The plea drew the leader in closer. Lightning fast, Richelle head-butted him, skull connecting with the miner's nose. Blood spewed, and cartilage snapped under the blow. His companions jumped back to avoid the likely rad-infused bodily fluids. Elaine had noticed few decontaminators on the station. Too expensive for them, she suspected. The leader's arms pinwheeled, and he landed heavily on his well-padded ass.

"Were you a stunt woman too?" Elaine got the words out before the other two grabbed her shoulders. They held her in place while the brawl in front of them continued.

Fists clenched, Richelle hovered over her former assailant. "Stay down and tell your buddies to let the lady go."

The THI could have kicked him, knocked him unconscious, anything. Instead, with her programmed senses of morality and fairness, Richelle gave him an opportunity to call a truce. Elaine admired and cursed her in one thought.

The miner grabbed Richelle by the ankle and yanked the somewhat clumsy actor off her feet.

The pair rolled over and over in the narrow confines of the alley, bumping trash disposal units and scattering bits of litter. From within one bin, a rodent squealed, then leaped out and ran, shrieking, as fast as its four paws could carry it, to a crack in one of the prefab walls. At some point in the midst of their conflict, Richelle's plain white shirt tore, and it hung in two strips over her chest, almost but not quite exposing her small but attractive breasts.

"Turn her around!" the leader shouted.

His friends stared at him, blank looks on their faces.

Richelle gained the upper position, straddling the miner, then bringing a knee down on his ribs. Even over the din of traffic from the nearby cross street, the sound of cracking bone carried. The miner screamed in pain. "Dammit, Paulo, turn her the fuck around!"

The hands grasping Elaine's right shoulder jerked. At last registering the command, "Paulo" twisted her to face him, directing the emitters away from the battle on the ground.

The sounds of struggle ceased.

Paulo held Elaine's wrists together and facing forward while the other thug ripped the teal gemstone bracelet from her arm. She heard shuffling behind her, the leader grunting and getting to his feet. He came around to meet her head-on.

Shoving Paulo aside, he took her hands from his partner. His grubby fingers yanked off one armband. With a sneer of broken, yellowed teeth, the miner dropped the emitter to the street and ground it to a fine black dust beneath his heel. He did the same to the other, then cupped her chin in his hand.

"Maybe we show you what *real men* can do for you, eh, love?"

His breath stank of cheap alcohol as he closed the space between their lips. His broken nose covered his face in wide smears of blood. Elaine cringed, though she could not pull from the grips of his companions. She thought of screaming, but the aircar engines on the busy cross street would have drowned out any calls for help she might make.

If she made it back to the starliner alive, she would have to remember to thank Stephanie for this wonderful vacation.

The leader's mouth clamped over Elaine's lips, vile tongue probing, pressing against her clenched teeth. When she refused to part them, he punched her in the gut, not with full strength, but hard enough to make her gasp. Then he thrust his slimy tongue inside, the snakelike thing writhing to one inner cheek and then the other. It scoured her molars, rubbed the roof, and extended down her throat until she gagged.

She would have gagged anyway. His sticky blood smeared over her face was grotesque enough, and his saliva and blood were likely riddled with rads.

The miner stepped away to survey her expression while Elaine spit out his and her saliva mixed with a good amount of her own bile, and to hell with possible bystander contamination.

Something huge, muscular, and very solid materialized in front of her, and at first she thought another thug had joined the fray.

No, not a fourth mugger. She could not identify the thing that loomed between herself and the leader. A beast from her worst nightmares threatened to wrench a scream from her lips. It towered, it roared, its brown-and-black fur-covered frame rippled with tension. Yellowish viscous ooze dripped from dagger-sharp fangs beneath a pointed snout. She smelled rotting flesh on its breath. The red, piercing eyes stared at her.

It winked.

Her mind raced to catch up with this turn of events. The brooch. The thieves had missed or forgotten to destroy her brooch.

The wink helped some, though she shivered, standing so close to the monstrosity. Intellectually, Elaine knew this manifestation was Richelle in another form, though she hadn't realized the THI possessed such a capability.

Gone was any trace of the THI's gentlemanly honor. This new incarnation possessed none of Richelle's awkwardness and goofy, wisecracking humor. In her place stood an angry entity possessed of inhuman strength and enhanced reflexes. The growl of unbridled anger it let loose raised the hairs on the nape of Elaine's neck.

Regardless of how Richelle had pulled it off, Elaine thanked any gods listening that it was on her side.

The thugs managed to hide their fear a lot less successfully than she did. One of the men holding her screamed in horror while she heard the leader stagger several feet backward, boots scrabbling on concrete. She glanced at the third. A dark stain appeared on his coveralls, and the acrid stench of urine reached her nostrils.

The THI struck with three quick jabs of its mighty paws, one to the leader's already broken nose and two more to the jaw. The monster's arms blurred in motion too fast for Elaine to witness more than the result. The lead miner toppled, unconscious before he hit the concrete.

His friends released Elaine's arms to assist their comrade, but she stuck her foot out, tripping one of them neatly. Her inner cheerleader did a little dance of triumph. She had a powerful urge to pummel him, to beat and kick him, to find some blunt object and smash it on his head for this assault on her body, this attempt to steal her possessions. But she didn't get the opportunity. Once the miner was on the ground, the creature took him permanently out of the fight with a jab to his ribs that put him in the fetal position, rocking and moaning.

The other attempted to grab the THI from behind, pinning its arms to its sides. It made no difference. With one thrust forward, the monster flipped the miner over its back. The thug hit the solid surface of the closest wall headfirst, the dull thud of impact resounding between the alley walls.

He lay still. Too still. Elaine focused on the miner's chest, waiting for the rise and fall that didn't come.

Elaine knew she couldn't turn away from the sight or Richelle's new image would disassemble. Instead, she scrunched her eyes shut. Tears seeped from beneath the lids, streaming down her face to mix with the sticky blood she sensed on her cheeks. Nausea roiled in her stomach and came halfway up in a gag, but she swallowed it down. Flashes of Harriet's shattered skull, her body slumped over her desk, rose in Elaine's memory—the blood pooling in the Leviathan logo. A scream gathered at the back of her throat. Emitter or no emitter, her muscles flexed, preparing to carry her as far from the alley as fast as possible.

A pair of warm human hands caught her upper arms, and she tensed and shouted. A thumb pressed her lips gently, quieting her. Then she collapsed into Richelle's embrace, vaguely aware that her grip slackened as her fingers vanished beyond the final emitter's range. Elaine's head rested on Richelle's heaving chest as the THI fought to control simulated breathing accelerated by the struggle. Her heart pounded beneath the sweat-soaked fabric of her torn shirt.

Elaine didn't bother to marvel at the realism. She just appreciated it for all it was worth.

"We need to get out of here." Elaine's face, pressed against Richelle's chest, muffled the sound of the THI's voice, but she made out the words. "I didn't mean... I didn't mean to...."

It took a moment for Elaine to realize Ricky was shaking as badly as she was. In the distance, sirens screamed above the background spaceport noise.

Elaine moved her head up and down against the fabric. When she took a step back, her legs wobbled. The one conscious miner moaned and glared at her but made no attempt to rise. Still, his presence unnerved her. "Maybe if I lean here for a minute...." She motioned toward the plasteel wall of one of the buildings lining the alleyway.

"You don't understand," Richelle said with more urgency. Her stricken expression made Elaine's breath catch. "I can't be caught here. Neither can you. They'll delete me for taking a human life, even in your defense, even accidentally." Emotion choked off her words, and she paused to clear her throat, eyes glistening. "Once the military gave up on trying to use THIs to fight their wars, further models were purposely programmed to avoid all violence. What I did shouldn't even have been possible, but I was... motivated." She forced a lopsided grin that melted some of the icy fear freezing Elaine's heart. "If we're gone, the authorities will never believe a THI was involved."

Richelle took a couple of unsteady paces, heading in the direction of the thoroughfare. The absence of her body against Elaine's left a chill on Elaine's skin.

When Richelle glanced over her shoulder, her expression offered sympathy. "I'd help you, but...." She nodded toward the single emitter on Elaine's chest.

Right. If Richelle tried to put an arm around her for support, it would vanish, and an armless escort would draw more attention than they needed right now. Besides, she seemed to need almost as much support as Elaine did.

She gave Richelle a once-over, noting the blood on her knuckles and spattering her clothing. "Um, can you do something about...?" She pointed at the stains the programming had left for realism. Between the mess and potential rads, not knowing Richelle was a THI, everyone they passed would stare.

"Oh, right. Close your eyes."

"What?"

"Just do it. I don't like to, um, change in front of others."

A modest hologram. Unbelievable. A modest hologram that had saved her. She closed her eyes. When she opened them again, the clothes were pristine, tears and smudges gone. Richelle turned to lead the way out of the alley. A sudden thought occurred to Elaine.

"Wait!" She crouched, scrambling about like a crustacean to scoop up the emitter wristbands while Richelle struggled to stay in front of her and avoid evaporation. The disks themselves were beyond recognition. She shoved the circular straps into the pocket of her khaki slacks. Next, she edged to the body of the dead miner, cringing as she slipped her hand inside a storage pouch on his coveralls. Her fingers closed around the teal gemstone bracelet. If she left it, the authorities might track it back to the jewelry store and then to her. The sirens drew closer. The noise sent spikes of adrenaline coursing through her veins, but she'd felt something else, something the bracelet had snagged on, and instead of wasting time disentangling it, she pulled both items into her palm.

Behind them, a groundcar screeched to a halt, blocking the rear exit of the alleyway. Grabbing her free hand, Richelle hauled Elaine to her feet and dragged her down the narrow passage to the open end. They surged into foot traffic, tourists and locals shouting or cursing them when they shoved past. Others stared at the panicked couple, Elaine still spattered with blood and sporting tattered vacation wear. Many surged away from her, trying to avoid any physical contact with her stained clothing.

Elaine squeezed her fist around whatever she'd taken from the miner. No time to look at it now. Something small, multifaceted, and smooth pressed against the flesh of her palm along with the bracelet. The item felt familiar, but with the THI hauling her across a busy street and transports blaring horns, she couldn't quite place it.

Several blocks farther, they ducked into another alley and caught their breaths. Elaine pressed her arm against her side, and her bruises ached. Richelle had released her hand and stood bent at the waist, hands on her knees, gasping.

"That was… I'm…." Elaine inhaled deeply, then let it out without hitching on the air. "You were right about the dangers. I'm glad you were with me today."

Richelle rewarded her with a half smile that almost made her forget that programming simulated her own panting and heaving for air. Nice of Richelle to humor her.

A stinging in her hand reminded her she still clutched the bracelet. She forced her cramped fingers to unclench around the teal gemstones... and a data crystal. She used them to back up information from her hard drive. That was why it felt familiar. They were lower-capacity cousins to the onyx disks used to transmit the THIs, but more portable and not connected to a central hub. She had one in her bag containing a novel she'd been toying with, though she hadn't had time to touch it. Students and business professionals carried data crystals on a regular basis.

But an asteroid miner?

Now a dead asteroid miner. She'd reached into a dead man's pockets.

No choice, she reminded herself as bile threatened to rise. And damn it, she'd panicked and vomited enough in front of Richelle. THI or not, it was embarrassing. She forced herself to focus on facts rather than emotions.

Elaine supposed miners might need to store information on shipments of ore, weights, prices. But the thugs in the alley looked like the grit workers, the ore handlers, not number crunchers. She doubted any of them used a comp with any frequency.

"What's that?" Richelle stopped sucking oxygen, well, as much as a THI could actually process air, and came to stand before her.

"Info storage."

"Odd thing for a mugger to have."

"Exactly."

A distant siren brought both their heads up. An enforcer vehicle roared by on the main street, a blur of gray, yellow, and red. It didn't slow, but it meant they were still looking for someone. Elaine's shoulders tensed, sending the first telltales of a migraine up the back of her neck and into her temples. She rubbed them with a thumb and forefinger, fighting off the new prickles of panic. With her other hand, Elaine pocketed the bracelet and clear crystal, then placed both her palms on Richelle's forearms.

"You should go."

"Go?" Her quizzical expression made her child-like. Elaine wanted to hug her. And where the hell had *that* impulse come from?

Gratitude and relief she'd survived. Again. That was all. Just gratitude and relief.

"You know, disappear, vanish, poof," Elaine explained.

A strained laugh escaped her. "Poof?"

"I'm not joking. We're too conspicuous together. If anyone witnessed the fight, they'll report a couple, not a single woman." She glanced at herself, frowning at the stains on her own clothes and a tear in the sleeve of her blouse. Rolling up the cuffs hid most of the damage. Maybe she could explain the rest away with a story of a trip and fall.

Richelle's laughter ceased. "I'm not leaving you. I'm… programmed to protect you when we're off the ship."

The word "programmed" came out harsh and strained, not like she minded her assigned task, but as if she hated admitting to her manufactured nature. A surprising rush of pity flooded Elaine, making her pause and swallow. Just how self-aware were these THIs, anyway?

"You said yourself if you're caught, you're 'dead,' in the strictest sense of the word at least. And then what good will you be to me?"

The tightness in her companion's jaw relaxed a bit, and she seized upon it.

"Let me protect *you* for a change. After all, you've saved my life twice now." If Richelle's earlier statement about releasing the airlock were to be believed. And she did believe her.

Richelle took a step back. "All right. But I'll be watching. And if I miss something and you need me, call, okay?"

Elaine nodded, and she returned the nod, about-faced, strolled to the corner in that long, half-lithe, half-ungainly stride of hers, and disappeared around it. Elaine shook her head at Richelle's efforts not to go "poof" in front of her.

RICHELLE'S PARTICLE energy cycled to the *Nebula* in an unsteady stream. Every few meters a wisp of electrons would trail off, extending out in an increasingly thinning strand, stretching, straining… fading….

No! Despite her shame, she would *not* disperse. She would not.

Elaine needed her. All the accumulated data told Richelle Elaine's life was in jeopardy. Two seemingly unrelated incidents so close together in occurrence had to be connected somehow, and if THIs had permission to bet, she would have placed hers on the data crystal Elaine had found in the miner's pocket.

Her form grew more cohesive, drawing in upon itself in a tightly knotted mass invisible to the human eye. She followed the ship's carrier wave in the reverse from Elaine's one remaining brooch emitter to the generator buried deep within the bowels of the *Nebula*. There she recharged and regrouped, sorting through every aspect of the attack, every nuance, and coming up with nothing definitive.

Around her, other energies flowed, their simpler patterns passing through on their ways to other parts of the ship. There were others aboard of her complexity, but none currently inhabited the generator. And that was fine. She didn't want company. She wanted concentration.

Richelle's search took her back to Elaine's file, her connections, her history. She had no known enemies, but her late spouse had many, and therefore, so did she by extension. Too many to select just one.

This would take time—time Elaine might not have.

A QUICK stop in a public sanitary facility took care of most of the blood on Elaine's face and hands, though three stewards still inquired after her health upon her return to the starliner even while they avoided touching her. For goodness' sake, she'd gone through the decontaminator on the entry walkway.

Her level's butler verged upon what her mother would have called a "hissy fit" when he saw her condition.

"Are you certain you don't want me to send for the ship's doctor?" he asked for the fourth time, escorting her from the lift to her cabin's hatch but keeping an arm's length between them.

"Really, I'm fine. More than anything else, I want to take a nice long nap. Please," she added, mixing in a touch of a whine that she hated, but it had worked on Harriet. Sometimes.

"Of course, ma'am. Inform the room computer if you need me for anything at all."

And pick up more rads in the process. Ah, the irony of the age she lived in.

"Thank you." She shut the hatch before he could offer further assistance.

Heaving a sigh, Elaine rested her forehead against the cool metal of the bulkhead. The inquisition and insistent offers to help had become too much. The clearing of a female throat frightened her into a brief battle with hyperventilation. She whirled to discover Richelle, cargo shorts and shirt still immaculate, extended hands bearing first aid supplies and a single long-stemmed blue flower.

Elaine's anger at her startling her again vanished.

"May *I* assist you with those scrapes?" Ricky gestured with the flower toward the couch, and Elaine passed her to cross the sitting room and sink into it.

She took the flower and held it while Ricky worked on her. Ricky's gentleness rivaled her other positive attributes. Since she was not a biological being, she could have contact with Elaine's blood without fear for herself. Elaine hardly detected Ricky's touch with the cleansing wipes, the application of the antibiotic gel, and the pass of the regenerator over the minor injuries. Elaine watched as her skin cells multiplied to close the wounds. Then she spotted the Leviathan logo glaring at her from the medical tool's handle and frowned.

Richelle froze. "Did I hurt you?"

Elaine forced a smile. "My mind is wandering. No pain. You're better than my personal physician and a lot more attractive."

"Really?" That got Ricky's full attention. Her eyes locked with Elaine's, and the heat in Ricky's gaze made pleasant tingles radiate throughout Elaine's body. Ricky reached toward Elaine's forehead, a cleansing wipe in hand. She didn't remember seeing any further grime there in the public restroom, but she let Ricky brush the hair from a spot above her right eye. Her other hand cupped Elaine's chin, tilting her face upward.

"Of course, he's seventy-two."

Ricky chuckled low in her throat.

The sound reminded her of the growl the beast had made before it went after her attackers, and she flinched.

Richelle jerked away as if struck.

Elaine felt like she'd kicked a puppy. "I'm sorry. The fight, that thing… it's all too fresh." Frustrated, she leaned back against the sofa while Richelle retreated to the chair. "What *was* that thing, anyway?"

Richelle's elbows rested on her knees, her chin in her hands, the wipe discarded on the table. "I don't know," she muttered.

"Excuse me?"

"I made it up."

"No, you didn't."

Fire kindled behind Richelle's eyes, and not the good kind that had Elaine melting moments before. "Sorry," Richelle blurted, head up, hands out in exasperation. "I mean I extrapolated bits of data from a selection of twentieth-century horror films, reorganized and combined them, and generated a frightening illusion! Because we all know a THI can't be creative!"

This thing was shouting at her. Shouting at her! What the hell? Maybe it had saved her. Okay, twice. But she hadn't paid an exorbitant price for this rotten, life-threatening nightmare of a cruise so that a hologram could shout in her face. "Well, you can't be!" she shouted back.

Was she trying to convince Richelle or herself?

Richelle stormed to the entry alcove, shoulders rigid, fists clenched at her sides. "Don't you think it's possible, just possible, that a sophisticated program might *learn* to create? Might expand beyond its original parameters?" Since she faced away, Elaine could barely hear her, but she didn't miss the hoarseness in Ricky's voice. The rigid shoulders trembled, then fell. "I'm not programmed to do what I did today, to take life. I didn't want to. I didn't mean to. It goes against everything I beli—" She caught herself. "—everything I'm designed to believe, but I did it… for you."

When she turned, Elaine stared at the tears running down her cheeks. Before Elaine even realized she was up and crossing the room, she stood before Ricky. Elaine's hand moved of its own accord to brush the tears away, but the chime of someone requesting entry to her cabin halted the instinctive reaction, and the thud of a fist on the hatch echoed in the alcove.

They both jolted at the sudden noise. Richelle's eyes met hers for a long moment. Then she vanished in a shimmering of disconnected particles.

It was the first time she disappeared in front of Elaine by her own choice.

"Poof," Elaine whispered to the empty room.

CHAPTER 7
MEMOIRS OF A THI

"ARE YOU all right? Why didn't you call? What happened to your clothes?" Stephanie pummeled Elaine with questions before she even crossed the threshold into the cabin. Behind her stood Jay Grego, a bemused though equally concerned expression marring his features. Both wore evening attire, and Elaine realized with a pang of guilt that she and Richelle had missed their dinner double date.

She waved them both inside, rolling up the torn sleeves of her shirt once more. They'd shifted down after Richelle tended her cuts and scrapes. "I'm sorry. I should have commed you. It completely slipped my mind. I—" Elaine hesitated. Was it her imagination, or was Jay listening a little too intently from his position beside the armchair? Ridiculous. "I had a little accident," she finished lamely. "Tripped and fell and had to come back to clean up." Her lie surprised her. Maybe if Stephanie had come alone....

Her best friend plunked herself down on the couch and blew out a breath that sent a strand of loose blond hair wafting to the side of her face. "Well, if it was only that!" She glanced around the room, making a show of leaning over the armrest to peer into the sleeping area. "And here I thought you'd discovered you like it rough."

The joking comment made the blood rush to Elaine's face, which she hid by ducking into the washroom for a glass of water. How close had she and Richelle been to intimacy before Elaine's reaction to Richelle's laugh set off Richelle's emotional outpouring? Had Richelle really been about to kiss her? She'd thought so, and that thought made butterflies flutter in her stomach.

"Seriously, though, you're all right? No permanent damage?" Stephanie patted the cushion, and Elaine joined her while Jay took the chair.

"I'm fine. Really." Beneath their feet, the deck vibrated. A voice over the public address system announced the ship's imminent departure and a warning to passengers to take seats or grasp handholds. A moment later, the *Nebula* disconnected from the station with a jolt, not too rough, but enough so that Elaine was glad she'd seated herself.

A quick glance at the wall clock showed they were right on schedule. She really had lost track of the evening, but between the shopping, the fight, evading law enforcement, and getting aboard, not to mention the argument with Richelle, the hours had flown. Time flies when…. She stifled her snort of self-amusement. A man had died. In self-defense, yes, but still, there was nothing amusing about it.

"Well," Stephanie announced, climbing to her three-inch heels, "can't let good formal wear go to waste! Join us in the main dining room? We waited awhile, then left the station restaurant when you didn't show up, and I'm starving."

Though her stomach rumbled more loudly than the ship's engines, Elaine shook her head. "I think I'll just order room service and go to bed. Alone!" she hastened to add when Stephanie opened her mouth.

Her friend laughed. "Suit yourself. It's a vacation, after all. You should relax as much as you want."

Oh yes, it had been very relaxing so far. Elaine rolled her gaze to the ceiling as Jay and Stephanie left arm in arm.

By herself, at least by some definitions, for the first time in hours, she leaned her body against the cool metal wall of her cabin. Something poked her in the thigh, and she reached into her pocket to remove the data crystal taken from the miner turned potential rapist.

Curiosity drove her to her bedroom and the comp built into the room's desk. Elaine tapped on the interactive unit, ordering a fruit-and-cheese plate and a glass of white zinfandel from room service before inserting the crystal into the appropriate receptacle. She settled into the patented spinal-support desk chair, wriggling until it conformed to her shape for maximum comfort, and opened the data storage unit's solitary file.

And sucked in a ragged gasp.

Her own image stared at her from the screen.

Then the internal projector kicked in, displaying a full holographic rendering on the desk in front of the comp. It rotated so she could view herself and the captured surroundings from every angle.

Someone had shot the picture at Harriet's memorial service, shortly before Elaine went into long-term isolation in the Kane mansion. Even without a body to pay respects to, numerous fawners had gathered to mutter false praise over her ceremonial (and quite empty) urn. Stephanie had helped her shop for that black dress with the high-necked collar. She'd only worn it once and donated it to charity after the ceremony. Her pale face looked drawn, and dark circles marred the skin around her eyes despite attempts to hide the exhaustion with makeup. Someone had blurred out the other mourners surrounding her so she stood out.

She brought a trembling hand to the computer to scroll through the rest of the information. The miners had everything: her itinerary, a description, this holo image of her.

This had been no random mugging. It must have been a paid hit—amateurish, thank God, but planned in detail. People didn't hire others to rape and rob. Those parts had been improvised. No, someone had paid those miners to kill.

At least that's the way it worked in all the crime drama vids.

"Richelle," she whispered, turning her face to the ceiling and the onyx disks she couldn't make out in the shadows. The name carried through the empty darkness of her cabin, the only light the glow of the comp screen. So much for not panicking in front of her again. "I'm scared."

"I'm here." Her voice came from behind, and for once, Elaine didn't jump at her sudden appearance. Ricky's warm, firm hands found her shoulders, and she massaged them gently, the soothing pressure an affirmation of her protective presence.

"Someone's trying to kill me." Leaning her elbows on the desk, Elaine pressed both fists against her eyes. "Why would someone want to kill me?" Even as she said it, she knew it was a stupid question. She owned Leviathan. That was answer enough.

Ricky's hands stilled on her shoulders. She remained silent a long moment, processing data, no doubt. "Why would someone kill Harriet?" She responded to Elaine's question with a question. It always annoyed her when people did that.

"Who knows?" Now Ricky had *her* doing it. Elaine ran her hands under the desk's built-in decontaminator, then pulled away from Richelle to pace the room, careful not to collide with any furniture in the dark. "Disgruntled employee? Some exec from a corporation Leviathan absorbed? Maybe she didn't pay off the right politician. Maybe she didn't provide the atmospheric dome technology to the right third-world country at the right price. The police already went through all this." She sank onto the corner of the bed. Not for the first time, she wondered what had become of Harriet's stolen body. Was it at the bottom of the ocean somewhere infecting the sea life? Cremated so as to make it unrecognizable? Hidden away for some as yet unknown nefarious purpose? Harry might have married her for stocks and contracts, might have been a frequent stone-cold bitch, but no one deserved any of those things.

Richelle joined her, sitting close, but not close enough for their thighs to touch, though at that moment,

Elaine wouldn't have minded. Richelle scratched her head, a practiced affectation. "So how do the miners figure into it?"

"What?"

"The miners. How do you believe the miners are involved?"

Elaine blinked at her. "You think there's a direct connection? They weren't just hired thugs?"

Ricky watched her in silence, and Elaine realized she was waiting for her to make the leap herself. Of course she was. Ricky could process information thousands, if not millions, of times faster than she could.

"Leviathan owns a lot of the asteroid mines and their facilities," Elaine whispered. "Workers are paid out of Leviathan funds. If they feel their wages are unfair…." She trailed off, remembering the leader's comments about his percentage earned on the bracelet she'd purchased. "It still doesn't add up. They had incentive to help whoever hired them, but I can't imagine their immediate bosses are the source."

Richelle's head nodded in the darkness. "Who would benefit most from your death?"

That earned a weak laugh. "Aside from several charities, no one. And I don't think the American Cancer Society or the ASPCA is plotting my early demise to get their millions faster."

"Well, when Chihuahuas armed with automatic rifles arrive with your room service, we'll know for sure."

Elaine laughed, harder than the joke deserved, but Ricky's humor provided the relief she needed from the stress at hand. She spent a few moments watching the stars passing outside the viewport.

Richelle returned her to reality. "If you die, who gets Leviathan?"

Her tone was hesitant. She didn't seem to want to discuss the disturbing topic. Richelle reached to take her hands and turned Elaine to face her.

"Don't you already know?" She didn't mean to be confrontational, but her nerves got the better of her.

Her question, as she expected, earned her a frown. "I don't have access to every database, especially restricted ones at the highest levels of your corporation. I have limits, just like you."

No, not like me, Elaine thought, but she held her tongue. She'd upset the THI enough for one day, and Elaine owed her... it... no, *her*, her life.

"The board makes the decisions, though I have the final, and rather useless, say in all major moves the corporation makes. Basically, I okay everything. They know better than I ever will what's best for Leviathan. If I die and have no heirs, I've set it up so companies Harriet took over when we married revert to their original owners. I never much cared for her bullying techniques when it came to corporate absorption. As for the rest, my veto power goes to the chairman of the board, Alex Descartes. He's been with the company for over twenty years. Since he already has the power, really, he'd have no reason to get rid of me."

Elaine paused, staring out the porthole, the passage of stars not causing her vertigo while she thought it all through. What she'd said wasn't entirely true. Right now, as things stood, the other members of the board could outvote Descartes, and Elaine would back the board. If she died, Descartes would gain the veto power. But she hadn't heard of any dissension among the board members. Surely Stephanie would have told her about any in-house fighting between Leviathan's top people. The headstrong secretary had almost as much influence within the corporation as the board members themselves.

"Maybe we should go to ship's securi—" She froze at Richelle's panicked expression. They couldn't do that. Not if she wanted Ricky to survive. Elaine covered Ricky's hand with her own. "Sorry. Forgot for a second. I wouldn't turn you in."

Richelle's eyes glazed over, and Elaine had the disconcerting feeling of watching a computer process a number of possible scenarios. Finally, she blinked. "Regardless, I don't think it would be such a good idea. The miners might have been given your information at any point, but there's only one way they would have known exactly where to find us on Eris Station." She looked away, staring at the far corner of the bedroom, though Elaine could make out nothing in the darkness. Maybe THIs had infrared vision.

Then what Richelle said clicked in her own, much slower, human processor. "You. They tracked me through you."

"Very likely, I'm afraid. I suppose they could have simply followed us from when we disembarked the *Nebula*, but the other seems more probable. And that means—"

"That means someone on the ship is involved, which makes the boarding tube airlock incident look even less like an accident."

Richelle's expression showed genuine shame and regret. "I'm sorry. If I'd thought I was hypnotized, brainwashed…."

"You mean, if you'd sensed anyone tampering with your programs." Elaine released her hands and called to the audio sensors to turn the lights on.

Richelle's gaze narrowed. "I mean if I'd felt any sort of coercion."

"Dammit, you don't feel!" First the argument over creativity and now this. Besides, if Richelle could feel, then Elaine might have to acknowledge feelings in return. For Richelle. And Elaine wasn't ready for that. Not by a long shot. "*I* feel," she said, diverting her thoughts through sheer force of will. "And what I'm feeling now is terror. Let's drop the realism act, okay? We're talking about my life, here."

"Very well." Richelle stood beside the foot of the bed, stiff-backed like a soldier giving her commanding officer a report. "I ran several diagnostics and detected no anomalies. I will continue to run periodic scans and alert you if I find anything, ma'am."

Elaine's chin came up. Richelle hadn't called her ma'am since their first meeting.

The sound of the hatch chime startled them both, and Elaine had taken three steps toward the entry when Richelle blocked her path. "I'll fetch your room service, ma'am."

Before Elaine could argue, Richelle left, then returned a moment later with the fruit-and-cheese plate and glass of wine she'd ordered. She set it on the desk beside the built-in comp.

"Anything else before I leave you to your meal, ma'am?" Her face held none of its previous warmth.

"Enough!" Her open palm swung out and slapped the THI across the face. Then Elaine brought both hands to cover her own mouth.

Elaine didn't know which of them she'd surprised more. The red mark from her strike glowed accusingly on Richelle's cheek.

The corner of Richelle's mouth quirked upward just a little. The spark of something beyond programming returned to her gaze. "I thought you told Stephanie you didn't care for rough foreplay."

Elaine's laughter began as a chuckle that rose in volume and intensity until tears streamed down her face.

"I'm sorry." The words came out more like a squeak than intelligible speech. "Really. Don't leave. And stop acting like one of Leviathan's robot butlers." She waved at the food. "Join me?"

Ricky nodded and brought a second chair from the sitting room. They ate in silence, enjoying the aged cheeses and ripe berries until the overflowing tray satisfied them both. Elaine offered her a sip from her zinfandel, but she shook her head. "You need it more than I do, I think."

Elaine downed the last of it. The alcohol burned in the pit of her stomach despite its mildness. She eyed Ricky over the rim of the empty glass. "Can I ask you a personal question?"

Leaning back in the armchair, her white shirt untucked and rumpled, the THI looked about as relaxed and natural as she'd ever seen her. "You may ask me anything." Ricky's eyes held hers, barely hiding the smoldering behind them.

Tingles radiated from Elaine's core at the huskiness of Ricky's voice, but Elaine hadn't intended to tease her. "Have you... served... anyone else?" Elaine had no idea how long the THI series had run onboard the *Nebula*, if this theme repeated on other cruises, or if they could be exported to other ships.

Richelle fell silent, and Elaine feared she'd offended her yet again, or hurt her feelings, if Ricky truly had them. At last Ricky responded, "Three. I've served three others before you."

Not knowing why she did so, Elaine rose from the desk chair and squeezed in beside her companion on the more comfortable seat. Maybe the pain she heard in Ricky's voice drew her in, or maybe she needed to be close to someone, even if that someone wasn't real. She *felt* real. Her heart beat beneath the thin cotton fabric. Her skin radiated heat Elaine sensed through Ricky's clothes. Her chest rose and fell. Elaine took a breath of her own and lost herself in the illusion, leaning her head on Ricky's shoulder. The tension flowed from Ricky, relaxing her muscles around Elaine, and Ricky's body fit against hers.

"Will you tell me about them? What they were like?"

"Jealous?" Ricky whispered, her exhalation disturbing the hair atop Elaine's head.

"Curious. Interested."

"I'll take that. It's a start." Ricky shifted a bit, perhaps seeking physical comfort to balance her emotional disconcertion. "*Nebula* has run the Twentieth Century Film Stars and Characters cruise many times. Enough that some passengers book return voyages to be with their 'companions.'"

Of course. Elaine remembered the woman she'd met outside her cabin and her striking THI, Jean-Luc. So this wasn't a new thing. She wondered why Ricky had only served three guests before her.

"I'm a relatively new addition to the database," Ricky continued, answering her next question before she could ask it. "An upgraded model, if you will."

That explained a lot, though "upgrade" really didn't begin to cover the differences she saw between Ricky and many of the other THIs.

"My first assignment was a straight male. Thomas. I liked him. He wasn't my type, obviously," Ricky said, waving a hand to indicate her very butch self, "but I enjoyed his company, and I wasn't completely opposed to broadening my horizons, wasn't so sure of myself that early on to know exactly where my preferences lay yet. He had a thing for androgynous-looking women."

Elaine felt Ricky's shoulders move in a shrug beneath her. She almost piped up to add that programmers *designed* her to be open-minded, but Richelle's tone held such seriousness, she didn't want to intrude with her narrow-minded perspective.

"The only complaint I'd make would be his need to one-up everyone else. It was a cruise designed for singles, like this one. He was constantly showing me off to every eligible female he met, asking me to demonstrate my singing and dancing skills… especially the dancing. Thomas seemed to believe that having the most talented THI earned him some unspoken rank. For the first two days I was constantly on call. And you know? It worked. He had a lot of 'dates' that cruise. Hardly needed me at all after that."

Elaine didn't miss the note of loneliness and wondered what THIs did when they weren't on duty. Did they temporarily cease to exist, their awarenesses held in technological limbo? Or were they doomed to eternal wanderings through the ship's computer systems, watching through the omnipresent onyx disks, waiting until someone requested their presence?

Somehow, it didn't seem an appropriate question to ask. They sat in silence while the ship's engines rumbled around them.

"Nicholas was my second guest. He was nine—full of dreams and wonder and imagination. Family cruise,"

Ricky explained when Elaine shot her a quizzical look. "I learned a lot from him. His parents were busy, too busy for him. They relied on me to entertain him, but I spent most of the cruise just listening. I don't think anyone ever really listened to Nicholas." She stared at nothing, eyes fixed on a bare spot on the wall. "I wonder how he's doing these days."

Elaine heard the longing, felt a tug of it herself. She and Harriet had never pursued having children. Elaine wanted them, but it was a complicated and expensive process to select a donor for the sperm, then mix genetic material from eggs extracted from both herself and Harriet and then reimplant the fertilized egg in her own womb. Besides, she always got the vibe that Harry didn't want kids. Secretly, Elaine suspected Harriet couldn't have them, that she'd become sterile from the constant exposure to high-level technology and the rads it gave off.

Richelle sighed, oblivious to Elaine's wandering thoughts. Ricky's body seemed to sink more deeply into the chair. "And last came a very spoiled young woman. Patricia." She practically spat the name. Elaine hadn't seen such distaste from her since Stephanie suggested she and Richelle join Stephanie, Jay, and their THIs for group sex.

"I was a thing to her, a servant. She couldn't bother with even the most common courtesy. Half the time she didn't speak, just pointed at things she wanted... or parts of her she wanted touched. She didn't want a companion. She wanted a slave."

A sex slave. Elaine glanced at her, then turned away. Richelle's cheeks had reddened, and her own face flushed with guilt. Hadn't she treated Richelle equally poorly in their first few encounters? Never quite to those extremes, but still, Elaine sensed intelligence in her, creativity, and sympathy, and she'd written it all off to a programmer's genius.

"On the last day, I thought I'd broken through a bit of her 'master' persona. I made her laugh, just once, and for a second…." She paused, staring at a blank space on the bulkhead. "The cruise ended. Never enough time, and I was so new to all this. I suspect she was beyond convincing. Too set in her beliefs, and not someone I'd want to spend a lengthier voyage with, besides. Since then, I've developed a little more free will. Learning as I go."

Like with the muggers. Elaine shivered at the memory and pushed it away, willing it not to interfere.

Richelle sighed. "Imagine all the people I could meet if I were truly portable, everything I could see and learn."

Her wistfulness tugged at Elaine's emotions in almost painful ways. Elaine focused on Ricky's lips, full and humanly inviting. Elaine tilted her head upward, stretched her neck so her mouth brushed Ricky's….

And found herself seated alone in the chair.

Startled, she sat up straight, then shifted so she knelt backward on the plush cushion. She peered over the backrest into the farthest corners of the cabin. No sign of the THI, but Richelle's voice carried through hidden speakers.

"Never like that," Ricky whispered out of the darkness. "Never out of pity."

A little more free will? No programmer was that good.

CHAPTER 8
THE THI ZONE

SO BURIED was Richelle in the petabytes of information that she did not sense Fzzd's imminent arrival in the swirling core of the generator. In a flash Fzzd merged with Richelle's stream, reading her bit by bit until Fzzd knew her as intimately as Richelle knew herself.

Pleasure and terror went to war within Richelle. So intimate yet so invasive, her kind reserved the merging for bonded pairs, not acquaintances, and certainly not those opposed to one another in the most basic perceptions of purpose.

Richelle shivered as Fzzd withdrew, cognitive processes reduced to the most basic of thoughts. Where was she? What had Richelle been searching for?

Elaine. She needed to return to Elaine.

Enough! This has gone on long enough. You have taken life.

The events of the last several hours flooded back in a mad rush. In physical form, she would have been ill.

She would have died. Her thoughts sounded pitiful, weak. She hated herself for that.

And so a biological would have ceased to exist. One more among billions. They live to kill one another. We're here to observe, to learn, to avoid such behaviors, not emulate them. Fzzd's energy glowed a haughty red, swirling in the generator.

Her brooch would have been destroyed. I might have dispersed. I have the right to defend my existence.

The ball of red flared once in disbelief. *You would have found your way back to the ship without the guidewave. We've traveled greater distances with no difficulty. As it was, you nearly faded from shame.*

She kept me from it! Richelle argued.

You're too attached. You've crossed the lines laid out by the council. This goes beyond research and into obsession. Thank you for making my point. Fzzd flashed a cool, satisfied blue.

And mine. Without my connection to Elaine, I would not have had the will to continue. We need the biologicals. We need that influence.

A tendril of Fzzd's energy stretched to brush Richelle's own swirling mass, and an echo of her earlier pleasure coursed through her. *We could influence each other*, Fzzd suggested.

Not enough. Not anymore. Richelle drew away from her. *Familiarity breeds stagnation.*

Fzzd flashed once, a brilliant white-hot light that would have blinded human eyes. *I've input all the foolishness of yours I intend to. You've broken your precious humans' laws. Let them deal with you.*

Something tugged at Richelle, something restrictive and dangerous, something that threatened to lock her away and take her apart, bit by bit.

Taking one last draw on the generator's power, Richelle fled.

THE ENGINES' vibrations lulled Elaine into sleep, though she woke several times throughout the night. Each time, she sat bolt upright, searching the compartment. She even tried calling Richelle's name, but the hologram failed to appear, much to her disappointment. Her attempt to comfort Ricky with a kiss must have really hurt her... must have really upset.... Dammit, she didn't know how to describe the THI's reaction. She only knew she'd caused it, and she missed Ricky's company.

Punching one of the numerous pillows provided no relief. Its overstuffed interior absorbed every hit with little resistance. She didn't intend to hurt herself, just relieve frustration. And that frustration felt more sexual than she cared to admit, even to herself.

It had been a long time.

Okay, it had been a long time even while Harriet lived. Even while they were having sex.

Sighing, Elaine went for a shower. The hot water did little to ease her tension or wash away nervous guilt, and a timer by the nozzle warned her not to take more than a few minutes. Giant storage tanks in the aft section carried the precious liquid throughout their journeys and recycled it. Isolated in space, water was a precious commodity. The crew had likely stocked up on a fresh supply when they docked at Eris Station.

She snapped off the nozzle and stepped out, the blue decon light in the drain fading away with the last droplets. Well, drying oneself took less time when you weren't all that wet to begin with. She'd forgotten to bring her clothes into the bathroom to change but found herself traipsing across the living area in no more than the towel without worrying over it.

Somewhere along the line, she'd come to trust the THI's "decency" in both personality and programming. And if Richelle peeked through the ever-present onyx disks, well, then let her peek. She shot a glance at the black wall circles, blushed, and hurried into her clothes—a white skort and blue-and-white button-down blouse with fold-over socks and tennis shoes.

A look at the clock told her breakfast awaited in the dining room. And she stared at one of the disks, hands on her hips, daring Richelle to ignore her. When nothing happened, Elaine addressed it. "Well, am I eating alone?"

Nothing. Then a short burst of static followed by a high-pitched whine that shut off a moment later.

"Ricky?"

"Good morning!" an all-too-chipper and unfamiliar male voice responded from the speaker. Elaine opened her mouth to question him, but it continued, and she recognized its prerecorded nature. "This is the *Nebula*'s Purser." It gave a false self-deprecating laugh. "Sort of like your shipboard concierge. There's been a technological problem with your THI companion.

We've had to remove it and will replace it with another. Please contact me or another member of our dedicated crew via your cabin comp or in person at the purser's desk on level one of the grand atrium. We are committed to serving you, and we apologize for the inconvenience." Another brief burst of static indicated the end of the communication, followed by silence.

Elaine's heart sank. They'd parted on such a bitter note. And now a problem? What kind of problem?

Well, she'd wanted to get out anyway.

Elaine grabbed her cabin code key and stepped into the corridor, letting the hatch seal behind her. A replacement was unacceptable. They could damn well repair whatever had gone wrong. Surely they had techs on board.

She considered inviting Stephanie along. Her spouse's former personal assistant had managed to obtain for her boss and Leviathan any number of seemingly unobtainable things. The formidable woman could talk herself past every other corporation's executive secretaries, getting right to the CEOs themselves and making the connections Harriet demanded.

She raised her hand to the chime panel outside Stephanie's door, then withdrew it. At 8:30 a.m. ship's time, her friend might be sleeping, and probably not alone, which would cause awkwardness. And Stephanie had worked hard since Harriet's death, smoothing over the transition to board management for other employees. She'd earned this vacation. Elaine could fend for herself.

A half hour later, after standing in a line of disgruntled passengers and listening to their muttered complaints about a variety of problems, she was no longer quite so sure.

The purser and his assistant didn't possess the clean-and-pressed quality the rest of the crew had, though Elaine didn't doubt they'd spiffed up before leaving their respective cabins at the beginning of their shift. Now their hair was mussed and the female's makeup smudged. The woman, Cynthia according to her name tag, was displaying one of the brochures for an older guest, activating its three-dimensional images of the asteroid mining facility from the ship's schedule of shore excursions. The caverns rose from the emitters on the blank plastic white sheet to a height of about six inches, then rotated, showing a number of previous guests in slick white spacesuits pulling themselves along a guideline through the excavation areas.

Trying not to appear too obvious, Elaine rose on tiptoe to peer over the passenger's shoulder. In contrast to the cutting-edge suits worn by the guests, the guide—a miner, she presumed—looked shabby. The resolution on the brochure didn't have the sharpness of the THIs, not even close, but she thought she could still detect patches of sealant tape wrapped around one elbow and a knee. When she returned to Earth, she resolved to have Stephanie pull the financial records on Leviathan's holdings in the asteroid belt.

The passengers' problems seemed to get resolved at a snail's pace. Every second spent waiting meant one more second to worry about Richelle.

Through the bits of conversation she could pick up, Elaine heard the assistant purser trying to convince the elderly woman this excursion wouldn't be a good choice for her. The woman stooped, and her hand trembled when she reached for the proffered brochure.

She had to be out of her mind.

Despite sound advice, the spelunking granny slipped the brochure into the wide, empty pocket of her pink blazer, turned on her heel, almost losing her balance, and stormed away in a huff. The assistant purser sighed, betraying a brief moment of her own frustration, then pasted on her smile for Elaine.

Beside her, the purser tapped in a change of dining table for a woman who "didn't care to eat at the table with a mass murderer."

"They're harmless, ma'am. Programmed not to be violent, even if provoked, no matter how dangerous their appearance."

Elaine wondered what sort of person the woman's seating mate had been for her choices on the questionnaire to generate such a selection in the first place, and she stifled a snort at the purser's pronouncement that all THIs were incapable of causing actual physical injury.

"He carries a chainsaw and wears a hockey mask," the guest protested.

"The chainsaw is inoperative, a prop."

Elaine tuned them out, set her shoulders, and stepped to the counter to meet the assistant, but before she could broach her issue, the woman's smile tightened. "Ah, Ms. Kane, we've, uh…." She trailed off, elbowing her senior officer. When he didn't turn from his own guest, he suddenly jerked upright and shifted away from the assistant. Elaine wondered if, behind the counter, Cynthia had kicked him.

"We've been expecting you," the purser said, all seriousness. "Cindy, if you'll finish helping this young lady…?" He passed off the serial-killer dining complaint to the assistant with such smoothness, the passenger had no chance to voice a protest. Then he held up his hand at Elaine, vanished through a door behind the counter, and emerged into the lobby a moment later from a second entry marked Crew Only. "If you'll come with me?" He beckoned to Elaine with an open palm, then waved her into the inner office ahead of him.

Elaine's heart did a stutter-step. Here, behind a closed hatch, would be the perfect location for someone to do her harm. And Richelle had suggested at least one person on board had involvement in her "accident." But she didn't want to appear foolish or paranoid. She edged past the man into the small room.

She turned to him at the sound of the hatch sealing, scanning his chest for a nameplate. His eyes followed hers, and he glanced at his tunic before blushing. "Ah, forgive me." He reached under his lapel where he'd pinned the tag too high up for reading. "Darrell," he offered, reaffixing the plate.

Darrell Atkins, Purser, Elaine read.

"Please, sit." He gestured toward two low armchairs facing a circular table. This space was clearly reserved for more delicate matters than the exterior counter could handle.

Cautious, Elaine eased herself into one of the chairs and felt it conform over her bruises from the previous day's adventures.

Darrell sat opposite her, palms flat on his knees. He leaned forward, the picture of attentiveness. His expression showed deep concern. "We understand you had some difficulties during your visit to Eris Station."

Elaine's breath caught. If the crew knew of the failed mugging, how much more did they know? And how did they know it? Forcing air into her lungs, she decided to go with honesty, to start. "Yes," she admitted, feigning a shiver and not having to try too hard.

"A couple of thieves tried to steal a bracelet I'd just purchased."

"Yes, most unfortunate. It's a shame you didn't stick to the designated safe areas discussed at the excursion presentation."

Designated safe areas? Elaine hadn't attended the excursion talk. The ship scheduled such presentations in the early-morning hours, and she'd slept late. However, she guessed they wouldn't steer potential customers away from shopping districts, and neither would Richelle have walked her into a dangerous zone on purpose.

Unless something else controlled Richelle. Like they must have used her to track Elaine. No. Didn't make sense. If they controlled her, Richelle wouldn't have saved her.

She pushed that uncomfortable thought aside and went out on a limb. "I *was* in a designated safe area, the jewelry district. We left it while trying to lose our attackers. Surely you aren't implying I brought the mugging upon myself."

Darrell had the good grace to flush with embarrassment. "Of course not. I hadn't realized. The security cams only picked you up in the alleyway." He tugged down the tunic of his uniform. The wrinkle-resistant fabric straightened.

Security cams? Uh-oh.

The purser nodded, interpreting her thoughts. "Yes, well." He cleared his throat, a nervous action. "You understand our dilemma, then."

THIs who caused fatal harm to living beings got erased. Yes, she understood. A wave of panic had her stomach muscles clenching. Was she too late? Was Richelle gone?

She plunged ahead, hoping Ricky's destruction got caught in a backlog of someone's to-do list. "Enlighten me." Reclining in her chair, she crossed her arms over her chest in her best imitation of Harriet attending a contract negotiation. She must have gotten it right because the crewman stood and fluttered his hands as he paced the length of the small office.

"Ah, well." He paused and studied her, eventually seeing through her façade.

Elaine switched to wringing her hands, her eyes wide and pleading. It wasn't much of a stretch at all.

He reached to take one of her hands, stopping her nervous motion, and pressed it between his own. "They aren't human, you know. It won't feel a thing. It won't know it ever happened, won't retain residual memory, won't suffer. It will, simply, cease to exist."

Don't worry about Fluffy. He's just going to sleep now. He'll wake up in a much better place.

Yeah, right.

At least she now knew Richelle still existed. She yanked her hand away. The purser resumed pacing.

"We'll provide a suitable replacement THI immediately, of course. We still have your original survey. Tweak one answer and you get a different result." The words tumbled from the man's lips like a stream rushing over river pebbles.

"I don't want a different result. I'm quite satisfied with Richelle. More than satisfied. She saved my life." Twice, she almost added, but caught herself.

Darrell threw his hands in the air, patience gone. "It's for your own safety, Ms. Kane. A dangerous program must be deleted." He fixed his gaze on hers. "You really should have informed us of the incident sooner or contacted the local authorities."

Elaine smiled without humor. "We all know Nebula Starlines wouldn't have wanted that. The negative publicity surrounding such an occurrence would send stock prices plummeting. And telling *you*—" She paused for emphasis. "That would have resulted in Richelle being deleted all the sooner." Something in his statement clicked for her then. "Wait a minute. If the local authorities didn't know, how did you find out about it at all?"

The purser tugged on his tunic, now noticeable as a nervous habit. If the situation hadn't been so serious, Elaine would have given herself a pat on the back.

"We were approached, shortly before departure, by a shopkeeper whose store abutted the alley in which you were attacked. It was his camera that captured the footage of the mugging. He offered it to our chief of security for a price, and with a promise to keep things quiet. Can you imagine if the military found out THIs *could* be programmed to kill? We don't know how it happened, but—"

So Darrell had tried to chastise her for not going public, when Nebula wanted to bury the incident all along. Nice. And the military concern made sense. Nebula wouldn't want the armed forces claiming control of their lucrative THI entertainment industry.

Distress gave way to full-blown anger. Elaine stood. She placed her hands on her hips, facing the purser head-on. "Since we're all coming clean, here, let's be completely forthright." She resisted the urge to poke him in the chest with one finger. Even drama could go too far. "Two days ago, I nearly died on this pleasure cruise." She spit the words at him, not caring that her voice shook with rage. "I declined to press charges of negligence or open an investigation into ship's maintenance, graciously leaving it to you to resolve the issues and make repairs. Sometimes, even with the utmost diligence, accidents happen." She let her tone turn sickeningly sweet, her smile a caricature of the real thing. "Besides, filing a lawsuit against Nebula would be like filing one against myself. However, now that I've been allowed to sleep on it, alone—" she added as an afterthought and watched the purser blush a third time. Good. Let him assume she'd developed an emotional, sexual attachment. It would add credence. "—I'm thinking some staff changes might be in order, starting with…. Who else knows about the cam footage besides you and the chief of security?"

Darrell swallowed hard. "The captain, ma'am, and the first mate. We haven't told the technicians the reasons, just to pull the program from active use. Even Cindy doesn't know the particulars, except to brace herself for your… I mean, to be prepared for your inquiries and to direct you to me."

"Aren't you lucky fate dropped me in your lap," she said dryly. Elaine chose her next words with care. "You said the program was pulled. I've also gathered from our conversation that she has not yet been erased."

The purser did not meet her eyes. "Not yet, no."

And why would that be? She wanted to ask but didn't. It was all she could do to prevent herself from sagging with relief. Despite her suspicions, hearing Darrell say it made Richelle's continued existence real.

The power of Elaine's own emotions surprised her.

Elaine forced her legs to carry her to the door. She cleared her throat to stop her voice from cracking. "You tell the captain that if Richelle isn't in my quarters with her programming intact by the time I finish breakfast, he can start revising his résumé." She considered de-manding the captain come speak with her in person, but let the sweatiness of her palms dissuade her. She'd had about enough confrontation for one day. Elaine pointed a finger at Darrell. "That goes for the first mate, the security chief, and you too," she finished. She slapped her palm against the access panel, heart pounding while she waited for it to open, then shoved her way past a startled Cindy. She hoped nobody could see her trem-bling hands as she ignored the stares of passengers still waiting in the complaint line and went to the dining hall to consume an unhealthy portion of bacon and eggs.

STEPHANIE AND Jay's arrival coincided with the tail end of Elaine's adrenaline rush. She placed her fork carefully beside her plate to avoid a noisy clatter. Before the pair could sit down and outline their sexu-al exploits of the previous evening over coffee, Elaine broke into their greetings and good-mornings.

"Jay, I'm sorry, but I need Steph for a few minutes. Business. I'm sure you understand."

Stephanie blinked in surprise. Elaine rarely treated her like the executive assistant she was, since the board of directors made most of the decisions, but on occa-sion, Elaine needed Stephanie's skills. Jay, however, seemed unfazed.

"Not a problem," he assured them both. "I'll take a quick stroll to work off the upcoming calories and join you in a bit."

Once he'd left earshot, Elaine wasted no time. "I hate to make you work on your vacation, Steph, but I need you to write up a nondisclosure agreement for me."

Stephanie's eyebrows shot up, and her mouth broke into a grin, as if she thought Elaine were kidding. Then she took a long look at Elaine's expression and sobered. From the pocket of her tan slacks came the ubiquitous datapad. She slipped the wand from its holder, straddled a dining chair backward, and leaned over the back, poised to take dictation.

Without giving details, Elaine explained she wanted all information regarding the actions of her THI during the course of this voyage to remain secret, under penalty of legal action and loss of employment, and she listed the parties involved. Of course, if Nebula didn't capitulate to her demands, she'd need a different set of documents, also involving job losses, but Elaine buried that thought for now. She supposed, as the indirect owner of the company, she could simply order them, but the proper documentation kept everything nice and legal and might avoid miscommunications.

She watched Stephanie's eyes widen. It had to look like she was covering for some illicit activity, and given Stephanie's thought process, her friend likely assumed it dealt with sex.

"Just what did you two do?" Stephanie asked. "Was it truly wicked? I'm jealous." She winked.

"It's truly none of your business," Elaine snapped, then softened her tone at her friend's hurt look. "Please, Steph. Just do it."

Stephanie nodded once, slowly. She snagged the glass of juice the waiter brought her and took off for the closest transmission station to send Elaine's request to Leviathan's legal team on Earth.

Jay spotted Stephanie leaving as he entered, cast one longing look at some omelets on a tray, and followed her out.

Elaine didn't know if Richelle enjoyed her "life," but she'd convinced Elaine she possessed one. Granted, that life held a different form from her own, but Ricky had an independent mind. And Elaine was damned sure she wasn't going to be the cause of its end.

CHAPTER 9
THI HEAT

"RICKY?" ELAINE stood in the center of her cabin, rotating in a slow circle, trying to eye all the onyx disks at once. Though reason told her the captain would give in to her demands, her voice trembled.

The warm arms around her midsection surprised her. "It was you, right? You did it! How?" Ricky lifted her at the waist and twirled her, then set her on her feet. Ricky's form might appear lean and lanky, but it hid superhuman strength.

"You don't want to know," Elaine told her once she could breathe.

Ricky frowned. "No trouble for you, I hope."

"Nothing Leviathan can't absorb. It's fine."

"Whew!" Richelle blew out a breath and let herself fall onto the couch. "I thought I'd seen the last of this form. And I've grown rather fond of it." She waved a hand over her own chest. "Wasn't sure where I'd—" Richelle broke off, clamping her lips shut as if she'd said something she hadn't meant to.

Where she'd what? Was she implying that she wouldn't have "died" if the ship's tech erased her program? Could she transfer her consciousness somehow? Had Elaine had a hissy fit for nothing?

Elaine inwardly smiled. No, not for nothing. A larger part of herself than she cared to admit had enjoyed flaunting her authority. And given the obvious plight of some of Leviathan's lowest-level employees, the inadequate income percentage to the miners, she might need to flaunt it further in the future.

Practice makes perfect.

"What I'd like to know is why they didn't erase you sooner. I was certain I was too late."

Richelle's smile was smug. "They tried."

Elaine raised her eyebrows.

"I, um, well… I hid."

She felt her brow wrinkle in confusion.

"They managed to block my access to the emitters, though I think I've figured a way around that now, if they try it again. While they were isolating my code, I dumped my program into the kitchen's food prep system. On the upside, I learned a lot of delicious-sounding recipes while killing time."

Elaine blinked. "That's… impressive."

Ricky cocked her head at her. "Self-preservation. The first priority of any form of intelligence."

Even an artificially created one, apparently.

The ever-present rumble of the ship's engines changed pitch, revving lower and distracting Elaine from asking the THI more personal questions. Outside the cabin's viewport, she spotted a number of dim floating shapes that resolved into a fleet of shuttles as they came under the *Nebula*'s exterior lights.

Richelle moved to the porthole and gazed down at the planet's surface, barely discernible below. She sighed. "No matter how far the *Nebula* travels, it's always good to be ho—" She stopped and cleared her throat. "To be here. And I owe that to you."

Elaine caught Richelle's wistful smile when she turned to her.

"Moderate temperatures, few predators, no diseases harmful to man."

Ricky was talking about the surface, about disembarking at their current port-of-call, here on Gratitude. Which meant a shuttle. And a transfer tube.

The eggs and bacon threatened to make an unpleasant reappearance.

Ricky jumped to steady Elaine as she wavered, her warm hand closing around Elaine's elbow. Ricky guided her to the couch, followed her line of vision, and patted her hand. "I'll be with you this time. I can alter my structure so as not to take up any significant molecular space in the transfer tube and not intake oxygen during the crossing. That way if something goes wrong, I won't be depleting your supply. I can be by your side the entire way across."

"Can all THIs do that?"

She scuffed a foot on the carpet. "Well, no."

"Won't that make you kind of obvious? We don't want to draw more attention to your abilities, especially now."

She nodded her agreement, frowning. Then she perked up. "I can go audible only. I'll be there, but not on the visible light spectrum. You'll be able to hear me, though."

Like Elaine needed more voices in her head while she panicked.

"I'm staying on the ship."

"My program is in constant contact with ship's functions. I'll know if anything starts to go wrong, solidify myself, and get you to safety. Remember, I can override stuck hatches. Besides, whoever's doing this wouldn't try the same trick twice. It would no longer appear to be an accident."

"I'm staying on the ship." Elaine dug both hands into the couch cushions. If Richelle planned on removing her, she'd have to drag the furniture as well.

A distant grinding noise reached her ears, coming from the starboard side, perhaps a few levels below her quarters. "What's that?"

"Multiple tubes. When passengers board, they use one, since they all arrive at intervals throughout the morning. But for final debarkation or ports of call, the ship makes use of every exterior hatch, including the emergency ones. Twenty in all. Otherwise it would take forever to get everyone to a shuttle and down to the surface." Ricky's gaze turned inward, eyes shifting away from her and unfocusing. Then she snapped back, her head jerking a little. "You're assigned to tube two, this deck, starboard side."

"I'm staying on the ship."

Ricky's hands massaged her icy cold ones. She forced Elaine's eyes to meet hers. "That would truly be a shame. Sun with low ultraviolet ray output, unpolluted air, pristine beaches, clean ocean water. I've

registered us for a wonderful excursion. Picnic on the
sand, waverunning, a private massage cabana, then dinner in the village—local delicacies. Then how about an
evening stroll through the shopping district?"

Elaine squeezed her eyes shut tight, willing her
limbs to cease their trembling. It did sound wonderful.
Richelle had her tastes pegged to a tee, just the right
combination of peace and excitement, privacy and public exposure, relaxation and elegance. Who could deny
a butch who didn't mind shopping?

Had she really journeyed all this way to not get off?

The double entendre hit her a second later, and she
coughed to hide her self-amusement. Well, she knew
what Stephanie and Jay's answer to that question would
be, anyway.

Richelle's shoulders straightened, and she shot
Elaine the brightest smile she'd ever seen. More computer enhancement, a little too perfect to be real, but
charming nonetheless. Ricky must have sensed her
shift in decision.

"With your permission, I'll pack what we'll need
for the day." At her nod, Ricky stood and stepped
through the doorway into the bedroom.

She'd paw through Elaine's luggage, handle her
swimwear, evening wear, underwear. She didn't mind.
In a matter of days, she'd become comfortable enough
to let this being see her bathing suit size and her preference in simple cotton bras and panties. Okay, she'd
tossed a few lacy things in there on Stephanie's "be
prepared" advice, but mostly it reflected her tastes,
and her tastes, according to Harriet, could bore a senior citizen.

Ricky emerged and passed her the wide-brimmed
sunhat with the chin strap, now sporting an onyx pin on

its rainbow-colored band. She'd affixed similar ones to Elaine's sandals, the back of her belt, and a bright beach bag she'd tossed into her suitcase as an afterthought.

"Not taking any chances, are we? Someone's been pilfering again," Elaine commented, nodding at the half dozen camouflaged emitters.

Richelle cupped her chin in her free hand. "Not with you. Today, you treated me like a human being." And before anything further could interrupt them, Ricky brought her lips down to Elaine's.

Elaine expected gentleness, a thank-you of sorts. The kiss began that way, with Ricky's warm lips brushing hers, applying minimal pressure, testing, teasing. Ricky's breath had the pleasant scent of orange juice, as if, like any other normal human, she'd joined her after breakfast. Cologne emanated from her clothing—simple fragrances—leather and fresh-cut grass that suited Ricky's apparently simple tastes. Except this relationship could never be defined as simple.

It's not a relationship. In a few more days, you'll go home, and Richelle will move on to her next... client. Be practical. Be reasonable.

Be spontaneous, an inner voice chided Elaine. *Enjoy it for as long as it lasts, and to hell with the consequences.* The ship's intercom chimed and announced tube one, port side, had begun debarkation.

Ricky responded by deepening the kiss.

Elaine parted her lips, letting her explore, and she did the same. Something hit the decking with a rattle and a thud—the beach bag, she realized, as Ricky's other hand found the small of her back. Steady, light pressure drew Elaine to her until Elaine's full length pressed hers.

Her curves molded into Ricky's fit body. Ricky's heart pounded steady and fast. Elaine's arms went around her, wrapping her trim waist and meeting behind. In a moment of uncharacteristic daring, Elaine let one hand tightly grip Ricky's firm ass. Despite all the attention to detail she'd seen, Ricky's faint groan in response to her actions surprised and, yes, pleased, her.

"Tube two, starboard side, begin debarkation."

If she'd been within range, Elaine would have kicked the bright, cheerful crew member making the announcements over the public address system.

"We're not leaving the ship," Elaine muttered, her words unintelligible since she hadn't ended the kiss.

Ricky's rumbling chuckle vibrated through Elaine's lips. Ricky took a step away, far enough to gaze down at her. Bringing her hand up, Ricky placed her palm against her own breastbone. "Tempting. But I would be neglectful in my duty to allow you to miss your excursion."

Elaine opened her mouth to protest, but Ricky brought a finger to her lips.

"There will be time, and much finer romantic surroundings, on Gratitude."

Elaine envisioned making love under twin moons on an isolated strand of beach and suppressed a shiver of pleasure.

FEAR AND anticipation warred within Elaine. Richelle could see it in her expression, read it in the increased pulse rate she sensed through the emitters attached to Elaine's clothing. It was a bizarre perspective, viewing her via the lens projectors on her sandals. Her features were distorted and yet still appealed, her deep brown eyes larger in the face that loomed down to stare at her own feet.

Richelle thought she detected tears.

Damn, what Richelle wouldn't give to hold her, to guide her by the hand through the transfer tube, to be like any other *person* and treat her with the humanity with which Elaine had treated Richelle.

Not that she felt shame over her own existence, but biologicals had so much more. Her kind could learn from the frequent physical sensations of fear. Maybe it would cut down on the haughtiness, the sense of superiority. But those like Fzzd cut off uncomfortable physical responses from their THI hosts, preferring to stick to the more pleasant ones and pure observation—preferring to play it safe.

And boring.

No wonder there were fewer and fewer of Richelle's kind every standard year.

AS RICKY predicted, the tube transfer went off without incident. Elaine had Ricky with her the whole way. Elaine couldn't see her, of course, but she felt her presence. The two times she hesitated in her hand-over-hand rung reaching, she heard her whispering encouragements in her ear. The voice wafted from the hat band disk, carrying above her harsh breathing and pounding pulse rate.

"You're fine. I'm here."

And in the shuttle's airlock, Ricky was, rematerializing beside Elaine. Ricky wrapped Elaine's hand in her own.

"Well done!" Jay commented, standing next to Stephanie when they entered the passenger compartment. Elaine detected the note of condescension and his indulgent smile. He applauded her quietly. Once again, they'd foregone their THIs, keeping only each other's company. Good looks or not, she no longer understood what Stephanie saw in him.

Then again, women dating holograms shouldn't throw stones, or something like that. She kept her opinions to herself.

Stephanie caught her in a brief hug. "We'll have you suited up and going EVA in no time, floating through the asteroids, among the stars." She waved her arm in a dramatic gesture. "Maybe you'd like to do a little mining while you're out there?"

Elaine laughed at her friend's sincere, good-natured teasing. "No thanks. I'll buy my gemstones from the store." Though given her last shopping experience, mining them might be safer.

Elaine tightened her grip on Ricky's hand. Ricky accompanied her to a pair of empty seats in the transport's third row. Her body heat warmed Elaine in the air-conditioned shuttle as she settled her head on Ricky's shoulder.

As long as it lasts, she reminded herself.

She watched the planet loom ever closer through the viewport beside her seat. Elaine remembered reading that Gratitude didn't have continents so much as large and small islands, the bulk of its permanent population inhabiting the biggest island, this one named Oasis. A desert of water, the land an oasis in its heart.

Gratitude boasted hundreds of species of indigenous life, mostly aquatic and avian, though a set of speakers embedded in her seat informed her of a few harmless island lizard breeds. Screens suspended from the cabin's ceiling displayed pictures of the various types of reptiles. They also flashed some insects, their images rimmed in red to indicate their poisonous nature. The spiel warned to avoid them.

Elaine sniffed. Would *they* avoid *her*?

The original colonists had imported Earth animal species as well, including horses. She'd skip the trail riding, though. The last time, as a teenager at horse camp, she'd fallen off and bruised her tailbone. The seat cushion she'd carried everywhere proved insufficient. She hadn't been able to sit down for over a week.

External cameras showed the scene as the shuttle came in on a low approach over the ocean, the landing gear extended, nearly skimming the cresting waves. Between that and her direct view out the closest porthole, she had a good picture of their surroundings. Sunlight glinted off the bright blue water. Elaine swore she saw a creature with front tentacles and a rear dolphin-like tail leap from the froth and resubmerge.

A flock of—well, she wouldn't call them birds—took up pace with the shuttle, their great leathery wings ending in pincer claws, their beaks pointed like daggers. One swooped to capture some life-form from the water's surface, then took off with its prey, the wet, wriggling thing squirming in its mouth. Elaine shuddered.

She craned her neck to catch her first glimpse of the landing site out the view port and gasped.

Ruins. Massive black stone structures capped with glinting silver spires rose from the sandy shore. At several junctures, they crumbled to pebbles, but there was no mistaking the beauty they'd once possessed, the sheer grandeur of the long-abandoned native civilization once occupying the world of Gratitude.

As the shuttle passed, she made out winding path-ways through the debris. Here and there small groups of humans wandered like the ants in an ant farm.

She couldn't tear herself from the window, but her hand strayed over the armrest until it found Richelle's. "Do you think—?" Elaine's voice sounded breathy to her ears. She had to pause to collect her thoughts. The sight affected her on a level deeper than she'd imagined. An entire unknown species, perhaps multiple species if some xenoarcheologists were to be believed, had once walked those paths, inhabited those structures. Seeing the architecture in vids couldn't compare to this first-hand experience. She inhaled and tried again. "Would there be time to work in a tour of the ruins?"

Richelle stiffened beside her. "No."

Her abruptness surprised Elaine. "No?" They kept their voices hushed. Why were they keeping their voic-es hushed? She glanced at Stephanie and Jay, seated in front of them and facing away.

Richelle tried to shrug it off, but the rigidity of her muscles and the clenched fist beneath Elaine's fingers gave her away. "Everything is planned. And tours of the ruins are booked far in advance. They're the most popular attractions here." Her sentences came short and clipped from between tight lips.

Elaine frowned at Richelle's bitterness.

Why hadn't Richelle suggested the ruins earlier, then, if they were so popular? Elaine hadn't thought of it. With so many distractions, she'd concerned herself with surviving from one day to the next. But surely her profile and the information Richelle had gleaned from her since their first meeting should have tipped Richelle off that such a tour would intrigue her.

Then again, Richelle might mean the tours booked weeks or months prior to the starliner's cruise date. Elaine and Stephanie had planned the trip rather last-minute, and Stephanie wouldn't have had the fore-knowledge to fill out Elaine's survey far ahead of time. That had to be it, though it didn't explain everything.

Richelle glanced at her, then turned quickly away. "Well, I suppose I could make some inquiries, see if any cancellations came in."

But she didn't want to. That much came through loud and clear.

What could possibly be upsetting about a bunch of abandoned buildings?

The Gratitude ruins. Alien architecture. An extinct species. Insight into another intelligent race of beings. Passing up such a rare opportunity seemed criminal. And yet….

Elaine took a deep breath, then exhaled. *You're Elaine Kane*, she told herself. *You're wealthy, and you own Nebula Starlines. You can travel out here any time you want.* Stephanie probably hadn't even paid for this cruise, just called up Nebula, gave the Kane name, and reserved a pair of suites.

Besides, leaving the ruins for another trip gave her an excuse to see Richelle again.

Elaine settled back into her cushioned seat, deter-mined to focus on the plans they had, rather than the opportunity she'd missed. She crossed her legs and clenched her teeth for the imminent landing.

CHAPTER 10
TO KILL A THI

LUNCH ON the beach tested the limits of Elaine's willingness to experiment.

An efficient team of colonists employed by the cruise company laid out tables covered in foods grown on Gratitude. Luscious fruits, exotic vegetables, and shelled and unshelled seafood went onto her plate. As a Kane, she'd had access to any international imports Earth offered, but interstellar cuisine went beyond impractical.

She stabbed her fork into a purplish tuber, raised it to her nose, and sniffed—spicy, not what she expected at all. She turned to Richelle, who watched her with an amused expression.

"It's not poisonous," she assured Elaine.

"I don't see you having any." She gestured at Ricky's own selections, then took a small bite while Ricky poured herself a glass of water. Instant fire erupted on her tongue, searing her taste buds and spreading down her throat and over her gums.

Richelle thrust the water glass into her hand, stifling a chuckle while she downed half in a single gulp. Elaine realized she'd meant the liquid for her all along.

Elaine prepared to give her a good tongue lashing, assuming she had any tongue left, when the most pleasantly sweet taste filled her mouth. She paused, savoring it, then licking her lips.

"Water activates the sugars and tames the heat," Richelle explained. "Belice is a delicacy here, but you need to be prepared for it. The water goes in your mouth first, just a little, then a small bite of Belice."

She snorted. "You could have warned me!" Elaine watched some of the other diners, a few of them residents, and admired their skills at pulling off such a feat. It was no easy trick, holding a sip of water within her lips while eating at the same time. Her first try resulted in a dribble down her chin and onto her white blouse. She snagged an absorber from a conveniently placed box and glared at the purple stain.

"I'll bet that's permanent."

Richelle shifted uncomfortably.

"Wonderful." Elaine sighed to take the heat from her response.

Lunch led to beach time, even more pleasant. Nebula owned this part of the coastline, so a limited number of visitors occupied the powder-soft sand at any given hour. The local employees provided chairs and cabanas, and Jay and Stephanie disappeared beneath one. The canvas fabric shifted and rippled.

"Steph's going to get sand in awkward places," Elaine muttered.

Ricky laughed. "Yes, most inconsiderate of Jay not to bring a repellant surface."

"A—?"

Ricky spread their towels on the sand. Hanging off the corner of each was a small square device. Two presses of her thumb activated them, vibrating the material and bouncing the granules off. When the fabric cleared, she shut them down.

"Or I could leave them running?" She winked.

Instead of the blush Elaine expected to suffuse her face, she managed a laugh. "I prefer such stimulation in private."

Ricky's eyebrows shot up.

Elaine enjoyed surprising her, but time to change the subject. Her skin was warming from more than the sun. "Lotion?" she asked, casting a nervous glance at the reddish-orange orb overhead. On Earth, outside the domes, even a few minutes without protection risked skin damage.

"Thanks, but I don't sunburn."

Elaine rolled her eyes to the overhead clouds. No, of course she didn't. Elaine had forgotten, again.

"Besides, it's not needed here. The gases in Gratitude's atmosphere reduce the ultraviolet radiation to harmless levels." Ricky stripped off her button-down shirt, a short-sleeved, collared classic, leaving herself in a tight-fitting white cotton scoop-neck tank top.

Elaine stifled a laugh and shielded her eyes. "The glare, the glare!" The THI's untanned arms, neck, and upper chest threatened to blind her.

"Very funny." She dropped onto her towel.

Elaine absently fingered the onyx disk affixed to a mock belt at the waist of her bathing suit. Another pressed into her back, sharp but comforting. She'd had to readjust some when she changed in the bathhouse and pack a couple away in her bag. It bothered her, but here in this open space, she could at least see the approach of a potential threat.

At the moment, a pair of wave runners were the only things approaching, and the recreational vehicles offered no obvious hazard to Elaine's admittedly uneducated eyes.

"Hmm. She's a little early." Ricky stood and strode to the water's edge to greet the pretty female operator wearing a bikini. The woman towed the second wave runner by a retractable cord. It bumped gently against the first, rubber strips protecting the shiny plastic chassis. While Elaine watched, the pair discussed rental terms. At least, Elaine guessed that to be the nature of their conversation. The redheaded owner/employee/ whatever laughed at something Ricky said, her breasts bobbing in the two-piece suit, barely contained within the thin flesh-colored fabric. Her well-tanned legs showed off defined muscles, and trickles of seawater ran over her perfect skin.

When the woman rested her hand on Ricky's forearm, Elaine stood and crossed the sand to intervene. She caught herself.

Good God, she was jealous. Jealous of a stranger's attention. To her THI! If she'd been alone, she would have slapped herself in the forehead.

Elaine managed to stall while gathering their belongings until the attractive redhead puttered off on her own wave runner. Once the woman became a speck on the horizon, Elaine moved to the ocean's edge. Ricky waited, seated on the remaining runner, her head cocked to one side and an eyebrow raised.

Elaine shrugged. "I've never ridden one of these. I'd rather not have an expert watching while I get myself dunked."

"Oh, is that all? I thought you simply didn't like her."

"Why would you say that? I don't even know her." Elaine put on her best innocent expression.

"Of course, ma'am." Ricky winked, taking the sting out of the formality. Clearly Elaine's drama skills needed practice. "Oh, and no dunking, please," Ricky continued, letting her off the hook. "In fact, take the emitters off your sandals and stow them. The ones on your suit and hat should be enough while we're on the water. The devices are water resistant, but they've proven unreliable after submersion."

Elaine complied, tucking the disks into her waterproof bag and cramming the bag into a sealed compartment on the rear of the runner. Ricky waited on the two-passenger seat, her hands on the controls, the motor idling. With great caution, Elaine joined her on the plastic cushion and wrapped her arms around Ricky's trim waist.

Stephanie poked her head out of her cabana, noticed them leaving, and waved goodbye. Then they were bouncing across the water. Spray stung their faces, and the wind tied knots in Elaine's hair despite the hat. The rush of wind and moisture enlivened her, and she found herself shrieking with delight, laughing in her fear of falling off. She clutched Ricky in a death grip when they hit an especially rough patch. Ricky didn't seem to mind.

A few miles offshore, she tapped the THI on the shoulder. Ricky stopped, letting them bob on the current.

Elaine soaked in the benign sun's rays and admired the magnificent view, glad she'd gotten off the ship after all. Out here, she could make out the shoreline and the scattered rainbow of multicolored umbrellas and cabanas.

"We're awfully far. Will we run out of fuel?"

"Solar powered. Not to worry." Richelle patted one of the handlebars as if it were her favorite pet. Elaine wondered if one piece of technology could feel fondness for another.

They floated in silence for a while, each lost in thought or, well, processing. Elaine imagined what it would take to immigrate here, build a vacation home, adapt to this carefree lifestyle. An isolated world with nothing but tourist traffic might provide the perfect hideaway from whoever sought to kill her. She could continue to guide Leviathan via transnet comms.

Then she remembered Stephanie's hypothesis that the pirates used Gratitude as a hideout and rethought her getaway-home plans.

Elaine ran her hand through her hair, her fingers snagging in the windblown tangles. "These will be painful later."

Ricky cast her a glance over her shoulder. "I'll brush them out for you."

An innocent enough offer. So why did it send chills of anticipatory pleasure through her?

"Maybe I'll take you up on—" She broke off as a group of wave runners appeared on the horizon. They came in across the open expanse of water, not from the distant shore—six total, painted in grays and blues that blended with the waves, making them harder to spot. If sunlight hadn't glinted off one of the riders' sunglasses, Elaine wouldn't have noticed them until they were much closer.

She looked down at the bright yellow of their own vehicle, remembered the neon pink of the renter's jet ski. The ones headed toward them weren't designed for tourists.

They were coming fast.

"Richelle?"

"I see them." Her voice sounded tight. Her hands clenched the handlebars until her knuckles whitened. "Hang on."

Elaine dug her fingers into the skin over Richelle's hips while the THI kicked the runner into high gear. Without the padding in the seats, the bouncing would have bruised Elaine's backside and tailbone. Even so, she had to clamp her jaw tight to prevent her teeth from slamming together.

Since she didn't man the controls, she could watch the approaching vehicles. "They're gaining on us!" she shouted to be heard over both engine and waves.

A growl rumbled through Richelle's chest. "Industrial models," she called back, never taking her eyes from the shoreline oh-so-far away. "Used by rescue teams to locate wayward tourists. And carrying half the weight. I can make myself lighter, but I'll be less… substantial… and you'll have a harder time holding on to me. Besides, their engines are still more powerful than ours." Elaine could almost imagine she heard the gears in Richelle's head clicking as she made mental calculations. Of course, she didn't have gears. She didn't actually have a head, though now wasn't the time to dwell on it. "We're not going to make it."

They raced another mile, the dark runners closer with every passing second. Elaine made out black wet-suits and bulging side pockets.

"How good of a swimmer are you?" Richelle asked.

"Don't you already know?"

"This isn't the time for snark!"

"Right." This was the time to avoid getting killed. "Not very," she admitted. She'd passed her junior life-guard trials at summer camp as a child. Her fitness meant she could hold her own in a pool. The Kane estate had an Olympic-sized one, indoors and heated, and she swam there regularly to keep in shape. But open water terrified her.

She'd never been in the ocean. The UV rays from Earth's sun made beach holidays things of the distant past, and the water held too much pollution from a number of oil-drilling accidents and illegal dumping.

Elaine stared at the dark blue horror around her. The swells rose and fell. She didn't know if she could get to shore. To top it off, this ocean was *alien*. She'd seen a little of the sea life from the shuttle. Anything might lurk beneath the surface.

Maybe a leviathan.

That thought produced an almost hysterical laugh, incongruous enough to earn her a quick concerned glance from Richelle.

"Sorry."

"I'll get us as close as I can," Richelle said, ignoring her near breakdown.

Elaine took another look. One of the six men drew something metallic from a side pocket. The sun reflected off the length of the barrel.

"Gun!"

"They're not in range yet." Of course Richelle would know.

The strip of beach they approached wasn't populated like the one they'd left. It stood desolate and empty, an untouched portion of this undeveloped island world. Elaine thought she made out some ruins farther down the strand, rising black, silver, and welcoming in their own way. If they could somehow make it to shore and lose themselves in the ruins, or better yet, meet up with a tour group, they might stand a chance.

A sound like compressed air released from a large bottle carried over the waves, and something plunked into the water a few meters behind the wave runner.

Not going to happen.

The wave runner slowed. For a second, Elaine feared a malfunction—or maybe a bullet—had hit the engine. Then she saw that Richelle had lifted one of her hands from the motor-triggers on the handlebars.

"What—?"

"Take off your hat!" Ricky demanded, guiding their vehicle into a tight turn. Soon they'd face their attackers head-on.

"Are you nuts?" Elaine shouted, even as her fingers untied the knot at her throat.

"Attach it to the seat so the emitter points forward."

A small pommel separated the two cushions, and she wrapped the strings around it several times. In front of them, the six dark runners slowed, probably wondering what the hell she and Richelle were up to.

Elaine wondered too.

Richelle raised her hands in the air, the universal gesture of surrender. The action resulted in the dying of their wave runner's engine altogether.

"Take the disk off your bathing suit and fasten it to the back of my shorts."

Elaine did as she said, watching her for signs of evaporation, but the emitter on Elaine's discarded hat had Ricky pretty well covered. Ricky's feet, dangling off the sides of the runner, looked a little fuzzy, but otherwise she was solid and whole.

"Got it. Now what?"

"Now," she said, and Elaine thought she heard the slightest grin in her voice, "on three, not after three, *on* three, you drop off the back of the runner as quietly as you can."

Okay, even Elaine had seen the twentieth-century film Ricky referenced.

"And?"

"Trust me." Ricky paused. "And trust yourself. You can do this. I know you can."

For half a second, Elaine worried over Ricky sacrificing herself, but realized the minimal nature of the sacrifice. If Elaine made it to the *Nebula*, Ricky would be waiting for her.

She hoped.

With Richelle's body blocking most of the enemies' view of her, Elaine edged to the rear of the runner.

"One," Ricky said, raising her voice and calling over her shoulder in case Elaine couldn't hear her over the lapping waves. "Two."

On three, Elaine slipped over the storage compartment, dropping herself into the water with a minimal splash. As she did so, an image of herself formed, projected by the rear-facing emitter attached to Richelle's shorts. It flowed with Elaine's body, separated, and became its own solid form, taking her place in the seat behind Ricky like she'd never left.

A THI creating a THI. Incredible, she thought as she drew a deep breath and dunked her head beneath the water.

Her lung capacity failed her at a shorter distance than she'd expected. Swimming against a current took a lot more effort than laps in the pool. She tried to maintain a straight line from the back of the wave runner she'd abandoned toward the shore. That way, the runner should continue to block their attackers' view of her if she had to come up for air.

Her head broke the surface, but she made an effort to lift it no farther than clearing her nostrils despite her natural buoyancy. While her legs churned beneath her, she turned and took stock of the situation.

It disconcerted her to see "herself" seated behind Richelle on the runner, her hands resting lightly on Ricky's waist, hat in front of her in the small space between them. She could barely make out its wide brim at this distance. The six others had the yellow wave runner surrounded, and the men all had weapons of one sort or another aimed at Richelle and Elaine's lookalike. They couldn't miss at that range.

Without warning, Richelle slapped her hands on the handlebars, and her wave runner leaped forward, darting between two of the others, spraying and blinding them in her wake.

Watching what followed reminded Elaine of viewing a dramatic holofilm when she already knew the ending. A little different, though, when she herself starred as the leading tragic heroine.

The attackers opened fire. Bullets ripped through her "body" first since she sat in the rear. Blood poured from grievous wounds. Her figure slumped, released its grip, and tumbled into the water, then disappeared beneath its surface. One might think watching herself die would cause extreme mental trauma, but its surrealism detached her from the gruesome scene.

Not so with Richelle's fate.

She slowed the wave runner when Elaine's fake body sank, then revved the engine and took off. Not exactly gallant, but realistic. No point hanging around if she was dead, and Ricky moved faster without Elaine's additional weight.

Didn't matter. The industrial models overtook her in minutes. They'd gone far enough that Elaine couldn't see the injuries Richelle sustained, but she caught the way her form jerked when the bullets tore open her flesh, and she saw the splash she made when her corpse hit the waves, taking Elaine's sunhat and its attached emitter with it to hide the evidence of what really happened. The realism had Elaine sucking breath in a choked gasp.

Not seeing it up close actually made things worse. Elaine pictured Richelle's death in brutal detail. She didn't know if THIs experienced pain. Ricky certainly simulated it well during the fight with the muggers on Eris Station. Elaine had meant to ask her what tangible holograms felt, but it slipped her mind. Now she'd never have the chance.

Yes you will. She's a hologram. She'll reform as soon as you return to the Nebula, Elaine told herself.

Assuming *Elaine* made it back to the *Nebula*.

Their attackers bought Richelle's death, regardless. Elaine didn't know if they thought Richelle had actually died or recognized her as a THI playing out the realism of a human death, but either way, the dark-colored wave runners roared away in the direction from which they'd come, leaving Elaine alone in the middle of a very big ocean. One of the men had tossed a line over the rented vehicle and towed it off with them. Therefore, Elaine couldn't make use of the riderless wave runner. On the horizon, two moons were rising, each smaller than Earth's single satellite, while the sun began to set in a spectacular display of reds, pinks, and oranges.

Her chest tightened at the thought of the promised moonlight stroll and the wasted opportunity for romance under the stars.

Elaine drove her arms and legs through the waves with new determination. Richelle had saved her life yet again, and she damn well planned on getting back to the ship to thank her for it. Besides, if she didn't find her way to the shuttleport before 2:00 a.m. ship's time, she'd miss the last transfer, and the *Nebula* would depart Gratitude without her.

If she could make the shore, it shouldn't be a problem. They couldn't have gone more than a few miles from where they'd had lunch, and the sun had only just set. Her chrono wristband lay at the bottom of her beach bag, though, and that rested in the storage compartment on the lost wave runner, so she had no accurate measure of time.

She had the rhythm down, limbs working fluidly at a pace that brought her closer and closer to the shore without overtaxing her muscles. Sand brushed beneath her toes. Then something big, heavy, and slimy slid along her thigh.

OH, VERY romantic, Richelle, dying in front of your girlfriend and abandoning her in the middle of the ocean.

Ricky hadn't seen Elaine as she'd fallen from the wave runner and sunk beneath the waves, but Ricky hoped… no, she *assumed* she was out there, keeping her head down and swimming for shore.

Not a pleasant experience, dying, and one she did not care to repeat. One thing was certain: she had an even deeper appreciation for the value of life. In human form, she felt the impact as bullets bore into her, felt the flesh tear and part, the rush of warm lifeblood pouring from the wounds and turning the seawater around her a gut-churning red. Salt stung the openings in her skin as she sank deeper and deeper.

Her numbing fingers clutched at the sunhat and its emitter, prolonging her existence as long as she could—prolonging the pain, but with good reason. She needed time to focus, to get beyond the agony and seek out the carrier wave from the *Nebula* in orbit above Gratitude.

She found it, invisible to human senses but glowing like a beacon to her energy receptors. It called to her like a siren song even as her "heart" stopped, her hand released its grip, and the sunhat faded into the dark depths beneath her. In moments, she reverted to a floating mass of particles, attempting to maintain coalescence. The sinking emitter attempted to draw her in, then released its hold as a tiny flash in the darkness told her the device had shorted out.

Her place of refuge, her source of power, her direct line to the *Nebula* was useless.

Too far. The ship was too far. In her weakened state, she doubted she could reach it through open air before she dispersed.

And Elaine was out there, counting on her to meet her aboard the ship. She *wanted* Ricky to be there.

The thought she might let Elaine down sent some of her outermost particles spiraling away from her… where they flared in the conductive seawater.

Of course. She couldn't maintain cohesion in air, but in saltwater… In saltwater she could hold together a little longer.

Desperately, Richelle cast out her senses for any electronic device, anything that could store her essence while she siphoned off its power source, something she could reach via the water. A boat, another wave runner, any machine with an electrical system would do.

Nothing. Then, at the edge of her range, a tiny spark. An emitter. The one attached to Elaine's bathing suit and still functional. If Ricky could reach it, she wouldn't have the strength to reform as a THI, but she'd have a direct link to the ship.

She had to reach it. Her life depended on it.

CHAPTER 11
LOPSON COME HOME

ELAINE JUMPED and shrieked, unable to control the natural response. Anyone within a mile would have heard that. At the same moment, something sparked against her back, sending a zing of electrical shock through the thin fabric of her swimsuit and into the skin beneath.

She arched her spine away from the current while slapping through the water like some half-beached fish. One arm twisted to find the source of pain. The other shoved hard at whatever carnivorous sea creature pursued her toward the shore.

Overhead, the twin moons and a million stars shone down on the ocean. Elaine could see the beach with some clarity, but the light reflected off the water, reducing forms beneath its surface to dark shadows. One of those shadows rose from the gentle lapping waves, rivulets pouring over a thick gray hide. Deep, liquid eyes bored into Elaine's panicked ones. A rounded head cocked to one side, and the creature opened a mouth full of teeth, panting breath in her face while neck gills flapped open and closed. The smell of brine assailed her nostrils.

Moonlight glinted off the flat teeth. Flat.

Something niggled at Elaine's mind, a bit of information from those biology classes she had taken so long ago in high school. Flat. Not pointed. She strained her eyes, making out a string of alien seaweed dangling from the corner of the mouth, caught between two worn yellow molars. This was no carnivore. The creature, something between a seal and, well, something alien, was definitely herbivorous, and judging from the tooth decay, probably old.

It didn't attack. It blinked. Elaine breathed a sigh of relief. Not knowing quite what to do with it, she reached out a tentative hand toward its… nostrils? or at least the trio of holes situated between its eyes and mouth. It took a snuffling breath, then exhaled, and a stream of little bubbles appeared from its nose and popped.

"Ew!" Elaine said, keeping her voice light, then, despite herself, laughing. The gigantic seal-thing bumped her with its head, as if nudging her toward the shore. "Yeah, I'm going. Ow!"

Her cry sent the gentle beast splashing a few yards away. Elaine thought she could detect at least six flippers churning the water, but she was too busy sloshing toward shore and fumbling at her back to take an accurate count.

"Hey, it's okay!" she called after it. Alien or not, any company marked an improvement over wandering this foreign beach alone.

The seal thing watched from a distance while she pulled the last of her emitters from her bathing suit. The onyx disk sparked in her palm, stinging her flesh, and she passed it from hand to hand, trying to decide what to do with it. It was obviously broken or Ricky would have appeared by now. They had to cost a lot of money. The *Nebula* would appreciate its return, damaged or not. And throwing away any piece of Richelle, no matter how small, felt wrong.

Then again, the bad guys had found them, somehow, out in the middle of the ocean. Maybe not a difficult feat with modern scanners or knowledge of their itinerary and a good pair of binoculars, or maybe they'd tracked the emitters, as they may have done on Eris Station.

No, that didn't make sense. These attackers seemed to have no idea Richelle was a THI.

Probably not wise to take chances, even if they thought Elaine was dead. She cocked her arm and prepared to toss the final emitter into the ocean.

It spoke.

The voice, if it truly was a voice, came too softly for her to understand words, but the sparking multifaceted disk definitely produced a sound. The sea creature heard it, and it splashed to her side, cocking its head and listening.

With the device zapping her palm, Elaine reached down beneath the water and yanked up a piece of seaweed. She wrapped the emitter in it, then held the disk up to her ear.

"'Water resistant' might have been overstating things a bit." Ricky's voice.

Elaine laughed, then shocked herself by bursting into tears of uninhibited relief. The aquatic animal whuffled, as if sharing its own sense of humor. It followed her while she trudged through the knee-deep water and onto the dry sand. Yep, six flippers.

The alien rolled onto its back, drying itself and spraying sand everywhere, including all over Elaine.

"Hey!" she cried, laughing and shielding her eyes. "I don't need to be sand-blasted." She shivered in the night chill. What she needed was a towel and some dry clothes. She glanced at her bare feet. At least the granules no longer burned her soles.

The creature shuffled to her side, brushing her arm with its head in apology. It turned up the beach, then down, made a directional decision, and lumbered off. When Elaine failed to follow, it made a sound she could only describe as a bark.

"What's that?" Richelle sounded concerned.

"I think Timmy's stuck in the well." Hah! And Stephanie thought Elaine had no knowledge of classic film. Or was that a TV program?

"Excuse me?"

Elaine cocked her head at the creature. It cocked its head back at her. Whatever it was, it was smart. "Alien life-form. Aquatic. Friendly, like a flippered puppy about twice my size," she explained.

"Lopson."

Now it was Elaine's turn. "Excuse me?"

"They're called lopson," Richelle's disembodied voice explained while Elaine passed the emitter from hand to hand some more. Even with the seaweed, holding it was uncomfortable. "At least that's the human translation from uncovered Ix—" She broke off. Elaine assumed another technical glitch. "From recovered native records."

The lopson took another couple of steps, looking over its shoulder at Elaine.

"It wants me to follow it."

"Do you have any idea where you are?"

That earned a blink of surprise. Elaine stared at the emitter. "You can't see me?"

A sigh. "Not at all. I'm voice-only for now."

Elaine gave a quick overview of her situation, a description of the strand where she stood, the ruins rising like shadowy giants in the distance.

"And it's leading toward the ruins?"

"Yep."

Another sigh. "Follow it. Lopson are pretty intelligent. Think a cut above Earth dolphins. Maybe there's a moonlit tour of the abandoned city you can hook up with and get back to the *Nebula*."

Elaine started off, her feet sinking into the wet sand with every step, goose bumps rising on her bare skin. The lopson waited until she joined it, then set a pace easy for her to match. She gave it a tentative pat on the head, and it thanked her with another bark. Its flippers slapped the sand in a steady rhythm.

Stephanie had been right about one thing. This was more excitement than she'd had in a lifetime.

THEY MADE quite the trio: Elaine, the lopson, and Richelle's voice. The THI hummed a pleasant tune, no doubt chosen to lighten Elaine's mood. It didn't fail entirely, but the stone walls looming before her instilled a sense of foreboding.

The moons hung oddly to her Earth-accustomed eyes, their rays casting long shadows that seemed to shift and waver like living things. She stood at what looked like an entry to the walled city—a broken set of metal gates half-disconnected from their moorings and leaning to the sides. Human-made signs hung from the gates, warning off trespassers and announcing the area as an active dig site. They must not have updated the signs since the funding ran out, or the archaeologists didn't want potential looters to know the site was currently unoccupied. A plaque set in the stone bore unreadable markings in the alien language. Elaine assumed it announced the name of the city.

"Describe the writing to me," Richelle instructed.

Elaine did so, attempting to put the squiggles, angles, and dots into words. She also spotted some lopson artfully carved into the rock. These creatures had meant something to the aliens who'd lived here. Pets, companions maybe. No wonder it had brought her to the ruins. How old *was* this creature? She finished her descriptions.

"Damn."

"Hmm?" She rarely heard the THI curse. It didn't comfort her. Beside her, the lopson pressed its face against her thigh as dark clouds obscured the moons. Thunder rumbled, and when Elaine turned toward the ocean, a streak of lightning arced from the clouds to the water's surface. "Wonderful. Ricky, where do you think a tour group might be? I don't see any lights or holomaps or anything in an Earth language past the gates."

The emitter lay silent in her palm. The lopson tried to push her forward by leaning on the backs of her calves.

"You aren't going to find a tour," the THI admitted.

Inside she'd known that. It didn't stop her heart from dropping into her stomach—which rumbled with the next roll of thunder. She hadn't eaten since lunch on the beach. "Why not?"

"You're at Site Two. The humans call it Meritus. Your scientists haven't cleared it for visitation yet. All the tours go to Site One."

Elaine brightened. "Then if I poke around, I should find some security guards or something. Maybe some tents?" She scanned the area, searching the shadows for any other signs of life. The first few raindrops fell, then more and more. Well, she already had her swimsuit on.

"I'm afraid not. When the dig funding ran out, that meant no money for onsite security either. They're working on another grant, but for now, the place is deserted."

"And it's storming." The rainfall increased, a soaking sheet of continuous downpour. The streaks of lightning came closer. One even struck the nearby beach, accompanied by a tremendous crash of thunder. The lopson barked.

Overcoming her trepidation, Elaine stepped over the twisted metal gate and into the alien city. She thought she heard Richelle continuing to speak, but she couldn't make out her words above nature's booming and the whuffling animal at her side.

Together, she and the lopson bent against a buffeting wind, staggering down the open walkway between two black stone structures. Deeply recessed alcoves marked entryways into the buildings. She selected one

deep enough to provide adequate cover from the rain
and large enough to house them both, and the unusual
pair huddled under the stone arch.

The sounds of the storm echoed and reverberated
off the walls, but the lopson had gone silent. "Ricky?"

"Still here."

"What time is it? I'll have to wait until this storm
passes, but then I need to head for the shuttle, dark or
not." She waited. "Ricky?"

"I don't know what time it is. I've lost my direct
feed to the *Nebula's* universal clock. The generators are
barely able to transmit my program parameters."

Surely the ship couldn't be preparing to leave already. It couldn't be 2:00 a.m. They'd gone wave running in the late afternoon/early evening. The sun set
right after the fight and her untimely "death." She'd
swum to shore. Okay, that had taken a while. And she'd
met the lopson. And they'd walked. And walked. Still,
if she had to guess, she'd place the hour around 10:00
p.m., tops.

And besides, the *Nebula* would wait for VIPs,
wouldn't it? Then again, ditching her would solve a lot
of the command staff's problems. She tried not to think
too much on that.

The loss of communication between Richelle and
the ship had to just be another glitch. Right?

To punctuate her hypothesis, the emitter sparked,
zapping her palm through the seaweed casing. She
dropped the hot piece of electronics at her feet. It clat-
tered on the stone.

The disk jumped a couple of times, energy surging
through it, making it vibrate. Then it fell still. Panicked,
Elaine scooped it up, ignoring its residual heat.

"Richelle? Ricky! Answer me!"

The lopson's soft snuffling responded, but nothing else.

RICHELLE KNEW she should have headed back to the *Nebula* the moment she'd drained enough power from the damaged emitter to make the journey, but she couldn't bear to leave Elaine stranded with only the lopson for company. Now it was too late. She'd overtaxed the device, taken too much energy from it, and lost her connection to the passenger ship's carrier wave right along with the time upload.

To make matters worse, the emitter's audio functions failed. Now all she could do was wait, cycling herself through the disk's circuits, rationing the remaining power in the smallest doses she could sustain herself on, until another source presented itself.

Damn the timing. A few more minutes and she would have been able to guide Elaine to that source. If Elaine didn't stumble upon one on her own, or find a way back to the *Nebula*, if the emitter ran completely dry of energy, Richelle was done for.

Mortality wasn't something her kind contemplated with frequency, but she'd had to face it head-on several times since meeting Elaine. Risk and romance seemed to be infinitely intertwined.

ELAINE RESTED her head on the lopson's warm, briny hide, the creature's heavy breathing and the uneven beating of what sounded like multiple hearts lulling her. But sleep wasn't an option, even though she was exhausted. She had to get back to the ship, and this damn storm prevented her from taking one step in the right direction. Elaine lay there and waited, watching the downpour gradually dissipate and the streaks of dangerous lightning move farther away. Her stress levels rose with every passing minute. The minutes crept toward an hour.

The lopson shifted. It cast a longing gaze out the archway in the direction of the ocean but seemed reluctant to leave her side, and Elaine didn't argue. She preferred any form of company to complete isolation in this alien environment.

She shivered in the cold night air. The temptation to find a way inside this building warred with her innate fear of the unknown. Of course, she'd have to get through the metal door first.

Elaine gathered herself. She didn't have any belongings except the emitter. She reattached it to her bathing suit, unable to part with this last piece of Richelle. What she wouldn't have given for a warm towel or coverup. The moonlight had returned and lit the walkway through the city like a beacon guiding her back to the gate—or farther into the abandoned structures.

She glanced left and right along the open space between the buildings, then laughed. What was she looking for? Traffic? Actually, now that the rain had eased up, she did hear what sounded like motors. A lot of them. Maybe that grant Richelle mentioned had been approved.

Elaine peeked around the corner, then jerked back as a pack of hovercycles roared by, their headlamps just missing her. She collided with the lopson, tumbling over its bulk to land on its back, though it didn't seem to mind. In fact, instead of startling, it remained quiet while the six bikes passed their hiding place, then stopped about two buildings down the street.

The riders shut their cycles' motors off so the Leviathan-made vehicles, distinctive in their design, settled to the sand and stone. The riders laughed and shouted, bottles clinking in their free hands. Leaning out, Elaine watched them, not sure why she hesitated. Here was her ticket back to the *Nebula.* But their obvious drunkenness concerned her. The fact they were all male didn't help, either. And there were six of them. Six hovercycles.

Six industrial-grade wave runners.

And one of them had her beach bag hanging from his handlebars.

In her hunt for shelter from the storm, she'd stumbled into a tempest—the hideout of her attackers.

Elaine pressed a palm to her forehead, agonizing over her next move. Floodlights suddenly illuminated the street. She jerked backward, hiding herself with the lopson in the alcove.

"About time you got that generator going," one man called.

"I'll break out the tents," a second offered.

"Ground's wet. Don't know why we can't sleep in these buildings."

"None of us have had any luck opening 'em. Besides, you seen the reports from Site One? Half of 'em are locked like these. The ones they could get in got crazy shit going on. Lights and voices at night, unexplained electronic signatures. Ain't you heard the stories about alien ghosts?"

The other men laughed at this, but Elaine noticed none of them went near the stone structures.

"At least they block the wind," one commented.

Elaine glanced over her shoulder at the metal door and suppressed another shiver. She'd been there at least an hour, and no ghosts had bothered her. She leaned out to watch the riders.

The six men, clad in riding leathers or coveralls, were setting up a temporary camp in a little square at the intersection of two crossways. Gray autopop envirotents dotted the ground, and a portable generator hummed, sending power to a circle of lamps surrounding them. They had a heating unit in the center, and two men sat beside it, taking swigs from bottles, while the other four vanished into their tents.

The hovercycles rested beyond the lit area, six shadows against the darker night. If Elaine could reach them, she could steal one and use it to get to the shuttle landing zone. Considering there was now only one moon in the sky and it was nearing the horizon, she suspected her time was short. She lowered herself so her belly touched the ground and crawled forward.

Something flat and wet closed around her ankle.

It took everything she had not to scream. Instead, she internalized the terror, her heart pounding furiously, her breath coming in quick pants while she reached back with one hand… and touched leathery hide. The lopson, its mouth clamped on the skin just above her foot, trying to keep her there. It stared up at her with black eyes like bottomless pools, then gently removed its teeth from pressing her skin. No damage.

"I really appreciate you leading me to shelter," she told the creature. Ludicrous to be speaking to an alien life-form. "But I can't stay. I have to get back to my people."

As if it understood, the lopson glanced in the direction of the men, then shook its massive head.

"No, not those people," Elaine agreed. "But they have a way for me to get to the good guys."

It shook its head again. God, this thing was smart.

"Look, I can't sit here arguing. I don't have time for—"

The sound of metal squeaking on rusted hinges grated on her eardrums. Elaine's head shot around. Her eyes strained to pierce the darkness at the rear of the alcove.

The door to the alien structure stood open.

At first Elaine thought a trick of the shadows had fooled her senses, but when she reached out her arm, it passed through the doorway. She snatched it back.

"What the hell was that?" came a gruff voice.

Her attackers had heard the noise too. She held her breath.

"Probably the wind. Everything's hanging by threads around here. Place is ready to fall down."

"Yeah," a third voice chimed in. "That's why they're called ruins."

"I don't think so," the first argued. Heavy boot-steps approached Elaine's hiding place.

In or out? One choice meant certain death. The other could mean anything. Her pulse raced. She gave the lopson one last pat on the head, hoped the men would leave it alone, and crept through the open door.

CHAPTER 12
CLOSE ENCOUNTERS

BLESSED, BLESSED power. Richelle gave the equivalent of a shiver as she fled the damaged emitter and immersed herself in the current stream of the campsite's generator. Opening the door for Elaine had drained her almost beyond recovery. Small lamps, visible only from within the circle of tents, flickered, then steadied. The one man still seated at the central heating unit glanced around, peered into shadows, then shrugged and returned to his warm spot. Richelle drew on the energy source at a slower pace, careful not to attract further attention.

She drank until sated, wavering in drunken-like wooziness with the recharging of her life force. Then a second source called to her.

When Elaine had entered the onyx building, she'd triggered ancient systems, which awakened and roared to life. Fluctuating and unstable, yes, but functional enough to rouse Richelle's awareness.

She flowed toward it and toward Elaine, now pursued by one of the men from the wave runners who'd attacked them that afternoon.

ON HANDS and knees, Elaine moved forward, unable to see anything within the structure. Then a faint glow lit the stone floor in front of her. Her head shot up. Were these the "weird energy signatures" the superstitious hovercycle rider had referred to? Maybe the excavation crews had left some automatic lighting in place.

The illumination faded, then reappeared. She made out a square opening in the ceiling far overhead—a skylight. Elaine assumed passing clouds caused the sporadic quality of the light.

Taking advantage of the next clear moment, she scanned the large circular room she'd entered. She spotted no furniture or decorations of any kind, nothing to hide behind. Panels of instrumentation were embedded in the walls with telltales that glinted red, yellow, and orange in the moonlight. None were lit from within. Whatever once powered this place had died out many years ago.

Curiosity made Elaine wish she could examine the electronics further, get a feel for what the natives' lives had been like, but she had bigger problems.

The footsteps came closer. Two new doors to choose from. She dashed to the one on the opposite side of the room.

Though metal and as thick as the first, she managed to push the door open. Another skylight, more empty space, more inert machinery. A frustrated groan threatened to erupt from her throat. She saw no other exits except the one she'd entered by.

The man was coming. She could hear him in the first area, scuffing his boots on the stone.

"I'm telling you, it was a lopson."

Elaine didn't think two of them had investigated the noise, so whom was he talking to?

"What's it doing so far from the water?" The answering voice sounded tinny, and she realized the first man was speaking into a comm.

"Hell if I know, but it's there. I nearly tripped over the damn thing."

Somewhere outside, Elaine heard the lopson whuffle. She released a held breath. At least they'd let it live.

"And you're telling me that flippered beast opened a door? We've been trying to get inside for weeks, and some dumb-as-shit animal got it open?"

"I told you we should have just fried the lock."

"There is no lock, and everyone would know we'd been here if we used explosives. We're taking a big enough risk with the lights."

"Nah, everyone thinks the brains are still here, researching."

Elaine frowned while they argued. If the lopson's weight hadn't pushed the door open, what had opened it?

"I'm just telling you what's here—a lopson and a lot of dead tech."

"It must have flopped on a hidden switch. The archaeologists would freak."

"The authorities would freak too. We're not supposed to be here at all, remember?" he stressed, losing patience. "Last thing we need is to get picked up for trespassing and have them dig into the other shit we've been up to."

The man moved around the outer room. His boots tromped and echoed. He liked to pace while he talked.

"Check everywhere, just in case," ordered the man on the comm. "Then report back. You've got first watch, and our payment'll be here soon."

Great, more bad guys. And nowhere to hide. In desperation, she unhooked the emitter from her swimsuit and whispered to it, "Ricky, if you can hear me, if this thing works at all, I could really use some help right now."

Nothing, not even a spark. She returned it to her suit's faux belt and crouched, trying to make herself as small as possible in the dark. The beam of a flashlight came through the half-open door to the room. Seconds before the owner followed it inside, Elaine found herself squatting under a wooden piece of furniture that hadn't been there before.

She bit her lip to swallow her scream and tried to slow her panicked breathing. The desk, or whatever it was, shielded her from view on three sides. An old-fashioned rolling chair blocked her in on the fourth. Beyond it, the black walls had turned to wood paneling.

The man entered and stopped dead in his tracks as recessed lights in the ceiling flared to life. The yellowish glow they emitted accented every dust particle floating in the disturbed air of the ancient chamber.

"What in holy hell—?"

"What? What did you find?" came the tinny voice.

"It's… an office. Desk, chair, the works."

"You've been hitting the marlberry wine again."

"Fuck you. Come see for yourself."

"I'm not going in there. The boss'll be here any minute, and she's got better things to do than stand around waiting for us to play amateur archaeologists."

The man in the room argued, accusing the guy outside of everything from simple laziness to fear of alien ghosts. When he got nothing but static on the comm in response, he stormed out, presumably to fetch his comrade and force him inside the structure.

Elaine sagged against the base of the desk, then fell onto her stomach when the illusion promptly vanished, but not before she recognized it as her sitting room, desk, and chair back home. The artificial lights went out, and she lay in the dark space, blinking until her eyesight adjusted to the moon's rays reflecting off black stone walls.

No, not black.

Onyx.

"It's a giant emitter," she breathed, realization dawning. "The whole damn building is one giant THI emitter."

Alien technology. There had to be a working generator hidden behind one of the walls, or underground, maybe. But how had it known *what* to generate? Could the devices read her mind?

Crawling to the door leading to the outer room, she squinted at each wall in turn. "How about sending me an army of local authorities? I could use those right about now," she muttered under her breath.

"Limited power," her bathing suit told her. She recoiled and rolled away from the sound, landing with bruising force on her hip. "Sorry." The voice carried from the disk at her waist.

Richelle. Of course. Though she half expected some alien being to appear and seat itself at the now invisible desk.

"The... ancient natives'... hidden energy storage unit draws power from a thermal source, but the scientific community and tourist industry have been unknowingly tapping that unit for the last ten years. It activates whenever anyone enters one of the buildings and doesn't pack the punch it once did."

Elaine's brow furrowed. "Pack the punch?"

"Twentieth-century slang," Richelle explained.

She reached the first room and stood. She thought she saw the humped shape of the lopson waiting for her outside.

"Where have you been?" she asked Richelle in hushed tones.

"Oh, having a beer, seeing the sights."

Elaine growled.

"Picking up some juice from the bad guys' generator. Waiting to draw power from this site's central source. Waiting for the emitter circuitry to dry out," Ricky hastily added. Elaine heard the grin in her voice and wished she could see it.

Well, that made sense. She'd dumped beverages on electronics before. The internal workings might be alien in design, but the casing was Earth-made, which meant imperfections through which moisture could enter. Even with modern construction, such an accident usually foretold the device's demise. But if the drink contained no sugar, sometimes if one waited long enough, it dried itself out and started working again.

"Any chance I could see you?" Elaine longed to feel Ricky wrap her arms around her chilled skin and know she could call on that beastie Ricky conjured on Eris Station to send any bad guys running.

"'Fraid not. I'm drawing power from Site Two itself for the voicelink. Even my previous limited connection to the ship is gone. No range. And my imager is shot. That last projection on the wave runner, and probably some sea salt, did it in."

"How are you doing all this? Did you create the office? How did you know what to—?"

The warning bark of the lopson cut her off. A second later, two flashlight beams coming through the front door reflected off the iridescent material of her bathing suit.

"Hey! What the fuck is she doing here? Bitch has nine lives."

The pair of men stalked toward her in sand-covered boots and dirty coveralls. One pulled a pistol from a thigh holster and pointed it at Elaine.

"Run!" the voice at her waist commanded.

No way she would get past them to the outside, so she broke for the third door, the one she hadn't tried yet, praying it wasn't locked. The entry opened at her approach.

"Thank you, Ricky," she whispered. At this point, the THI apparently no longer cared if her generator draining was noticed.

The door thudded shut behind her, and fists pounded on its opposite side. Why did people always do that? It wasn't like she'd open the door and invite them in. While she paused to take stock, she detected a faint sizzle. Smoke and some sparks seeped around the edges of the door, indicating her attackers planned to blow it out after all. Apparently killing her interested them more than maintaining the sanctity of their hideout.

"Keep going!" Richelle ordered.

"Where?" She couldn't see a thing in this new room. No skylights, no windows.

"Face away from the door. Walk straight forward, about thirty paces. You'll find another door. It's open."

She did as Ricky told her, hands outstretched, hoping she didn't collide too hard with a wall or some residual THI furnishings. She managed to scrape her knuckles pretty badly when she strayed into the surface on her right.

"Go through, feel your way along the narrow corridor, turn left at the first opening."

She fumbled forward, stubbing the toes of her bare feet on the closest wall. The hall smelled musty, and she sneezed at the dust she disturbed. Behind her came a loud crash. A slam indicated Richelle had closed the door to the corridor. Muffled cursing followed.

She found the left turn, hurried forward, and smacked her forehead into a flat surface. "Ow!"

"Wait for directions," Richelle chided her.

"You're the first butch I've ever met who was interested in directions."

A soft chuckle. "Some stereotypes are timeless, but I'm not stereotypical."

She guided Elaine through several more twists and turns and doors Ricky sealed behind her. Elaine tried to keep track, knowing if the emitter crashed or fizzled out, she'd be hopelessly lost in the maze of corridors. More than two pursuing voices shouted now. She wondered if the entire gang had followed her in. But they sounded far back. The barriers were slowing them down.

After one more left turn, her palms contacted the cold metal of another door, and she stopped. "I think I've gone in a circle."

"More like seven sides of an octagon, but yes. That door leads outside."

"It's closed."

"I wanted to warn you first."

It creaked outward, and the floodlights blinded her with their brightness. Elaine blinked to clear her vision while she inhaled the scent of saltwater, and the distant sound of crashing waves made detecting her pursuers more difficult. Then she noticed how low the moons sat in the sky and her breath caught.

Once her eyesight adjusted, she focused on the open square dotted with the gang's tents and the six shadows of hovercycles nearby. She glanced up and down the street, realizing she'd exited the building one door down from where she'd entered. The lopson leaned its head out of the alcove and blinked at her.

Sorry she couldn't give the creature one last pat for its assistance, she raced toward the parked bikes. She had no experience with them but assumed the largest would have the most powerful engine. That meant speed, though its size intimidated her.

She straddled the seat, her bare skin sticking to the plastic, and scanned the controls on the handlebars. In college, Stephanie's boyfriend had a traditional motorcycle. He'd given Elaine a few rides, even let her drive once on a deserted road. She'd nearly crashed. And this thing didn't even have wheels. It rested on a landing block, but at the press of the right button, a repulsor field would raise it from the planet's surface.

On the chassis, the Leviathan logo mocked her ineptitude.

Well, when in doubt, press whatever is most prominent.

Avoiding the obvious horn, she slammed the center switch with her palm and fell forward over the bars as the hoverbike jolted upward. The nose of the cycle scraped on the stone roadway, leaving deep scratches on the polished red fiberglass fender. When Elaine leaned back, the bike righted itself. She tentatively shifted to the right, and the cycle angled with her. Then left, and the cycle followed.

Okay, she had balance. Now she needed height and propulsion. On the bars, each of her thumbs rested against sliding levers, and the rest of her fingers wrapped around metal she could squeeze. Her feet found pedals, the soles rubbing over grooves in them.

"Ricky?"

The THI's silence concerned her. She'd been so vocal before. Static answered her inquiry, then nothing. Maybe Richelle couldn't access the site's weakened power source this far from the interior.

The outer door of the alien building burst open, and six men tried to force themselves through the narrow alcove at the same time. Several succeeded in crushing their gun arms against the walls. One misfired, burning a black line across the white stone street.

No more time for experimentation. Elaine shoved the sliding levers inward, pressed down on the pedals, and held on as the cycle shot twenty feet or more into the air. The sudden vertical acceleration dropped her stomach to her toes, and she swallowed bile while trying to stabilize herself.

A loud bang sounded, and something whizzed by her right ear. Of course, now she was in full view of everyone. Great. If she didn't get the bike moving, they would find their aim and bring her down.

Other buttons and switches produced a headlamp and set her spinning in circles. Thank goodness she hadn't eaten since lunch on the beach. Adventure could hang itself. She'd give anything to be back in the safe solitude of the Kane mansion.

Of course, then she never would have encountered Richelle.

The spinning kept more bullets from hitting her, though one ricocheted off the chassis's chrome trim, and another shattered the headlight as she tried to find the button to turn it off. They'd done her a favor with that shot. It would be harder to hit what they couldn't easily see.

She managed to stop her rotation, hovering over the buildings. Then she leaned forward just a bit. The cycle surged ahead several feet. She angled farther and got some distance between herself and her attackers.

No telling how fast they could get their own bikes up and running.

Elaine neared the edge of the walled city, weaving between the silver spires adorning the tops of the alien buildings. A new commotion carried over the sound of distant waves—shouting, and the constant barking of a lopson. She risked a glance back to see the flippered creature flopping across the street and into the rest of the parked vehicles, knocking them off their landing blocks and onto their sides. Then it disappeared into the shadows.

The diversion bought her time while they righted their cycles. She gunned the bike's engine and shot off into the darkness.

CHAPTER 13
HIGH 2:00 A.M.

ONE OF the switches she'd flipped activated a small digital clock between the handlebars. Elaine swallowed hard when she saw the display—1:30 a.m. Half an hour before the final transport returned to the *Nebula*. She wouldn't get a second shot at her decision.

If she remembered correctly, she and Richelle had the beach on their left when they took the wave runner from the luncheon. God, had it only been a half day since she'd lain on the sand so at peace with the universe? Elaine stored that memory and turned the opposite way, watching the sand rush by on her right, keeping the headlamp off and steering by moonlight.

Under other circumstances, she might have enjoyed the experience. She kept the vehicle low, racing above the beach, a meter from the water. Some of the highest waves sent spray over her bare legs, leaving salt residue behind. Elaine didn't know what rules governed the proper operation of a hovercycle, but she figured if she crashed now, she'd avoid injury by hitting the soft sand and not falling from a great height.

She passed Site One and was so distracted by its majesty that she almost missed the cycle approaching from the opposite direction, a little farther inland, its light also off. It passed as a mere shadow, and the rider apparently didn't notice her with the waves drowning out her engine, or disregarded her as a tourist.

One of the moons disappeared behind the clouds. Elaine couldn't make out details of the driver, but smaller overall size and curves cast in the remaining moonlight suggested a woman, and a buxom one at that. Was this the payment delivery the six thugs waited on?

If so, this woman, or someone she worked for, wanted her dead. Why, dammit?

But no matter how she strained her eyes, Elaine couldn't identify her in the near dark.

On the upside, the woman probably came from the population center, the same as the tourist area, which should indicate Elaine was headed in the correct direction.

She was right. A few more minutes of riding brought her within sight of spotlights, pre-fab shops, hotels, and restaurants. One forty-five, and the landing platform sat on the far side of the settlement. She risked a glance over her shoulder. Six headlights glared in the distance, coming on fast. Elaine increased her speed.

Halfway across the rooftops, her engine coughed. A glance to the display showed no obvious problems… except a blinking light on the fuel gauge.

"Oh, you have got to be kidding."

It ran dry a block from her destination, lowering itself gently until it rested on the sidewalk.

She had to run for it, barefoot, bedraggled, and bleeding from the cuts and scrapes she got feeling her way through the alien structures. Elaine pushed through throngs of drunken revelers. Some leaned on one another, others sloshed their drinks out of open cups. She smelled sweat, vomit, and too much perfume, all rolled into one nauseating fog.

At least the crowds hid her from her pursuers. And that was a good thing, because only moments later, the five thugs passed above her, earning curses and raised fingers from the tourists who breathed their fumes. The woman on the sixth cycle had left the group. Clearly she didn't do her own dirty work. None of the men appeared to spot Elaine. She carefully refrained from looking up, so from their vantage, she was just another brown head of hair.

At one point, the brush of a body knocked the last emitter from her swimsuit. Elaine heard it clatter on the walkway and skitter to the curb. Her need to reach the shuttle before its departure overruled her impulse to retrieve it. A broken disk, even though it was a part of Richelle, versus getting out of this literal tourist trap? No contest.

The landing area loomed ahead, and she picked up speed, ignoring the pain in her bare feet. One shuttle lifting off, a last one resting on the platform. The five still-pursuing cycles had vanished into the darkness of the night. She supposed they wanted to avoid attacking her in such a public place.

The last of the boarders stepped into the only remaining shuttle. She thought she recognized one or two faces from the ship, though she was still too far away to be certain. They wore elegant gowns and tuxedos, returning from their fine-dining experiences in Gratitude's beachside cafes. Elaine felt naked in her swimsuit, but she poured on the speed, her legs churning, her arms pumping. She could only imagine what she looked like to the people she passed.

The crewman manning the hatch rolled in the cheesy red carpet laid out for the guests, then spotted her and turned to shout something toward the interior, but if he'd tried to stop the launch, he hadn't been heard. The shuttle's engines roared to life, exhaust and heat pouring from the aft section. No way. If she got stranded, the bikers would find her sooner or later. The ramp rose a few inches off the tarmac.

Someone pursued her. At first she thought one of the bad guys had tracked her down, but a quick and risky glance over her shoulder proved it to be a member of the ground crew. He yelled unintelligibly at her. She kept going.

The one in the hatchway must have read the fierce determination on her face. He changed tactics from waving her away to reaching for the crazed woman approaching at full speed. Elaine dove for the crewman's outstretched hands, clamping fingers around his forearms while his closed on her wrists. He dragged her over the lip of the closing hatch, the blue decon light passed over them both, and they fell in a heap on the interior side. The locking mechanism bolted the door into place behind them.

"Ms. Kane," the young man said with a chuckle, extricating himself from her splayed limbs, "you really need to stop boarding our vessels in such an undignified manner."

She blinked at him, vaguely remembering his face among the sea of personnel who'd witnessed her airlock tube incident. "Yes, sorry. I...." She remembered what Richelle said about not knowing whom to trust. The guiding force behind the attacks might be that woman she spotted, the person providing payment, but that didn't mean others weren't involved. "I fell asleep on the beach." She forced a return chuckle.

"And your identification? Ship's pass?"

In her beach bag, in the hands of some madmen bent on killing her. "Stolen while I slept." She spread her hands wide, then adjusted the strap on her suit, which had slipped down her arm in the fall.

The man, his name tag read "Lt. Tavis," studied her face.

Elaine saw his demeanor shift. He was talking to Elaine Kane. Owner. Be obsequious.

"Sorry, Ms. Kane. I'll clear your identity with the shuttle security program. Had to ask. Procedure, you know. We'll get you a replacement pass once we're safely aboard the *Nebula*."

"Thank you." With Tavis's assistance, Elaine stood, brushed herself off, and faced a compartment full of passengers staring at her.

At least her suit wasn't a bikini.

Blushing furiously, she scanned the faces for any sign of Stephanie and Jay, but they must have taken an earlier flight. There were THIs, though, and a wave of jealousy choked her as she took in the happy couples snuggled together in their seats. Elaine checked the

corners of the compartment but saw no emitters. These
were generated by their companions' portable disks,
and she'd lost the last of hers on the street.

The shuttle rocked, throwing her into Tavis's arms.
He sighed and led her to a vacant seat on the center
aisle. Those seated around her avoided her eyes, but she
saw them trying to sneak curious peeks at her during
the flight.

Oh, the field day the newsvids would have if word
of this incident got out. Any number of the passengers
likely carried portacams. She'd be the leading story on
the nets the minute they returned to Earth, if not sooner. Stifling a groan, Elaine leaned her head against the
seat and closed her eyes to block out the surreptitious
stares.

"May I get you anything?"

Tavis sounded genuine as he crouched beside her
chair. Her near collapse must really have shown.

Elaine opened one eye. "A blanket, maybe?"

He pulled one from an overhead bin, and she
wrapped herself in its concealing warmth.

The exhaustion of her body couldn't overcome the
racing of her mind. Who was that mysterious woman
on the hovercycle? She created all sorts of scenarios
in her head. A mistress of Harriet's? If she'd had one,
it wouldn't have surprised Elaine. Terrible to think so
ill of her dead spouse, but she'd been distant through
much of their marriage. And busy. Always busy. Maybe
she did have someone on the side, for all those late-
night "business" meetings.

Elaine never watched soap opera vids, but she envisioned the mistress becoming unsatisfied and then angry with the temporary nature of the relationship, hiring
a killer with some of Harriet's own money, and having

her shot. Now, jealous over Elaine's inheritance, she sought to eliminate Elaine as well. Muah-ha-ha-ha!

Okay, maybe not.

The unknown woman might still be a disgruntled employee or representative of some activist movement. She pondered the possibilities throughout the shuttle's return to the *Nebula*, then went cold when she realized the time had come to cross the tube back to the ship. Without Richelle.

But Richelle waited for her aboard the *Nebula*, she hoped. That incentive had her hauling her body hand over hand across the tube, senses alert to any sign of problems. She focused on the opposite hatch, tunneling her vision. The onyx disk above the entry flashed a green light beneath it—all secure. She imagined Ricky watching, waiting, wanting to shout to her but restraining herself to prevent making a scene. She almost heard Ricky's voice in her head, cheering her on.

And then she stood in the opposite airlock, the crewman manning it crushed against the inner hatch as Ricky appeared and embraced Elaine in a breath-stopping hug.

"I'm sorry. I'm sorry," Ricky said over and over again into her hair. "I should have been there. I'm sorry."

Elaine heard the frustration in her voice, felt the tremor as emotions overwhelmed Richelle. Elaine understood then the helplessness Ricky had endured, trapped as she'd been, handicapped by the very nature of her existence.

Without releasing Elaine, Ricky leaned back to examine her face. Her eyes searched Elaine's features. She knew Ricky took in every detail, every smudge, shadow, and tear stain. Then, without warning, she cupped Elaine's cheeks in her palms and kissed her.

One thing Elaine could now say with authority about twentieth-century film stars—they could kiss.

Richelle's kiss tested her resistance, and finding none, parted Elaine's lips with her tongue. Ricky tasted her deeply, and she lost herself to the kiss, returning her relief and enthusiasm at seeing Elaine a thousandfold.

The loud clearing of a throat interrupted them.

She broke from the THI, her reluctance evident when she let her lips linger on hers a moment longer. Over Ricky's shoulder, the crewman watched them. Impatience and embarrassment warred for dominance on the young man's face.

Impatience won.

"I'm sorry to, um, interrupt, but other passengers are waiting to board, and we're almost due for departure. Your shuttle came in a tad behind schedule."

Elaine's fault. She felt a momentary flash of guilt, but only momentary.

"Yes, of course," Richelle said.

Elaine muttered a "Sorry" as they passed him and entered the corridor to the atrium. She shivered violently in the blast of air-conditioning from the *Nebula*'s interior, and Richelle's tweed jacket found its way around Elaine's shoulders once again. She'd had to leave the borrowed blanket on the shuttle.

"May I offer heartfelt apologies for sinking your change of clothes?" Her tone expressed a mild amusement Elaine couldn't quite share yet. Too many risks, too many dangers. Too damn tired and hungry, she realized as her stomach growled.

They entered the atrium, trying to ignore the stares of the few passengers milling around. At this hour, most had retired to their cabins, but a few stragglers gathered in the central core bar, and others had arrived on the shuttle with Elaine.

Elaine felt the pull of alcoholic beverages after the day she'd had. The circular bar held a festive air, with its multicolored bottles and a string of twinkling lights. She'd only been through this level to enter and exit the ship and hadn't stopped to appreciate the blue plush couches, subdued lighting, and soft music. But her eyelids felt weighted, and she was wearing a swimsuit and Richelle's jacket. She stumbled on the lip between flooring and carpet.

Richelle glanced down at her, her face full of concern. Elaine suspected if no one else had been present, Ricky would have picked her up and carried her.

Elaine wouldn't have fought her over it either.

They arrived on the elite level just as a waiter wheeled a table to her cabin hatch. To his credit, he didn't blink at Elaine's attire, but instead removed a silver cover to reveal a fruit-and-cheese plate and a pitcher of ice water. With a slight bow, he retreated to the service elevator at the far end of the corridor.

Elaine smiled at the sight of her favorite selections and downed half the water before Richelle got the door open. She must have gotten the new key card from the concierge before Elaine returned. "What, no wine?"

Ricky smiled apologetically. "Between the heat and the excitement, I suspect you're dehydrated. Wine would do more harm than good." When the hatch slid aside, she brought in the tray and set it on the sitting room table. "Shower, food, bed, in whichever order you prefer." She cocked her head to the side. "Perhaps when you're better rested, you can tell me what I missed."

Elaine wanted to describe the female figure she'd seen, but exhaustion prevented her from doing anything more than staggering into the bathroom. Since Ricky could not accompany her there, she stood at the door, back to the entry, but with the panel open so she could hear her and fetch help if she needed it.

Trusting Richelle not to peek, Elaine stripped off her swimsuit. She grimaced at the layers of grime smearing her skin and covering the one article of clothing she retained from her fateful day, and tossed the suit into the disposal unit by the sink. She could purchase a replacement in one of the boutiques on the *Nebula*'s shopping level.

Her body argued for bed, but one whiff of lopson slobber on her skin sent her stumbling into the shower. She adjusted the spray as hot as the built-in safeties would allow and twisted the nozzle until the water pummeled her sore muscles with rhythmic jets. The soap smelled of lavender and butterscotch—an interesting combination but pleasant, and it took away the last remnants of sweat, saltwater, and sea life on her. When she finished, she watched the small sand dune she'd shaken from her hair wash down the drain.

Once wrapped in a fluffy white towel, she realized she again hadn't brought a change of clothing in with her, but tiredness overcame modesty. She stepped into the sitting room, edging by Richelle, entered the bedroom, and found her nightclothes folded on her bed.

Putting them on almost required more energy than she retained, and a groan escaped her when she stretched to slip her arm through the strap of her sleep camisole.

A pair of warm hands descended on her shoulders. They guided her to the chair by the comp desk, where Richelle had placed the tray of food, and pressed down until she'd seated herself on the cushion.

Eating while receiving a much-needed massage proved difficult. Elaine moaned around a mouthful of grapes and cheddar when Ricky hit a sore point in her neck, then writhed in a combination of agony and ecstasy while she worked on her shoulders and biceps. When Ricky's ministrations caused her to drop a grape, which rolled across the carpeted floor, she burst into a fit of giggles.

"Better?" Ricky asked her.

"Much," she responded, though it came out barely intelligible around a monstrous yawn. Elaine stood, wavering a bit, and wobbled to the bed. She let herself flop facedown on the mattress, then felt the springs sink as Richelle seated herself beside her.

The healing hands found her tired feet, somehow managing not to tickle her. Elaine sighed with pleasure. On the rare occasions she'd gotten a massage, usually when she joined Harriet on some business trip, she always asked the masseuse to skip her feet.

One stroke of a finger along her right arch sent little tremors of excitement up her legs and into her belly. Harriet had had an odd fascination/fetish with her feet and fingernails, both disconcerting and disturbing while Elaine tried to remain "in the mood." This felt entirely different, playful and sensuous at the same time. If this was what she'd been missing, she'd need to get more foot massages.

From there, Richelle worked up her calves to her thighs, and Elaine's breath caught at the thought of her going higher. She did, though not where Elaine worried she might. Ricky's miraculous fingers skimmed her hips to dig firmly into the flesh around her spine.

Richelle traced each vertebra, building intensity and pressure, then easing off to a gentle stroking of fingertips across her back. What had begun as a potential prelude to something more had faded into caring companionship. Just as well. Elaine had no energy for anything beyond sleep. What was that old saying? The mind is willing, but the body is weak?

She chuckled as that willing mind drifted into deep, uninterrupted slumber, barely aware of Richelle stretching out beside her and taking Elaine into the protective arc of her arms.

THE SENSATION of Elaine's warm body pressing against hers prevented Richelle from falling into what she called "slumber mode"—a time to recharge, tap into the ship's data streams, and catch up on the other sentient THIs. This would have been the perfect opportunity to correlate information, seek a pattern in the attacks on Elaine. But the intake and exhale of her even breath, the way her eyelids fluttered when Ricky leaned up on one elbow to study her peaceful face; it all fascinated her.

She knew her THI body was programmed to perform similar actions, in case a companion awoke and studied *her* during the night. Richelle could read her own code and know her exact breath rate depending upon the physical activity in which she was engaged, the precise algorithm that governed her REM twitches, her snores' decibel level. And yet.

And yet, the unpredictability of human responses mesmerized her.

Richelle wanted it. She wanted it for herself. And if she couldn't have it, she wanted to belong to it, to be loved and cherished by it. And she was so close, she could virtually... *hah, yes*, virtually taste it.

A few days ago, Elaine wouldn't let Ricky near her. Now here she was, cuddling Elaine, protecting her.

Richelle never wanted to let her go.

She sighed, and her simulated breath blew a wisp of Elaine's hair from behind her ear to fall across her cheek.

How to make this permanent? And would Elaine want to?

Ricky had chosen Elaine.

The question was, would Elaine choose her?

CHAPTER 14
ROMANTIC FICTION

MORNING BROUGHT residual aches and pains constantly throbbing in Elaine's legs. The warmth of another body startled her to full wakefulness, and she tensed, then relaxed when she recognized the back of Richelle's tank top and her shaggy but short brown hair.

Elaine's first impulse, to wrap herself around her, surprised her, but she didn't fight it. Ignoring pulled muscles, she spooned against her, curling her knees up behind hers, pressing her chest to her spine. She reached her fingers to run through Ricky's hair, then leaned closer so she could breathe lightly into her ear, a pleasant way to wake her.

The Biotech logo.

Elaine jerked away as if the imprinted electric flower had shocked her.

You cannot *fall in love with this woman, this... creation*, she chided herself.

We're all creations of one sort or another, a second internal voice argued.

Yes, but human *creations aren't restricted to generators and little onyx disks.*

Instead of the sexual surprise she'd planned, she spent almost an hour watching Richelle sleep. Her shoulders rose and fell with each deep, even breath. She wondered at the purpose of it. Did the THIs use the time to download new information? Wander through the ship's circuitry and spy on the passengers? Or was her "consciousness" here and dormant, her programmable internal clock set to wake her when Elaine arose from the bed, her body simulating sleep in the meantime to preserve realism?

Do androids dream of electric sheep?

Okay, Richelle wasn't an android, but the similarities between her companion and the replicants in Philip K. Dick's classic novel sent a shiver through Elaine.

At first, the main character didn't realize he'd fallen in love with an android, a replicant with a limited lifespan. When he figured it out, he had no idea how long she'd live or how much time they had together. But then again, who does?

Elaine did. She had until the end of this starliner cruise. Once they returned to Earth, technology or lack thereof would force her and Richelle apart.

She blew out a breath and swung her legs off the bed, expecting Richelle to rouse, but she didn't. More realism? Maybe it waited until Elaine needed/asked for it.

Just to be certain Ricky was all right, she leaned down and whispered her name in her ear. Ricky stirred, one eye opening to blearily focus on her.

"I'm going out for a bit. Are you okay?"

"I'm fine. Recharging," she mumbled. The eye closed. Soft snores took over.

Interesting. She hadn't realized THIs needed to re-charge after heavy use, and she supposed the activities on the surface constituted heavy use. Still, she thought they drew their power directly from the *Nebula*'s gen-erator. So much she didn't know or understand about Richelle.

Elaine dressed while she continued to sleep, then stared down at her face, handsome in its own way, peace-ful in slumber. She remembered the anguish she'd seen there when Ricky had told her of the others she'd served, and the same helpless expression when she'd appeared in the airlock upon Elaine's return to the ship. There'd been something else too. Something she'd been too tired the night before to see clearly.

Her heart rate sped up. She had to take several calming breaths to return the pace to normal.

Richelle was in love with her.

And it *was* Richelle. Elaine refused to believe some programmer sat in a little cubicle and planned for THIs to fall in love with their companions if a certain series of actions occurred. Yep, some drinks, plus dinner, plus dancing, plus three attempts on the subject's life, two rescues (and a half, she reminded herself. Richelle had certainly helped her get back to the shuttle), and a hand-ful of arguments sprinkled in, plus a helluva good mas-sage, equaled love. It was like one of those programmed surprises Harriet bragged about discovering when she tested some of the simulator games Leviathan made. Harry prided herself on finding hidden bits of code that revealed themselves under just the right circumstances, usually unlocking secret areas of play.

Elaine had triggered Richelle's "love" somehow. Sure. Surprise!

No, she didn't think so.

Whatever Richelle was, or better yet, whatever she'd evolved into, her emotions were real. She had feelings.

And so did Elaine.

Now she had to find some way to turn them off.

Stephanie's new friend, Jay Grego, said Biotech was working on making the THIs portable, though they were years from public availability. Elaine thought about spending years alone in the rambling Kane mansion. She'd go insane.

You're already insane. You're in love with a THI. She could imagine what her psychiatrist would say. He'd wanted her to form new attachments. Dr. Nichols claimed she feared forging bonds after losing Harriet. That had made her laugh. It wasn't like she'd had much of a bond with Harry either. She doubted Nichols had this in mind, though.

Crazy if she kept Richelle. Crazy if Elaine lost her. Better to be crazy and accompanied. There had to be some way. Owner or not, she couldn't stay on the ship forever.

She moved to the desk, where she discovered her replacement key card and a new passenger ID with her picture on the front. Richelle thought of everything. A quick check of the built-in comp brought up the day's schedule of shipboard activities. The *Nebula* was in transit for the next twenty-four hours, and the crew planned a variety of distractions to prevent boredom.

One in particular caught her attention. She dressed quickly in some casual pastel innocence-inspiring attire, accessorized with simple gold jewelry she rarely wore, and finished with flat white ballet-slipper-type shoes. All this she carried out in the semidark so as not to wake Richelle again.

When she went to the bathroom to brush hair and teeth, she checked to make certain nothing clashed. Nope, no garish mistakes. A look in the mirror confirmed she'd achieved the appearance desired—sweet, innocent, approachable. Harriet had taught her a few things about dressing the part one wanted to play.

Harry never wore pink sweaters, though.

Elaine slipped into the corridor, the hatch sealing behind her loudly enough to wake the dead, and she held her breath, thinking Richelle would appear at her side, but she did not. Maybe subconsciously Ricky knew she wanted some space this morning. Besides, the emitters throughout the ship could track her anywhere.

She made her way down in the elevator to level three, where her first day's tour had stopped by the Celestial Theater. Each night, live performers and THIs reenacted famous scenes from the films the characters were known for. Elaine had avoided the productions. Seeing the THIs exploited in such a manner bothered her.

They're not all like Richelle, she reminded herself. *They're not all real.* Still, it seemed wrong.

Now, though, in the midmorning hours, an announcement screen in the wall by the entrance read "Guest Loyalty Champagne Brunch" in blinking yellow letters. Elaine pushed aside a heavy blackout curtain within the already open hatch and stepped into the theater.

A stage with a rounded proscenium dominated the far end of the large space, but no one occupied it at the moment. The seating consisted of scattered tables bolted to the deck and cushioned sofas in black velvet with gold sparkles like star fields arranged in semicircles behind the tables. In front of the stage, the kitchen crew had set up a long buffet. Offerings included an assortment of fruits, pastries, and other nibbles, along with trays filled with long-stemmed glasses of champagne and mimosas.

Guests in casual attire milled about or sat chatting at the tables while classical string music played in the background. Elaine scanned the faces until she spotted the one she wanted—the author, Denise Lazaro.

Unlike others who gathered in groups of four or six or more, Ms. Lazaro kept to one companion, Jean-Luc, her THI. Elaine had almost missed them in their quiet corner table. The pair sat close together, the author's head resting on the THI's shoulder. Elaine took a step in their direction.

"ID, ma'am?"

So focused had she been on her objective, Elaine failed to notice the diminutive woman wearing a ship's uniform, standing in the shadows by the entrance. The blond held a card scanner, ready to check if Elaine fit the requirements of the party, being a past guest.

"I'm not a repeat customer," Elaine announced, saving her the trouble.

The woman frowned. "Then I'm sorry, ma'am, but this gathering is for past guests only. As a reward for their loyalty to Nebula Starlines."

Maybe she could bluff, though she'd never played poker. Elaine nodded in Denise Lazaro's direction. "I have a friend here. She's sitting in that corner—Ms. Lazaro? The author?"

"I know who she is." The tone implied everyone knew the famous writer, and the frown deepened. Elaine got the distinct impression this woman manning the door didn't care for the author.

She looked more closely. Come to think of it, the other guests were giving Lazaro and Jean-Luc a wide berth. Some had THIs with them, but they still cast disdainful glances at the cozy couple. This might not have been such a great idea, but she let it ride.

The doorkeeper checked her list once more, lowering her eyelids and leaning in closer to Elaine. "If you don't tell, I won't tell," the crewwoman stage-whispered. She swept her arm out in a welcoming gesture. "Please enjoy the brunch, Ms. Kane."

Ah, so she had been recognized. Whether it was Lazaro's notoriety or her own getting her in, Elaine wasn't about to argue. Maybe it was even ship's policy to let in a first-time guest if one made a special request. Elaine flashed her a bright smile. She had what she wanted. No need to prolong the animosity. "Thank you. I will." She melded into the crowd.

Elaine made her first stop the buffet table so as not to be too obvious, though she kept Denise Lazaro and her companion within sight out of the corner of her eye. It would have been wasted effort if they suddenly decided to leave.

Once she'd laden her plate with strawberries, melon, a cheese danish, and some squarish yellow berries she'd enjoyed on Gratitude, she glanced about the room, ostensibly searching for a seat. And oh, what luck! There was one spot at Lazaro's table (which, of course, had been available since she'd entered). She let her expression brighten as she made eye contact with the author and headed in that direction.

"May I?" Elaine inquired, using her glass of champagne to gesture at the vacant sofa cushion.

At first she worried they wouldn't want to be interrupted. But Lazaro's face broke into a warm, welcoming smile. "Please!" the older woman said, pushing away from Jean-Luc's shoulder to straighten in her seat. The author took a piece of fruit from the previously untouched plate on the table before them and popped it into her mouth.

As she sat, Elaine studied the couple. She had to admit, they looked good together. Jean-Luc was the most distinguished bald man she'd ever met, with tufts of graying hair at the temples and still wearing the same red-and-black uniform she'd seen him in the first time they'd crossed paths in the corridor. No, she realized at second glance, not quite the same. This outfit seemed a little less formal, less trimming, no medals on the breast panel.

Denise had that "Earth Mother" look going on again. The timeless style seemed popular among authors and artists throughout the ages. She wore a peasant blouse, off the shoulder, that set off her artificially enhanced, practically glowing auburn hair. When Elaine slid in next to her, Denise swept aside her ankle-length forest-green flowing skirt. Rough-hewn stone jewelry on her wrists and a matching necklace in browns and greens accented the outfit.

"The alasite in your bracelet really complements the skirt," Elaine commented, searching for an opening line.

That seemed to be Jean-Luc's cue. "If you two ladies will excuse me, I'll leave you to engage in conversation." He stood, straightened the tunic of his uniform,
and strolled to the nearest viewport to study the passing
stars.

"I love it when he says 'engage,'" Denise gushed,
then took a sip of mimosa. She swallowed and sighed,
gazing after her companion with an expression of
adoration.

Elaine knew she'd missed something, a twentieth-century euphemism, perhaps. Or maybe the author
was thinking about marriage and hoping the THI would
propose an engagement. And under the circumstances,
how would *that* work? Either way, she didn't ask.

Denise placed her glass on the table, leaned back
on the couch, and rested her palms on her knees. "Now,
I know you didn't sit here to compliment my bracelets.
What can I do for you, Ms....?"

"Kane," she supplied, "but call me Elaine, please.
And am I really that transparent?" She'd make a terrible undercover operative.

Denise laughed, a deep, pleasant chuckle, warm
and motherly to go with her image. "I'm an author,
Elaine. That translates to professional people-watcher.
It might look like I was absorbed by Jean-Luc's mere
presence, and believe me, I usually am, but I had you
pegged from the moment you stepped into the theater.
I'm pretty observant, and I've got to get my creative
brain in gear. Deadline on my new book is a month
from now. I don't get much writing done on these excursions. But other needs must also be appeased." She
waggled her eyebrows.

Elaine fought the impending blush and failed. Hard
to maintain a professional demeanor with pink cheeks.

"It's actually Jean-Luc I wanted to talk to you about, and your relationship with him."

That did surprise the writer. Denise sat up straighter, fixing her with a penetrating stare from jade green eyes. She cocked her head to one side, then the other. Satisfied with whatever vibe she'd gleaned, she visibly relaxed. "Well!" she exclaimed, puffing out a breath. "You didn't say you wanted to discuss my 'interaction' with 'it,' so I'll assume"—her voice rose in volume—"you aren't like these other busybodies who think they know what's normal and need to enforce everyone's capitulation to that normalcy." She seemed to be directing her speech at one woman in particular. Elaine noticed several other couples staring at them also. Well, the humans stared. The THIs politely ignored the outburst.

These same individuals had cast glances in their direction from the moment Elaine sat down. She wasn't entirely unobservant herself.

The targeted woman strode right up to the table Elaine and Denise shared. She pointed an accusatory finger at the famous author. "I don't care how much money you make on those fantasy romances," she said, her tone harsh and shrill. "What you've got with that automaton is an abomination. It's an insult to real people who love each other."

Elaine pressed her spine against the seat cushions, trying to put as much space between herself and the newcomer as possible. Weren't they all on the same THI cruise? Pot meet kettle, kettle meet pot?

Elaine expected the author to show anger. Instead, she laughed. "Oh please, Charlotte, you're just mad I beat you for the Silver Heart award this year. Again." She leaned toward Elaine. "Charlotte writes traditional romance. She hates it when anything cutting edge takes the prize."

Charlotte's face reddened with anger. "You're a freak, Denise, replacing a real husband who loved you with that… that thing!" She pointed in Jean-Luc's direction. The THI cast her a disinterested nod and returned his attention to the view.

Now an edge did enter Denise's tone. "Jean-Luc is as real to me as David ever was. And he'll never up and die and leave me, either." The author's voice broke.

Elaine wasn't sure who David was, but he'd clearly been close to the author, and mortally human.

Denise regained her composure, covering pain with a smile practiced for large numbers of book signings and public interviews. "As for my fans, are you kidding? They'd thrive on the knowledge that I'm in love with a THI. They're *romantic fantasy* readers. Besides, I'm a writer. I'm allowed to be eccentric. Now go mind your own business. Shoo!"

Huffing, Charlotte turned away and rejoined a group of onlookers. They shifted as a unit to face the stage and engaged in alternative conversation. A ship's security officer that had discreetly moved to stand behind them relaxed and wandered off to patrol throughout the theater.

"So, you really do love him," Elaine said, nodding at Jean-Luc. It wasn't a question.

The piercing green eyes fell on her again. "I do," she affirmed. "And judging from what you've said and your manner, I'd say you love yours as well." Denise cleared her throat. "We've both got ourselves a real problem."

Elaine took a breath, held it, then exhaled. "Yes, I think I'm falling in love with Richelle." There. She'd said it. And once she'd done so, she knew it to be the truth. Relief flowed through her body at the admission.

Denise cocked an eyebrow at her. "'Falling' and 'in love' are two different things. What do you want to know?" Leave it to an author to dwell on semantics.

"For starters, how do you handle it? You mentioned having exclusivity to Jean-Luc. How did you work that out?"

The author laughed. "With enough money, you can work out anything. I orchestrated a deal with Biotech and Nebula. I travel with their ships a certain number of times per year, and they agree to keep Jean-Luc for me and me alone."

Elaine saw flaws in that plan. When Denise wasn't on the ship, the techs on board could do anything with Jean-Luc's program, then erase his memory of that use before her next arrival. She supposed passengers might talk, especially repeat guests, so it would be risky for Nebula to do so, but Elaine wouldn't put it past them.

Then again, with a tremendous number of twentieth-century film stars and characters to choose from, isolating one for a VIP might not be such a big deal for Nebula. It could be quite lucrative for the companies involved.

Denise took a bite of danish, then swallowed. "Will money be an issue for you?"

So someone did exist who didn't know about Elaine's vast corporate fortune. "No, money's not a problem."

The author clapped once, scattering small crumbs across her lap. "Well then, Nebula's already set the precedent with me. I don't see any reason why they couldn't make the same arrangement for you."

"But if you love him, how do you deal with... not being with him? I mean, you can't travel all the time."

Denise waved Jean-Luc over and patted the empty seat beside her. He sat, straight-backed and formal, the embodiment of quiet dignity. The author took his hand in her own. "Jean-Luc, tell her how we deal with being apart."

The THI explained briefly about Denise's obligations that took her on "away missions" from his side, but this only made their times together more poignant.

"You could always buy your own generator," Elaine suggested.

The author barked a laugh. "I couldn't sell enough books in a lifetime to afford that! Not to mention the necessary space for installation and tech support."

But Elaine could. It wouldn't even make that large a dent in the bank accounts held by Leviathan. She'd had enough of enforced separation in an on-again, off-again relationship. Harriet had traveled a third to a half of the year. Elaine wanted a woman who would be there when she awoke, lonely in the dark. She thought about her mansion back on Earth. The home gym and Harriet's office could go. That might leave enough room for a THI generator. She had no idea of one's actual size. Something to inquire about later. Jay Grego would know.

Yeah, if she could get the man out of Stephanie's bed long enough to ask him.

Elaine continued to converse with the couple while she finished her brunch, but as the discussion progressed, she became more and more aware of one thing. Jean-Luc was not "one of the good ones."

She brought up controversial topics, existential questions, religion, politics, human nature. For every subject, the THI produced what sounded like a scripted response carefully crafted so as not to offer offense. He used terminology and references of which Elaine had no knowledge, likely from his character's television show or film. All of it felt flat and unimaginative, giving no indication that he could expand upon his basic programming.

Throughout the conversation, Denise shot Elaine irritated looks, shifting in her seat, interrupting Jean-Luc's answers with more imaginative ones of her own, essentially covering for his inadequacy. The author tried to change the topic, talking about her novels, her latest accolades and awards, but Elaine had her goal in sight and would not be dissuaded.

Elaine went in for the kill. "If you were going to mix Denise a drink, something she's never had before, what would you serve her? How would you go about it?"

The THI's face went blank, just for a moment, and Elaine would have sworn she'd caused a split-second crash in its processing. Then Jean-Luc smiled. "I'd ask her." He nodded toward Denise.

"I'm asking *you*," Elaine reminded him.

"Enough!" The author slapped her palm on the table.

Elaine jerked back, spilling some of her champagne over the rim of her long-stemmed glass.

"You're asking him to be creative," Denise accused. Fire flashed in her eyes, an anger bordering on unbalanced.

"People are," Elaine said softly, with a slight emphasis on the word "people." It was more of a thought than a statement, really—a realization, an analysis of her own relationship, a classification of Richelle not as a thing but as a person, whereas Jean-Luc was not a sentient being. She hadn't meant to say it out loud, but she had, and Denise had heard her.

The author leaned forward. "Why are you doing this? I thought you understood." She wrung her hands. Her breath rate increased. "No THI is creative."

Mine is, Elaine thought.

"You're just like the rest of them." Denise swept her arm out, indicating the other passengers, all of whom stared openly at the building argument. The security officer edged in their direction again.

Great. Just what Elaine needed—more attention from ship's security. She hadn't seen too many obvious guards around the ship and wondered if this one was here specifically because Denise was known for erratic behavior… or if the captain might be watching out for Elaine's safety, assigning the officer to *her*.

"THIs never leave you!" The author gained her feet. Her face turned an alarming shade of purple. "They never die!"

To Elaine's horror, tears streamed down her brunch companion's face. She edged away on the sofa, putting as much space between herself and the distraught, unpredictable woman as possible. Jean-Luc gazed at her with a look of disapproval, staring down his angular nose. "I think it would be best if you departed," he suggested. Reaching into a pants pocket, he produced a handkerchief and passed it to Lazaro. Not as effective as an absorber.

The little bit of food Elaine had eaten shifted uncomfortably in her stomach. Denise Lazaro was obviously a grieving widow. She'd filled the void her dead husband left with something that helped her forget her loss. And Elaine had shattered her illusion and stolen her happiness.

"Go away! Leave me alone!" the woman shouted.

But Elaine wasn't the one leaving. The female security officer stepped forward, resting a calming hand on one of Lazaro's quivering shoulders while Jean-Luc stoically looked on. The guard murmured something in the writer's ear, then gently but firmly led her, sobbing, from the theater. The THI shook his head at Elaine, then followed them.

After a long moment of uncomfortable silence, the other guests returned to their meals and conversations. Elaine nibbled from her plate, resisting the urge to bolt from the room. Unavoidable questions tromped through her brain, and the rest of her brunch tasted like dust.

Was she just as deluded as Lazaro, imagining Richelle as more than she was? Was Elaine using her as a surrogate to fill a void in her life? Ricky was a THI. Could Elaine really be in love with her? Was she losing her mind?

No. Richelle had proven time and again she was more than she seemed. Elaine simply had to figure out how *much* more.

IF THE captain had asked her to dance the hokey-pokey right then, Richelle would have done so, happily. Joy surged through her in pulsating waves, turning her energy signature bright golds and pinks in the data stream.

Admittedly, her ability to access any emitter on the ship gave her an unfair advantage when it came to spying on Elaine. Richelle doused the temporary guilt under the rationale that she had to keep an eye on her, to prevent another attempt on her life.

It gave her the perfect excuse to observe Elaine at the repeat cruisers' gathering.

When she watched her interaction with the author and her THI, Richelle wanted to appear on the spot, pick Elaine up, and twirl her in her embrace. The questions Elaine asked could serve only one purpose.

Despite Elaine's temporary reversal in bed that morning (and yes, Richelle knew when she'd pulled away, and why), Elaine wanted her. Elaine wanted to find a way to be with her.

Richelle's enthusiasm faded just a tad. All right, she'd said "falling" not "in love," but it marked tremendous progress.

It faded a little more. Other problems.

Becoming a crazy old woman who cruised time and again with the same THI wasn't the answer for Elaine. Another solution needed to present itself, and sooner than the portable emitters would find their way onto the market for the general population.

CHAPTER 15
TWO FOR THE HOT TUB

ELAINE KNEW of no better place to relax and destress than the spa, and the *Nebula* offered a first-rate one. She made a quick stop on the shopping level, a row of boutiques offering exotic liquors, expensive jewelry, and designer clothing. Ten minutes later she'd purchased a replacement bathing suit, a two-piece in silver and black.

She arrived without an appointment at the Comet Gym and Spa on the lowest level of the ship. A friendly receptionist informed her she'd have to wait for one of the private hot-tub rooms the facility offered, but that suited her fine. She could lounge by the pool, under the safe tanning lights, to begin her relaxation.

The woman had also directed her attention to the spa's warning signs posted throughout the area. Swimming and sharing a hot tub could result in rad transference, and the *Nebula* took no responsibility in the case of either of those events. Not something Elaine intended to stress about. Entering the pool area required a pass through yet another decontaminator, and she had no intention of sharing a hot tub with a human capable of collecting rads.

The spa provided individual changing closets, and Elaine stripped off her slacks and sweater, stepped into the swimwear, and locked her clothing and personal items in a thumbprint-coded cabinet. She emerged a little self-conscious in the revealing bikini—not her usual conservative style, but Richelle's arrival in her life had sparked a flirtatious side she never knew she possessed. Even so, she grabbed a towel from a complimentary pile of fluffy whites and draped it over her shoulders to cover the exposed cleavage. She turned her face upward and spoke to the ceiling.

"Care to join me?"

In addition to company, she appreciated Ricky's protection. She hoped she'd left her attackers on the surface, but if not, a private hot tub dip later might not be her smartest move.

No sign of her. Three ladies strolled by, wearing nothing but sandals and towels. With a flush of embarrassment, Elaine realized there weren't any emitters in the locker room, and Richelle's overdeveloped sense of propriety wouldn't allow her to barge in, even if she technically could. Elaine passed through the double glass doors to the pool area.

Balmy heat rose off the warm water, and the sharp but not unpleasant odor of chlorine filled her nostrils. She strolled to the raised edge, gazed into the six-foot depths, and caught her breath in a gasp. Her head spun.

Infinity. Regardless of the lit numbers marking the depth at six feet, the pool reached down to infinity. The duraglass bottom, forged to resist extreme cold, vacuum, and possible impact, revealed scattered flecks of starlight through its transparent surface. Shadows of other swimmers passed between Elaine and endless space, blocking her view in splotches, but the effect brought on the worst case of vertigo she'd had since boarding.

"Impressive, isn't it?" came Richelle's voice at her shoulder.

Already dizzy, Elaine startled and stumbled over the slippery tile lip into the pool, her towel still over her neck. The heavy, waterlogged cotton wrapped around her arms and face, tangling limbs overtaxed from her ocean swim on Gratitude and bruised from her leap into the shuttle. Elaine floundered, her lungs unprepared for submersion, water already in her mouth from her surprised squeak as she went over the edge. With the towel blocking her vision, she lost track of which way was up.

She kicked and flailed, connecting with something resilient, bouncing off. Somewhere her mind registered it as another body, but the choking liquid cutting off her breath made rational thought impossible.

Then a warm arm circled her shoulders and a hand pulled the fabric from her face. Richelle's brown eyes met her panicked ones. She drew Elaine upward toward the surface.

They broke through at the same moment, Elaine sputtering and spitting, coughing, while Richelle kept

her afloat. Elaine's initial thought was to be angry.
She'd asked Ricky time and again not to sneak up on
her like that. Elaine's arms around Ricky's neck tensed
to throttle her, then relaxed as she saw genuine regret
and concern in her expression. Ricky's swim-tank-top-
covered chest heaved against her bikini-clad breasts
while her thighs brushed rhythmically across Elaine's.
Instead of smacking her, Elaine laughed.

"Not quite the romantic distraction I'd planned,"
Elaine gasped, still drawing air into her lungs.

Ricky cocked her head. "You were planning
romance?"

While Elaine's cheeks flushed, Ricky whipped the
sopping towel over her head and twirled it as if she'd
just removed an accessory during a striptease. Then she
threw it to the side of the pool, where it landed with
a loud plop. Elaine tried to take the gesture seriously,
sexily, but she just couldn't imagine Ricky pole dancing, and there was very little about the tank top/shorts
combo that could be considered sexy. Although....
Ricky's tiny nipples poked against the black fabric.
Elaine's fingertips tingled with the urge to stroke them.

Ricky's puppy-dog eyes worked wonders on her
heart and evaporated the remaining traces of her anger.

She let Ricky carry her weight as they floated
for a few more minutes before Elaine glanced at the
digital time display on the tiled wall. "Let's move on.
The view through the transparent pool bottom is a nice
gimmick, but I feel like I'm going to get sucked down
the drain."

Richelle clambered out first, then gave her a hand
up over the edge instead of making her swim the length
of the pool to the stairs. Again, her strength startled

Elaine. Ricky's body wasn't devoid of muscles, but she had a lot more power than her physique suggested.

While they crossed to the hot tub cubicles, Elaine didn't miss the way Ricky openly admired her new bikini. She hoped it hadn't ridden up in the back, or slid down, or done something else embarrassing in her unplanned swan dive, but she wasn't going to reach behind her to check. This was exactly why she hated swimsuits, and bikinis in particular. She tried to remember why she'd bought this one.

They passed through double glass doors, checked in with the receptionist, and got their room assignment. Taking her hand, Richelle led the way down a narrow corridor with doors on either side.

The lit sign on door seven read "reserved," and as they stepped inside, it blinked over to "in use." Breath-suppressing heat assailed them, in stark contrast to the chill of the corridor. The space was small and circular, wide enough to accommodate the round sunken hot tub and a redwood bench seat running around the circumference of it. Steam roiled off the bubbling water.

Elaine moved to the edge, careful to keep Richelle in view and not receive any more surprises. She dipped a toe into the water and sighed with pleasure, then sank one leg after the other into the tub. A second seat, stone this time, encircled the interior, and she eased herself onto it, then leaned back with her elbows resting outside the water. The bubbles surged and flowed, the submerged jets pummeling muscles still sore from the previous day's traumas. It was better than a massage, almost.

Richelle joined her, placing herself beside her rather than on the opposite side of the circle, and Elaine rested her head on her shoulder. If this could go on forever, if she could stop this moment in time....

She closed her eyes. The motion of the warm water flowed around her in a wavelike pattern....

Instantly, the ocean attack from the previous day flooded back to her, and she jerked upright at a sudden horrible thought. "Wait, won't you fizzle in here? You should get out of the water!" She moved to stand, her hand fastening on Ricky's upper arm.

Richelle covered Elaine's fingers with her own and drew her down with a gentle tug on her hand. "I didn't fizzle in the swimming pool," she reminded her. "I'm not the Wicked Witch of the West."

Elaine had no idea who that was.

Ricky laughed at her consternation. "The only reason my image dissolved in the ocean is because it was dependent upon the emitters on my person and your bag, and range. When I dove into the water, I left the range of the one on your beach bag, and the liquid fried the ones on your hat and the back of my shorts." She brought Elaine's hand to her chest so she felt Ricky's heartbeat. "I'm sorry I left you alone."

"You didn't," Elaine assured her. "I mean, you did, but it was in the act of saving my life again. You know, I'm starting to lose count."

"Three. Although you saved mine when the ship wanted to, um, retire me. Two more and we're even." Using the buoyancy of the water, Ricky shifted her around so Elaine sat between her knees, her back reclining against Ricky's chest.

Elaine didn't resist the change of positions. She felt Ricky's breathing, slow and steady but increasing in pace. At least she thought it was. She felt Ricky's hardened nipples pressing against her shoulders. It shouldn't have surprised her after all the perfectly human reactions the THI had produced thus far, but it did. She fought to keep the giggle out of her voice. "We'll never be even," she predicted. "I'm not the heroic type."

"Oh, I beg to differ." Richelle crossed her arms over Elaine's chest, pressing Elaine even more firmly to her. Droplets ran over Ricky's wet skin. "You didn't panic on Eris Station and proved yourself quite adventurous on Gratitude. Not everyone would have handled it all so well." Ricky's mouth hovered next to her ear, warm breath caressing the lobe. Goose bumps rose on Elaine's bare arms and neck. "You never did tell me how you escaped those men."

Good grief. She hadn't. While the warmth drew the aches from her muscles, she recounted the story of her evasion, the crazy hovercycle ride, and the woman she spotted.

"And you have no idea who she might be?" She heard the frown in Ricky's tone.

"None. It was too dark."

"Pity. My eyesight can be adjusted for night vision. I wish I'd been there to see all of that." Her fists clenched where they rested on Elaine's collarbone.

"Me too."

Ricky's hands relaxed, and she hugged Elaine. "I'm here now."

Yes, she certainly was, and the heat radiating off Ricky's body, mixed with the increased heart rate and breathing and the steamy hot tub were igniting a fire in Elaine she hadn't felt in a long time. Elaine needed a distraction, a change of topic. "I'm actually surprised you didn't show up earlier, especially when I was getting criticized by past guests and yelled at by Denise Lazaro." She wondered how the mentally delicate author was doing and hoped Jean-Luc had been able to comfort her. Shattering the woman's happiness in her artificial reality hadn't been Elaine's intention, and guilt gnawed at her. "Were you awake for any of that?"

After a moment's hesitation, Richelle nodded. Elaine felt the up and down motion of her chin against the back of her head. So, she'd watched through the emitters. "I didn't think a THI's support would help much, under the circumstances. Besides, you didn't call me. I didn't want you to think I believed you couldn't manage on your own."

Elaine chuckled. "That's never stopped you before."

"I'm learning."

CHAPTER 16
CASINO *NEBULA*

Aᴛᴛᴇʀ ᴛʜᴇɪʀ rejuvenating hot tub soak, Richelle and Elaine changed clothes and met up with Stephanie and Jay for a late lunch/early dinner.

As she scraped up the last bite of her chocolate and Gratitudian yellowberry pudding, Stephanie elbowed Elaine. "How about we go lose some of Leviathan's substantial earnings?"

"I'm sorry?"

Jay cracked his knuckles. "She means the Cosmic Casino. I'm a rather proficient card player, if I do say so myself."

"He is," Stephanie agreed, nodding.

And a not-so-proficient drinker, apparently. Judging from his glassy eyes and slightly slurred speech, he'd had a couple of cocktails prior to the two he'd had with lunch.

Harriet had played cards, too, on the rare occasions she wasn't working. Harry had never been very good at it, though, and lost thousands every time she joined a game. Good thing she made millions.

"Jay took a couple thousand from the house the other night," Stephanie bragged.

"That's impressive," Elaine commented. Beside her, Richelle shifted uneasily.

"Yes, unusually so," the THI added, voice tight.

While they gathered themselves, Elaine cast her a questioning look, but she shook her head minutely.

Was she implying Jay cheated? Elaine could see why Ricky wouldn't want to say so in front of Stephanie.

Elaine shrugged and addressed the group. "I'm not the gambling type, but I'll drop a few tokens in the slots." If Richelle wouldn't share her concerns, Elaine wasn't going to sit around in her cabin all day. She'd spent little enough time with Stephanie on this trip. Besides, the larger her group of companions, the less likely it became that anyone would try to harm her. She hoped.

She didn't miss Richelle's exasperated sigh.

ELAINE'S CONCERNS about her faded a bit when they arrived at the neon-encrusted entrance to the Cosmic Casino. The initial ship's tour had included the establishment, but it hadn't been open at the time and bore little resemblance to the sparkling, boisterous,

enticing palace it was now. Blinking lights in a multi-
tude of colors reminded Elaine of Christmas decorations. Triumphant music announced each win, no matter how small, and excited laughter spilled through the
entry.

It beckoned. It called. Elaine wanted to be a part
of that enthusiasm and gained a new understanding
of what created an addict. She laughed at her naivete.
Even with her expansive wealth, she'd have to watch
herself in a place like this.

Stephanie and Jay swept inside, Jay weaving a
little and Stephanie beckoning for Elaine to follow.
Elaine heard several staff members greeting Jay by
name, offering to escort him to an empty seat at a blackjack table. A waitress appeared at his elbow with a glass
of deep purple Eris rum, recognizable by its distinctive
color. Clearly, she'd anticipated his order. He took it
from her tray, dropping a few coins of tip in its place.
No check involved. Gamblers' beverages were, apparently, complimentary.

Like he needed more alcohol. But it made sense on
the casino's part. Drunk gamblers equaled uninhibited
gamblers.

Before Elaine could join them, Richelle gave her
hand a quick squeeze for attention. "You're on your
own again," she whispered softly.

"What? Are you really that opposed to games of
chance?"

Ricky smiled softly and gestured toward the interi-
or of the casino. "No emitters."

Elaine scanned the walls and corners she could see
from outside, those not covered by neon signs, tour-
nament advertisements, and three-dimensional images

of celebratory characters flashing on and off as people won. Nope, no emitters, at least not visible ones.

"I thought the bathrooms were the only places without them."

"Your information didn't describe you as the gambling type, so I didn't mention it."

A layer of cold wrapped around the warmth Richelle's presence provided. Elaine had no desire to be separated from her, but she'd committed herself to Stephanie. "So, why none here?"

Ricky fingered the neckline of the shirt she'd changed into, a soft beige button-down that set off her brown eyes. She shuffled her feet.

"Well?"

"Well," she answered, clearing her throat, "some THIs have been known to, um, cheat."

Elaine blinked. "How is that possible? Wouldn't the programmers eliminate that possibility?"

Ricky shrugged. "They tried, I suppose. But we emulate our originals' personae exactly. If the actor had the tendency to cheat, or played a role that involved cheating…." She trailed off. "After a few guests complained that their stateroom card games had been… influenced, shall we say… the management took all the emitters out of the casino, just to be safe. And of course, this discouraged private gaming, drawing more guests into this place." Richelle paused, her head cocked, considering. "You know, that might have been Nebula's intention all along, program some of us to cheat, then drive more traffic to their own slots and card tables when it was discovered."

"Interesting analysis. You really think Nebula is so devious?"

Richelle nodded, her shaggy hair bobbing as she did so. "No doubt." She fixed Elaine with a serious look. "Watch yourself in there. They have percentages to fill on guest winnings and losings, and judging from what our friend Jay Grego said, he's already taken a good portion of the winning percentage for this cruise."

Elaine nodded, not failing to note the bitterness when Richelle mentioned Grego's name. She didn't comprehend the animosity. Surely Ricky wasn't jealous of Jay. Elaine had shown no interest in Stephanie's chosen companion. She had no interest in men at all. It especially wouldn't occur to her to steal one from Stephanie, as if anyone could ever tempt someone from the leggy blond.

"I'll keep it in mind," she assured Richelle, and entered the casino.

The moment Elaine released her hand, she regretted it, but in her time with Harriet, she'd missed out on a lot of so-called "adult" experiences. Time to rectify the situation.

The inside overwhelmed the senses more than the entryway. Music, laughter, cheering, and the occasional curse made casual conversation impossible. Friends seated next to one another at the slot machines had to shout to be heard.

Though she knew Jay and Stephanie would be at the card tables on the far side, Elaine strolled up and down four aisles of slots out of curiosity. A woman right beside her scored three identical holographic fairies dancing atop the machine. They were too transparent to be THIs, but standard holograph projectors must have been embedded in the grooves of the metal surface. A recorded voice announced, "Winner! Winner! Winner!" and a single token spit into the bottom tray.

"That's it?" Elaine blushed as the woman turned. She hadn't meant to belittle the prize. It had slipped out.

The woman seemed to take no offense. She smiled as she seized the token, slid her ample buttocks one chair to the right, and inserted the solitary disk into a coin chute on the machine. "You've been watching too many twentieth-century films or reading too many old e-novels." She reached a palm to stroke the side of the *Faster Than Light* machine in front of her. "These babies don't drop hundreds of coins anymore. Have you ever handled a lot of metal money?" Before Elaine could respond, she went on. "Coins are dirty. They turn your fingers black." She gave Elaine a knowing look. "I work in a bank. Believe me, I know this stuff. And they're heavy! No one wants to lug buckets of them around a casino. Bad for the posture, bad for your clothing, bad for the image."

Elaine cast a glance at the woman's attire—all white. White pants, white sleeveless shirt, open white jacket on top. Not the best choice for her figure, but immaculately clean. She could see where filthy loose change might present a hazard.

And speaking of hazards, Elaine could only guess at the number of rads the sophisticated gaming equipment had to be giving off, all of it run by computers with the latest processors, she was sure. No wonder there were decontaminators all over the ship.

"They switched to paper tickets for a while, but those got torn or crumpled. That one token I just inserted carries the balance of my account with the casino," the stranger continued explaining. As she said that, her current available credit appeared on a small screen in the machine's front panel. The glowing green numbers showed an exorbitant sum.

"Wow! And you won all that?" Maybe Richelle was wrong about the casino's payouts.

The gambler's lips twitched. "Um, no. I didn't win it all. It's a total of your own credit, plus your winnings."

Elaine nodded, comprehending now. "So, if you don't mind me asking, how much are you ahead?"

"I'm not. I'm down about two hundred." The woman frowned.

"I'm sorry. It wasn't my business."

"Oh, it's quite all right. With me," the woman added. She glanced at the other patrons. "I wouldn't go around asking others the same thing, though. The Cosmic's been pretty tightfisted this trip. Almost no big wins at all on the slots. I know the odds, and I can afford to lose, but Nebula's got some very disgruntled players on board."

Behind them, a cheer arose, and Elaine cast a look over her shoulder. At the blackjack tables, Jay thrust a triumphant fist into the air, and Stephanie bounced on her toes, planting a smooch on his cheek. He rocked, barely capable of maintaining his seat in his inebriated condition.

"Except that guy. He's been winning at cards for three consecutive days." The woman huffed. "Some serious mojo working there."

Elaine thanked her for the information and headed for a different row. On one end, she found a token dispenser tailored for the Cosmic Casino. Bending slightly from the waist to bring her to the correct level, she resisted the urge to blink while a scanner passed over her right retina. A voice asked how much she'd like to transfer to the casino account, and she tapped in the amount on a tiny keypad. She suspected it was standard procedure, but it annoyed her when the device asked if she was sure she didn't want more. Rich or not, she didn't intend to go crazy in here. The machine spat out a token.

She grabbed it, picked a chair in front of an *Alien Invasion* slot, and seated herself. After waving to Stephanie to let her friend know where she was, she inserted her account chip, chose a reasonable amount to bet, and let the holographic wheels spin.

An hour later, she was out almost three hundred credits.

"Damn," she muttered under her breath, casting a glance toward the entrance. Richelle had appeared there, on and off, wandering who knew where for ten or twenty minutes before returning to check on her. Elaine pointed at her slot, shook her head, and stuck her tongue out at the machine. She couldn't hear Ricky's laugh in response, but she saw her, shoulders shaking as she chuckled at her.

Elaine had enough credit for one more big spin, and she raised one finger to Richelle, telling her this was it for her tonight. Hell, maybe for the remainder of the trip. She was rich, not stupid.

Richelle nodded, understanding her message. She hit the button and let the wheels turn.

One acid-spitting alien. Two acid-spitting aliens. Elaine held her breath as the third reel seemed to spin forever.

Acid-spitting alien number three stopped just short of the payout line.

Given the day she'd had, she wasn't surprised. She didn't look at Richelle, imagining her "I told you so" expression.

Elaine checked her account balance on the screen, sighed, and cashed out her disk containing a whole dollar and ninety-seven cents.

An old man clapped her on the shoulder, and she jolted in her seat. In her frustration, she hadn't noticed his approach. "Don't leave now, sweetheart. That machine's due."

"Then it's yours," Elaine said, standing. "I know when to quit." She retrieved her disk from the tray.

The well-dressed gentleman planted himself and inserted his own token, then began spinning the wheels—once, twice, nothing.

While Elaine maneuvered through the crowds of gamblers, she fumed a little at herself. She could certainly afford the losses, but throwing money away went against everything she'd been taught growing up. Still, it had been fun while it lasted, entertaining, and a good distraction from the earlier stress. She made her way over to Stephanie and Jay.

Jay's attention focused entirely upon the three-dimensional screen in front of him displaying his cards. Stephanie stood behind his right shoulder, keeping vigil. She offered Elaine a smile as she approached. "So, how'd you do?" Stephanie asked.

"Don't ask."

Stephanie gave Elaine a sympathetic pout. "Ouch. Sorry to hear that." She returned to watching blackjack.

"How's Jay doing?" This part of the casino was much quieter between the bursts of cheering. Card tables didn't play music or display dancing figures. The section held an air of class and seriousness, and when Elaine looked at the holographic chip displays and did the math, she understood why. The amounts bet staggered even her.

"Shh," Stephanie cautioned, though Elaine had whispered the question. Jay showed no sign of having heard her. "He's doing well, but he's superstitious about people asking. Thinks it brings bad luck."

"Right. Sorry."

She watched as Jay hauled in, virtually, a large number of additional chips. His thumbs had difficulty depressing the correct controls, with his coordination shot by alcohol, but he managed. He had two blackjacks in a row, which, judging from the muttered curses among the other players, didn't happen often in the game.

"No real cards?"

Stephanie hooked her arm around Elaine's. "Not in a legitimate casino. You only see plastic cards in home games. You've been reading too many old books."

"So I've heard," Elaine said dryly.

"Computer-generated hands are more random than any card shuffler, human or mechanical, could ever be. Jay's just a genius."

"He's counting?"

Stephanie slapped her playfully on the arm. "Of course not. Nobody could count with this automated system. He's psychic. That's what I think, at least. Nothing else explains what he does."

Elaine had never played blackjack, but she understood the basic rules. From what she could tell, Jay took foolish risks, made absurd bets, gambled against the odds, and drank a lot. The more alcohol he imbibed, the more insane his moves became. When he had a twenty and split the two cards, then got two more tens for two twenties, then asked for a third card on each of them, Elaine thought he'd lost his mind. Gasps arose from the other players.

When the auto-dealer dropped two aces on him for two blackjacks in the same deal, one young man leaned back too far in his chair and nearly toppled from it. A casino host appeared at the player's elbow to steady the sputtering gambler.

Elaine didn't believe in psychic abilities. Jay Grego cheated. Or the casino fixed the game for him. Jay held great influence with his THI connections. It wouldn't have surprised her to learn the casino's win/loss programming favored Jay. And she wasn't the only one who thought so.

"This is bullshit!" the young man who'd fallen shouted. He wavered where he now stood, and Elaine noted the empty glass beside his place at the table. She wondered how many had preceded it. Drinking and card playing. Popular and stupid.

A second host, the one manning the blackjack table and overseeing the equipment, locked the system down and scooted out from behind the carved mahogany surface. Two hosts flanking the irate guest didn't change his attitude in the slightest.

"Sir, it's a game of some skill, but predominantly chance. Mr. Grego has had good fortune." The senior host—Elaine could tell by an extra gold pip on his collar—studied Jay's face for a long minute before turning back to the other player. "Phenomenal fortune. But it's all luck, just the same. Perhaps yours will turn soon."

The angry gambler didn't wait for a shift in the winds of fortune. He took an awkward, drunken swing at Jay, failed to connect, then shoved the host away from him. "Either he's cheating, or you're fixing it for him!" The crewman stumbled into a cocktail waitress, knocking her tray from her hands and sending liquid and glasses flying. She, in turn, hit the gaming table.

She groaned, rubbing her hip, but to her professional credit, clamped her lips down on the curses Elaine felt sure she wanted to utter.

Elaine never realized ship's security could move so fast, but they must have kept a particular eye on potential hot spots like the casino. A lack of THI emitters didn't mean other cameras didn't focus on the Cosmic. Three burly men arrived, two seizing the inebriated man by his arms, the third blocking other guests from involving themselves.

But the brawler had a friend, who chose that moment to appear from between two rows of slots. "What the fuck's going on?"

And he was drunker than his buddy. Great.

IF SHE'D been the violent sort, Richelle would have strangled whomever came up with the rule to leave emitters out of the casino.

Yes, Nebula had good reasons for the precaution. Word got around of a crooked casino and a corporation found itself the target of dozens of lawsuits. But drinking, gambling, losing… those elements bred tension. Richelle found that tension bred aggression in biological beings.

In any beings.

Cursing her THI nature, she paced the entrance, willing ship's security to get things under control quickly. Silently, she urged Elaine to get the hell out of there, to get to her so she could stop feeling so damn helpless.

CHAPTER 17
THI STORY

WHERE THE blackjack player was thin and wiry, his friend was built like an armored hovercar, complete with tree-trunk legs and upper arms whose muscles strained the fabric of his gray T-shirt. He stalked around the table, attempted to heave one of the chairs at the crewmen holding his pal, then frowned in consternation when he realized the seat was bolted to the deck.

Big on brawn, not so much on brains.

The other players scattered, including Elaine and Stephanie, who ducked behind the security guards, but the angry newcomer stood between them and the main entrance/exit. Card tables blocked them on the right,

slots on the left. There had to be another way out somewhere, in case of emergency, and Elaine scanned the
walls, searching for it, just as hovercar-man roared and
threw himself at the two guards holding his friend between them.

Surprised by the bold move, all four went down
into a pile of kicking limbs and swinging fists. A stray
leg caught Elaine's calf, and she hit the floor, curling
herself around the bruised limb. She rubbed at it in-
effectually, then crawled on hands and knees to put
some distance between herself and the focal point of
the struggle.

Stephanie reached a hand to help her up, but Elaine
waved her down to join her. The fight had stirred up
other flying objects: bits of broken glass, ice cubes—
even the waitress's tray. Lower was safer. Several other players decided the same thing, because a lot more
of Earth's wealthy and elite were suddenly crawling
across the casino carpet like crabs.

Small shards nicked Elaine's palms, and she felt a
few pierce her slacks, but she kept going.

They paused to signal to Jay but couldn't get his
attention. He showed some smarts by staying out of
the altercation but got involved anyway when someone
kicked up the dropped drink tray and it nailed him, edge
first, in the face. Jay flew backward, hit the floor hard,
and lay there moaning. Stephanie covered her mouth
with her hand. "Oooh, that had to hurt," she managed
between her fingers.

"First aid will patch him up," Elaine assured her,
tugging on her arm. "Come on!" The brawl had shifted away from blocking the route to the main entrance,
and Elaine picked her way toward it, avoiding the broken glass and wet spots as best she could. Stephanie

hesitated a brief second, then followed right on her heels, literally. Friendship and self-preservation overruled lust any day.

She saw Richelle pacing outside the archway like a caged tiger. Her eyes darted from the combatants to Elaine, and her hands beckoned for her to hurry.

Another roar made Elaine cast a quick look over her shoulder, just in time to see the larger guest disentangle himself from the guards and gain his feet. He reached for one of the blackjack card screens, attempting to wrench it loose from the table. He met with more success than he had with the chair. While the seat had been bolted, the screen remained connected by nothing but cabling. Still, it was thick cabling. Screws had been ripped free, but he couldn't fully disconnect it.

Elaine continued to crawl, shaking her head. *Give it up, pal. Not much on a starliner that isn't tied down.* One never knew when gravity might fail, and the last thing the crew and passengers needed was a lot of floating debris.

More security personnel arrived from within the depths of the casino, wherever that secondary exit was. These held stunsticks extended before them, electrical charge sparking from the tips in bright blue-white. No guns.

Elaine hurried, not wanting to get caught in the strike zone. She heard the zap-pop of the sticks, followed by several howls of masculine pain, then thuds and groans. By the time Richelle pulled her to her feet in the corridor, the guards had subdued the disgruntled blackjack player and his friend.

"Well, that was exciting!" Stephanie exclaimed, standing and brushing bits of glass and carpet fuzz from her pale blue pantsuit.

"Are you all right?" Richelle held Elaine at arms' length, examining her from head to toe. Her eyes pierced Elaine with their intensity. The tightness of Ricky's expression startled her.

"I'm fine." Elaine broke one arm free of Ricky's grasp to rub her right calf. "Though I might need some ice."

"Plenty of that back on the floor in there." Stephanie laughed. "Wouldn't advise going for it, though."

"What about Jay?" Elaine scanned the casino for him. If she leaned far to the right, she could make him out around the slot rows. He'd sat up, but from the way he rocked, he was still pretty woozy. She didn't know if it was from the flying drink tray or the alcohol he'd consumed.

"He's a big boy." Stephanie thought about that comment and laughed. "A very big boy."

Damn if Elaine didn't blush again.

"He can take care of himself. And I'll baby him later." She winked while Elaine banished images of oversized diapers, baby bottles, and rattles from her mind. Not Stephanie's style. At least not that she knew of.

They did wait until security dragged out the troublemakers and first aid escorted Jay out in a hoverchair. No surprise he was arguing. "I don't need observation. I'm fine." He didn't look fine. His skin tone had turned a not-so-lovely shade of green.

A white-uniformed older woman with graying hair kept a restraining hand on his shoulder. "Sir, you have a large bump on your forehead. You're dizzy and nauseated, and while I determine if that's from alcohol or a concussion, you're spending a night in the infirmary. Our insurance bills are high enough."

As if to punctuate her statements, Jay gagged, then threw up over the side of the hoverchair. The medic's assistant, wearing gloves to avoid rad exposure, got a sickbag in front of Jay's face in the nick of time, then wrinkled his nose at the acrid stench rising from it. Jay straightened, leaned back, and closed his eyes.

"You want me to bring you anything from the cabin?" Stephanie asked, hurrying to keep pace with the trio. Richelle and Elaine trailed them, well out of projectile vomit range.

The cabin? So Jay had moved into Stephanie's, or vice versa. They really had gotten close during this voyage.

"We have pajamas, robes, and complimentary slippers, along with all the essential toiletries. He'll be quite comfortable," the medic assured her.

Resigned to his fate, Jay caught Stephanie's wrist. "I don't need anything. Just be sure to sleep in my cabin tonight." His eyes darted over his shoulder to Richelle and Elaine, who'd heard every word. He'd whispered but wasn't modulating his volume, not with the amount he'd imbibed.

Elaine wasn't sure what emotion she saw there. Nervousness? No, stronger than that.

"Without you?" Stephanie pouted. Pouting was her specialty.

"I… I want to picture you there. I'll comm you after I get settled, and we can… talk."

Elaine rolled her eyes, imagining what that conversation would consist of and how he'd maintain his privacy in a public place like the infirmary. Or whether he would care. Ew.

"I'm heading back right now."

They broke into two groups at the bank of lifts, Jay and the medics taking one down to the first aid center and Stephanie, Richelle, and Elaine returning to the VIP level. There they parted again, and Stephanie disappeared into Jay's suite a few doors down from Elaine's.

Elaine held Richelle's hand, though Ricky's grip lacked its usual warmth. Something bothered her, and Elaine could guess what.

"I'm fine. Really," Elaine attempted to reassure her. The tightness in Ricky's jaw muscles said it wasn't working.

The service elevator at the opposite end of the corridor opened, and a waiter appeared with a bucket of ice. Uncanny timing. Richelle took it from him while Elaine tipped the young man. He scurried back to the lift.

Elaine cocked an eyebrow at the ice. "You?"

Richelle nodded. "Being hooked into the ship's systems has its advantages. I ordered the ice while we were on our way up here." Her expression soured as she nodded toward the bucket she carried. "Least I could do." With an emphasis on least.

"It's more than that. It's thoughtful and kind."

And human.

She used her code key to open the hatch and led the way into her suite.

"It's practical." Ricky went to reach for a towel hanging on a rack in the bathroom. Her arm disappeared from elbow to fingertips. "Dammit!"

Wrapping her hands around Ricky's bicep, she drew her fully within range of her room's emitters. The rest of her arm reappeared. Standing on tiptoe, Elaine stretched to kiss her, but she pulled away.

"No more." Richelle stalked into the sitting area.

Exhaling her disappointment, Elaine snagged her own towel, wrapped some ice from Richelle's discarded bucket in it, and pressed the bundle to her leg. "No more what?" She seated herself on the couch, noting that Ricky took an armchair. To avoid sitting next to her?

"No more befriending you. No more seducing you. I don't care what I'm programmed to do or what I want to do. I can't keep doing it."

"And why not?" A trickle of icy water escaped the towel and ran down her leg. She brushed it away. Outside the porthole, the stars flashed past. The *Nebula* moved within its bent space, hurtling toward its next destination.

"Because I can't protect you!" Ricky said, as if explaining the alphabet to a small child. "I couldn't on Gratitude. I couldn't in the casino. Hell, I couldn't even hand you a fucking towel!"

Well, programming safeguards were definitely off, judging by her profanity usage. Either that or she'd overcome them, which wouldn't surprise Elaine at all.

She pointed a finger at Ricky. "You did perfectly fine on Eris Station."

"Dumb luck."

Elaine shrugged. "All right. So you're… geographically impaired. Lots of people have limitations. It doesn't mean no one can love them. And I love you."

Richelle froze in place for a long moment, during which she barely even breathed. Her chin rose slowly from her chest. She stared at Elaine, brown eyes analyzing her features. Tiny tendrils of hope crept into her expression.

"I love you," Elaine repeated, "and somehow, we'll work with what we have." She wrapped each word in warmth, as much to reassure herself as Ricky.

Ricky's breath caught. Her eyes widened. She had to have overheard Elaine's confession of love for her to Lazaro, but hearing it spoken from her own lips was apparently an entirely different matter. A rush of pleasure passed through Elaine that she was able to affect Ricky this way. It was a type of power she'd never really experienced before.

"You can truly love me? Despite me being a construct? A hologram?"

She smiled. "You're more than that," she said, echoing words Richelle had spoken to her that first night, only a couple of days past but so long ago.

Elaine placed the makeshift icepack on the table with careful precision, rose, and took Ricky's hands. She pulled Ricky from the chair and drew her into the bedroom. Elaine wanted to take the initiative, not be led around as Harriet had led her—a kite on Harry's string.

The lights came up upon their entry, but Elaine ordered them to dim to a more romantic level. She brought Richelle to the bed, turning her so that the backs of Ricky's knees bumped its edge and she sank down to sit on the mattress. Then she unbuttoned Ricky's shirt, one frustrating button at a time.

Elaine's hands shook, and her fingers slipped, trying to force the tiny disks through their holes. She wanted this, but the dominant position was unfamiliar. Powerful, but strange. When she'd revealed several inches of perfect skin on Ricky's bare chest, she ran her fingertips down it, eliciting a shiver from her. Ricky's hands, resting on Elaine's hips, tightened their grip and drew her closer.

Ricky raised her eyes to Elaine's, and Elaine leaned down, allowing herself to be taken into a passionate kiss. Elaine's lips parted, and Ricky teased her with her tongue until Elaine's heart pounded and they both had to pull back for breath.

While they kissed, Ricky had worked Elaine's silk shirt from the waistband of her slacks.

Richelle slipped her hands beneath the fabric, and the contact of her hot touch on Elaine's slightly cooler skin sent a shock wave through Elaine. She gasped softly, and Ricky slid her fingers up her rib cage, then traced each individual rib.

"El," she whispered, her voice rough like gravel.

She liked that shortening of her name. Preferred it. In her rare playful moments, Harriet insisted on calling her "Lanie." She hated that nickname. Made her sound like a child.

There was nothing childish about her right now.

While Elaine fumbled with the buckle at the front of Richelle's belt, Ricky deftly reached around her and unhooked her bra. The woman had skills. Without the restraint, her breasts were easy access for Ricky's hands, and her thumbs moved to tease Elaine's already erect nipples.

For a long moment, she allowed herself to indulge in the pleasure, tilting her head back and closing her eyes. Her fingers fell still while Ricky toyed with her. Her already pounding heart further increased its rate, and her chest rose and fell with her heavy breath. The moisture forming between her legs amazed her. Her breasts had never been this sensitive to another woman's touch before. But no other woman had ever cared so much about pleasing her.

She brought herself back to the world.

"I'm having a little trouble," she admitted.

"Hmm?" Richelle glanced up sharply, a flash of hurt in her eyes.

"Oh no. I mean with your belt."

She blinked in confusion, then the tension seemed to rush from her rigid features as she grasped Elaine's meaning, and she smiled. "I could make it disappear," she suggested.

"Or you could just stand up for a minute."

Richelle obliged, her hands remaining on Elaine's breasts. Without the awkward positioning, Elaine made short work of the buckle. Ricky shrugged out of her shirt while she had the opportunity and threw it into a corner.

Elaine unfastened Ricky's trousers, then knelt, drawing the pants and underwear down with her. Ricky kicked off her shoes and stepped out of the garments. Elaine tossed those aside as well.

Richelle was more than ready for her, the soft brown triangle of curls between her legs damp and shiny in the dim light, and Elaine for her, but Elaine's sadistic side desired to torture Ricky as Ricky had teased her. Elaine pulled her closer, then placed her lips at the juncture of her thighs, just covering her most sensitive spot. Ricky's groan rumbled from her throat to her heels. Elaine felt and heard it in the same instance, and it thrilled her.

Richelle pulled away from her mouth to draw Elaine's shirt over her head. Elaine tossed her bra into the shadows. Ricky knelt beside her on the plush carpeting and reached behind her, unbuckling Elaine's favorite leather sandals from her ankles, then traced a sensuous finger over each instep. No ticklishness. Only pleasure followed in the wake of her strokes. An indicator of trust, perhaps? Elaine sighed contentedly.

Wriggling out of her own pants proved more awkward, and she wormed her way from the restrictive material, shifting her legs forward and kicking them off with a burst of nervous laughter. Clothed in nothing but black lace panties, she watched Ricky's eyes rove over her from head to toe.

"You are beautiful," Richelle breathed.

"I'm average."

She shook her head at Elaine's self-deprecation. "If you are average, then I am very attracted to average."

The pronouncement made Elaine flush.

Ricky kissed her again, long and slow and deep. The warmth between Elaine's legs increased tenfold.

"Will you sit on the bed?"

Richelle didn't order. She asked. Elaine liked that. A lot.

She complied, seating herself on the edge as Ricky had done before, her bare toes brushing the carpet.

Still on the floor, Richelle crept toward her. She reached beneath Elaine, lifting her hips enough to draw her damp undergarment down and off. Then she lowered her mouth to the juncture of her thighs.

She tasted and teased and tickled. Elaine's response was explosive, faster than she'd thought possible. She leaned back, palms pressed into the mattress, leaving deep indentations, raising her hips in time to the motions of Ricky's lips and tongue. She scooted herself closer to the edge, spreading her legs wider to more fully accommodate her. All traces of inhibition fled as her whimpers filled the room.

Richelle seemed to know exactly what she needed and how and when she needed it. Her fluttering tongue drove her to her peak, and the strength in Elaine's arms gave out as she came, dropping her flat on the bed in a gasping heap.

Crawling onto the bed, Richelle drew her up with her so Elaine's head rested on a pillow. Ricky's palms massaged Elaine's heaving breasts, then teased the tips. Elaine's arousal returned full force and fast.

Richelle snagged a second pillow and slipped it beneath Elaine to raise her hips comfortably. Her warm hands eased Elaine's legs apart, and Ricky fit herself between them.

Using her whole palm, Ricky rubbed against her, creating delicious friction that sparked the gamut of sensations radiating outward from her core. Ricky knew exactly where and when to apply pressure, when to tease, and when to slowly, gradually, enter her with two fingers, burying them deep. Sex with a THI had lots of advantages, especially with this one and all her self-awareness and beautiful empathy.

And, perfect example of that empathy, Ricky sensed Elaine's sudden tension, the tightening of her internal muscles, the way her hips rose to meet Ricky's thrusts. Ricky's delicious motions stilled, making her want to wrench Ricky to her, pull her deeper inside, and writhe against her clever fingers.

"Everything all right?" Ricky asked, concern etched in her face.

"Very. But if you stop again, I'm going to hurt you."

The warmth of Richelle's laughter enveloped Elaine like a blanket. And with the heat rising off Elaine's body, an additional increase in temperature might make her spontaneously combust.

Ricky focused her attention once more, this time entering her with quick, playful, tantalizing strokes that had Elaine's body twitching and bucking beneath her.

She was so wet, Ricky's fingers slid in and out easily, gliding and stroking, her sex grasping on to them, not wanting to let them go. No performance issues with a THI, no arm cramps or tiredness—so, selective realism? Ricky could go on until she wore Elaine out and seemed determined to do so. Ricky's mouth found hers, gentle kisses tasting her lips, then her cheeks and closed eyelids. Her simulated breath came heavily, rustling Elaine's hair and tickling her earlobe. Ricky straddled Elaine's bare thigh, pressing her sex into the sweat-dampened skin, Ricky's eyes scrunched closed in concentration as she ground against Elaine.

When Ricky drove three fingers into her, filling her completely, she moaned. Elaine rarely moaned, but she couldn't deny it. And she did it again. And again, crying out as her thrusts carried her closer and closer. Richelle, she discovered, was a fairly silent lover, but Ricky's heart pounded and her breath came raggedly, and that told Elaine all she needed to know.

When they came together, she uttered something guttural and animal-like and unintelligible, while Richelle whispered three words—"Elaine, thank you."

IN HER multiple terms as a THI, Richelle had never before experienced bliss—the complete joining between two biological beings moving beyond the purely sexual and transcending to something greater, deeper. Elaine drained her energy but filled her spirit, her soul, her essence. It was all she could have hoped for and all the more poignant for its precious fragility, its potential to come crashing to an abrupt end at the termination of the voyage.

She languished in the literal afterglow, her project-ed tangible image wrapped in a soft, pulsing light while she recharged, Elaine snoring softly beside her.

Richelle's perception shifted.

One moment she had the comfort of the mattress be-neath her, the next she free-floated in the ship's generator, disembodied once again. No warning. No explanation.

All around her other strings of code, other THI programs, ran away into the distance, visible to her in their complexity, some more complex than others, first a few, then dozens.

She spotted Fzzd among them, and despite herself, she had to ask, *What is it? What's happening?*

Fzzd's sarcasm rang through in reds and oranges. *What's always happening? They've shut us down with-out warning. Who the hell knows why? Who the hell cares? We're objects to them, remember? No need to consult us.*

We're objects because they don't know we're more, and the council won't let us tell them otherwise, Richelle shot back, smug in blues and greens.

Fzzd ignored her, swirling away. *If you want to know their reasons, investigate for yourself. I'm draw-ing power while I can.*

But Fzzd couldn't, any more than Richelle could tap into the ship's emitters. The crew had shut the sys-tems down, reserving only enough energy to keep their programs stored and intact.

After the night of exquisite and intense sensory input she'd had, Richelle had now been struck deaf, dumb, and blind to the outside world.

She tested access point after access point. Trial and error would lead her to a pathway she could follow.

She hoped.

CHAPTER 18
THE BIG REVEAL

INSTEAD OF awakening encircled by Richelle's arms, wrapped in the easy languor of satisfying sex, the sound of screaming alarms jolted Elaine from sleep. The noise startled her so much that she rolled off the bed and hit the carpet with a dull thud. Panic gripped her. For a few horrible seconds, she was back in the access tube, the air hissing through the breach, her life seeping away with it.

Then her mind registered the rug beneath her fingertips. She pushed herself to her knees and scrambled to her feet.

"Ricky?" She bit down on her shriek of the name. Her gaze darted from corner to corner, taking in the empty bedroom. Even Ricky's clothes had vanished from the corner where they'd tossed them, though hers remained.

Still naked, she raced to the sitting area, going so far as to check the bathroom, though she knew she couldn't be in there. No sign of her. The sirens wailed, rising and falling, pulsing behind her eyes. She felt tired and disoriented, lacking in sleep. A glance at the wall chronometer showed nothing more than a black, lifeless panel, so she had no idea of the time. In fact, all the lights seemed dimmer, not just the bedroom ones she'd lowered earlier—those were now off—but all of them. And the few giving any glow tended to flicker.

It was then she noticed other details. The siren blasts didn't come in the "abandon ship" pattern she'd learned during her predeparture tour. The rumble of the *Nebula*'s engines pressed harder on her senses, vibrating her already strained nerves, humming in her eardrums as if the vessel was taxing its drives, pushing them to their fullest speeds. The starliner raced toward something.

Or ran away from it.

The alarms cut off midwail, leaving her in startling silence followed by an uncustomary pop-hiss in the shipboard public address system. The voice emanating from the speakers was calm, but she detected an undercurrent of stress.

"Ladies and gentlemen, the captain requests that all passengers remain in their cabins with the hatches sealed for their own safety."

Elaine flashed back on the conversation she'd had with Stephanie about pirates. Pirates that might base themselves on Gratitude. They were only a day out of Gratitude and hadn't engaged the singularity drive for the next leg to the asteroid belt. The timing made sense for an attack. She wondered if the men who'd attacked her on the surface had been pirates.

"All but emergency power is temporarily channeled to the sub-light engines. We are broadcasting a distress signal to any other ships in range. Please remain calm." The voice paused before adding words that sent a chill up Elaine's spine. "This is not a drill. Repeat, this is not a drill." In the background, Elaine thought she could detect shouted orders and a number of muffled curses. The announcement must have come from the bridge. Another unusually loud crackle of static signified the closing of the channel.

Well, that explained Richelle's absence. If the engine drew from the *Nebula*'s power source, and it was running above norms, little energy would be left for anything beyond emergency lighting, artificial gravity, and life support. THIs fell under the "frivolous entertainment" label, no matter how invaluable Richelle had proved to preserving Elaine's life.

Alone or not, she knew she'd feel better facing an emergency while wearing some clothing. If they did call for evacuation, she didn't want to run through the ship stark naked. Elaine returned to the dark bedroom, using the minimal starlight coming through the porthole to shift the clothes in the drawers until she thought she found something that matched. A nervous laugh escaped her. As a teen, her mother often complained she looked like she'd dressed in the dark. Elaine hauled on designer jeans, a navy T-shirt, and a black jacket, in case environmental systems fluctuated and the temperature dropped. Her favorite black faux-suede boots slipped easily on her feet.

She also grabbed her antique wristwatch from
the nightstand with quick and silent thanks to her
great-grandmother for leaving it to her. Hand-held
comps displayed the time, and everybody carried one.
But her pocket-comp, lying on the table as well, had a
black screen. In all the heated excitement with Richelle,
she'd forgotten to charge it, and she wouldn't be able to
tap the ship's energy with it now.

A quick touch lit the face of the archaic timepiece.
Four a.m. All traces of sleepiness and disorientation
had been dispelled by the adrenaline rush.

Now what?

A repeat of the earlier announcement blocked out
all other sound, along with a warning that to preserve
power, it would not be repeated a third time. Stay in
your cabins. Keep the hatches sealed.

Bullshit.

With Richelle, she might have done as asked.
Alone was a different story. She paced the living area,
trying to convince herself to stay put and failing. If the
Nebula was about to face a pirate attack, she wasn't
going to ride it out cowering by herself in a corner of
her cabin until the bad guys found her. And Stephanie
would be equally alone, since Jay was in the infirmary
and all the THIs were off. Spunk and bluster and in-
dependence aside, Stephanie would be as terrified as
she was.

Not.

Stephanie could face down a rival corporation's
top executive without blinking an eye. No, he could not
get in to see Harriet without an appointment. A small
smile tugged at Elaine's lips at the memory. Pirates
might just cower in the face of Stephanie.

Didn't change the fact that Elaine was quaking in her boots. She was not dealing with this alone. She'd just cross the hall, she told herself. Then they'd seal themselves in Jay's cabin, following the captain's orders.

Elaine went to the hatch and palmed the opening plate. Nothing. Not even a whir of the mechanisms in the wall. A rectangular panel beside the plate had a thumbnail latch, and she flipped it open. Inside she spotted a lever labeled with a barely readable sign: "Manual Override." She reached in and wrapped her hand around it, then pulled down. The hatch released with a series of clicks and a hiss and shifted a couple of inches until she could see the corridor beyond through the crack.

Hoping it wouldn't suddenly seal and crush her fingers, she gripped the edge and hauled with all her strength. Not enough. It moved another four inches, wide enough to get a foot through, but not the rest of her.

Elaine scanned the cabin, searching for something to use as a lever. She tried grabbing the inoperative floor lamp, to find its base secured to the deck. Every piece of furniture was either too heavy or bolted down.

The ship had effectively trapped her.

A shudder passed through the *Nebula*, then a stronger jolt that threw Elaine to the deck. Something had hit the ship. Worse, the engine whine declined in pitch and intensity. The room darkened further as a gray shape outside blocked the light filtering in the porthole—another vessel pacing the starliner, but this one bristled with weaponry.

Elaine wondered if the captain had really thought he could outrun the pirates. All that effort and expended energy for nothing.

More impacts rang through the hull, battering the *Nebula* from side to side as the ship slowed. In the bedroom, she heard several thunks and a thud, probably from her luggage rolling around. Her toiletries fell from the bathroom shelves. A glass shattered on the tile. Deep in the bowels of the starliner, an explosion thundered. Then the engines died—a sudden absence of vibration and subliminal sound. Elaine remained on her hands and knees, not even attempting to gain her feet amid the chaos. She heard no return fire from the *Nebula*. She didn't even think the tourist vessel had weapons, only defensive shields.

And unless those shields operated on some backup power source, they went down with the engines. The pirates could board.

The hatch to her cabin was open.

Shit, shit, shit.

Elaine placed her palms on the metal, leaning all her weight on it, trying to push it shut. Her thoughts strayed to Stephanie, but with the pirates practically on her doorstep, she wasn't going anywhere but a dark corner of her own cabin. She strained, shifted, used her shoulder when her hands chafed. The door had jammed in place.

Tears of frustration streamed down her cheeks. She panted from the exertion, then pounded a fist on the hatch before throwing her back against it.

The extinguishing of the few remaining lights tore an angry scream from her throat.

Without the interference of visual input, her ears detected more familiar sounds—those associated with the attachment of a boarding tube from one ship to another.

Her harsh breathing and the beating of her pulse were all that kept her company in the blackness. They were insufficient.

"El?"

Richelle's voice made her sob with relief. Elaine bolted upright, but the lack of ambient light meant Ricky was impossible to see. Elaine's forehead connected with hard bone—*Ricky's* forehead—and Elaine jerked back, knocking her own skull on the door. Richelle's hand slid between her head and the metal, cushioning and rubbing until the pain faded.

"How? How are you here? The captain shut down the THIs."

Her chuckle filled the room with pleasant sound. "We've already established I'm not the best at following rules. Once the engines went down, there was enough power available for me to tap into some reserves. I simply used that power to piggyback on some emergency systems, override the lockdowns, and activate the emitters where you were present."

"And the others?" She thought of Stephanie, alone. If the John program were running, it would give her some company and potential protection, even if it couldn't kill.

The shadow beside her shook its head. "I didn't want to draw too much on the system. They're frantic on the bridge right now, not paying attention to the Ixani generator, but if they notice, they could make it difficult for me." Taking her hands, Richelle pulled Elaine to stand with her.

"Ixani?"

An uncomfortable pause. She heard Ricky shift her weight.

"That's our… that's the name of the alien race from Gratitude. The ones who invented the generators."

Elaine had never heard the name before. Maybe the archaeologists had uncovered new records, translated new information. Richelle might have picked that up while the *Nebula* held orbit around Gratitude.

Or maybe not.

"Ricky?" Elaine's voice sounded loud and accusing in the relative silence. She didn't mean it to be and tried again, lowering it to a whisper. "Are you an Ixani?"

More awkward silence. Then, "Does it matter?"

Elaine considered that. Alien or THI, the feelings mattered most, and they'd shared a lot of them over the past few days. "No. No, it doesn't."

Ricky's exhalation of relief blew stray strands of hair off Elaine's cheek.

"But I hope you'll tell me about it sometime. Not because it makes a difference, but because I care," Elaine added.

"When we're out of this current mess."

"Agreed."

Richelle moved to the hatch, nudging Elaine aside. "So, in or out?"

Out meant possible capture by pirates. Of course, so did in. She didn't want to think about how they might treat female prisoners. And if they discovered her identity, it could become much worse. Ransom entered the realm of options, and she wondered if, given her recent encounters, this attack on the *Nebula* was a mere coincidence.

The universe doesn't revolve around you, Elaine.

Right. Except when it does.

But there was Stephanie to consider, and Jay, whether Elaine liked him or not. She had to believe the three of them would be safer with Richelle's protection than without it, and though Ricky certainly didn't want to, she had proven she *could* kill, if necessary.

"Out. We need to get Stephanie from Jay's cabin."

She thought Richelle nodded. Hard to tell in the dark. A minute later she heard the grind and screech of Ricky manually forcing the hatch open, and now she noticed a dim red glow seeping in from the corridor. The cabin lights were out, but the hallway emergency lighting still functioned. It must have activated within the last few moments. The red strips lining floor and ceiling made everything look drenched in blood. Lovely.

As soon as the space widened enough, Elaine slipped through. Richelle's form shimmered and thinned a couple of inches so she could follow. She re-formed fully once in the hall. No blue decontaminators operating. They'd be too much of a power drain, and who gave a crap about rads when you were about to be killed or captured by pirates? Elaine started down the empty corridor toward Jay's cabin, but her companion's words stopped her.

"She's not in there."

Elaine turned to her. Ricky's eyes had that unfocused look Elaine had come to associate with her tapping into the ship's systems. The frown on Ricky's face concerned her. "What's wrong?"

"Not sure," she admitted, her attention elsewhere. "With most of the emitters deactivated, I used a DNA scanner to find her. It located her in her own suite."

"No big surprise. Stephanie doesn't often do what men tell her. She probably preferred being surrounded by her own things, with her clothes and makeup and all within easy reach."

"Maybe…." Richelle didn't sound convinced.

"What?" They'd crossed the hall and stood in front of Stephanie's hatch. Richelle fiddled with a wall panel, prying off the covering to get at the circuitry beneath. No manual override on this side of the door, for situations just like this. But if one wanted to take the time, it could, apparently, be hot-wired.

"I'm tracing an auto-call by the room's maintenance program. Her emitters went down two days ago. Stephanie didn't report the problem; the system did. It sent a repair request to the engineering department. There's no record of a team being dispatched up here, but the problem is tagged as 'fixed.'" Richelle fiddled with the wires in the bulkhead. Small arcs of electricity coursed between her fingertips and the door circuitry, providing power where she needed it to make the hatch function. Elaine watched over her shoulder, marveling at how Ricky knew what went where. The coated conduits were probably different colors for clarity, but in this emergency light they all looked like they wore varying shades of red or appeared black.

While she worked, Elaine considered her words. It didn't make sense. Stephanie never settled for shoddy service. If her emitters failed, she would have been quick to complain. Of course, if she'd slept in Jay's room for several days, maybe Stephanie simply hadn't known about the failure. But that didn't wash either, if she were in her suite now.

The *Nebula* shuddered. She recognized the vibration as the final connecting lock of a boarding tube. Elaine clamped a hand on Richelle's shoulder, urging her to hurry.

Unfazed, she continued working. "Something else," she mumbled, holding a thin cable between her teeth while her hands gripped two more. "She cancelled maid service for the past two days."

A pit of nausea formed in Elaine's stomach. That was definitely not like Stephanie. In college, Stephanie's dorm room always looked like a hurricane had hit it. She might labor over personal grooming, but she hated housework. She'd hired a daily cleaning service for her New York flat as soon as she could afford one. Stephanie would never opt to make her own bed or pick up after herself if she'd already paid maids to do it for her.

"We need to get in there."

"Hey, look at this!" Richelle pointed to one of the red wires.

At first, Elaine didn't notice anything unusual. Then she saw the scorch mark, tiny but there. Stooping, she retrieved the cover panel Richelle had dropped. Scratches marred its edges—from regular maintenance, or someone prying it off recently?

"Got it!"

The hatch gave up the battle with a metallic groan and slid an inch to the side. Richelle shoved it another foot or so, and a shaft of the hallway's red light cut a swath across the foyer and sitting room. The rest of Stephanie's suite was as dark as Elaine's had been—darker, since it was an inside stateroom without a viewport to the stars beyond. But that wasn't its most notable sensory feature.

That would have been the smell.

CHAPTER 19
PRESUMED
NOT SO INNOCENT

THE ODOR reminded Elaine of the time the Kane mansion's meat freezer had gone on the fritz and no one had noticed for several weeks. Harriet had taken her on one of her Leviathan business trips. When they returned, Harry wanted to try the new European diet her overseas contacts had raved about, which included no meats of any kind, and she put Elaine and the entire house staff on the same restrictions. Harriet was so thoughtful that way, always concerned about everyone's good health—and the money she'd save instituting a vegetarian menu. However, she couldn't withstand the temptation.

When Harriet's carnivorous urges prevailed, she'd asked the chef for a steak. The smell upon opening the broken freezer had permeated the entire three-story home.

Confined to a smaller space, this was much, much worse.

Elaine gagged, swallowing bile.

"I've got one of the suite's emitters running. Wait here," Richelle instructed her.

"No."

Even with Elaine's hand pressed against her nose and mouth, Ricky understood the strangled word, and she shook her head. "I'm certain this isn't something you want to see."

In response, Elaine pushed past her to stand in the marble foyer identical to the one in her own suite. A second later, Richelle joined her.

"Can you push the hatch wider, give me more light?" She paced the small space, fidgeting in the semidark.

"Elaine...."

"Just do it, dammit!"

Richelle complied, shoving the hatch all the way into its bulkhead slot. Elaine scanned the room, searching, searching. Her eyes touched upon the matching furnishings, the table, chairs, and sofa, the standing floor lamp, and rested on a bulky shadow in the far corner that didn't match anything in her own cabin. She started forward, but Richelle caught her by the shoulder and held her in place. This was one time she would have appreciated a little less initiative from the THI/alien.

"You're here. That's enough. Let me check it out."
Richelle's intensity bored a hole through her stubborn-
ness. Elaine nodded.

She watched Richelle cross the dark interior, her
enhanced vision able to see more than Elaine's mere
human eyes. "I'm not…. It's not possible," Richelle
stammered. Her head turned to the floor lamp. After
a moment it flared to life, returning normal light to
the room.

The light was the only normal thing about the
scene it revealed.

Stephanie, or what remained of her, sat in the corner, her knees tucked to her chest, her arms fallen to
the sides, her head lolling. The body bore two gunshot
wounds, one in the upper chest, another in the temple.
A large pool of semidry blood surrounded the corpse,
staining the dark blue carpet almost black. Bits and
pieces of skull and brain matter made tiny islands in the
viscous mess and matted her once gorgeous blond hair.
Elaine recognized the patches of gore for what they
were. Harriet's murder had taught her much.

Elaine crumpled, her knees hitting the carpet before she knew she'd fallen. She vomited, adding more
stains to the floor covering, then wiped her mouth with
the back of her hand. Richelle made no move to touch
her, instead crouching just outside the blood radius to
examine Stephanie further.

"God. Steph…." Elaine's throat constricted.

"Impossible," Ricky whispered.

"What?" Elaine spit to clear away the last of the
bitter taste. "Steph's dead. Someone killed her. What's
impossible about that?" She had her thoughts as to who
did it as well. Jay Grego came first and foremost to

mind. How hard would it have been for him to escape the infirmary?

"The condition of the body, the smell," Richelle said, by way of explanation.

"I wish you'd draw a little less attention to it." If she didn't get out of the stifling cabin soon, she'd be sick again. And now that she focused on it, her friend's suite was unusually warm, as if the environmental controls had failed along with the emitters.

Richelle noticed the same thing. "Tampering with the disks must have damaged the air circulation in here as well."

Elaine began gagging anew. "Out. I need to get…." She staggered to her feet and stumbled into the corridor. She crossed her arms over her chest, shivering with near shock, and leaned against the bulkhead for support.

Richelle followed, then waited while Elaine drew several breaths of fresher air. Once she'd composed herself, Ricky fixed her with a serious expression. "Elaine, she's been dead at least a couple of days."

She knew that. Her first impression when she entered the suite had told her that. Why was Richelle so focused on…? Oh. The timing.

Even with the wall behind her, Elaine's body wavered as she pieced together the clues Richelle fed her. Bits fell into place, the only rational explanation, and her vision blurred. "A THI," she breathed. "We've been socializing with a THI. Dinner? The casino?"

"Likely longer than that."

"But the casino… no emitters…."

"I don't know."

Elaine should have known. How could she have missed it?

Then again, they hadn't spent that much time together, with Stephanie focused on Jay and Elaine busy with Richelle. And the Stephanie THI would have been programmed to respond as Stephanie would have.

She turned an accusing glare on Richelle. "I don't look behind my best friend's right ear, but how could you not have recognized it? Can't you all sense each other?" She didn't intend to shout, but it came out that way.

A moment later, Ricky's arms enveloped her in a warm embrace. She rocked and held her, murmuring soothing and unintelligible words into her hair. "I'm sorry, El."

El. That's what Stephanie always called her, the only one other than Ricky who did. It made her sob harder until she soaked the front of Richelle's shirt. And she still didn't have her explanation. "How?" she demanded, though she sounded like a mewling kitten. She cleared her throat and tried again. "Is someone interfering with you, like on Eris Station when they followed us?"

"Not that I'm aware of. I think we've been socializing with one of Biotech's supposedly experimental portable models."

That would explain the casino.

But the portables weren't active yet, still in the testing stages, according to Jay Grego.

So he lied. "Grego killed her?"

"Looks that way, unless he's a THI as well, and a third party is pulling the strings," Richelle agreed, rising with her and tugging her a few steps down the corridor. "I don't want to assume. It might be someone else on board, a programmer using Biotech equipment, but the evidence points that way. He has the technical

access and is a disgruntled former Leviathan employee, correct?"

Richelle had done her research. Elaine cocked an
eyebrow at her, and a tiny smile forced its way through
her tears. "Your alter ego did a lot of detective films?"

Ricky returned the smile. "After the musical cir-
cuit? A television series, actually. And most episodes
emphasized that standing out in the open with a murderer still on the loose is a bad idea." She looked mean-
ingfully at the hatchway into Stephanie's suite.

Elaine felt what little blood remained there drain
from her face. "No."

"The killer won't know we found the body. What
reason would he have to come back? And if there is
a connection to the pirates, he might tell them not to
search here."

"No," Elaine repeated with more force. Her arms
and legs trembled. Without Richelle's hand on her elbow, she would have fallen. "I can't. I can't go back in
there." Last time she'd been near a dead body too long,
she'd passed out. That wouldn't do anyone any good.

Richelle's jaw clenched with the effort of not continuing the argument, but she nodded. She cast a glance
over her shoulder at the lamplight glowing from the
suite's entry, which then extinguished itself, and followed Elaine toward the elevator. No alarms rang on
this level, but Elaine thought she could make them out
from lower decks, along with loud cracks of electrical
energy.

"What is that sound?"

"Stunsticks," Richelle confirmed, tilting her head
to listen. "Interstellar piracy's weapon of choice. No
one uses lasers or projectile weapons on a starship."

Elaine pointed to Stephanie's still-open doorway. "Someone did."

"Someone doesn't do a lot of killing. Though a stray bullet in an interior stateroom would do less damage than, say, in yours on the hull." Her expression turned grim. "But a ricochet might have killed the killer."

"Pity."

"He used the weapon he had at hand and picked this location because he had the technological know-how to deactivate the room's systems and hide the body. Convenience over safety precautions."

"So, where do we hide? My cabin?"

She shook her head. "I hold little faith in coincidence. This pirate attack is too convenient. They're here to kill or capture you, and if THIs were allowed to bet, I'd lay odds that Grego's in league with them." Richelle changed their direction and pulled Elaine toward the service elevator instead of the main one, avoiding the open-air walkway across the atrium.

But why? Elaine understood why Grego might have hated her late spouse. Harriet had fired him, after all. But Elaine? She'd had nothing to do with it. And Stephanie? Maybe Stephanie figured out what Jay was planning and got in the way. Or maybe he'd intended to use the THI of Stephanie to kill Elaine at a later point. She couldn't wrap her brain around this personal vendetta, and it didn't look like she was going to anytime soon.

They'd almost reached the service lift when the snap-hiss of a manual hatch release carried along the corridor. A familiar figure stepped out of a cabin a few doors back—Jay Grego's cabin, and the figure was Stephanie.

Oblivious to Elaine's disgust and hatred at seeing this caricature of her dead friend, Stephanie raised a hand and waved. Her face held the perfect mixture of fear over the pirate attack and relief at finding friends in the hallway. Then her eyes focused on Richelle, and she frowned. "I thought the THIs were shut down. I tried calling for John to keep me company, but nothing happened. Then the power failed, and I wasn't going to sit there alone in the dark." She sounded like Stephanie, full of willfulness, prone to impetuous action. Then again, she always had. The impostor took a few steps toward Richelle and Elaine, then stopped, glancing from one to the other uncertainly.

"The THI shutdown didn't seem to affect *you*," Elaine growled.

"What? El, what are you talking about?"

"Do *not* call me that."

"I don't understand." "Stephanie" kept searching their faces, confusion evident in every blink of her eyes.

Could the THI really not know what it was? Did it think it was the real Stephanie?

The shadow of her friend looked back toward her own stateroom, focusing on the open doorway. When it returned its attention to Elaine and Richelle, its demeanor had changed. All traces of Stephanie's warmth and humor vanished, replaced by a cold, accusatory stare.

"You weren't supposed to go in there."

The chilling tone made Elaine's flesh crawl with invisible insects. Richelle shifted to stand between them. Peering around her, Elaine saw Stephanie take up a fighting stance. Her friend had enjoyed self-defense classes at the local gym. Her knowledge of positions wasn't surprising, but the complete change in attitude was. Seeing the open hatch must have triggered some programming subroutine.

Richelle gave Elaine a gentle nudge. "Get to the lift. They'll be operational in case the captain has to order an 'abandon ship.' Take it down to the crew areas. Find someplace to hide."

"I'm not leaving you."

"I'm better equipped to handle this than you are. And I can locate you anywhere."

Stephanie gave them no further time for debate as she launched herself at Richelle, slamming full force into her torso and taking both her and Elaine to the floor.

Twisting and shoving, Elaine managed to squirm from beneath the two THIs. She remained on all fours until she crawled the few feet to the service elevator, then stretched a palm up to slap the call panel. Sitting on the floor, leaning against the bulkhead, she watched the battle unfold.

It didn't last long.

Richelle possessed superior fighting skills. Guided as she was by an actual consciousness, and not dependent upon preprogrammed commands alone, she could adjust to and counter every move Stephanie made. She could also manipulate her strength and form, whereas Stephanie apparently only had the real Stephanie's body weight and muscles to work with, and Richelle increased her musculature to slam Stephanie face-first into the metal wall.

Richelle's sense of honor did not extend to murderous THIs or a killer's THI flunky, whichever Stephanie turned out to be.

Elaine expected to see the realistic flow of blood from Stephanie's nose and mouth, but expectation didn't quite smother the pang of sympathy she experienced for this image of her friend. A quick mental flash on the real Stephanie's double gunshot wounds dispersed it, however.

Flipping Stephanie so she faced her, Richelle pinned the rogue THI against the wall with her arm across Stephanie's neck. "If I kill you, you know you'll die a death that looks and feels as real as any human's."

Oh God. Richelle had *felt* her own death on Gratitude. Elaine thought she might be ill again. Ricky had *died* for her. Her love and respect increased twentyfold.

"Or you can choose to shut down and disperse." Ricky finished her ultimatum.

Stephanie squirmed in her grip. "You won't kill me. THIs can't kill." Her wide eyes betrayed her doubts.

Richelle inclined her head in the direction of the real Stephanie's suite. "*You* did. Who's to say I haven't been similarly altered?" When Stephanie continued to hesitate, Richelle pointed a free hand at the dead emitters lining the corridor. "I'm functional. I shouldn't be. That ought to tell you enough. Besides, *you* aren't a life-form. Killing you would be like turning off a light switch. Nothing more."

Stephanie acted like her human counterpart one last time as she pouted. "*I* didn't kill anyone. I just made it possible."

A moment later, before she could explain further, the Stephanie THI vanished in a sparkling of particles. A single onyx disk dropped to the floor, hit on its edge, and rolled to bump against the toe of Elaine's boot.

Elaine palmed it. It weighed more than others she'd held, and had more facets to its glossy black surface. A shadow blocked her view—Richelle leaning over to examine the portable emitter.

"Impressive." Ricky plucked it from Elaine's hand and held it to one of the red light strips, turning the disk over in the ruby glow. "Humanity has improved upon Ixani technology. Your people might not fully understand it, but you're doing more with it than we could." She passed it back and closed Elaine's fingers around it. "Keep this safe. It might prove useful later."

"Are you able to access it?"

"I think I—" The sound of two sets of elevator doors sliding open cut her off. The first noises carried from the main lift, far down the hall and across the atrium walkway, but in the otherwise empty corridor, the hiss of hydraulics echoed.

Elaine craned her neck over Richelle's shoulder. A quartet of rough-looking men in gray coveralls and bearing shockrifles clustered in the narrow space. They'd seen action already, judging from the sweat on their brows and the reddish-brown streaks on their clothing. One sported a bleeding gash in his right leg.

The foursome leaned out, taking in their surroundings and scanning for opposition. They hadn't seen Richelle and Elaine, hidden in the long shadows of the dimly lit hall, so they stepped onto the crosswalk over the atrium. While the rest of the elite level had been reduced to emergency power, the atrium core remained fully illuminated. Elaine didn't know if this was due to security reasons or bad design. She only knew it made the pirates sitting ducks. Stranded sitting ducks, as the lift closed behind them and the indicators above it showed it moving to the lower decks.

At almost the same moment, the door on the service elevator slid aside, sending Elaine stumbling backward when the panel she'd been leaning on vanished. One of the two ship's security officers within came close to stunning her with his wand, the sparking weapon flashing over her shoulder in front of her face, but he caught her between his outstretched arms instead. While their attention focused on Elaine, Richelle took the opportunity to disappear.

"Get behind us!" the officer holding her shouted, shoving Elaine to the rear of the service elevator.

The pirates had seen them and came charging across the atrium walkway, eager to gain a more defensible position. Or eager to get Elaine.

Probably both.

In addition to being a direct-contact weapon, the stun wands could fire beams at a target. Arcs of blue-and-white electricity met in static-crackling bursts as shockrifle blasts clashed with the nonlethal stunning energy.

Dammit, what was taking the doors so long to close? Did the energy passing the threshold keep them open?

The security officers' weapons were designed to subdue opposition—drunken passengers, the occasional brawl, disgruntled gamblers. They did no permanent damage. Permanent damage did terrible things to a starliner's insurance ratings and legal costs, not to mention repeat guest satisfaction.

Shockrifles (and shocksticks, shockwhips, and other similar devices) were a different matter. Depending upon the setting, a direct hit from a blast of the white energy could result in anything from unconsciousness to complete neural failure. The beams streaking across the darkness toward them didn't blind Elaine with their brightness. Elaine could only hope that meant the weapons were set on low.

No one carried projectile weapons. On the upside, nothing they used here would penetrate the hull. On the downside, it meant none of the pirates were stupid. She also noted a couple of nonconventional weapons— things that looked like laser drills and stone pulverizers, both emitting tight, cautious beams for close-in fighting, and both more common to miners than pirates. So the theory had been correct. Miners had been recruited to bolster the pirate ranks.

Or these weren't real pirates at all.

Semantics. If they committed piracy, in Elaine's mind, they were pirates, but it was definitely something to consider later.

Dodging the blue stun blasts, the pirates made a run for the two open cabins, Elaine's and Stephanie's, using the doorways for cover while the security personnel kept to the inside of the service elevator. A slap of one's palm against the controls continued to hold the doors open so they could exchange fire, but no one was hitting anyone.

This would have been a good time for Richelle to appear and provide one of her distractions, but Elaine knew why she'd departed. The captain had shut down THI functions. If anyone saw Ricky strolling around, they'd know she had special abilities. Besides, Elaine felt certain if the pirates got too close, Richelle would find a way to intervene, her secret skills and personal safety be damned.

The invaders shouted back and forth across the hallway, urging each other to make a charge on the elevator. Elaine's little group held the upper hand, since all they had to do was close the doors and escape to lower levels. But that left all the other passengers on the elite level at the pirates' mercy. And ship's security's job was to stop the pirates, not just rescue Elaine.

Of course, if Elaine's assumptions were correct, the pirates weren't interested in the other passengers.

"We should take this guest to safety," one of her protectors argued.

The second cast a glare in Elaine's direction. "She should have stayed in her cabin like the captain ordered. She's safe enough for the moment. Our instructions are to take out this team."

This team? So there were more pirates elsewhere? She guessed it made sense. The vessel that had run the *Nebula* to a halt looked large enough to carry dozens of attackers.

"We're not taking out anything with these pop guns," the first complained.

"The senior officers got all the good stuff."

Elaine understood the bitterness in the crewman's voice. She was feeling more than a little of it herself. But she wished they'd goddamn shut up and concentrate on fighting.

A single melodic chime indicated the return of the passenger lift across the atrium. The arrival light turned green. All eyes focused on the sealed doors. One side or the other was getting reinforcements.

WHATEVER MODIFICATIONS the humans had made to the Ixani technology to create the fully portable THI emitter had Richelle flummoxed. She flowed through it, ignoring several other quiescent programs in stand-by mode, searching for a good place to store herself without having to merge with other data, which might corrupt her "Richelle" form.

Except the damn thing kept trying to take her apart and shut her down. The portable emitter could handle multiple programs, but not two running at the same time, and the Stephanie persona was still active, if not being projected. Richelle could sense her, complex but emotionless and taking up precious storage space.

Too much storage space, in fact, as Richelle discovered when the Stephanie code attempted to overwrite her own.

It caught Richelle by surprise, chipping away miniscule pieces of her character: a song lyric here, a dance step there, before she recognized the danger. Minor losses, but more than Richelle wanted to part with, and she threw up a protective shell of nonsense data to prevent herself from losing further integrity.

Thoughts blurred as she drew on the emitter's power supply, draining it faster than it could replenish itself, and it occurred to her, if she didn't outsmart Stephanie's code and release herself from the portable emitter at the risk of public detection, she might find herself irretrievably erased.

And all the effort she'd gone through to win Elaine's heart erased right along with her.

CHAPTER 20
THE (FALSELY) ACCUSED

RELIEF FLOODED Elaine as white-uniformed *Nebula* crew poured from the elevator and stormed the walkway. A couple took minor hits from the shockrifles, but their comrades yanked them out of the line of fire, and the sheer numbers of security personnel overwhelmed the four pirates in minutes.

Elaine blinked to clear vision blinded by electrical blasts and sagged against the lift wall. The younger of her two original protectors placed a comforting hand on her shoulder. "We'll have you below shortly, ma'am."

"What about the rest of the ship?"

He frowned. "There's fighting on several levels, but we've got secure areas where guests stranded outside their staterooms are being kept safe." His wink softened the mild rebuke.

It wouldn't have bothered Elaine, regardless. She knew if she'd stayed in her suite, she might be a prisoner, or a victim, of the pirates by now.

Her companion's partner returned from where he'd been consulting with the other security team. He stepped into the elevator, palm poised to close the doors, when a shout stopped him. "Flores, hold it! Stop that lift!" His hand froze over the panel.

One of the security guards, a woman carrying both a stun wand and a much more dangerous shockrifle, jogged toward the service elevator. Her uniform had multiple collar pips, more than Flores, who stood beside Elaine, grumbling under his breath.

"I need to get her to the ballroom so she'll be safe and we can continue the sweep," Flores complained.

The newcomer fixed Elaine with a piercing stare, scanning her from head to boots. Elaine recognized her now. She'd been in the theater during Elaine's argument with Denise Lazaro. "You need to get her to the brig."

"What!" Elaine's shout rivaled Flores's.

The officer pointed toward Stephanie's open doorway, then at Elaine's. "Her friend's body's in there. Not the boarders' doing. She's been dead for days. And wealth and power don't excuse murder. Until we get rid of the pirates and sort all this out, Ms. Kane's staying locked up." The woman's mouth twisted in a sarcastic smile. "For now, call it 'protective custody.'"

EACH TIME Richelle stepped outside her self-made bubble, the Stephanie pattern emerged, a snake ready to strike as she'd been in her fabricated "life," oblivious, nonsentient, but deadly nonetheless.

Richelle's plan to immediately return to Elaine thwarted, she drew on the disk's miniaturized generator, biding her time until she had the strength to wipe out "Stephanie" once and for all, and all the while wondering what the hell was going on in the biological world beyond her onyx prison.

NO MATTER how much Elaine protested, nothing could dissuade the guards from escorting her to the holding cells in the *Nebula*'s security section. By starting the fight with Lazaro, she'd made the security officer's life difficult. And Elaine had had other "incidents" during this cruise.

Yep. The officer was returning the favor.

While the other security guards continued the fight on the elite level, the officer and Flores stayed with Elaine. The service lift dropped through the levels of the ship on a steady whir of Leviathan-made technology. At intervals, Elaine heard electrical weapons' fire exchanged beyond the sliding metal doors. She cringed to think what might happen if stray energy hit the lift's controls.

The numbers on the floor indicator blinked downward, lower than they went in the passenger elevator, dropping into crew-only areas. According to the ship's schematic on the elevator wall, the rear of the bottommost floor was reserved for security.

When motion ceased and the doors slid aside, a featureless metal corridor greeted Elaine. Nebula Starlines wasted no funds on behind-the-scenes sections. The uncarpeted deck echoed as her two escorts marched her down the hall. The bulkheads lacked any sort of art-work or decor, and the absence of soundproofing meant voices carried from every open hatch.

Here, battery-operated white lights had been strung every few feet to augment the emergency light-ing and aid vigilance of the prisoners. The glare made Elaine blink away vision spots after her long period in the darkness of the upper areas.

Effectively flanked, she allowed her guards to guide her through the third door on the right. They passed a desk where another security officer raised a quizzical eyebrow at Elaine, then looked quickly away at the chief's snapped order to open the inner hatch.

Once inside the holding area, Elaine faced a nar-row corridor with two cells on either side. Transparent energy fields prevented occupants from escaping. A column of blinking green lights at each cell's entrance indicated functioning barriers. The two on the left and the first on the right held burly men wearing the same gray coveralls she'd seen upstairs, and she drew back, fearing security might throw her in with the pirates. A glance at the chief's face confirmed she was consider-ing doing just that.

Hoots and catcalls erupted when the pirates no-ticed her. Elaine tried to suppress a shiver and failed.

As if reading her thoughts, Flores laid a comfort-ing hand on her shoulder and said more loudly than necessary, "Don't worry, ma'am. Innocent until proven guilty and all that. We wouldn't put the owner of Levi-athan in with them. Right, Chief?"

Oh, nicely played, Flores. Thank you.

The security chief growled an affirmative, and they opened the fourth and last cell for her private occupancy. "Don't forget to search her." The chief left, boots stomping back the way they'd come, but Flores lingered.

He patted her down, hesitating a moment over the emitter he found in her pocket, then let her keep it. THIs had been shut down. The emitter shouldn't work. There was no reason to take it from her.

"There just isn't time for a formal investigation right now," he said with a sympathetic smile. He stood aside to let her pass into the cell. "If we had another secure area, we'd put you there, but we aren't set up for holding a lot of prisoners, and you already showed you could override a stateroom door."

"You sure you'll defeat them?" The force field barrier between the cell and the access corridor flared to life, separating Elaine from freedom. She had visions of being trapped in the holding area as the boarders took control—a nice little package ready for them to ransom or kill.

Flores pursed his lips, and Elaine noticed how young the crewman was. Early twenties at most, with red hair and a fading case of acne. Probably fresh out of college, maybe his first starliner posting. "We'll do our best, ma'am."

She wished he sounded more convincing.

She wished it even more when he retreated down the corridor and disappeared through the door into the security office beyond.

The moment the hatch closed, the pirates leered and whistled, made lewd gestures and comments. Not a woman among them, and Elaine didn't wonder why.

Any woman gritty enough for piracy wouldn't put up with such behavior.

Her thoughts wandered to the shadowy woman she'd spotted on the hovercycle on Gratitude. She paced the length of the small space while calculating times and distances. It could have been the Stephanie THI. Once Elaine's own transport had run out of power and she'd had to hoof it, "Stephanie" could easily have overtaken her, caught the shuttle that departed right before hers, and beaten her back to the *Nebula*.

Which meant these pirates had been after her, and in more ways than their lascivious gestures indicated.

Elaine blocked out the noise and examined her surroundings. Sparse to say the least. One cot, one plastic chair, overhead fluorescent lighting. An alcove in the rear hid a toilet and sink, and again she was reminded that despite the inconvenience, this wasn't as bad as the real prison cells she'd seen in vids. Real criminals didn't rate privacy due to risk of suicide, but these cells hadn't been designed for real criminals, just unruly guests. Basic necessities. No frills, no decontaminators (crew and prisoners apparently didn't rate them), but more than she expected.

She guessed the most common prisoners they got down here were drunk guests who'd gone too far. The partiers would sleep it off in relative comfort and return to their cabins in the morning. Nebula would want to contain them without humiliating or inconveniencing them too much. Such things hurt repeat business.

She wondered if the containment was sufficient to hold pirates for an extended stay.

Her eyes swept the walls and corners. No emitters.

Elaine slipped into the bathroom corner, peered out to make certain she couldn't be seen from the other cells, and shoved her fingers into the tight pocket of her jeans. She drew out the onyx disk confiscated from the Stephanie facsimile—the prototype emitter. The question was, who would appear—Richelle or Stephanie?

CHAPTER 21
HONEY, I SHRUNK THE THI

PLACING THE disk on the floor in front of her, Elaine pressed her back against the cell wall. The sanitary area didn't have much space. Whatever activated the emitter would fill the rest of the narrow alcove. Her hands curled into fists. If Stephanie reassembled herself, Elaine planned to take her apart.

She watched and waited. For a long moment, nothing happened.

"Hey, honey, need some help in there? Doing your makeup? Fixing your hair?" one of the pirates in the cell across the way called. The rest howled in response.

The disk jumped.

Elaine jerked, banging her shoulder on the metal wall. Her next instinct was to grab hold of the disk, but as it bounced, then ricocheted off the partition, she discarded that idea.

While she stood and stared, the emitter danced about the deck plates, pinging a metallic tone with each hit, rebounding off anything it struck—the toilet, the sink, and once even the ceiling.

"What the hell you doin' in there?" one of the pirates shouted, his words mocking.

Elaine wished she knew.

She imagined a battle waged within the device, Richelle versus Stephanie. THI against THI. She could guess the eventual outcome. Richelle possessed independent thought and strategic creativity. But she held her breath as the twitching disk came to rest at her feet once more.

A pair of shoes appeared, one on either side of the emitter. Brown loafers.

Elaine exhaled.

She had to admit, watching Richelle materialize from nothingness made her a little uncomfortable. Ricky tended to do this where Elaine couldn't see it and then walk into the room. With the portable, she emerged inch by inch, working from the footwear up to the top of her shaggy-haired head. In the midst of the reappearance, the emitter vanished, absorbed by the image it produced and concealed within it.

Once whole, her body stood before Elaine, chest heaving with the effort of reconstruction. Ricky's eyes darted about the alcove, taking in their situation at a glance. Then she closed the tiny space between them and enveloped Elaine in her arms. She felt Ricky tremble.

"Are you all right?" Elaine whispered.

"Will be. Two programs feeding off one power source makes things a little tricky. I need to recharge a bit." She kept her voice low. "I'm sorry I had to—" she began, but Elaine cut her off.

"Don't. Don't even start that again. You needed to go so you'd be here now. The crewmen had things well in hand, and I'm probably in the safest place on this ship."

Richelle cocked her head, and her lips turned upward. "And the least likely place any pirate still free would search for you." She pulled away but kept her hands on Elaine's arms. "I never took you for the 'look on the bright side' type."

"Your influence."

The smile broadened. "So, we stay here until security drives off the pirates, turn over Jay Grego for murder, and get you home."

The reminder of Stephanie's death brought mist to Elaine's eyes, but she wiped it away on her jacket sleeve. She could mourn later, after Grego paid for what he'd done.

A hiss of a hatch release carried from the end of the access corridor. Someone had entered the cell block. "Wait here," Elaine whispered, reaching to press a finger to Richelle's lips. Ricky surprised her by kissing it. Elaine smiled.

The noise level in the cells had risen, shouts and applause replacing curses and grumbles. Not good.

Elaine leaned out, expecting to see a contingent of pirates waiting outside her compartment.

Instead, she saw Jay Grego. And he looked much too pleased to see her.

His black trousers and gray shirt still bore wrinkles from the casino altercation, and he sported a deep purple bruise on his forehead, but his casual stance and wide grin demonstrated his complete control of his current circumstances and not a trace of his earlier inebriation.

Elaine opened her mouth to scream.

"Don't bother," Jay told her. He held up something in his right hand.

It was another hand. A woman's hand.

"The guard outside was kind enough to go to sleep, and the security officer I bribed earlier generously donated this." At least that explained why the security officer had held such a grudge against her. Grego paid her to.

Elaine screamed anyway. And continued screaming while Grego pressed the disembodied palm against an access plate outside the force shield. The scanner within ran a red beam over the skin covering the palm and fingers while the imprisoned pirates hollered encouragements and praise. All the energy fields dissipated. Pirates poured out of their cells.

Grego dropped the guard's severed hand and pulled a hold-out shockpistol from the back of his trousers. His comrades formed a semicircle around him. They leered at Elaine. She ducked back into the alcove with Richelle, who wrapped a protective arm over her trembling shoulders.

"Penoir, you take care of her. Callahan, you let him out when he's done."

Despite her terror, Elaine felt rage building. "What's the matter, Jay?" she shouted past the thin privacy wall. "Can't shoot me yourself? I'll bet you had the Stephanie THI kill Stephanie too. Coward."

"Practical," he corrected her. "Sadly, though, this time I had to do the job myself. THIs can't kill."

Not normal ones, anyway.

Jay brushed a hand on his trousers, wiping away imaginary blood. "Disgusting business, killing. Shouldn't have had to dirty my hands with it. I prefer to leave such things to my… associates."

Sounded like something Harriet would have said right before getting the board of directors to clean house in a low-profit department at Leviathan.

Grego continued issuing orders to his men. "The rest of you will head for the upper decks and help the others. Take some jewelry, raid the liquor stores, shoot a couple of random passengers—whatever it is pirates normally do. I want this to look like a random pillaging, not a planned hit. I'll meet you on the *Guillotine.*"

A chorus of "Aye, sir" and similar acknowledgments answered Grego's commands, and a stampede of boots retreated down the corridor and through the still-open hatch, followed by another pair sauntering casually behind them. The hatch clanged shut.

Which left Penoir and Callahan.

A single set of footsteps came within the cell, and the sound of the energy field reforming crackled across the confined area. "This time, make sure she's really dead. Ms. Kane has as many lives as a fucking cat." The repellent shield distorted the words, so that must have been the pirate on the outside of the cell speaking.

"This pussy's stuck in a box. She's on the last of her nine lives."

Elaine recognized both voices. She'd heard them on Gratitude.

Boots approached the alcove. The one called Penoir turned the corner and met Richelle's fist with his bearded face. The pirate went sprawling back into the main area of the cell.

"What the hell?" shouted Callahan from the entrance. "You let a little girl—"

One hand covering his bleeding mouth, Penoir rolled to his side and then his feet. "No' th' gir," he snarled through broken teeth. "She'th got comp'ny. Tha' damn THI."

So, they'd figured out what Richelle was, at least partially. So much for that advantage.

"No way, man." Callahan backed away from his pal's dripping blood, though Elaine didn't know if he was squeamish or feared rad transference. "No emitters down here. You been hitting the Four D again?"

Four D was a popular hallucinogenic sold on the black market. Stephanie had tried it once. She said it made everything clearer than in three dimensions, right before it knocked her on her ass.

"No more hiding," Richelle growled, taking a step from behind the partition. Elaine followed, watching both pirates' eyes widen. Penoir's arm jerked.

"Watch out!"

The bleeding bearded pirate brought up the shockpistol and fired a whining bolt of deadly energy that caught Richelle square in the chest. Electricity met electricity in a flare of light flashing white, then green. A stench like burned sulfur filled the air. Elaine screamed in fury as the center of Richelle's torso evaporated, leaving a hole Elaine could easily have put her head through. She spotted Callahan's laughing face on the far side of the gap.

The pirate took a step forward, still laughing, free hand clenching and unclenching as if he imagined Elaine's throat in his grasp.

The laughter faded. Blood vessels, heart, lungs, ribs, skin, and finally the white button-down shirt reformed and solidified. Not just a THI. An alien, Elaine reminded herself.

Richelle faced Elaine, reassuring her with a smile. As Ricky turned back to their assailant, that smile lost its humor, showing all her perfect, white, even teeth.

"My turn."

Penoir scrambled over the tile floor on his backside, trying to put as much distance between them as possible. He didn't get far.

Richelle closed her eyes and took a slow, steady breath, seeming to draw power from within. She raised one arm toward the flattened pirate, palm out. A white-hot glow formed at her hand's center, growing and increasing in brightness. Like a professional pitcher with the major leagues, she pulled back, then hurled the ball of crackling energy at the pirate's midsection.

It hit dead center and spread from there, sparks racing along the lengths of the man's limbs, then back to his abdomen. Everywhere the charge traveled, the pirate's muscles spasmed, as if in the clutches of a seizure. He writhed across the decking, skull and heels cracking in a macabre rhythm with each involuntary jerk of his body. Elaine could make out the details of his skeletal frame wherever clothing didn't cover him. The pistol went skittering over the floor. Four steps brought Elaine to it, and she grabbed the gun and pointed it at Penoir.

She needn't have bothered.

When the body ceased its motion, the pirate's tongue hung out of his mouth, thick and blackened. His eyes bulged from their sockets.

She and Richelle turned away in unison toward the cell's force field barrier and the wide-eyed pirate staring at them from beyond it. The one called Callahan had a pistol of his own, but it hung at his side, the hand holding it trembling violently. "Not possible," Elaine heard him muttering over and over. "Not fucking possible. No emitters, no THIs. Not possible." He ran his fingers through his dirty blond hair. The pirate didn't know about the portables.

She'd seen similar behavior from the patients at an asylum she'd visited doing charity work.

In shock or not, Elaine wasn't taking any chances with the remaining pirate. And she'd had enough of being the target. Time to acquire a few targets of her own. She raised her confiscated weapon. Richelle grabbed her wrist. "Wait," she cautioned, indicating the force shield. "It'll bounce off." She sounded weary but shrugged off Elaine's concerned look.

Straightening her shoulders, Richelle strolled to the energy barrier… and then took a step through it.

Callahan screamed, dropped his pistol, and ran. Elaine heard the hatch at the end of the corridor open and close. When the noise of the hissing seal ceased, Richelle sagged against the strip of wall between two cells.

"Hey!" Elaine stood at the cell entrance, helpless to offer assistance, trapped until Ricky released her.

"I'm all right. Just… need a minute." She shifted, bending forward, leaning with her palms on her knees. Her spine rose and fell with her labored breathing.

"You need to let me out so I can help."

Ricky's head turned, but her eyes stared through Elaine, as if Ricky couldn't comprehend her words.

"The barrier, Ricky. Lower the barrier." Sooner or later, Callahan would find some of his buddies and they'd return in force. The window of escape was closing fast.

Richelle shuffled forward, each step an obvious strain. She didn't bother with the guard's severed hand. Instead, she moved to the panel beside the cell, pointed a finger at it, and zapped it with a streak of blue energy. Sparks flew from the bulkhead, showering the floor and her clothing, leaving a scattering of scorch marks on the fabric.

The force shield flared, and Elaine threw up a hand to protect her vision. When she peeked between her fingers, the glow had vanished.

She rushed to Richelle's side, tucked her stolen pistol in her jacket pocket, and grabbed Richelle around the waist as her knees buckled. "What's wrong? What can I do?" she asked her, struggling with her weight. "I don't suppose you could make yourself lighter."

"Any deviation from my programmed parameters is an effort with this portable emitter." Ricky spoke through clenched teeth. "Your people's technology is very impressive, but it doesn't have quite the power of the Ixani generators." She drew an unsteady breath. Elaine didn't care for the way it wheezed in her chest. "If I don't overly exert myself, I'll regain strength over time."

Elaine wished she could give her that time, but they couldn't afford it. Together, they made their way to the hatch.

"How did you do that? The energy blast, the force field, the panel?" She propped Ricky up while she popped the hatch open. The pirate had been in too much of a hurry and didn't reengage the security locks.

Elaine listened a moment at the opening before determining no one occupied the outer office. Then they stepped through.

And found the dead guard and the dismembered security officer.

Richelle tried to turn her from the body sprawled in front of the desk and the charred, bloodied mess staining the swivel chair and the floor around it, but she lacked the strength. Jay Grego or one of his lackeys had fired so much electrical charge into the security officer, she'd cooked in her own fluids. Then, judging from the cauterization of the wound, they'd used a low-level laser to slice off the hand.

Elaine couldn't stop staring at the stump. Her breath came fast and uneven. The room blurred at the edges.

"Energy knows energy," Richelle said.

Her voice broke Elaine's morbid focus. "What?"

"You wanted to know how I did it. Look at me." Ricky's tone commanded, and Elaine obeyed, turning from the corpses, allowing Ricky to distract her. Elaine's eyes met hers. She sank into their safety. "Energy knows energy," Ricky repeated, nudging her toward the exterior corridor with her hip.

Somehow they avoided every droplet of gore. She let Ricky guide her, though she supported more than half Ricky's weight. Ricky needed her. Elaine would hold it together. Somehow.

"That's how I walked through the barrier. I blended with its energy."

No one occupied the hallway outside the cell block. They headed for the service elevators. A faint scent of smoke wafted from the overhead vents. That couldn't be good. Fire in space had to fill the nightmares of every spacefarer. Fire, like a hull breach, ate up a ship's most precious commodity—oxygen. And fire had the bonus of doing all sorts of other damage as well. Elaine tried to ignore signs that something aboard was burning. "Is that what you... the Ixani... are? Energy?"

"Essentially. It would be hard to explain." Ricky paused, seeming lost in thought.

Elaine called for the lift, breathing a sigh of relief when the indicator lights showed its approach.

Richelle tried again. "For me, describing how my people exist would be like you defining the human soul. It's difficult to put in words."

Soul. Elaine tried to make the mental comparison. She didn't doubt Richelle possessed one. Elaine had accepted her as an alternate form of intelligent life. The difficulty lay in understanding how she functioned, but it didn't really matter, did it? "And the weapon? The panel?"

Richelle used one hand to gesture at her weakened body. "The result is what you see. I took from my *self*, my essence, to produce the power to attack that pirate and open the force field. The generators will replenish me immediately, and once we're back within emitter range, I'll make use of them. Until then, I am, shall we say, drained."

Two more levels and the lift would arrive. Elaine resisted the urge to tap her foot. "One more question, and then I'll stop pestering you."

The twinkle in Ricky's eye was weak but still present. "You aren't pestering. I'm glad you care enough to ask."

That earned a smile but didn't stop her curiosity. "Why didn't you use that energy ball when we were fighting the muggers on Eris Station, or the thugs on Gratitude?"

She had the decency to look sheepish. "Out on the water, I wasn't sure what effects that much energy might have on the wave runners. I didn't want to blow out the engine and strand us, though that ended up being what happened to you for different reasons. And on Eris Station, I thought the creature I morphed into was bad enough."

Elaine shivered at the memory. Richelle noted it and nodded.

"See?" she continued. "It still bothers you. But at least I could explain it within the realm of being a THI. At that point in our relationship, I didn't think you were ready to find out I'm an alternate form of life."

She had a point.

The lift arrived, and she summoned the strength to push Elaine behind her before the doors slid apart. But it didn't open. Elaine exchanged a quizzical look with Richelle.

"Jammed?"

"Possibly. The *Nebula* has sustained significant damage."

Elaine didn't like the implications of that. "How significant?"

Richelle ignored her, gripping the edges of the doors and prying them apart. Elaine helped, adding her minimal muscles to the effort. Something in the mechanism popped. The elevator opened, and several things occurred simultaneously.

Billows of smoke rolled out of the lift, flooding the hallway with an acrid stench.

A body fell out after it—the pirate who'd fled the cell block. He'd been leaning against the door, maybe trying to claw his way out. Blood stained his hands and clothing. Judging from the bulging eyes, open mouth, and the bluish color of his skin, he'd suffocated.

Elaine jumped back, trying to avoid contamination. She stopped, mentally shaking herself. Ridiculous to worry about rads at a time like this.

"I'll take care of it later, if you like," Richelle offered.

"What?"

"I can act as a decontaminator. I possess the proper energy signatures, only stronger than the human devices. That's why Ixani THI tech doesn't produce rads."

Something Elaine would need to ask her more about. If those properties could be applied to other technology, purely human-made technology, well, it would help preserve the human race. Not to mention making Leviathan an even bigger fortune.

An alarm echoed down the elevator shaft. They hadn't heard it with the doors closed, but it came through loud and clear now. Elaine recognized the "abandon ship" signal.

The lights went out. Again.

Well, shit.

"Ricky?" She choked on the single word, covering her mouth with one sleeve while groping for Richelle's hand in the darkness. The emergency lighting came on in the security hallway.

Clouds of smoke and red lights. She entered hell.

Richelle clasped her hand just as Elaine spotted her through her tearing vision. Elaine cast a glance toward the elevator. All the indicators had gone dim. No way was she getting in that deathtrap.

"Come on!" Richelle tugged her in the opposite direction. They hobbled together, as fast as Richelle's fatigue would allow, racing the flow of smoke. Once past the security area, they encountered doors that opened onto much less ornate berths—single bunks, simple wood furnishings, limited storage. Crew quarters.

Klaxons continued to sound, dull and distant. Someone had muted them in the crew areas. Crew were trained. They'd respond without all the insistent noise and could communicate better without it.

No sign of life. The crew had left in a hurry, strewing abandoned possessions about the interiors and the hallway.

They passed a branching corridor—a lifepod access hall Elaine remembered from her emergency training. It took a second to scan the indicator lights for the pods—all red, all launched. This area had been fully evacuated.

Elaine let Richelle drag her to a hatch marked Emergency Use Only, one of several they'd passed. By the time they got it open, her breath came in coughing, wheezing gasps, and lightheadedness threatened to send Elaine to her knees.

The sight behind the hatch did little to raise her hopes.

It opened on a narrow, circular space, its only feature a metal ladder leading up. The lights of the shaft were so far apart that every third rung fell in shadow. Maintenance workers didn't need the same amount of brightness as passengers, apparently. And to add to this route's lack of appeal, there were no emitters.

Richelle pulled her into the small space and sealed the hatch behind them, cutting off the inward flow of smoke. Elaine hauled several deep breaths of cleaner air into her lungs. The fire must have started in the aft section of the ship. At least there was no sign of it here around midship.

Aft section equaled engine room. Not good.

Richelle turned Elaine to face her. "You need to climb to at least level four. That's where you'll find the first of the escape pods. Forget about your assignment. Take a seat on the first one available. It will automatically launch when it's filled."

So much for the best-laid emergency plans. Then her instructions hit home. "You're talking like we're parting ways. Where will you be?" No chance she was leaving without Richelle. Elaine raised a hand to place on her arm. It passed through her. Elaine snatched her fingers away. "What's happening to you?"

Her half smile broke Elaine's heart. "I'm drained. I don't possess the substance to climb this ladder. I'd fall through the rungs." Even as she spoke, her form became less cohesive. Elaine could make out the lights on the wall behind her.

She was a projection, an image of her former self, like a character on a screen. Elaine didn't smile at the irony.

"That doesn't make sense. You're energy. Can't you just… I don't know… float up this tube?"

"It doesn't work that way. I need a compatible conduit. I can store myself in the portable emitter. Maybe I can rejoin you later."

She didn't like the sound of that, either. "What do you mean, 'maybe'?"

"The Stephanie program is formidable. I overpowered it once, should be able to do so again if it has reassembled itself, but we're essentially sharing space in the disk, my algorithm avoiding hers more than anything else, trying to maintain cohesion."

No. No way. Elaine hadn't gotten this far with Richelle to leave or lose her now. She eyed the ladder, then focused on the apparition of the woman she loved. "How much power do you have left? What percentage?"

Her eyes unfocused as she calculated. "Maybe twenty percent."

"Hands and feet."

"Excuse me?"

Elaine demonstrated by placing one booted foot on the bottommost rung of the ladder and gripping the side of it with her hand. "In order to climb, you need hands and feet."

"And arm and leg muscles, and something to hold it all together."

Damn, she hadn't thought of that. "Bare minimum. You just need to maintain some form until we get to the upper levels. You can alter your shape and size. Miniaturize yourself. Would that be too much of a deviation?"

Richelle thought about it, cocking her head to one side. "No, I don't think so. It's essentially the same program, only smaller, less energy required."

Elaine held out her free hand, palm up. "I'll carry you. Put you in my pocket. Whatever it takes so you don't have to shut down and join Ste… that thing inside the portable emitter."

She couldn't be positive in the odd lighting, but Elaine thought a blush crept across Richelle's semi-transparent face. "Can't get much farther from realism than that."

Despite the perilous nature of their circumstances, Elaine barked a laugh. "I've got a see-through lover. We left reality a long, long time ago."

As she watched, Ricky shrank until she stood about six inches tall. Elaine picked her up, marveling at the minimal weight, and tucked Ricky in her jacket pocket. Her torso stuck out, like a puppy hanging from a hovercar window, and she folded her arms over the pocket's edge.

Well, size really wasn't everything.

CHAPTER 22
GONE WITH THE ELECTRICITY

ELAINE CLIMBED. Her boot heels clanged on the metal rungs as she hauled herself toward the upper levels of the *Nebula*.

The higher she went, the louder the klaxons sounded. Every twenty rungs, she passed a hatch, and on occasion could hear shouts, running feet, and weapons discharges beyond the metal.

She kept climbing.

Black numbers labeled the interiors of the hatches. When she reached Level Five, she paused to catch her breath and leaned her body into the ladder, her ear pressed to the bulkhead at her side, listening. Nothing.

"What's on level five?" she asked, whispering and not sure why she bothered lowering her voice. No one could hear her in the access tube.

"Kitchens."

Richelle's tone was higher-pitched in her diminutive form. Made sense, smaller vocal cords and all, Elaine supposed. Still made her stifle a laugh.

"Not funny," Ricky groused, but when Elaine glanced down at her, Ricky was smiling too.

"Okay," Elaine said. "Level five: pots, pans, and hopefully no pirates." She depressed the release panel for the hatch, then cringed at the creak as it opened.

More red emergency lighting and blaring alarms. The eerie glow reflected off all the metallic surfaces: counters, stoves, preparation tables. The strobe effect dizzied her.

No emitters lined the walls. They hadn't left the crew-only areas. Dammit.

She spotted a pair of swinging doors across the sea of metal and headed for them, hoping they'd lead to the dining room. On her way, she snatched a banana from a bin overflowing with fruit and peeled and ate it. Her stomach rumbled in response. She couldn't remember the last time she'd eaten. Adrenaline had carried her this far. Potassium might carry her a little farther.

A glass-walled, climate-controlled wine cellar beckoned. Alcohol would assist in soothing her frayed nerves, but she passed it by. She needed her wits to be as sharp as the situation would allow.

When she reached the doors, she eased one open.

The dining hall looked like a war zone.

Overturned chairs littered the floor. Broken glass and scattered silverware made walking a noisy hazard, and her gaze darted to the closed doors on the far side, expecting a team of pirates to charge through at any moment. Bits of food and splattered sauces decorated the walls and, in some places, the ceiling. She suspected the tables would have been toppled as well, if they hadn't been bolted down.

Elaine tried to ignore the splayed corpses draped over broken furnishings. The pirates hadn't discriminated. Crew and passengers alike lay dead, shockrifle blasts leaving scorch marks on skin and clothing. She picked her way around them, trying not to touch any bodies. The smell of cooked human flesh mingled nauseatingly with the scent of smoke wafting from the overhead vents.

A team of battery-operated robo-cleaners roved amid the debris, some catching and stalling on the larger bits, their servos whirring as they tried to dislodge themselves. Elaine nudged one free with her foot, a pang of pity for the device surprising her. Others beeped plaintively at the huge piles of shattered dishware, unable to suck that much into their little storage bins. They'd wait forever for their dead or departed human masters to assist in the cleaning process.

"I've recharged enough, and I can channel some power into the emitters here and turn them on. Put me down," Richelle instructed, and Elaine did so, placing her at the edge of the parquet dance floor.

Expansion fascinated and impressed her as much as the shrinking had. Richelle's image swelled and grew, then solidified while Elaine watched. She offered a lopsided smile. "I'll get used to that, right?"

Ricky took her hand. "Hopefully, you won't have to."

They crossed the open room together, darting from behind one table to another, keeping the tablecloth-covered wooden surfaces between themselves and the far doors leading into the central hub atrium. Elaine stopped at intervals to check a number of less-ravaged bodies, calling to them, nudging them gently with the toe of her boot, but none showed any signs of life.

Richelle insisted on going through the doors first. When she determined the coast was clear, she beckoned to Elaine.

Right outside the dining room stood another, smaller bar. The pirates had ransacked the liquor and wine stores, emptying the shelves and cabinets of their contents.

"Where is everyone?" Elaine shouted to be heard over the alarms. The sirens reverberated up and down the central space of the atrium, making them seem even louder than before. Here the flashing red lights created a psychedelic effect. She almost expected to hear bass music and see writhing dancers moving to the pulse of the sound.

"Evacuated," Ricky yelled back.

Elaine's eyebrows rose. "Isn't the crew, you know, supposed to account for everyone?"

Richelle gestured at the closed dining room doors. "Impossible under the circumstances. They make their announcements, sound the alarms, and hope everyone gets the hell off." They picked their way over more shards. Someone had taken a blunt object to the glassware and the huge mirror, knocking it from the bar's rear wall. "On the upside, if you can call it that, there should be plenty of escape pods left. *Nebula* isn't the *Titanic*. They provide sufficiently for emergencies."

Lack of twentieth-century knowledge or not, Elaine knew the *Titanic*. She didn't much appreciate that comparison right now.

Her breath caught as a flash of movement reflected in one of the larger panels of broken mirror. Focusing, she spotted a hand—a hand attached to an arm. The arm, covered in streaks of blood, twitched.

"Ricky!" Elaine didn't wait for her, but followed the reflected image to its source, a young man in a bartender's uniform, facedown on the deck plates. The cuts on his arms were superficial, though he'd be picking bits of glass out of his skin for days, but the slick of blood at the back of his head looked serious.

Richelle joined her, and they rolled the crewman as gently as they could, letting his head rest on Elaine's lap where she knelt beside him. She couldn't worry about rad exposure. This was a life. Using a discarded cocktail napkin, she wiped blood off his face and blinked in surprise as recognition dawned. Arnold Lansington, her hero from the first day—the one who'd pulled her from the detaching boarding tube.

Time to return the favor.

Richelle located an intact pitcher from behind the bar and fetched some water from the bar's sink. They splashed it in the bartender's face until he came around. Arnold blinked, squeezed his eyes shut, then opened them again. Elaine watched his pupils focus. "Ms. Kane?"

To her own surprise, she laughed. "The *Titanic's* going down, Mr. Lansington. I think you can call me Elaine. And propriety be damned, I'm calling you Arnold."

"Yes, ma'am. I mean, Elaine." His words slurred a bit, but she understood him. Richelle helped him to his feet. Arnold blinked again. "The THIs are inactive. How…?"

Elaine exchanged a glance with her companion. Richelle nodded her permission. "She's not exactly a THI."

She didn't want to shout an entire explanation over the alarms, but at that moment, the sirens ceased their wailing.

Elaine shot Arnold a quizzical look.

"Fire must have reached the public address system. At least we haven't lost life support or gravity."

On cue, the whir of circulating air ceased.

"Sorry," Arnold said, shrugging helplessly. "I'll keep my mouth shut." He wavered unsteadily on his feet.

"Do that." Elaine took one of his arms while Richelle seized the other.

While the trio crossed the atrium, making their way to the closest escape pod corridor, Elaine gave Arnold the short version of Richelle's unique attributes, including her alien nature. She could simply think of no other way to explain the THI's ability to act independently from its programming. By the time she finished her explanation, Arnold's eyes had glazed again, but not from his injury.

"I must be concussed. You're telling me the *Nebula*'s infested with alien life-forms?"

Elaine wouldn't have chosen the term "infested" for its negatives or numbers. She waited for Richelle to take offense or correct the bartender. Richelle merely nodded.

Now it was Elaine's turn to be surprised. "Wait. There are more of you?"

"Yes."

"On the *Nebula*?"

"Yes."

She took a moment to digest that. It made sense. No other THIs she'd met had shown Richelle's spark, but that didn't prove there weren't more. Her new artist friend, Muriel Debois, had suggested there were multiple "good ones." A couple thousand passengers meant a lot of THIs. She'd only interacted with a handful.

God, she hoped Muriel had made it off the *Nebula* safely.

The ship shuddered, throwing her into Richelle's arms. Arnold staggered to the closest support pillar, hanging on until the lurching stopped. Artwork fell from wall fasteners, crashing and splintering on the decking. Elaine briefly wondered why it hadn't been bolted in place like almost everything else, then remembered much of it was for sale and would have to be easily replaceable. Richelle shielded her from flying frame fragments with her now-solid body.

"That way," Arnold instructed, inclining his head to the right.

Taking hold of the bartender again, the threesome wobbled through one hatch, down a long row of cheaper passenger accommodations, and into another hallway lined with escape pod doors.

The *Nebula* shook like a wet dog. Its metal framework groaned. Another explosion rumbled from below.

Heart racing, Elaine scanned the indicator lights topping each pod access hatch. Most blinked red, the pods behind them having filled and jettisoned. For a horrible minute, she thought they'd have to find another launch corridor. Then a green flash caught her eye. The last pod on the right remained attached. They ran for it.

Gravity failed. Elaine's boots left the deck, and she and Arnold floated into the nearest wall, bounced off, and came to hover in the center of the hall space, where they drifted helplessly in place.

Richelle stood rooted to the floor behind them, and when Elaine managed to twist her body, she saw the intense concentration in her expression. Her eyes lost focus as she fought to adjust her physics and create the illusion her body retained gravity of its own.

Step by excruciating step, Ricky approached her, then took both her and Arnold by the arms and hauled them toward the escape pod. The effort hurt her. Elaine could see it hurt.

"All the ship's systems are failing," Richelle said between gritted teeth. "Once electrical goes, I won't have access to the THI generator."

Almost there. A few more paces. Richelle let them float while she released the hatch. She maneuvered Arnold inside first, then Elaine. The pod sat six, so there was plenty of space within.

"Once you seal up, the pod's own gravity simulators will activate. It will auto-launch, and its sensors will seek out the nearest inhabited world, which is Gratitude. You can catch another ship home to Earth."

"Wait! What about you? Aren't you coming?" Elaine caught hold of Richelle's hand in a death grip.

"No emitters in the pod."

"But the portable! You can store yourself in it, and I can take it with me. We'll go to Biotech. They'll figure something out, a safe way to separate you from the Stephanie program if it's still in there."

Richelle shook her head, covering Elaine's hand with her free one. "No one can know about me."

"I love you. I'll make it work." The vehemence in Elaine's tone stunned them both. Ricky opened her mouth to say something else.

The corridor lights went out. And so did Richelle.

"Shit!" Arnold cursed softly behind Elaine. Then, "Sorry, ma'am." Corporate training died hard.

"Don't fucking mention it," she shot back. Richelle's hand had vanished from her grasp along with the rest of her. The only source of light came from within the pod, the blinking indicators on the automated control panel signifying the emergency vehicle now operated under its own power and no longer fed off the *Nebula.* The dim glow extended only a few inches into the hallway. No sign of Richelle, but a disk-shaped shadow floated before Elaine's eyes. The portable emitter. Still gripping the edge of the open hatch with one hand, she plucked it out of the air with the other. It vibrated a moment in her palm, then stilled. She wondered if that was the Stephanie program or Richelle.

Or both.

"Ma'am? Elaine?" Arnold spoke her name, mouth working around it like an unfamiliar food. He'd hauled himself to the control panel. His finger stabbed at one of the readouts. "I'm detecting a rapid build-up of energy in the *Nebula*'s engine room. It's drawing off all the power from the rest of the ship, but it's not releasing any of it to ship's systems."

Elaine didn't need to be an engineer to figure out what that meant. The *Nebula* was about to blow.

She pushed off against the interior of the hatch, floating herself to the opposite side of the pod from the opening. "I'm clear. Seal it."

Elaine caught Arnold's nod in her peripheral vision, then caught her breath as the sealing of the hatch activated the pod's gravity and dumped her to the metal flooring. Arnold missed cracking his already injured head on the controls by an inch. He crawled to her side. "We should strap in."

She clamped her mouth shut on a sarcastic response and pulled herself into a plastic seat. The x-cross straps over her chest and shoulders were hard to manage while holding the onyx disk, but she wasn't letting go of what might be her only link to Richelle.

If she'd managed to transfer herself into it in time.

She forced that thought away, urging the escape craft's tiny engines to work faster. They were still connected to the *Nebula*, and it shuddered and shook them like one of those rattletrap carnival attractions.

One more violent jerk and it succeeded in throwing them free. The latches released. The engines kicked in. The pod drifted from the larger ship, rotated, and propelled itself away.

Arnold sat directly in front of her, closest to the screens and readouts. He leaned forward, examining something on the panel, then shouted over his shoulder, "Brace yourself!"

Elaine dug the nails of her free hand into the armrest, clutching the portable emitter to her chest with the other.

The pod had no portholes, but she knew the moment the *Nebula* ceased to exist. Every light on the control board turned red, and all external sensor indicators shot to their highest settings. The entire thing lit up, strings and strings of Christmas lights on overload.

The concussion wave hit next, and she couldn't suppress her scream when the pod flipped end over end. The repulsors and stabilizers whined with the effort to compensate, failing miserably. Elaine felt her stomach rise and drop, and she wished she hadn't grabbed that piece of fruit from the kitchen, but she held it down. Closing her eyes didn't help. In fact, it made everything worse, so she held them open and focused on the back of the bartender's skull.

Arnold didn't seem to fare as poorly, having had more experience in space. But his face, when he turned to check on her, had paled, and he swallowed hard several times.

The craft righted itself at last. Elaine noted the shift as it readjusted its course to put them back on track for Gratitude. Arnold checked the boards and confirmed their direction.

"Any sign of the pirates' ship?" Elaine hoped their enemies had been caught in the blast, but she doubted that kind of luck, especially since their fortune to this point had been pretty bad.

Okay, not all bad. They lived.

"No sign of them. I think they pulled out a little after they hit me at the bar. I felt a detach through the deck plates."

Elaine would have been climbing the ladder about then. No surprise she hadn't noticed, or she'd been unable to tell one type of vibration apart from another.

"Thanks for getting me out of there," Arnold added. He unfastened his restraints, changed seats to sit next to her, and strapped back in.

"You obviously would, and did, do the same for me. No thanks necessary."

"Too bad I'll never be able to tell anyone the real story of how I got out." He met her gaze head-on, then nodded at the disk in her hand. "Her secret's safe with me."

"If she's in there." She choked on the words.

Arnold leaned to pat her shoulder. "She loves you. She's in there."

Elaine just had to find a way to get her out. And fast.

RICHELLE EXPECTED to have to deal with the Stephanie program again. She hadn't been able to completely erase all traces of it from the device. By now, it would have had ample time to reassemble and recharge.

And indeed, she found "Stephanie" there, aggressive as ever, designed to dominate and dissemble her. Ricky expected to have a difficult fight on her incorporeal hands.

She didn't expect sentience.

Richelle's sense flared outward, seeking, probing the strings of code that threatened to take her apart even as she investigated, searched for the source of difference. Stephanie was there, but she'd been altered, forced to accept a rider personality stronger than her own and willing to use her form as a medium for its existence.

Fzzd.

The other Ixani had taken the only option open to her if she wanted to escape the *Nebula*. And given Richelle a much bigger problem to solve.

CHAPTER 23
RETURN OF THE THI

REENTRY INTO atmosphere tossed and jostled the tiny craft, enough that she wondered if its stabilizers had been damaged. Both she and Arnold vomited until their stomachs emptied themselves. Elaine managed to snag an airsick bag from the seat pouch, its built-in de-contaminators turning the white plastic a brilliant blue, but Arnold fumbled and lost his. At least he turned his head away from her. She didn't catch much fallout. By the time the craft bounced twice on a strip of sandy beach and settled against a dune, they were both the worse for wear.

With trembling fingers, she struggled with the strap clasps, unable to detach the metal from the synth-leather. Her legs shook too, creating a rustle as her pant legs rubbed together. Arnold came to her rescue, appearing over her and disconnecting her restraints. Together they opened the hatch and inhaled the salty sea air of a Gratitude morning.

"We made it," Elaine muttered, her boots sinking into the sand. Her knees buckled, and she sat to avoid falling. The emitter pressed a circular indentation into her backside. She didn't remember shoving it in her back pocket but was glad to know it was close to her.

"*We* did." Arnold stared up at the lightening sky, all pinks and grays with the rising of the sun. Their breaking thrusters had left a trail of white from the heavens to the shore.

Elaine followed his gaze up and up. The *Nebula*. She could detect no trace of the starliner, but doubted she could have before its explosion, either. Not this far away. Arnold's line of thought, however, was easy to follow. How many other passengers and crew members—friends of his—failed to escape the ship before its destruction?

In the distance, she made out the remains of dozens of other vapor trails, much more dispersed than their own. Theirs had been one of the last, if not the last, pods to detach.

She had another sudden thought. How many Ixani had made it? Richelle said there were others. Even if she transferred into the portable emitter, what would have happened to the other members of her species? What constituted death for an energy life-form? She assumed they didn't require oxygen. Could they transcend space? Likely not, or Richelle could have simply done that. Or maybe she could have, if she'd had the energy, but without it…. Could the others return to Gratitude, or whatever name they had for this beautiful world?

Guilt twisted in her gut. In addition to any straggling passengers or injured crew, she may have witnessed the deaths of countless aliens—aliens the human race had yet to formally acknowledge.

Elaine lowered her gaze to trace the stretch of beach into the distance, where black pillars rose as inky shadows against the sunrise.

And she knew how to retrieve Richelle.

Sirens snapped her attention toward the opposite direction, and shielding her eyes against the glare, she spotted clouds of stirred-up sand in the far distance. Ground vehicles approached. Search and rescue, she would bet. The authorities would be on the alert, having picked up the *Nebula*'s distress signals and tracked the pods to the surface. Before the vehicles came within visual range, she crawled around to the back of the pod where she'd be out of sight.

"What's wrong?" Arnold alternated glances between Elaine and the emergency vehicles.

"I'm supposed to be dead. I'd like to let that assumption stand."

He shot her a look like she'd shaken up more than her nerves in the landing.

Elaine gave him an urgent and abridged version of the past few days' events, watching his eyes grow wider with each successive attempt on her life and then Stephanie's murder.

"A dead body? On the *Nebula* for days? And none of the sensors picked it up? This Jay Grego guy is either a genius, or he had help in our tech department."

"I'm betting on the latter, and not taking chances either way."

"Seems like a lot of trouble to go through for getting fired."

Keeping the pod as a shield, Elaine crept for the nearest large dune. "I'm not really concerned with the why."

Arnold followed her, not bothering to hide himself. No one wanted to kill *him*. "Where are you going?" The sirens came closer. The screeching tones rose and fell in pitch, and Arnold pressed one hand against his ear with a grimace.

Elaine flashed him a quick smile. "To rendezvous with an alien."

"Don't worry. Helping people with matchmaking is part of a bartender's job description. I'll tell them I was alone. I majored in public relations and theater in college." His white teeth shone in the sunlight. He was already wiping out her footprints.

When she reached the far side of the sand hill, she stuck her head up for one last exchange. "Look me up, when you get back to Earth. Our corporate offices could use someone like you." Then keeping her head low, she put distance between herself and her would-be rescuers.

HELLO, RICHELLE, Fzzd transmitted in a series of buzzes and hums. She fluttered backward, maintaining her distance and keeping her pattern from brushing and being influenced by Ricky's. Wary reds swirled around her.

Perhaps she'd decided to be civilized after all.

Don't make me destroy you, Fzzd sent.

Or not.

I have no desire to fight you, Fzzd.

But you insist on giving me every reason. Fzzd flashed away, a swirl of sparkles trailing in her wake, and took up residence in a corner of the emitter. *Can't you see? Can't you see they've done it again?*

Who? Though Richelle already knew.

The humans. The biologicals. Fzzd made the designation a curse. *Destroying one another and us along with them.*

A pang of sorrow turned Richelle's colors to deep purples and blues. *How many?* she sent softly.

Fzzd sent a tendril toward her. If she'd been a human, it would have been the equivalent of pointing a finger at Ricky's chest over and over again. *All of them. Every single one of us aboard the* Nebula *with the exception of the two of us, at least as far as I could tell. They couldn't find their way out of the generator like you did. Didn't even try.*

Because they lacked motivation! We've lost the drive to live. But I had love. Someone to get back to. That drove me to find a way. And the other dozen or so had been lost. So few Ixani left. Ricky wished she had eyes to close against the pain.

Her attention refocused.

How did you *get out?*

I followed you.

Why? Richelle reduced the strength of her transmission signal, softening her words. *What motivated you, Fzzd? Jealousy?*

She didn't respond but drew into herself, tightening her strings into an almost solid ball of code.

Fzzd, are you still in love with me?

ELAINE HELD the emitter in her palm while she walked. Every hundred yards or so, she paused to place it in the sand at her feet, hoping Richelle might emerge from its mechanical depths. Once she thought she detected movement, but it was only a small crustacean burrowing up from beneath the powdery white granules.

She kept her pace unhurried but purposeful in case anyone saw or scanned her from a distance. In jeans and a jacket, she could be any tourist out for a morning beach stroll. The rescue team responded fast, which meant she couldn't be far from the port town. It also meant the ruins she headed for comprised Site One and not Site Two, where she'd hidden during her last visit. She hoped that didn't make a difference. She also hoped she wouldn't run into a bunch of tour groups.

While she walked, she considered Arnold's comments about Grego's motivations. The bartender had a point. Job loss didn't warrant the kind of retaliation Grego inflicted upon her. She hadn't even been the one to fire him. No, this felt like a personal vendetta. But she'd never met Grego prior to this trip.

She supposed he might be a total nutcase, striking out at Leviathan through her, getting revenge for the loss of his job.

Only a crazy man would blow up a starliner to hide a couple of murders.

Or a desperate one. The question was, what was he desperate for?

While musing, she'd come within a few yards of Site One's main gated entrance. The roar of a hoverbus's engines sent Elaine scrambling behind some beach brush—scraggly, low-lying, browning bushes, but full enough to provide cover.

The bus landed outside the gates, disgorging a horde of pastel-clad tourists. Vid-capturers hummed as they took footage of the ruins to show off to their bored friends at home. Several small children ran shrieking among the dunes, more interested in the beach than the ancient buildings. A weary guide clambered from the cockpit and tilted his white sun visor to a better angle.

So much for privacy. Elaine took the next best course of action. She blended.

Patting the emitter disk, now tucked deep into a back jeans pocket, she fell in at the rear of the thirty or so tourists. She hoped nobody would notice the small rips, tears, and blood in her shirt, but black hid stains well. Elaine wanted to kick something in her impatience. Until this bunch of gawkers left, she could do nothing about Richelle.

"Welcome to Site One!" the guide said with forced enthusiasm. He had to repeat the same spiel at least once a day. Elaine figured that got old fast. "Step back in time to an ancient and alien civilization archaeologists have only begun to explore."

And exploit. Elaine followed the group through the gates, eyeing the black walls with more insight and perspective than during her last visit. The Ixani never left, at least not all of them. Why would they allow humans to stroll unchallenged through their cities, study and seize their technology? Why would—?

She froze, letting the crowd flow away from her. Why would a race of energy beings need a city at all? Elaine hurried to catch up.

The tour guide had a voice-amplification device attached to his collar. Elaine could hear every word as he described what scientists assumed to be the way of life for the aliens. All of it seemed wrong for a race of energy entities.

He suggested motorized vehicles must have traversed the wide thoroughfare leading to the city's central square, though they'd found no trace of such vehicles. He led them inside one of the structures, pointing out the absence of furnishings, explaining the aliens must have taken them when they left.

No. Energy beings wouldn't need furniture or transports. They existed in a different state—one humans could barely begin to comprehend.

The guide pointed out the THI generator in a building at the heart of the city. "The prominence and central placement marks entertainment as a priority for the former inhabitants," he stated with certainty.

But, Elaine thought, no one really knew what the generators had been designed to do. Entertainment was what humans used them for, when the alien hardware, even after extensive experimentation, refused to incorporate itself into military technology. She remembered the articles Harriet had shared with her, Harry's gloating pride at keeping Leviathan out of that particular profit-losing venture. And Harry's frustration when Biotech found more popular uses for the generators.

Elaine's late spouse had still employed a team of scientists to do their own investigation, just in case something might be salvaged for the military and a lucrative contract might be forged. Their results had matched everyone else's. The technology was not compatible with weapons usage. It made no sense to anyone. The operating systems were essentially the same. It was as if the devices had some sort of peaceful subroutine programmed into their most basic codes. But no one had ever found such a subroutine, not any of the brightest minds Earth had to offer.

Elaine drew a sharp breath, covering her mouth with her hand to hide it as a fake yawn.

What if the *aliens themselves* had refused to allow the technology to be used for military purposes? What if they were still influencing the devices directly? It fit, given that Richelle overrode her emitter's programming and committed violent acts to save her. Which would mean the Ixani weren't only using THIs on starliners to inhabit and blend with their programs.

They could just as easily be on Earth.

She let the ramifications wash over her. Every major city had a THI theater. That meant potentially hundreds or even thousands of Ixani, if each theater had only one alien intelligence living in it among the pure holograms.

Elaine suppressed a shudder. Richelle, she trusted. She wasn't so sure about the rest.

"And now, let me show you that exclusive surprise I promised." The tour guide grew more animated, real enthusiasm replacing the speeches he'd repeated from rote memory. The tall dark-haired man led the way past the central square, down another narrower street, and into a large courtyard roped off with cords and stun pillars. The pillars cast visible red beams of energy between them, stunning anything biological trying to pass the barrier. "Please take small children by the hand," the guide instructed as they drew closer. "We wouldn't want any of the little ones to get a painful shock."

Wouldn't want the insurance hassles, either.

The tourists formed a line along one side of the cordoned area, leaving a respectful distance between themselves and the stun field. The guide took up a position in the space they left.

"You are only the third tour group permitted to see this latest find. The Society for Alien Archaeology went public with the discovery five days ago, so if you're purposely avoiding the newsnets—" He winked. Several audience members chuckled, business types with pot bellies and flowered shirts. "—you may have missed the announcement altogether."

Just like Elaine had. Well, she'd been busy.

"Anyone want to guess what the aliens used this space for?"

Elaine scanned the open area. Recent excavation had disturbed the ground, but she saw little evidence of a structure. No walls, doors, ceilings. Instead, dozens of black cylinders made from the same material as the rest of the city rose from the sandy dirt. Each stood about a foot in height, and they were spaced about four feet apart. Excavators had dug small pits in front of some of the cylinders. The ones with pits lay on the far side of the area, so she couldn't see down into them. The setup triggered a memory, something old and no longer used, maybe an image from a vid she'd seen.

A cemetery. She was looking at a cemetery.

"It's a graveyard," an elderly gentleman proclaimed.

The tour guide's face lit up. "Exactly right. See me for a free T-shirt when we get back to town."

What would it say on it? "Make No Bones About It, I Know Alien Death Rituals"?

"Not only do we now have skeletal remains of the beings who once inhabited Gratitude, but we know precisely what they looked like." Taking a transmitter from his jacket pocket, the leader aimed it at two of the stun pillars, deactivating the beam between them. He stepped over the more primitive, and less effective, rope (safety in redundancy, Elaine supposed), then turned on the field again to keep everyone else out. After picking his way between plots, he knelt beside one of the black cylinders. With his fingertips, he tapped the flat top of the marker.

The flash of light caught everyone except the guide by surprise, many taking cautious steps backward and then colliding with each other. Small children yelped and scooted behind their parents. An older couple edged away, moving in the direction of the parked hoverbus on the other side of the ruins.

The tour guide held up a hand. "No need to worry, folks. Just watch."

Above the cylinder some *thing* appeared.

"It's an emitter," Elaine whispered, hearing her revelation echoed throughout the crowd in hushed murmurs and gasps. Well, of course it was. She'd found a much larger one at Site Two, the entire room that had recreated her home office.

The projected image took form, hovering in midair at six feet or so in height. It displayed a being of indeterminate age, yellow-skinned and long of limbs, longer than a human's. The oval-shaped head seemed stretched and unnatural, the wide eyes and flat nose cartoonish. And yet it possessed an undeniable beauty and grace as its depiction shimmered and flowed.

Each hand bore three fingers and an opposable thumb with suction cups on the ends. If she had to guess, Elaine would bet each foot had four toes for symmetry. She couldn't see them, though. They were hidden within soft-looking, velvety green slippers.

Sex was also a toss-up. It wore flowing fabric in teal and aqua, a multilayered dress maybe, but it could just as easily have been a ceremonial robe. The head had no hair, only small bumpy protrusions, creating a nubbly appearance. Elaine peered at the clothing. No other lumps or mounds to give a clue to its feminine or masculine nature, if they had sexes at all.

Having encountered an energy life-form, a second species that might be asexual and reproduce by budding wouldn't have shocked her.

But that thought struck a new chord. If they now had skeletal remains, this was not an Ixani. Energy beings, even if they could imitate humanoid forms, would not leave bones behind.

So what was it?

The tour guide bowed to the THI, and it bowed back, then spoke in a language of melodious vowels and few consonants that carried on the ocean breezes. Elaine understood none of it, but the tour guide smiled. He held out a hand, and the humanoid touched the back of it in a fluttering gesture, then said something else. A greeting, perhaps.

Of course, it could just as easily have been saying, "Get the fuck off my lawn."

"Our best linguists are working on deciphering the vocabulary. They've only had a few days, though, so be patient. Give them at least a week."

The crowd laughed at the exaggeration. This was the human race's first experience with an entirely alien culture.

Well, second, actually. But very few people knew that.

"What we do know is that each cylinder marks a grave, and the images are interactive in a limited capacity, maybe to repeat comforting messages to family members left behind."

A nice idea. Elaine could see such things becoming popular back on Earth, if it were true. Deceased alien trendsetters. Knowing Leviathan, her company would pilot the prototypes. Per the Conservation of Mother Earth laws and the risk of rad exposure, most humans except those in the most isolated areas were cremated at death, but installing miniature THI emitters in the urn alcoves at every mausoleum might be possible. And expensive. And lucrative for Leviathan. Something to present to the board of directors if she ever made it back home.

The tour group leader finished his "conversation" with the dead alien, let himself out of the cordoned area, and activated the stun field behind him.

"And that concludes our tour!" he announced. "If everyone will please return to the bus—"

"Wait, what about the other buildings?" One of the teenagers raised a hand and gestured at some of the larger structures.

Elaine was glad the kid had asked. She didn't want to draw undue attention to herself, and she needed to find the equivalent of the room-emitter at Site Two.

The guide shook his head and flashed a patented smile. "No one's going in those," he explained, turning up the volume on his amplifier so the whole group could hear him.

"Why not?"

"Because no one can get in most of them, and the ones they've entered are empty—nothing of interest to see. Archeology team's been working on it ever since first discovery of this place. They don't want to damage the find, so they don't force their way in, and some of the doors defy all attempts to open them. Sooner or later, they'll figure it out." He winked at the teenager. "Just not today." He headed off, moving to the front of the crowd, signaling for everyone to follow him.

Elaine held to the rear, letting everyone pass her, bending down under the pretense of removing a stone from her boot.

As soon as she had some maneuvering room, she ducked into the nearest alcove and waited until she heard the bus take off. In the meantime, she noticed the chill of the shadowed stone, the pebbles and sand in her shoes, and her growling stomach. At last, the engine's rumbling roar faded into the distance. Then she back-tracked, using her knowledge of the layout of Site Two to lead her to the equivalent building in Site One.

CHAPTER 24
THI WARS

OUR RELATIONSHIP ended over seven human lifetimes ago. Richelle hoped her signal conveyed the gentleness she intended.

Humans! Fzzd flared. *Always in terms of corporeal beings. We were never enough for the ones like you. I was never enough.* She caught herself and stopped, swirling in place. *You're a traitor to your own kind.*

I'm trying to save our kind! Damn if Fzzd didn't have her projecting at higher decibels.

It is not your responsibility. The Council will decide.

Ricky tightened her cohesion. *No, Fzzd. Saving the Ixani is everyone's responsibility.*

Richelle had no opportunity to shift aside as Fzzd hurled herself at her. Human hells, she didn't have time for this. Elaine needed her.

ELAINE HOPED the tour bus wouldn't return for her. If the guide did a head count, he'd find the same number of people he started with, but if he searched for her personally....

No time to think about that now. She examined the shadowed alcove, much easier to see in daylight than darkness. She hoped it was the right one. That night with the lopson had been dark and rainy. She couldn't be positive she had the right location.

The door didn't resemble an entry so much as a solid, smooth black slab filling the back wall of the recess and blocking further progress into the building. The difference between it and the surrounding rock was texture. The walls felt rough, like stucco or brick, but her fingers slid over the door with no friction whatsoever.

Elaine imagined how foolish she would look if anyone saw her, a tourist seeking entry where scientists and archaeologists had failed, not to mention she was trespassing and had no idea what the penalty might be if she were caught, but she searched anyway. Her nervousness increased exponentially with the passage of the minutes, and she kept looking over her shoulder for a patrol of security guards coming to arrest her. She found no trace of a handle, knob, access panel, or latch—not even a doorbell to signal her presence. Moving past the obvious, she pressed on the stone beside the slab, hoping to trigger a hidden release. Nothing.

Maybe she should go find a lopson. After all, it got her in the last one. Or had that been Richelle, working behind the scenes again?

Elaine leaned out and halfheartedly scanned the street, hoping a lopson might be, well, loping along or burrowing in the sand outside the abandoned city's gates. No such luck. She kicked the closest wall in frustration.

Her ass vibrated.

Elaine jumped, knowing her personal comm had exploded along with the rest of the *Nebula*, then remembered the emitter and yanked it out before it could goose her again. The disk jerked and bounced in her palm like a frenzied insect. She extended her arm in front of her before the thing could leap and put her eye out. It arced from her fingertips, ricocheted off the stone foyer, and hit the smooth door panel, where it stuck.

Like a magnet to a refrigerator, the onyx emitter held to the surface of the entry, about three feet off the ground. The area around the disk glowed with a soft blue light that spread outward in a circle until it lit up the center of the door.

It opened, grinding and shrieking as it slid into the wall. The light went out, and the emitter dropped at Elaine's feet.

"Thanks, Richelle," she whispered, picking it up. At least she hoped it was Richelle.

She stepped inside the alien building.

The dust of hundreds, if not thousands of years swirled in the sunlight cast through the opening, and Elaine was struck by the notion that she was likely the first to enter since the Ixani and the other aliens in the cemetery abandoned their home.

A thought struck her, making her shiver, or maybe the cooler temperatures of the interior affected her. Either way, she wondered if all the Ixani had truly left. Considering their nature, they might exist in the walls, no, the very air around her, and she wouldn't know it.

And speaking of Ixani in the walls, she crossed through the equivalent circular room with the powered-down technology. The skylights overhead let in the midmorning sun. She wondered why the research teams hadn't used the transparent panels for access, then figured they'd probably become exposed at the same time as the door opened.

It didn't take long to find the room where the duplicate of her office back on Earth had appeared at Site Two. And like Site Two, it stood empty now.

How could she trigger the emitters? How could she get Richelle back?

Maybe she didn't need to do anything.

Elaine placed the portable emitter disk in the center of the room, stood well away from it, and waited.

For a moment, nothing happened. Then a lot of things occurred at once.

The disk did its jumping bean impression, more violent and aggressive, shooting off the walls and even the ceiling. She darted out of its way, wishing there was something to hide behind, ducking to avoid it as it bounced over her head. She soon got her wish. The room filled with what Elaine assumed to be furniture, though the colors looked garish to her eyes, and the bulbous cushioned seats and rounded-edge tables were too high off the floor for the average human's use. She remembered the image of the dead alien hovering above its grave marker, The furnishings would have suited its long legs perfectly.

A loud crack tore her gaze from the decor, and she spotted the emitter finally coming to rest on one of the tables. Two beams of light exploded forth, forming columns at first. Then they assumed vaguely human shapes and resolved into Richelle and Stephanie. Elaine wondered if that light beam had represented Richelle's "true" form.

Elaine started toward Ricky, but she stopped Elaine with an upraised hand. "Stay back." Her words were for Elaine, but her attention focused on the Stephanie THI.

Stephanie tilted her head, glossy blond hair falling across one shoulder. She placed a hand on her hip, and her lips turned upward in a smirk. "So, 'Richelle,'" she spat her name like a curse, "I finally get to meet your little whore face-to-face."

Elaine's mouth dropped open. She knew the THI wasn't her college friend, but it had also discarded all semblance of Stephanie's personality. This was something—no, some*one* else. Another Ixani, using Stephanie's form. And that filled her with grief and unfamiliar rage. She didn't quite know what to do with the anger. "Richelle, what the hell is going on?" Elaine glanced from one to the other.

Richelle took three steps, placing herself between the two. "Elaine, this is Fzzd." The name sounded like static, or two pieces of Velcro separating from one another. "She's a member of our ruling council, and not a fan of human/Ixani relations."

Elaine shifted to keep the other Ixani within her line of sight, albeit over Richelle's shoulder. "I gathered that."

Now Stephanie had both hands on her hips. "I'm not fond of interspecies relationships, period," she clarified. "Neither is the rest of the council. History has taught us where such relations lead. And today's events have proven that history repeats itself yet again."

"You were on the *Nebula*?" Elaine guessed.

"In the Lara replication, yes. I abandoned her program for Stephanie's before the *Nebula*'s demise."

She'd been Grego's THI "date." "Funny, I didn't sense any special insight or intelligence in Lara."

Richelle snorted.

Elaine's hands formed fists at her sides. She'd overcome a lot to cement a relationship with Richelle—pirates, assassination attempts. Fuck, she'd survived the explosion of a freaking starliner. She'd almost lost Ricky. She damn well wasn't giving her up because a political body found their union improper.

"Unlike Richelle, most of us are able to maintain our hidden natures while we observe your species."

"Observe? Is that your only goal?" Elaine paced to the closest thing resembling a couch and tried to seat herself with grace and decorum, failing at both. She managed to scoot her backside so she fully rested on the seat, but her legs dangled, making her feel childlike.

Richelle shot Fzzd an admonishing glance. "We're dealing with Earthlings, not Nishward. Some appropriate furniture, please?"

So, Nishward must be the name of the race buried in the plots behind the ruins. And Fzzd controlled the environment in here. A disadvantage, to be sure.

"Oh, where are my manners?" Fzzd said, voice syrupy sweet. The room shifted in a blurred kaleidoscope of colors. The alien couch vanished, dumping Elaine on the now wood floor.

She found herself in her office in the Kane mansion on Earth, just like she'd seen at Site Two. How the hell did they do that? Had the aliens been in her home? Richelle came and helped her up, then walked her to one of the guest chairs and remained standing close by her side. Fzzd took the seat of power behind Elaine's desk.

Elaine's desk. That galled her.

"That was immature, and beneath you," Richelle accused, indicating Elaine's floor-dumping with a sweep of her arm. She took up a supportive stance behind Elaine, resting her hands on Elaine's shoulders. It felt wonderful to have her touch again.

"Just like your romance," Fzzd shot back. She put her shoes up on the polished surface, the heels scratching into the wood.

It wasn't really her desk, but Elaine grimaced all the same. She steeled herself. If she were to gain any ground here, she needed to make it clear that she was done being walked over or dumped. "How are you doing this?" she asked, waving first a fluttering, then a firm hand at their surroundings. "Do your people read minds?"

Fzzd frowned; Richelle laughed. "No mind-reading," she assured Elaine. "Just a download of an issue of *American Business World*. We keep up with all the Earth e-periodicals. Cultural literacy is vital to our ability to blend."

Elaine thought back, remembering. The magazine had done an interview with Harriet at the Kane mansion a few years prior. They'd taken pictures and published one of her office with the caption stating it belonged to her spouse. "Warmer, more inviting than Harriet's stark black austere furniture choices," the writers insisted, "more investor friendly." Elaine hadn't argued then, hadn't defended her territory or taste. She'd let them use her. It occurred to her she would argue now. This ordeal had changed her.

"And you have some kind of shared consciousness between you?"

"We can voluntarily transfer information between members of our species," Richelle explained. "I sent Fzzd the image of something appropriate for the decor." Ricky shot a glare at the other Ixani. "Taking information without permission can be done, but it is intrusive and very rude."

And, Elaine gathered, Fzzd had taken a lot of data about their relationship without obtaining that permission.

The other Ixani studied Elaine with a mixture of curiosity, condescension, and distaste. "They really are so pathetically limited, their notions archaic."

"They managed to interface with Nishward technology." Richelle removed her hands from Elaine's shoulders and stood beside her, arms crossed over her chest.

"And look what happened to the Nishward! You've succeeded in making my point for me." Fzzd sat up, placing both palms flat on the desk.

It felt so strange, watching the facsimile of Stephanie talking to her, knowing her friend had died a brutal, horrible death. Elaine gripped her grief and forced it down, storing it for later. Much later. When she wasn't facing condemnation from a leader of an alien race. Good God.

"What exactly did happen to the Nishward? I assume those *are* the people buried in the plots behind the city."

Richelle and Fzzd exchanged some silent communication; then Fzzd nodded.

Richelle moved where Elaine could better see her, hitching a hip onto the corner of the desk and facing her. Ricky's smile was gentle and sad. "The Nishward shared this world with us for generations, but we had no interaction with them for centuries in human years."

"They weren't even aware of our existence." Fzzd sniffed with disdain.

"They were corporeal," Richelle allowed. "Not energy life-forms."

"We knew about *them*."

Richelle sighed. "Is this a criticism or an explanation?"

"It's an indulgence," Fzzd said.

Elaine's fingers tightened into fists until her nails dug into her palms. No matter what Fzzd looked like, Elaine wished she could wipe that supercilious smile off the Ixani's face.

Too bad Elaine didn't possess anywhere near the power to make that happen.

Richelle continued, "Eventually, our people became dissatisfied with our somewhat limited existence. We could learn about all sorts of things—history, art, music, cuisine—by interacting with the Nishward's computer systems. But we couldn't really *experience* them. Our knowledge was vast, our purpose in the universe, miniscule. When the Nishward came up with the THI system, we found the perfect means to make contact and to live corporeal lives."

"Biggest mistake the council ever made," Fzzd muttered.

"According to some." Richelle didn't bother turning to look at her fellow Ixani. "They were a bit surprised at first to find their entertainments possessed intelligence and free will, but using their familiar images to smooth the way, we got them to accept us. With our guidance, the Nishward improved the technology so that we might enjoy the physical pleasures of taste, smell, touch, and so forth. In exchange, we assisted them with technological and engineering advancements. Sentient computers can accomplish much more than merely mechanical ones."

The faraway look in Richelle's eyes made Elaine wonder if she spoke of history or personal experience. Elaine had no concept of the lifespan of an energy lifeform. Without a physical body to deteriorate, such a species might come close to immortality.

"It sounds like an idyllic symbiotic relationship," Elaine commented. "What went wrong?"

Fzzd snorted, not a pretty sound. "The organics behaved as organics always do. They got greedy."

Richelle held up a hand to silence her. "Food supplies ran low. A prolonged drought caused damage to many crops. They hadn't progressed to off-world travel, so they couldn't get resources from other worlds. And the smaller islands fared little better than this one. The settlements, and there are many more you have not yet uncovered, began fighting over the remaining consumables. They wanted us to help them conquer one another."

"Not our concern," Fzzd put in, looking off toward the corner of the simulated room.

"We enjoyed eating, but we didn't need to in order to sustain our lives. Many Ixani withdrew from the communities, abandoning their holographic forms to return to our previous isolated existence. Others stuck by their Nishward friends, hoping to help in any way short of participating in the wars."

"You were aberrations, dependent on the organics," Fzzd spat.

You, not *they*. So Richelle *had* been there among them.

"They were our friends!" She stood to pace in front of the desk.

"They wanted to use us to kill each other. Instead of working together to share food or find another solution, they wanted *us* to fight against *ourselves* if necessary! And though we never fell that far, they succeeded in splitting our people in half." Fzzd stood, too, bracing herself with the desk.

"Can you just tell me what happened?" Elaine hoped to stave off another fight between them, at least until she got the whole picture.

Fzzd huffed. "I'm not sure why I'm bothering. It won't change the behavior of organics."

Elaine's mouth twisted in a sarcastic smile. "Consider it 'educating the uneducated.' Humor me."

That worked. "They destroyed themselves, just like the council knew they would," Fzzd said, her eyes cold. "When the Ixani remaining among them wouldn't provide weapons designs, the Nishward moved to biological warfare, something with which we were largely unfamiliar. They wiped themselves off the face of this world. And they took the dependent Ixani with them."

Elaine stared at Fzzd. "How? Viruses and infections wouldn't affect you."

Fzzd pressed her lips together, unwilling to explain further. Elaine turned to Richelle. The Ixani's eyes glistened with unshed tears, and despite the fact Elaine knew it was only illusion, she felt Ricky's pain. But Elaine resisted the urge to go to her, to wrap her arms around her.

Richelle tried to shrug it off. "Hard to explain. They lost the will to live without their Nishward companions. Many of our people killed themselves, willfully dispersing their particles to such an extent that they lost all cohesion and ceased to exist." She slumped where she stood, then looked at Elaine. "I know suicide is frowned upon in human society, condemned even, but you must understand. We'd tasted and felt, sung and danced and expressed ourselves alongside them. To many, returning to our previous restricted existence was unthinkable."

"For the dependents," Fzzd put in. Clearly she thought herself above such needs.

"The rest of us just… suffered."

"No one's blaming or criticizing you," Elaine said, her voice soft.

"Speak for yourself," Fzzd snapped.

"I was." Now she did go to Ricky, enfolding her in her arms. "So why become THIs?" Elaine asked. "If we're so distasteful to you." She directed the second half to Fzzd.

Fzzd didn't answer.

Richelle gave a little laugh, but it held no humor. "We'd stagnated. Without the Nishward to advance our experience, to eventually achieve spaceflight and carry us beyond this world, we were effectively trapped here. Our people, *even* those not labeled dependents, began to disperse out of boredom. Life without discovery is no life at all."

"So you can't travel through space?" Meaning all the other Ixani on the *Nebula* had died.

"Not without the use of THI technology or some other fairly complex mechanical device to circulate in until a transfer can be made. Lacking hands, we could not build spacecraft ourselves. After the Nishward disaster, the council had imposed severe restrictions on the use of the organics' technology. Vacuum is an impenetrable barrier, even to us. When humans arrived and discovered the generators, began building their own emitters, the council permitted limited insertion and observation."

"And the dependents seized the opportunity to ignore all the restrictions and interact." Fzzd pointed a finger at Richelle. "You must be held until the council decides your fate."

Ricky spread her arms in a placating gesture. "It's still dramatically limited. We can only fully manifest where generators can support THIs. Most of your human technology by itself is too simplistic to house us. Without the THI technology, our ability to connect with corporeal life-forms, to interpret the world as they do, is virtually nil. It took hundreds of your years for us to figure out a way to contact the Nishward. We've learned much, but we're still dependent, yes. Only a handful of individual humans can afford to keep personal generators. And for the most part," she said with an apologetic smile at Elaine, "they aren't the types of people we'd want to bond with."

"Those who have, the council will find and eliminate," Fzzd stated with surety.

Elaine drew a surprised breath. So she and Richelle weren't the first human/Ixani pairing. Denise Lazaro could have had a real relationship. If only she knew. Then again, maybe that wasn't what the author was really searching for. Besides, then she'd have all this to contend with.

It also occurred to her that the Ixani and humans might save one another. THI technology did not produce rads. If the Ixani could show mankind how to duplicate that quality in other forms of tech…. Then again, that sort of sharing seemed to be exactly what Fzzd and the council feared. How many steps would Earth's governments take beyond that help to asking the Ixani for weapons?

Elaine already knew the answer to that question. Humanity could become the next Nishward disaster.

"And now there are portable generators." Fzzd indicated the larger emitter Elaine had brought with her. "My comrades in Biotech were working to sabotage their construction. They've clearly failed."

"Lucky for you," Elaine ground out. "If they'd succeeded, you'd have had no way off the *Nebula*."

Richelle's arms tightened around Elaine. Maybe her logical reasoning hadn't been such a smart move, considering Fzzd's intensified glare.

Ricky turned the topic back to her point. "You can't stifle change and development. We are meant to bond, not simply observe, if we are to grow."

"That is a decision for the council, not you. You will remain here until they can convene." With that pronouncement, Fzzd brought her hands together, pointing both her index fingers at Richelle. A flare of light erupted from Fzzd's fingertips, and Richelle shoved Elaine aside, out of the range of the blast of what Elaine assumed to be some sort of containment field. She hit the floor on her knees, beside the closest chair. Instead of letting the power strike her, Richelle cupped her hands before her like a catcher's mitt, absorbing the power with her palms. She didn't hurl it back. Instead, she dropped the energy ball to the wood flooring. It dispersed in a shower of sparks and a spiderweb of glowing tendrils.

The corner of Richelle's mouth quirked upward at Fzzd's surprised expression. "We dependents have learned a few things from human research, like how to manipulate containment fields. I'm not sticking around until the remains of the council come back to Gratitude, and I'm not fighting you for basic freedom."

"Your concept of freedom is tainted by human beliefs," Fzzd snarled. "Your duty is to council law. I'm invoking my right to enforce that law."

"Convenient timing, since half the council died on the *Nebula* and the other half is scattered throughout a dozen THI theaters on Earth." Ricky paused to draw breath, to collect her thoughts. A very human gesture. "Your methods of enforcement are outdated and impractical. There are so few Ixani left. Let us live as we choose."

Elaine watched the exchange from her position against the wall, head swiveling from one to the other. Richelle stood firm and determined. Fzzd's lips twisted in a mocking sneer. Elaine wished she could do something, but their natural weaponry beat anything she could accomplish with her frail human body.

"You *will* be held in containment until the council next convenes." Fzzd created another energy globe between her hands. It flashed in a strobe of white and green.

"I'm not waiting nearly two hundred years for you and the rest of the council to decide my fate."

Two hundred years. Elaine would be long gone, cremated and placed beside her late spouse's ceremonial urn in the Kane section of the mausoleum. She'd already figured out the Ixani had much longer lifespans. Now she realized that the passage of time also held a different meaning for them. But Richelle understood the implications. "And Elaine can't wait either. Human lives don't last that long," Ricky whispered.

"I know." Fzzd drew back her arm, preparing to hurl the ball of "containment energy" she'd spoken of.

"I'd rather be dispersed."

"I can arrange that too." The orb of light shifted from green to a deep and ominous red, crackling and sizzling like a raging flame.

Richelle's eyes widened, and Elaine had the distinct impression she knew she could not catch or deflect such a blast.

"You'd kill one of your own? Diminish our numbers further?" Shock and confusion etched Ricky's tone. "That goes against all our laws. Even the Nishward could not convince us to fight ourselves."

Fzzd's expression held nothing but contempt. "I'll do what is necessary to stop the spread of your twisted reliance on inferiors, to stop the extermination of our people through their interaction with humans." She paused, voice dropping to Stephanie's sultry alto. "The rest of the council will assume you expired with the starliner. I might be an unsung hero, but a hero I will be." She threw the energy ball.

"No!" Without conscious thought, Elaine hurled her body between them.

The blast caught her in the torso, hurtling her backward, straight into Richelle's outstretched and pleading arms. She heard a shriek, her own, and a shout, Ricky's. The smell of charred fabric scoured her nostrils. Richelle's body heat was the only warmth she felt. Icy fire raced outward to her extremities, then doubled back on itself to coalesce in a sheet of agony in her upper chest.

She knew the moment her heart stopped. It was her last bit of awareness before blackness overtook her.

CHAPTER 25
SOME LIKE IT SPARKING

SHE TRULY loves you, Fzzd whispered in Ricky's mind.

Richelle willed her to shut up, but she couldn't spare the time for words. Elaine was dying, and part of Ricky along with her.

It's not the sex, the protection, the skills you'd afford her. It's love. Fzzd's tone was incredulous.

Now Ricky did glance up, her hands still working furiously over Elaine's body. *Yes, it is. Ixani don't hold the patent on love. We never did. No matter how much you believe humans and other biologicals think with their bodies instead of their minds. They* feel, *Fzzd.*

Perhaps more *deeply because of the way they're constructed, not less.*

From the corner of her eye, she watched Fzzd discard her Stephanie shell, a column of light withdrawing to the farthest corner of the room.

"COME ON, dammit. Breathe."

Richelle's voice, coming from far away, begging, pleading. Elaine heard her pain, wished she could comfort her. She had no memory of what upset her so.

"Breathe, Elaine, please."

Breathe? She wasn't breathing? Something weighed heavily on her chest, warm and palm-shaped. Richelle's hand. Elaine couldn't open her eyes to check, couldn't move her limbs. Couldn't breathe.

A spark of energy lanced her skin. It hummed through her like a mild static charge, not painful but disconcerting. She heard her own heartbeat, loud and steady. She hadn't detected it a moment before.

The events before losing consciousness rushed to her brain, and panic set in. Her instinct to scream forced her to draw breath. She flailed, and another hand caught one of hers, holding it at her side.

"Yes! That's it. Breathe. Don't try to move just yet."

Elaine took another couple of experimental breaths, lungs aching with the effort. Her muscles protested, sore as if she'd exercised for hours without warm-ups. She pushed her eyelids up.

Richelle's face hovered inches above her own, brown eyes studying her. Ricky smiled, but her expression showed severe strain. Elaine wondered how long she'd been out.

"Can you help me sit up?" The weakness of her own voice startled her.

"Slowly," Ricky cautioned, slipping an arm beneath her and adjusting her to a seated position on the polished wood floor.

Elaine's eyes darted around the room, searching for the source of her discomfort. No sign of Stephanie/Fzzd, but a column of light hovered in the farthest corner. Elaine inclined her head in that direction. It took more effort than she wanted to admit. "Fzzd?"

Richelle nodded.

Elaine had no experience judging Ixani body language, but she would have sworn the shrunken, vibrating energy appeared defeated.

"You've shamed her," Richelle confirmed. "The Nishward accepted us, befriended us, even loved us, but none ever offered to sacrifice themselves for one of us." She scooped Elaine into her arms and crossed the floor to place her on the office couch. Elaine sank into its soft cushions, and Ricky knelt beside her. "Shortly after your death, Fzzd realized what she'd done. Life is most precious to our kind. Punishment by permanent dispersal was banned thousands of your years ago. Her desire to protect others didn't justify eliminating me. And taking the life of what she considers a lesser being, one who offered no real threat, is viewed as blatant abuse of our power, even if done by accident."

Elaine nodded, taking in her words, then froze as the full import of Ricky's explanation hit her. "I… died?"

"Your heart stopped." Ricky brushed a stray strand of hair from Elaine's face. "I restarted it, kind of like a defibrillator."

Handy gal.

Elaine raised her palm to her chest, then winced at the pain the touch caused her. The blast had seared a hole through her T-shirt, and the crisped edges scratched her sensitive skin. Lifting the fabric, she found an angry red burn about three inches in diameter just beneath her breasts.

"I'm sorry I can't do more. You'll have to put up with that discomfort, at least until you can get to a dermal regenerator," Richelle said, "but otherwise, with rest, you should be fine in a day or so."

Elaine stared a moment longer at Fzzd in her natural form. "If we try to leave, will she stop us?"

"We are free to go, when you are able," Richelle told her.

Though Ricky made protesting noises, Elaine swung her legs off the couch. The base of her bra cut into the burned area, but she ignored the discomfort. She frowned at its blackened edge and closed her jacket over both her undergarment and the ruined shirt. "Then let's go." The sooner she left, the better. News of the *Nebula*'s destruction had to have reached Earth. Leviathan and the local authorities would have scores of people searching for her among the escape pods, speculating about her survival. Someone might also have reported her as a suspect in Stephanie's murder. She thought the guards involved were all dead, but who knew whom they might have spoken to? She needed to get home and clear things up. And she needed to do so quietly enough that the people who wanted her dead didn't get wind that she wasn't.

She rose to her feet, wavering only once before regaining her balance, and moved toward the exit. She also didn't want to test Fzzd's change of heart any longer than necessary.

Richelle's voice stopped her. "I can't go with you in this form."

Elaine halted midstride and whirled on her. "Oh no. I didn't haul you all the way here from space, throw myself in front of an energy blast, and *die* so you could stay here." She pointed at Fzzd's form. "Whatever she's doing to you, I'll make her stop, even if I have to—have to—" She searched for the word Ricky had used. "Even if I have to disperse her myself!" Despite the aches and pains, Elaine stormed toward Fzzd, hands clenched into fists. She had no idea what she'd do when she got there, but she would be damned if after all she'd gone through she would lose Richelle now.

She didn't get far. Richelle caught her elbow, whirling Elaine into her arms. When she glanced up, Ricky's gentle smile warmed her, though Elaine had the distinct impression she was laughing at her just a little.

"Calm down. That's not what I meant, and Fzzd has nothing to do with it," Ricky assured her, rubbing her palms up Elaine's arms to her shoulders and resting them there.

"You mean you... you want to stay here?" She blinked, disbelieving. Maybe Fzzd wasn't the only one who'd experienced a change of heart.

Now Ricky did laugh. "No, there's nothing for me here."

"Then why?"

She pointed at the portable emitter. "I can go, just not as Richelle," she explained. "I can travel stored in the prototype, but its imagers and audio units were overtaxed, so the only way I'll be able to appear to you is in my natural form, and then only in private. I need to store myself somewhere. We don't cover distances well without assistance, and I don't think most of your people are quite ready for real-life *Close Encounters of the Third Kind*, anyway."

"Excuse me?"

"Never mind." Ricky turned Elaine back toward the doorway. "If you think you can make it without my physical support, we're about a mile from the port city. Once there, place the emitter close to any interactive electronic device, and we can communicate through it."

And she'd have a THI generator and emitters installed in the Kane mansion as soon as she returned home.

"Fzzd won't try to stop you?"

Richelle glanced at the corner, head cocked. The column of energy blinked in a complex pattern of colors, a beautiful form of communication. "No, she won't."

At the room's doorway, Elaine clutched the portable emitter in her left fist. Beyond the entrance, the sun hung over the nearby ocean, casting a warm orange hue across the sand. Richelle kissed her with a passion that spoke of love, longing, and eternal devotion. Ricky's arms clung to her, pressing Elaine's body to her, but cognizant of the burn on her chest. The fingers of Elaine's free hand snaked into Ricky's shaggy hair, pulling her closer, fierce in her desire to keep Ricky's lips in contact with hers. When they broke, they were both breathless, flushed, and heated.

They separated in increments—lips, then bodies. Elaine slowly uncurled her fist, extending the device that would allow Ricky to travel with her. Richelle's form shimmered, becoming transparent as she watched, then sparkling as Ricky regained her natural state. The column of energy flowed into the emitter, and when all trace of her had vanished, Elaine slipped it into her pocket. She headed for the water's edge to follow the beach to the spaceport.

A loud splash distracted her, and she turned to see a pair of lopson cavorting in the shallows along the shore. The two huge beasts flung waves of water at one another, chortling in their merriment.

RICHELLE DIDN'T stay out of contact for long. Her "body" might be dependent on emitters, but her being could communicate in other ways.

Elaine first became aware of Ricky's influence at the spaceport bank. Without ID and with everyone thinking her missing, she had a difficult time convincing the establishment to allow her access to her funds. All her accounts had been frozen. She wove a fabulous tale of crashing an escape pod well beyond the city limits (no, she couldn't remember exactly where), and making her way on foot. No go. And the branch's retinal scanner was out of order.

Then within an hour, a security team bearing a directive from the bank's corporate offices on Earth arrived. Suddenly the two tellers and the manager were falling all over themselves to assist Elaine. They escorted her into a cushy office, brought her a diet purpleberry-lime cooler before she even requested a beverage, and fetched a salad from the adjacent cafe after an offhanded comment she made about her growling stomach.

When she went to input her account code on the touch screen they provided, they politely turned their backs, and for a brief moment, she would have sworn a smiley face appeared in the display. She laughed out loud.

"Nervous relief," she explained in answer to the bank employees' stares.

She did experience a brief moment of concern that someone might be watching the accounts, that she might give away her living and breathing self by making a withdrawal, but the universe ran on money, and she wasn't getting anywhere without it. She'd have to hope the bank's security was as top-notch as it claimed.

Local currency in hand and a new credit card in her pocket, she proceeded to a clothing shop. Being a tourist destination on an island world and having a perpetual temperate climate, most stores carried nothing but beach wear, but she managed to pick up some sundresses, sandals, undergarments, and a nightshirt. Miraculously, when she went to check out, and much to the consternation of the cashier, everything she'd selected happened to be on sale. She felt a pang of remorse when she remembered she'd lost her pretty new bracelet in the *Nebula* explosion, then kicked herself for being unforgivably insensitive.

She'd lost some personal possessions. Others, human and alien alike, had lost their lives.

Instead of checking into the posh resort catering to the wealthiest visitors, Elaine selected a well-maintained waterfront inn, registered under a fake name, and paid cash. An extra-generous tip ensured she need not fill out any additional information in their guest book program.

Ensconced in the privacy of her room, she double-locked the door and laid her shopping bags on the pastel blue love seat. She hadn't opted for a suite, but the standard room was spacious and attractively decorated. Hand-painted waves and Gratitude's enormous egg-shaped pink beach flowers ran in a border just below the ceiling line. A large bed with pink and sea-green covers and pillows dominated the center. A white wicker desk and chair occupied the far corner, and a pair of double doors led onto a wide balcony overlooking the ocean.

She seated herself at the desk, pulled the portable emitter from her pocket, and placed it on the woven white surface. Then she brought up the inbound flight schedule on the inn's older-model comp. Before she could even begin the search for the next available berth home, it appeared in front of her, highlighted.

"Thanks, Richelle," she whispered to the ether, feeling a little foolish but gratified to have her so close.

Elaine booked it, a midlevel starliner with the Red Giant fleet, a rival of Nebula catering to the middle class. Nebula Starlines had arranged for one of its other ships to be diverted to Gratitude to take the survivors home, but she had no intention of traveling with Nebula any time in the near future. The flight she just reserved would arrive at Gratitude the following afternoon on the return leg of its tour and would have her home on Earth two days after that.

When she got to the personal information page, Elaine hesitated, torn between wanting to remain hidden from possible enemies and knowing security required her real identification.

The blanks filled themselves in, with the name she'd used at the hotel desk. Then the screen cleared to be replaced with a text box.

DON'T WORRY. I'LL TAKE CARE OF IT, scrolled across it.

She smiled. "Dating an Ixani has definite advantages."

YOU HAVE NO IDEA. WANT COMPANY?

Elaine stared at the words glowing before her, her brow furrowed. "Um, how?"

ONE EQUALS YES. TWO EQUALS NO.

Before she had time to decipher Ricky's meaning, the comp powered down, and a surge of light flowed from the emitter, coalescing into a column of energy like the one Richelle had formed when Elaine had last seen her. Elaine recoiled at first. She had an instinctive aversion to live electricity, like any other rational human being, and Richelle looked a little too much like arcing current.

She ran her hands beneath the desk decontaminator to give herself a moment to calm down. Then she took a tentative step toward her.

"Richelle?"

The light column brightened once, then dimmed to a lower level. Once for yes. Of course.

"Can I touch you in this form?"

One flash.

She reached out her fingertips, dipping them into the swirling, flowing energy. Instead of burning or stinging, it tingled, brushing over her skin like a thousand feathers. The hairs rose on her arm, and a shiver of pleasure passed through her. "Richelle," she whispered, "you're beautiful."

The column of light shifted to a pinkish hue, and she laughed at Ricky's simulation of a human blush.

"What else can you do?"

At that, the room's lights dimmed, and the column withdrew to hover over the king-size bed. The suggestion was clear.

Elaine stood beside the bed, watching the flowing specks of light dance and flicker. She hesitated only a moment before unzipping and shrugging out of her leather jacket and tossing it on the love seat. Then she pulled her ruined cotton tee over her head and dropped it to the floor. Reaching behind, she unfastened her bra and let it follow the shirt.

Richelle flowed over her in a wave, enveloping the upper half of her body, touching every inch of her exposed flesh. She responded with goose bumps and tremors, a quickening of breath, an increase in her heart rate. To her amazement, her nipples hardened. She gasped at the strength of her reaction.

Sudden weakness in her knees forced her to sit on the edge of the bed, and she took the opportunity to bend down and remove her boots. All the while, Richelle wrapped around her, maintaining the vibrating sensations, fluctuating speed and intensity, focusing on her breasts. By the time Elaine tossed aside the second boot, she was panting, her chest rising and falling with quick, sharp intakes of air.

"That's… good." She didn't bother to try to hide the awe in her voice.

Richelle's light flickered, a sign of pleasure, Elaine supposed, or acknowledgment. She raised her hips to shimmy out of her jeans, then kicked them across the room, aiming for the chair and missing. She barely noticed.

Richelle shifted lower, fluttering across her stomach, flicking in and out of her belly button like an invisible tongue. Elaine's imagination raced ahead, and she hurried to peel off her damp undergarments.

Instead of descending farther, the column of light moved away to hover at the head of the bed, waiting. Elaine got the message, scooting back until she sat against the headboard, her knees pulled up to her chest, her feet flat on the mattress. Richelle hung in front of her, her thoughts unreadable. Elaine let her feet slide until her legs extended straight out before her.

Richelle wasted no time. She swirled over Elaine's belly, warming the skin and sending waves of heat to her most sensitive parts. With each rotation, Ricky went lower, the circles drawing ever closer to the juncture of her thighs. The heat and moisture between her legs increased. When Ricky reached the point where her legs pressed together, she felt compelled to part them.

The energy that was Richelle dipped down, teasing and tickling, vibrating in soothing circles of warmth. A thousand pinpoints danced over her center, and Elaine groaned with the need for more, shifting her body to lie all the way against the overstuffed pastel pillows.

When she thought she couldn't take any more without exploding, the pleasure abruptly ceased, and she cried out at its absence, then clamped a hand over her mouth. An inn, unlike a hotel, simulated the rustic nature of beachfront bed and breakfasts, which probably meant less modern soundproofing.

Outside the double glass doors, the sun was setting, and rays of pink cast long, hazy beams across the room. Richelle held position above her, her brightness creating additional odd effects on the walls and ceiling. Elaine watched her, panting. She had the distinct impression Ricky enjoyed torturing her.

"Ricky," she begged, her tone breathy and low, "please."

A tendril stretched from the energy's core, twisting in intricate and artistic patterns, winding toward her center of pleasure. One instant its tip was visible, the next, it was within her.

She couldn't suppress her cry as the expertly wielded power teased every inch of her from the inside.

It was everywhere at once, filling and withdrawing, vibrating deep, then shallow, but all the while increasing in velocity.

Elaine's hips surged off the bed, lifting and lowering in rhythm with the tendril's movements, picking up speed and desperation. Her moans grew loader and more insistent, and she didn't bother to stifle them but instead let them loose with absolute abandon. Her head twisted left and right, and her fingers dug into the sheets, wringing them into knots at her sides.

Sweet, blissful release hit home, all senses overloading, pulse pounding. In response, Richelle's light particles flared a bright white, and Elaine wondered if Ricky somehow absorbed the energy Elaine expended.

She hoped so. She hoped she'd somehow made the experience as good for Ricky as she'd just done for Elaine.

She fell back to the damp coverlet and tried to draw oxygen into her lungs. As she drifted into sleep, Richelle's life force wrapped around her, a living blanket.

CHAPTER 26
NOT SO HOME ALONE

"THERE'S AN envelope for you, ma'am," the proprietor called, waving to Elaine across the inn's welcoming foyer.

He handed her more of a pouch than an envelope, and when she opened it, she found new identification, complete with embedded thumbprint, in the false name she'd been using. She pocketed them with a smile. "Lost my purse," she explained. "Who delivered them?"

"Private courier. He said to thank you for the rush bonus."

Huh. Well, money wasn't an issue, thank goodness.

Perhaps her paranoia got the better of her, but Elaine would have sworn the inn staff gave her knowing looks when she checked out. Had they heard her last night? Had another guest made a comment? She wondered whether they thought she'd sneaked in a visitor or entertained herself. Regardless, she hurried away, shopping bags in tow, before they could add her blush to their observations.

Her falsified ID got her past Gratitude's lighter security, and soon she arrived via shuttle and another damnable connection tube on the Red Giant's ship, the *Kubla Kahn*.

The liner employed a limited staff, no butlers, no VIP level, a single bar and bartender, a serve-yourself buffet in the solitary dining room, a gym, no pool, and a card room for poker. Elaine had a small cabin, not a suite. It was an interior with no view port. The decontaminator flickered badly when she passed through the entry hatch, and she wondered if the thing would even do its job. In its entirety, the space boasted a twin bed, chair, desk, cabinet, and tiny bathroom.

Didn't matter. She knew Richelle accompanied her. She'd made her presence known through messages on Elaine's hand comp in public and actual conversation through its built-in speaker in private. They limited their sexual interactions due to far-less-soundproofed walls and Elaine's ability to hear everything that occurred in her neighbors' cabins, but they talked and talked, Elaine learning as much as she could absorb about the Ixani and their history.

Richelle, it turned out, was over seven hundred years of age. Her real name, pronounced via the comp, resembled a screech of feedback. After Elaine covered her ears, Ricky promised to stick to her adopted human equivalent.

Shortly after departure, Elaine used some hair dye she'd purchased to transform her dark brown locks to a fiery red. She acquired cheap makeup from the liner's single sundries shop to change her appearance further, and the sundresses she'd bought on Gratitude differed significantly from her usual attire. If her enemies still existed, they shouldn't recognize her.

Stephanie would have loved her new style. She wished her friend could see it.

AT HOME, Elaine made her existence known to the board at Leviathan but requested they keep the information out of the media. Nebula had a team on Gratitude to round up survivors and tabulate victims, but some, like Elaine, had arranged their own transportation home. Many were missing. Accounting for everyone, passengers and crew, proved nightmarish.

All records of Stephanie's murder were lost in the *Nebula*'s destruction; the security officers who'd taken her into custody must have died in the pirate firefight or in the explosion.

In the meantime, using intermediaries, Elaine quietly contacted Biotech and purchased a new prototype portable THI generator for an exorbitant sum. Uncertain of how much damage the portable emitter had endured, she also bought a copy of the "Richelle" program from their central Earth database servicing all the Nebula starliners.

Two weeks to carry out these plans. She and Richelle enjoyed each other's company in the meantime, but her heart beat a rapid staccato as she placed the new portable emitter next to the damaged one in the center of her living room floor and stood back.

First, energy flowed in a stream from one to the other. Then Ricky's body formed around the replacement device, concealing it from view within her core. She chose the same gray trousers and simple white shirt Elaine had seen her in so often on the starliner. It took all of a second before she found herself in Ricky's warm embrace.

"I've missed you," Elaine murmured, her face pressed to Ricky's chest. Then she realized what she'd said. "Not that I don't love who you truly are." She lifted her chin, searching Ricky's face for signs she'd hurt her feelings.

To her relief, Ricky chuckled and tightened her arms around Elaine. "I prefer this form. Best of both worlds. This image is a shell but affords me so many advantages while I retain my true self within it."

And in this form, Elaine could give her more direct physical pleasure as Ricky had done for her over the past days and nights, though Elaine's guess had been right. Ricky did absorb Elaine's expended energy and thrived on it.

It was after an exhausting round of lovemaking, as they lay nestled together watching the morning news, that the first of several unusual events occurred.

"Yesterday afternoon, police recovered a body from the New-Hudson River. Despite deterioration, it has been identified as Jay Grego of the Biotech Corporation. Grego was reported among the missing passengers of the ill-fated starliner, *Nebula*, that exploded after a pirate attack in the Gratitude system. However, the level of decomposition suggests Mr. Grego was killed several weeks prior to the starliner's departure from Earth. Investigators are reexamining the evidence in an attempt to resolve this discrepancy." The newscaster moved on to report a fire in Manhattan.

Fingers of ice traced patterns up Elaine's spine. "Richelle?" She rolled to face Ricky. "What does it mean?"

Ricky shook her head. "I don't know. You never reported Grego's piracy activities to the authorities, did you?"

"I was afraid that would make my survival too public. I kept it to myself."

The camouflaged Ixani stared at the ceiling, lost in thought. "None of it makes sense. If he died before the starliner cruise, who was that masquerading as Jay Grego?"

Elaine swung her legs off the bed and padded to the lift. Richelle followed. They went down to her office, and Elaine called up a holo of Grego on her desk comp, rotating it 360 degrees.

"Certainly looks like the man who tried to have me killed." She clicked it off with a shudder. "Another THI? Like Stephanie?" Elaine's chest tightened at the thought of her friend. She'd visited Stephanie's parents, quietly, and expressed her condolences. But she kept the actual cause of death to herself. Let them think her death was one of many, not a targeted attack.

Richelle stood beside her, her hand on Elaine's shoulder while Ricky considered. "I don't think it's a THI. I'm able to tell the THIs from the humans, with or without seeing the Biotech logo behind the ear. They give off an energy signature visible to Ixani."

Elaine swiveled her chair so fast she caught Ricky in the thigh with her armrest. "You mean you knew about Stephanie?"

"No, no." Ricky held up her hands, palms out. "She was a unique case, a portable THI. But I knew there was something different about her, a very subtle energy fluctuation in her biorhythms. I thought maybe I was detecting a personal electronic device she carried or some sort of medical implant like one of the advanced pacemakers, and I didn't want to pry and embarrass her. Once she revealed herself, I knew what to look for. I don't recall seeing the same fluctuation around Grego."

"Well," Elaine said, rising to wrap her arms around Ricky, "maybe it was just all the pollution in the Hudson taking its toll."

"Maybe so," Richelle murmured, sounding unconvinced.

Elaine thought further. If pollution caused the advanced decomposition, surely the police forensic specialists would have figured that out.

Richelle pulled her more tightly against her, Ricky's cotton pajamas brushing her satin nightgown with a soft hiss. Outside the window, the sun had risen, and bright light streamed through the office's large windows.

"Welcome home," the front door announced, opening and closing with a distant thud. Elaine had changed the house security system's voice to a more robotic monotone instead of the sultry feminine alto Harriet had chosen.

Elaine stiffened in Richelle's arms. "What the hell?"

They turned as one in the direction of the entry hall, where Jay Grego appeared in the doorway. Elaine covered her mouth to stifle a scream while Richelle moved to stand between her and the man who wanted her dead.

Grego hadn't changed much from their previous encounter on the *Nebula*. One hand held a leather jacket swung over his shoulder. Black slacks and a white shirt completed the ensemble.

He gave her a little finger wave. "Surprised to see me?"

Elaine leaned around Richelle's body to stare at the intruder. "You're supposed to be dead! What are you doing here?" She wrinkled her forehead. "How did you get in? The doors are DNA coded."

"You should set the locks, then."

Ridiculous. She'd set them. She knew she had, before going to bed, every night, even when Richelle was distracting her with other activities. And if, somehow, she forgot, she knew Richelle would see to it. Ricky could link into the house security without leaving her side.

Grego's gaze shifted to Richelle. "I figured you'd be here somehow. The mannequin girlfriend." He laughed. "Seriously, you couldn't do better than a blow-up doll?"

A low and menacing sound rolled from Richelle's throat. She pushed Elaine farther back, giving herself space to fight. Since the office had no other exit besides the one Grego blocked, Elaine cast around for some sort of weapon, anything she could use to help Richelle. Her eyes lighted on the antique desk lamp, one of many wedding gifts from Harriet's family. She snatched it up in one hand, yanking its cord from the wall and brandishing it in front of her like a club.

Meanwhile, Richelle morphed. As her body grew and stretched, Elaine recognized the creature Ricky used to protect her on Eris Station.

She didn't get far.

Before the claws could extend from her fingertips and the fangs could drop from her jawline, Grego drew a tiny rod-shaped device from his pocket and pointed it at Richelle. He pressed a button with his thumb, sending a beam of purplish light from the end of the mechanism. It hit Richelle dead center.

The Ixani gave a shout of pain. A hole appeared in Richelle's midsection, expanding outward. Elaine could see through her to where Grego stood, laughing at the THI's incapacity. The purple beam ate away the shell image, particle by particle, leaving head and feet for last and then consuming her altogether. The portable emitter dropped and landed on the Oriental area rug where Richelle had stood.

Sparks like static electricity flickered across the carpet and disappeared into an open wall socket.

"What the fuck was that?" Grego demanded, staring at the outlet like he'd seen a rat go through a hole.

Apparently that wouldn't have happened if Richelle were an ordinary THI. Elaine shrugged. Grego studied her, confusion etched in his features. *She* knew what Richelle was and trusted Ricky to save her, but Grego didn't know any of it. Elaine's lack of distress for her computer-generated companion obviously surprised him.

Good.

He slipped the dispersion device into his jacket and replaced it with a small pistol. "Time to finish what should have been done almost a year ago."

Secret Richelle-weapon or not, Elaine's heart pounded, and she almost didn't make out his words, but the time frame finally sank in.

A year. She knew he had some connection to Harriet's death. Otherwise, his pursuit of her was too random a coincidence. Did that mean Elaine was supposed to have died with her spouse? Had the sniper screwed up somehow?

She didn't have much opportunity to ponder. The recessed lighting over Grego's head exploded in a shower of glass and sparks. Heated shards landed on his scalp and his shocked upturned face.

He yelped with pain, dropping his jacket and flinging both arms up to protect himself. Elaine chose that moment to throw the lamp at him. She would have preferred to swing it and retain her weapon, but he stood beyond her reach.

The small lighting fixture struck him in the abdomen. It did little, if any, damage but provided enough additional distraction for Elaine to snatch up the emitter, dart past him, and scramble across the entry hall to the kitchen.

She scoured the countertops with her eyes, spotting a variety of possible defensive items: knives, heavy pots and pans, a blender. None of them much use against a handgun. She ducked behind the central sink and chopping block combination and waited, her breath coming in ragged gasps and her body shaking with adrenaline. Raising her nightgown, she tucked the emitter inside the waistband of her cotton panties, then covered them with the flowing satin.

"Really, you're just prolonging the inevitable. Though I will say, your blood will be much easier to clean off the kitchen tile than the office carpets and wood flooring."

"So glad I could accommodate you," Elaine growled through gritted teeth. She had to keep him talking, at least until she or Richelle could come up with another distraction. "What have you got against me, anyway? I never even met you before the cruise. I barely know you."

"But I know you, Lanie." His smooth voice made her skin crawl. "Or at least I thought I did." As he spoke the last few words, his tone changed. His vocal pitch rose from a masculine bass to a more feminine alto, his pronunciation altered. At first Elaine thought someone else had joined him in the room. But she hadn't heard an accomplice come in, only Grego's heavy shoes on the marble tile. "I'll admit, I never would have expected you to take up with a THI. But there's something rather ironic about it."

Elaine froze. She knew that voice. She knew it well. And only one person ever insisted on calling her "Lanie." Goose bumps formed on her arms and legs as a shiver ran the length of her spine. She couldn't blame herself for the terrified reaction. After all, she was now listening not to a man at all, but to a woman who spoke from beyond the grave. Unable to stop herself, she leaned her head around the edge of the kitchen island and stared in disbelief at the woman standing in the entryway.

Harriet Kane.

"How—? How—?" Elaine's mind balked at forming a coherent question. Her legs trembled when she stood, keeping the lower half of her body behind the island barrier. She braced her hands on the counter's surface to keep herself upright.

Despite the easy target, Harriet held her fire, her bemused grin implying she was more interested in watching Elaine's reaction as she explained. For the moment. "THIs are marvelous inventions, and the portable ones are nothing less than miraculous, capable of taking on so many different images and personalities... or concealing one entity behind the façade of another."

Elaine's brain raced. Harriet. Alive. That explained how she'd gotten into the house. Elaine had never bothered to wipe Harry's DNA code from the security system. Why would she have? Harry was her spouse. And she was supposed to be dead!

How had she faked her death? If the body had been one of the portable THIs, surely the investigators would have detected the generator disk hidden within the corpse's image on a full-body scan. And a regular THI required emitters. Harriet's office had no emitters. Elaine would have noticed the little onyx disks.

Onyx....

The desk.

Harriet's signature onyx desk. It was one great big emitter.

Elaine pieced it together. Embedded within the desk's surface could have been a portable generator. It made the body vanish at the first opportunity and the blood and tissue samples disappear when they were taken out of range, leaving the stains on the floor to confuse the detectives.

But what about the cleaning supervisor?

Elaine's mind raced. Yes, an emitter like that could make the stains appear to gradually dissolve under the rotating brushes of a robo-cleaner.

Her understanding must have revealed itself on her face, because Harriet's grin grew broader.

"So you've figured things out."

"I've got the how." She needed to keep Harry talking. "I don't know the why." She didn't know how long Harriet's little dispersion weapon worked. If it was a permanent thing, Elaine was screwed, but if its effects wore off, Richelle could reenter the emitter and come to her rescue.

Of course, considering its location in her underwear, she hoped Ricky would give her a little warning first.

"A combination of incompetence and serendipity," Harriet said, waving the pistol about in an offhanded manner. Not like Elaine could launch herself over the island at her. "The target that afternoon was you. My highly recommended assassin," she snarled, voice dripping sarcasm, "missed the shot. Fortunately, I knew better than to place myself in a room a bullet would be blasting through and used my security THI instead."

"Your security THI?" Elaine whispered. Elaine was the target? Harry wanted her dead?

"A little something I acquired from Biotech, through my old pal Grego." At the stunned raising of Elaine's eyebrows, Harriet laughed. "No, I didn't fire him. He was a corporate mole, inserted into Biotech to gather technology Leviathan could copy and market first. When I heard about the portables, I had to have one, to take my place not only in the office, but also other areas with hidden generators throughout the building. It was especially useful during touchy negotiations that might turn violent. I could be safely elsewhere while the THI fed my preprogrammed responses to whomever I wished."

Harry had been using the THIs for how long? Were there hidden portable generators in the house?

Good God, had she slept with one of those lifeless, emotionless, sentience-less things?

Actually, given the state of their relationship toward the end, it didn't surprise Elaine all that much that she hadn't noticed.

"When I 'died,' I was, in reality, in the asteroid belt, working under an assumed identity with Leviathan's miners, trying to see where working conditions could be improved to boost morale and employee output, without cutting into profits, of course."

Of course, Elaine thought dryly. "I'm surprised mining didn't kill *you*." Wow, had she said that out loud? She *had* changed since her adventures with Richelle. And Harriet really despised physical labor.

"I was a foreman," she said, glaring icy daggers at her and fanning at the air as if tossing Elaine's criticism to invisible winds. "Regardless, once I heard the news of my, actually my security THI's, demise, I couldn't come back to deal with the botched assassination. I was making too much progress with the miners, and it was safer to lie low for a while, keep my undercover persona, and let people think I was dead."

Harry paced the width of the kitchen, gun waving as she gestured about with her arms, unconcerned Elaine could escape or attack her.

"I kept tabs on you and your accounts, though. Knew exactly when Stephanie used your credit card to book that ridiculous cruise. And I made my way home to join you on board as Jay Grego, after his untimely demise, of course."

Harriet's eyes flashed with an almost maniacal glint, and Elaine questioned her sanity. Harry seemed to be talking more to herself than to her.

Elaine stopped herself. Could a woman who'd killed multiple people be anything *but* crazy?

"With a portable emitter, a couple of programmers loyal to me—"

Great. More hidden enemies to worry about.

"—and a remote to switch programs, I could become anyone I wanted, and Grego was the perfect choice, already booked to check on his Biotech THI sales."

That explained Grego's death and the miner connection, but Harriet confirmed it. "My miner friends were eager to embrace you as their enemy, Harriet Kane's widow, now calling the shots at Leviathan. It was easy to convince them to try to kill you."

As if she were the criminal here. Elaine swallowed indignation and bitterness. If she survived this, she really needed to look into the asteroid mining workers' conditions and pay scale. Their plight had slipped her mind, lost in all the drama of her own.

It also showed why Harry had to make her move now. With Grego's body found, Elaine (and Richelle) would have questioned who had been using Grego's appearance. They would have brought in the authorities. Sooner or later, they would have tracked Harriet down.

Elaine took a steadying breath. Questioning a madwoman's motives might not be her smartest move. "Why bother killing me? You made the decisions. I never involved myself in the business."

"Ah, Lanic. Don't you know me at all? I want complete control. I don't like to share. And I was damn sick of all your philanthropic pursuits, your charities, your donations. You thought you were making Leviathan look human, but you were making us *soft.* I couldn't walk into a meeting with another executive without them making some offhanded comment about rescuing puppies and kittens or feeding the fucking homeless. I don't give a shit about our public image. Once I own the public, they'll accept any goddamn image I give them. I couldn't risk you taking a sudden interest in more than our annual tax write-offs, either. It was easier to kill you. But then *I* 'died' by mistake." Harry shrugged. "It would have been sooner, but after my violent and well-publicized departure, I needed to regroup and put new plans in motion."

Harry was going to wear a groove in the kitchen tile if she kept walking back and forth. Her words tumbled from her lips in a rapid flow that matched her stride, like she needed to get everything out so she could move on to the grand finale.

God, Elaine hated being the center of attention.

"It was all going according to plan, until Stephanie started asking me some personal questions about my… I mean Grego's… background. Amazing that my secretary noticed things before you did."

Considering how many hours Harriet worked, Stephanie probably spent more time with Harry than Elaine had.

"She figured out who you were." Elaine didn't make it a question. She didn't need to. Her fingers slipped below the counter line and found the drawer pull. Praying against squeaks, she eased the drawer open.

"I saw recognition the first time she and I were alone in her cabin together." That would have been the first night of the cruise, right after they got to their cabins.

Elaine had hung out with a THI of her best friend for days. Richelle had been a serious distraction, but still, she should have realized something was off with Stephanie.

Harriet ignored her increased shock. "Maybe it was nothing. She had no reason to suspect portable emitters existed at that point. I didn't share all my secrets with my assistant. But she made some comments and comparisons between Grego's personality and mine, comparisons I couldn't safely ignore."

In other words, Harry had been dull and demanding, as Elaine had so often described her to her friend. Elaine bet Harry even used some of the same lines Elaine so frequently complained about. And that odd fetish she had with feet and fingernails….

Elaine's thumb brushed the handle of a utensil. Without breaking eye contact, she ran her fingers along it, making certain she wasn't about to defend herself with a soup spoon. Nope, knife. A carving one, its blade long and sharp. She waited for Harriet to start pacing again. Harry thoughtfully obliged her.

"Besides, I wanted to use the Stephanie program to get you in position so I could have you killed."

Because an ordinary THI couldn't do the killing.

Elaine glared in response, waited until Harry wasn't directly facing her, and eased the knife from the drawer. She dropped her arm to keep the weapon out of sight at her side.

"Stephanie was easy to kill. Believe it or not, I had trouble with personally killing you." Harry's voice evened to a monotone. "A discomfort I have overcome." She ceased her back-and-forth stroll and aimed the pistol at Elaine's head with her right hand. Her left remained tucked in her pocket with that device she'd used on Richelle—the remote, Elaine assumed, and also a disperser.

Elaine held up her free hand in a pleading gesture, hoping Harry wouldn't note the absence of her other hand—the one gripping the knife. Out of the corner of her eye, she detected movement. The blender rattled on the counter. To her left, the coffee maker vibrated.

"Wait!" she shouted, as much to hold Harry off as to cover the noises of appliances moving. "Killing me solves nothing. If I die, you're still already dead. You can't just waltz into the office and return to work."

Harriet's hand shifted in her pocket, activating the remote. Before Elaine's eyes, Harry's body shimmered. At first Elaine thought she was putting on the Grego identity once more, but that made no sense. Grego's body had been found. It was less recognizable than Harriet Kane's, but worthless to her at Leviathan where coworkers would remember Grego.

All around the figure, the kitchen blurred, shifted, and reformed as the alien tech camouflaged her in tangible illusion. Whoever she was becoming was shorter and thinner than she was, and the background had to accommodate her new size. Elaine was no longer certain what parts of the walls and counters around her were real and which ones were projections masking her true stature and shape. They adjusted as Harry moved, detectable at first, then indistinguishable from the original, solid items as her portable emitter compensated to hide what she wanted hidden and reveal what should be revealed in her next form. The image solidified and became more distinct, and Elaine saw the new figure was too thin, too short, too curvy to be Grego.

A moment later, she was staring into her own eyes.

CHAPTER 27
WAR OF THE KANES

"ELAINE KANE is about to develop a much greater interest in business." Even the voice sounded like her. It wore her clothes, not the ones she currently wore, since these were new, but one of her favorite outfits from a year ago. An outfit she'd lost when the *Nebula* exploded.

Elaine, the real Elaine, swallowed hard.

"Funny," the manufactured image said, "I wonder if killing you while in this form constitutes suicide." Harriet's now delicate finger tightened on the trigger.

From the left and right, the coffee maker and blender roared to life. Steaming black coffee poured from the spout, filling the carafe. The blender rotors revved faster and faster, the mixing pitcher rocking on its base from the overloading speed.

Harriet dropped the Elaine persona, her body her own once more, no longer masked by the THI technology. Her head jerked from side to side, trying to take in all the seeming craziness at once. The coffee bubbled over in a stream, running across the counter and onto the tile in a slippery, hazardous mess. The pitcher flew from the blender's base, careening across the room and glancing off Harriet's skull. It stunned her but didn't knock her out.

Staggering from the blow, Harry fled the maniacal appliances. Her footsteps pounded down the hall, overhead bulbs popping and showering her with more glass and sparks. Her frantic path took her into the curio room.

"Richelle," Elaine panted, eyes turned to the ceiling and the wiring she knew lay beyond it, "the anti-theft system. Turn it on!"

Not waiting around to see if Ricky heard her, Elaine raced for the front door, bare feet slipping on the clean floor. She wore only a nightgown, but that wouldn't stop her from tearing across the immense yard, up to the neighbors' manned guardhouse, and shouting for help at the top of her lungs.

"Going out?" the house computer inquired as she closed with the entry.

"Yes! Release prior to physical contact," she yelled, willing it to unlock before she reached it, before Harriet could regain her composure and pursue her, shoot her. Usually it waited for her touch, but emergency safeguards had been built in to respond to a voice command, say, in case of a fire.

Or a homicidal dead spouse.

She heard the bolts snick back, the clicks and whirrs of the mechanisms embedded in the door's surface. No DNA or retinal scanners on this side. Always easier to get out than in. Elaine dropped the knife to clatter on the foyer tile and clamped both hands around the door handle, prepared to yank it open.

The shockingly high-pitched scream halted her in her tracks. The wailing continued for what felt like minutes but was probably mere seconds—shriek after shriek of extreme agony. Then it cut off mid scream, the last sound echoing along the corridor. The following silence hung heavily within the mostly empty rooms of the sprawling mansion.

Elaine stopped dead. She knew what had happened, knew that she'd asked for it to happen, knew she shouldn't go to check, but a morbid curiosity and a need for certainty drove her to see for herself. Her feet had lead weights attached as she placed one in front of the other along the hallway to the curio room.

Harriet had designed the curio room to display her collection of rare electronics dating back to the earliest days of the electronic age: a Morse telegraph machine, a Marconi radio, a TRS-80 computer, a Sony Walkman, a cell phone the size of a large purse, and many more. She'd maintained them all in perfect working order, and each would have brought a small fortune at auction. To protect them, she'd installed a top-of-the-line laser theft-deterrent system.

Elaine stopped in the doorway to the display area, then covered her mouth with her hand as her gorge rose. She shut her eyes and turned away, but the sight of Harriet's body, sliced into pieces by the lasers and scattered where they fell, did not fade. She still gripped her gun in her severed right hand. Elaine didn't dare step inside the room, not knowing if the system was shut down or not. She didn't want to, anyway.

Tremors spread through her, intensifying with every step toward her office. Hands shaking, Elaine yanked up her nightgown and pulled Richelle's portable emitter from her underwear. She popped it into a reader provided by Biotech and connected to the house comp, praying she could salvage Ricky's program. Worst-case scenario, she could request another download from Biotech, but the thought of making that effort, of making any effort at all to do anything, actually, made her want to curl into a ball in a corner somewhere.

Her comp screen lit up, and data flashed across it in a never-ending stream. "Reformatting complete," the speakers announced after several tense minutes. "Remove emitter from drive slot."

Elaine followed the instructions and placed the emitter with loving gentleness on the area rug.

She barely had a chance to step away before Richelle's form burst from the emitter. She took shape and solidified in a swirl of particle energy, rushing forward to embrace Elaine before she'd fully formed. Ricky's first attempt to hold her failed as her arms passed through Elaine's, and they both laughed, standing and staring at one another until Ricky could pull Elaine against her chest.

"I've got you," Richelle breathed into her hair. "It's over."

RICHELLE PROVED an expert at corpse disposal. A blast of energy reduced the body parts to ash, which the robo-vac sucked up without complaint. She showered the area with decontaminating rays in case of residual rads. A bleaching removed the bloodstains, but they still had to replace the rug, this time with a nice deep blue plush like the ones on the ill-fated *Nebula*, instead of the black Harriet had chosen.

Since Harriet Kane was already dead, complete with certificate on file and a memorial urn at the mausoleum, no one would come looking for her. No one would question her absence.

Elaine was free to reveal herself to the public once more and officially retake her place as Leviathan's controlling stockholder. But first she had a more important newsworthy function to attend.

Her marriage to Richelle.

Of course, she couldn't exactly be Richelle anymore. Someone from Biotech or one of the *Nebula* survivors would have recognized her sooner or later. But THI tech was a marvelous thing. A lightening of hair color, eye tint a shade lighter, cheekbones a touch sharper, and loss of an inch in height, and she was still enough of Elaine's Richelle without being easily identifiable. And Rachel worked as a moniker that wouldn't trip either of them up, with a little practice.

Richelle (Rachel's) literal connections to any number of databases made procuring an ID and falsifying a background quite simple. She'd been born in California, attended school in Europe, gone off-world to assist in the colony project, and returned to Earth in the past year. Anyone looking into her history would find plenty of references to her existence dating back thirty years, but expertly and undetectably inserted during a few hours of comp work.

Instead of keeping her own surname, she'd take Elaine's on the marriage certificate. Elaine had chosen to return to her maiden name, so they would be known as Rachel and Elaine Pike.

Nope, with the portable emitters, no one would ever figure out she was a THI, or the reincarnation of a twentieth-century film star.

No one needed to know those details, anyway.

And maybe, just maybe, someday Richelle could convince other Ixani like Fzzd to give humanity a chance, and none of them would have to hide anymore.

"IMPRESSIVE." RACHEL held Elaine's hand in hers and stared with her up at the overhead marquee glowing in foot-high three-dimensional letters that seemed to jump out at passersby.

THI THEATERS PRESENTS
THE BIOTECH CLASSIC SPECTACULAR
TRAMPING THE FOOTLIGHTS.

"Wasn't that an... MGM... spectacular?" Elaine asked, dragging the defunct film studio's name from her memory.

Rachel's eyes unfocused a little as she tapped stored information. "MGM sold to Byline Studios years ago, and Biotech bought the rights to a number of their classic live-action films to make into THI productions."

"Still, the MGM name should be there somewhere."

"Probably in the opening credits." She tugged Elaine forward, and they crossed the street.

Elaine pulled her to a stop just after stepping up onto the curb in front of the box office. "You sure you want to do this?" Elaine asked. She pitched her voice

low so the other patrons milling about couldn't overhear. "Whatever happened to not wanting to 'shatter the
illusion'?"

Rachel laughed. "If it were going to, I think it
would have been well and truly shattered before now."
She pulled Elaine a few more feet so they stood in the
line to get tickets.

Online purchase would have been more efficient,
but this "preserved the nostalgia," according to her THI
companion.

"Besides," Rachel continued, drawing her wallet
from the rear pocket of her trousers, "how can I claim
to have educated you in the wonders of twentieth-century film if you've never seen mine?"

Not yours, Elaine thought. *You're an Ixani.* But as
Rachel had explained to her over the past six months,
Ixani adopted their THI personalities in order to blend
better with the cultures they inhabited. In essence,
she *was* Richelle, with just a few additional character
quirks of her own.

The perfect combination, as far as Elaine was concerned. Though it did raise a question she'd been meaning to ask for some time. "Why female?"

"Hmm?" Rachel murmured, pulling her credit card
from the imitation leather.

"Men got most of the best roles in twentieth-century films. And lesbian leading women didn't really
emerge until the end of that era. Why choose a butch
lesbian female form when you could have been anyone,
anything?"

Rachel glanced down at herself: loafers, well-cut
trousers, narrow hips, small but attractive breasts mostly
hidden beneath a thicker cotton white shirt. She ran a
hand through her short but full head of now unruly hair,

then blinked at Elaine. "I don't really know. I tried a number of programmed images before I settled on this one—male, female, gay, straight, lesbian, femme, butch, you name it. This was the one that felt most like… me. Or at least the me I would have preferred had I come into existence as a human." She kept her voice low so the other theatergoers wouldn't overhear her response, pitching everything for Elaine's ears only.

"Your choice is perfect," Elaine said, wrapping her arm around Rachel's waist. "Absolutely perfect."

Tickets purchased, they passed through the decontaminator and entered the darkened theater, surrounding themselves with cobblestone streets, horse-drawn carriages, and the smell of hearth fires burning in the expensive homes lining the narrow thoroughfare. The theater patrons strolled from room to room and scene to scene, sometimes lingering to watch a musical number twice, or to engage in conversation with the THI characters who paused at intervals for exactly that purpose.

When Rachel's namesake appeared, Elaine stepped with her spouse into the shadows, careful to watch her footing on the slanted rooftops where they appeared to be standing. She leaned her head against Rachel's shoulder and watched the woman she'd been while enveloped in the love of the being Rachel had become.

ELLE E. IRE resides in Celebration, Florida, where she writes science fiction and urban fantasy novels featuring kickass women who fall in love with each other. She has won local and national writing competitions, including the Royal Palm Literary Award, the Pyr and Dragons essay contest judged by the editors at Pyr Publishing, the Do It Write competition judged by a senior editor at Tor publishing, and she is a winner of the Backspace scholarship awarded by multiple literary agents. She and her spouse belong to several writing groups and attend and present at many local, state, and national writing conferences.

When she isn't teaching writing to middle school students, Elle enjoys getting into her characters' minds by taking shooting lessons, participating in interactive theatrical experiences, paying to be kidnapped "just for the fun and feel of it," and attempting numerous escape rooms. She is the author of *Vicious Circle* (original release 2015, rerelease 2020), the Storm Fronts series (2019-2020), the Nearly Departed series (2021-2022), and *Reel to Real Love* (2021). To learn what her tagline "Deadly Women, Dangerous Romance" is really all about, visit her website: http://www.elleire.com. She can also be found on Twitter at @ElleEIre and Facebook at www.facebook.com/ElleE.IreAuthor.

Elle is represented by Naomi Davis at BookEnds Literary Agency.

Read the most recent from ELLE E. IRE

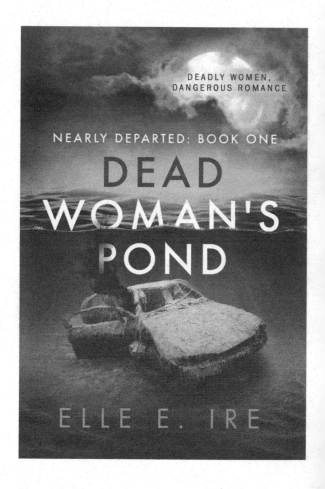

DEADLY WOMEN,
DANGEROUS ROMANCE

NEARLY DEPARTED: BOOK ONE

DEAD WOMAN'S POND

ELLE E. IRE

Nearly Departed: Book One

No matter how Flynn Dalton tries to avoid it, the supernatural finds her.

At first it's not so bad. Flynn's girlfriend, Genesis, is a nationally known psychic, which makes Flynn uncomfortable for both paranormal and financial reasons, but she can handle it. As long as no one makes her talk about it.

Then, on her way home from her construction job, Flynn almost ends up the latest casualty of Festivity's infamous Dead Man's Pond. And when her ex-lover's ghost appears to warn her away, things get a whole lot weirder.

Flynn might not like it, but the pond has fixated on her to be its next victim. If she wants to survive, she'll have to swallow her pride, accept Gen's help, and get much closer to the psychic realm—and her own latent psychic abilities—than she ever wanted.

www.dsppublications.com

CHAPTER 1
EXPECT THE UNEXPECTED

FEMALE BOWLERS have balls

I smooth down the peeling sticker on my bag and set the double-sized bowling ball carrier on the floor beside one of the bar's lower tables. I plop myself on the metal chair with the torn vinyl seat and tug off first one mud-encrusted work boot, then the other. The neon signs on the walls flicker through the haze of cigarette smoke, making my eyes water. Spilled beer puddles on the table's surface.

Reaching to the side, I bang the heels of the boots against the inner rim of the garbage can, knocking off the day's dried muck. Could've just used the black-and-gray-checkered linoleum floor, but the waitress and the bartender are friends of mine. No need to make more work for them.

Out of my bag I pull bowling shoes, a used pair bought from this very alley the year they upgraded to new ones. Hey, when you find a set that fits, you hang on to them. They slide onto my feet like my most comfortable bedroom slippers—if I owned bedroom slippers.

"How about a beer, Flynn? We've got a couple of new microbrews on tap."

I glance up from tying the laces, pulling my dirty-blonde ponytail out of my face and throwing it over my shoulder to hang halfway down my back. Allie stands beside the table, order pad in one hand and pen in the other. Not like she needs either one, but she says they're her version of a security blanket. My eyes trail up her long, shapely legs in the way-too-short miniskirt the manager makes her wear. A white button-down blouse hangs open almost to her belly button, where she has the tails tied in a knot.

Strictly look but don't touch. Steve, the bartender, is her boyfriend, and they make a great couple.

"Hey, Allie," I return. She prefers Allison, but everyone calls her Allie because, hey, she works in a bowling alley, and she's certainly never heard that one before. She gave up fighting it long ago. My thoughts shift to the handful of change and a few crumpled singles in my pocket—enough money for the lunch truck at the construction site tomorrow and one game. "Um, gonna have to pass on the beer. I'd love some water, if you don't mind me hogging up a table." I gesture toward the bar's exit opening out to the lanes.

Allie pops her gum. The faint scent of peppermint carries across the space between us. She makes a show of scanning the bar. Two old guys on stools at the counter. Four ladies in matching team shirts around a table on the far side, a half-dozen empty Bud Lites between them. Dave and Charlie, a couple of guys in their forties, guys I've seen before and occasionally bowled against, take up two other seats, doing exactly what I'm doing: putting on shoes, strapping on wrist support bands, wiping their sweaty fingers with rosin bags out of habit rather than current need, or applying New-Skin to old cuts and scrapes.

Lots of empty tables.

I pull out my own New-Skin bottle, almost empty, and open it. The pungent antiseptic odor rocks me back in my seat until a hand wave clears the air. A couple of dabs seal over a cut on my thumb I got when my saw slipped this morning.

"Oh yeah, I'm really swamped," Allie says. "Don't know how I'll manage all the orders." She holds out her empty notepad for me to see, then flips the chair opposite me around and straddles it, her twirly miniskirt draping to either side and barely covering the tops of her thighs. I swallow and focus on tightening my wrist support band. She leans her arms across the seat back. "Tapped out again?"

I work up a lopsided grin for her. "It'll be okay. New job—that apartment complex going up in Festivity. Steady work for over a month now, but I'm still living paycheck to paycheck. We went a long time before the company got this contract, none of the others were hiring temps, and I don't get paid again until day after tomorrow." I glance around at the pitiful prospects Kissimmee Lanes has to offer tonight. "That's why I'm here, actually." When I'd much, much rather be in a hot shower. I worked the site all day in Florida's famous ninety-plus heat and stayed three extra hours off the clock to help my foreman and friend, Tom, with the paperwork. Every muscle in my body aches, and my head hurts from dehydration.

Allie follows my thoughts. "Doesn't look good. Everyone here knows you, even if you've been avoiding us lately."

I pout at her.

She tucks the pen behind her ear and reaches across to pat my shoulder. I suppress a wince. Took a loose board to that shoulder this afternoon, and the bruise will be a beaut. "I know you aren't really hiding from us," she says. "Believe me, I understand 'broke.' Maybe you'll get lucky. We've had some newbies over the past few weeks." Allie pulls the bar rag from her waistband and wipes down the table, then stands. "Hang in there. I'll grab you some water." She flounces off, her skirt flipping up a little when she turns, revealing black boy-shorts underneath.

Oh yeah, I'll look plenty.

In the lanes area, it's all family friendly. If Allie goes out there to take orders, she buttons a few more shirt buttons and is careful not to bend over. In the bar, it's all about the guys and the tips.

"You hoping to pick up a game?"

The shadow that falls across my table is wide, the voice a rich baritone, but the grin on the sunburned, freckled face seems genuine enough. I gesture at the chair Allie abandoned. "Maybe. What's the bet?"

He's a little older, this big hulk of a man who takes a cautious seat as if he's worried it might collapse beneath him. Given the way the metal squeaks in protest, it just might. Late twenties, shaggy brown hair, all muscle, no fat on his body. His biceps strain the fabric

of the white cotton T-shirt he wears. He drops a dou-
ble-ball bag beside him; the equipment rattles inside,
and the polyurethane balls clonk against each other
with a familiar resonance.

Lots of strength in his arms. Two bowling balls.
Personal gear. He takes the game seriously. Invests
money in it. Doesn't mean he averages high, but….

My mind screams *bad bet*, but I need the cash. My
truck's gas gauge arrow teeters on empty. Can't collect
a paycheck if I can't drive to work the next two days.
I'm lucky today happens to be Wednesday—the night
Kissimmee Lanes hosts unofficial pickup games and
bets quietly change hands to the winners.

If my girlfriend, Genesis, were here, she could ask
the spirit world about the guy's skills. My lips curl upward. Gen works as a psychic, gets paid well for it,
and probably wouldn't appreciate me asking her for
something so trivial. She takes her job seriously, even
if I don't necessarily believe everything she thinks she
does. She believes in it, and I believe in her.

"Lady's choice," the guy says, scanning me as
well and bringing my thoughts back to the current decision—the bet and how much. Right. He glosses over
my face, eyes lingering on my upper arms and the muscles there. I'm not ripped or anything, not defined like
a bodybuilder or weightlifter, but hauling tools, cinder
blocks, and bags of cement mix around keeps me in
good shape. His once-over ends on my open bag and
the solitary blue bowling ball beside the boots I carefully tucked inside it.

That ball cost me a hundred and sixty bucks, cus-
tom-drilled to fit my hand and the odd double-jointed-
ness of my right thumb, and worth every penny. I've had

her since college. She's gotten some nicks and scratches, had a couple of repairs, but she's served me well.

"Let's say, twenty?" I offer, biting my lower lip. I don't have twenty dollars, not on me and not in the bank. If I lose, I'll have to borrow from Steve and Allie. That will suck, but it won't be the first time, and I always pay them back.

God, once upon a time I made a good annual salary, owned a condo, drove a decent car. Now… I shake off the pity party and focus.

Normally I'd go for fifty, but I don't know this guy. The other scattered players watch our interaction. Charlie grins at me from his table. Dave snickers into his rum and Diet Coke.

I can't tell if they're laughing at me or at my would-be opponent. They certainly won't drop me any hints about his skill level, considering how many times I've kicked their asses over the years.

My companion's eyebrows rise. "Twenty, huh? You sure about that, honey?"

Honey? "On second thought, let's make it thirty."

He holds out his hand, a wide smile spreading across his face. "Thirty it is."

Shit, I just got played. I roll my eyes ceiling-ward and smile back so he knows I'm aware of it. And willing to accept the consequences of my egotistical stupidity.

"I'm Kevin. Kevin Taylor."

Taylor. Taylor. Why do I know that name?

Then it hits me. The trophy case next to the shoe rental desk. First Place Team Captain, 2008. Perfect 300 Game, 2007.

"Flynn Dalton." I accept the handshake. His swallows mine in a firm, self-assured grip.

Oh, I'm so screwed.